"The Czar"

and

"World's Fair Goblin"

MW01071327

TWO CLASSIC ADVENTURES OF

DOC SAVAGE

REG. U S PAT. OFF.

by Lester Dent and William
G. Bogart writing as Kenneth Robeson

with new historical essays by Will Murray

Published by Sanctum Productions for
NOSTALGIA VENTURES, INC.
P.O. Box 231183; Encinitas, CA 92023-1183

Copyright © 1933, 1939 by Street & Smith Publications, Inc. Copyright © renewed 1960, 1966 by The Condé Nast Publications, Inc. All rights reserved.

Doc Savage #17 copyright © 2008 by Sanctum Productions.

Doc Savage copyright © 2008 Advance Magazine Publishers Inc./The Condé Nast Publications. "Doc Savage" is a registered trademark of Advance Magazine Publishers Inc. d/b/a The Condé Nast Publications.

"Intermission," "Postscript," "The Men Behind Doc Savage" and Lester Dent photograph © 2008 by Will Murray.

James Bama quotes originally appeared in *Windy City Pulp Stories* #8: "Bama's Favorites," © 2008 by Brian M. Kane.

This Nostalgia Ventures edition is an unabridged republication of the text and illustrations of two stories from *Doc Savage Magazine,* as originally published by Street & Smith Publications, Inc., N.Y.: *The Czar of Fear* from the November 1933 issue, and *World's Fair Goblin* from the April 1939 issue. This is a work of its time. Consequently, the text is reprinted intact in its original historical form, including occasional out-of-date ethnic and cultural stereotyping. Typographical errors have been tacitly corrected in this edition.

Walter M. Baumhofer cover classic edition:
ISBN: 1-932806-94-6   13 digit: 978-1-932806-94-6

James Bama cover variant edition:
ISBN: 1-932806-96-2   13 digit 978-1-932806-96-0

First printing: May 2008

Series editor/publisher: Anthony Tollin
P.O. Box 761474
San Antonio, TX 78245-1474
sanctumotr@earthlink.net

Consulting editor: Will Murray

Copy editor: Joseph Wrzos

Proofreader: Carl Gafford

Cover restoration: Michael Piper

The editors gratefully acknowledge the contributions of James Bama, Jack Juka, Tom Stephens, Jack Adler, Brian M. Kane and John Gunnison in the preparation of this volume, and William T. Stolz of the Western Historical Manuscript Collection of the University of Missouri at Columbia for research assistance with the Lester Dent Collection.

Nostalgia Ventures, Inc.
P.O. Box 231183; Encinitas, CA 92023-1183

Visit Doc Savage at www.shadowsanctum.com & www.nostalgiatown.com.

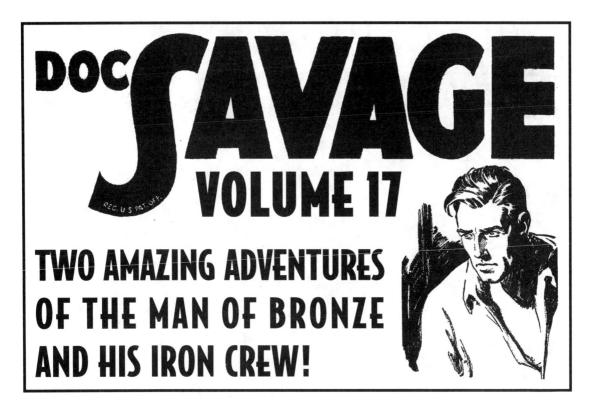

DOC SAVAGE VOLUME 17

TWO AMAZING ADVENTURES OF THE MAN OF BRONZE AND HIS IRON CREW!

Thrilling Tales and Features

Cover art by Walter Baumhofer (classic edition) and James Bama (variant edition)

Back cover art by Walter Baumhofer, Emery Clarke and James Bama (variant only)

Interior illustrations by Paul Orban

The Czar Of Fear

Strange, queer things happen in a thriving community, a rich section, bringing about poverty and desolation. A marvelous field for Doc Savage and his companions to show their mettle!

A Complete Book-length Novel

By KENNETH ROBESON

Chapter I
GREEN BELL

THE midget radio squawked away noisily beside a cardboard sign which read: "Our Special Today— Roast Beef Plate Lunch, Twenty-five Cents."

The man on the lunchroom stool sat sidewise, so he could watch the door. His eyes were staring; pale fright rode his face. He wolfed his sandwich as if it had no taste, and gulped at his fourth mug of

scalding coffee. He was tall, light-haired, twentyish.

One of the two women beside him was also tall and light-haired, and in her twenties. She was some degrees more than pretty—hers was a striking beauty. A mudfreckled raincoat and a waterlogged felt hat seemed to enhance her charm.

Her eyes were dark-blue pools of fear.

The other woman was a pleasant-faced grandmother type. Around sixty was probably her age. She had a stout, efficient look. Her cheeks were ruddy as apples, and pleasant little wrinkles crow-tracked from her eyes.

Her jaw had a grim set, as if she expected trouble, and was steeled to meet it. She was not eating, and she was watching the door more intently than the man.

The young man and the girl were obviously brother and sister. The elderly woman was no relative, but they called her Aunt Nora.

"You had better eat, Aunt Nora," said the girl. Her voice was liquid, quiet, with a faint quaver that went with the terror in her eyes. "It is more than an hour's drive to New York. And we may be very busy for several hours, trying to find Doc Savage."

"Eat!" Aunt Nora snorted. "How can I, Alice? The way you and Jim are acting takes a body's appetite away. Bless your Aunt Nora, honey! You children are acting like two rabbits about to be caught!"

The girl forced a faint smile, reached over impulsively, and gripped the older woman's arm.

"You're a brick, Aunt Nora," she said gratefully. "You are just as scared as we are. But you have control enough not to show it."

"Humph!" Sniffing, Aunt Nora grabbed her sandwich. Squaring both elbows on the white counter, she began to eat.

Rain purred on the lunchroom roof. It crawled like pale jelly down the windows. It fogged the street of the little New Jersey town. The gutters flowed water the color of lead.

The little radio made steady noise. It was picking up canned music from Prosper City, a manufacturing town in the Allegheny Mountains. Aunt Nora had tuned it to the Prosper City station when they first entered the lunchroom.

"Good little set," she said, nodding at the instrument. "Prosper City is quite a ways off, and the set brings in—"

She stood up suddenly, splayed both hands tightly to her cheeks, and screamed.

The young man whipped off his stool and spun to face the radio. His face was distorted; his eyes bulged.

His sister also leaped erect, crying out shrilly. Her coffee cup, knocked to the concrete floor, broke with a hollow crackle.

EVEN the noise of the breaking cup was not enough to drown the strange sound which had come abruptly from the radio.

It was a tolling, like the slow note of a big, listless bell. Mixed with the reverberations was an unearthly dirge of moaning and wailing. The din might have been the frenzied crying of some harpy horde of the ether, shepherded by the moribund clangor of the hideous bell.

The lunchroom proprietor got off his stool behind the cash register. He was startled, but more by the terrified actions of his three customers than by the hideous uproar from the radio. However, the bewildered stare he directed at the set showed he had never heard this sound before.

The fanfare in the radio ended as unexpectedly as it had arisen. The lunchroom owner smiled, evidently from relief at the thought that he would not have to pay a repair bill. The three customers stood in a sort of white-faced, frozen immobility.

Rain strings washed moistly on the roof and swept the street like the semi-transparent straws of a great broom.

Aunt Nora was first to break the rigid silence.

"Prosper City is around three hundred miles from here," she said hoarsely. "It's not likely the Green Bell was tolling for us—that time!"

"I suppose—not," blond Alice shuddered violently. "But that sound was the Green Bell, and it always means death!"

Jim made his voice harsh to hide a quaver. "Let's get out of here!"

They paid a puzzled, curious proprietor for their lunch, and also for the broken cup. He watched them leave, then shrugged, winked at his cook, and tapped his forehead. He had decided his three late customers had been slightly touched with insanity.

A somewhat ancient touring car stood at the curb, forlorn in the rain. The side curtains were up, but the windows were cracked, some entirely gone, and the car interior was almost as damp as the drizzling dusk.

"Got plenty of gas, son?" Aunt Nora asked with gruff kindness.

Jim roved his fear-ridden eyes alertly. "Sure. You remember we had her filled at the last town. The gauge isn't working, but the tank should be nearly full."

Starter gears gritted worn teeth. Sobbing, the motor pulled the old car away in the streaming gloom, in the direction of New York.

A few seconds after the elderly machine had gone, a blot stirred under the trees which lined the village street. In the dripping murk, it seemed to possess neither substance nor form.

Down the street, a lighted window made pale luminance across the walk. The moving black blotch entered this glow. It suddenly became a thing of grisly reality.

There was, however, little of a human being about its appearance.

It was tall, tubular, and black. It might have been a flexible cylinder of black rubber standing on end, had an observer chanced to glimpse it in the fitful light.

On the front of the thing, standing out lividly, was the likeness of a bell. The design was done in a vile green.

Close against the sepia form hung a tin pail of ten gallons capacity. It was full to the brim with gasoline. Gripped in the same indistinguishable black tentacles which held the pail was a long rubber siphon hose of the type used to draw fuel from automobile tanks.

The dusk and the rain sucked the eerie figure into a wet black maw.

A moment later, a moist slosh denoted the bucket being emptied. Smell of gasoline seeped along the street, arising from the gutters where the stuff was flowing away.

Silence now enwrapped the small town, broken only by the sound of the rain and the occasional moan of a car down the main street, which was traversed by one of the main highways leading to New York.

THE ancient touring car was laboring along at perhaps forty miles an hour. Jim drove, hunched far over the wheel, wan face close to a small arc the swiping windshield wiper kept clear of water.

The two women huddled in the rear, raincoats drawn tight against the spray which sheeted through the broken side curtains.

"I guess—that belling—couldn't have been meant for us," the girl, Alice, said jerkily.

"I wouldn't be too sure of that!" Jim called back sharply.

Aunt Nora leaned forward, jaw out, arms akimbo.

"Jim Cash, you know something you haven't been telling us women!" she said, almost screaming to get her voice above the roar of car and rain. "I can see it in your actions! You know more about the Green Bell than you let on—what the thing is, or something! You can't fool me! You do know!"

Jim Cash replied nothing.

Aunt Nora snapped: "Answer me, boy!"

"You're a good guesser, Aunt Nora," Jim managed a gray smile.

"What is it?" Aunt Nora bounced forward anxiously. "What do you know?"

"I'm not going to tell you."

"Why?"

"For the good and simple reason that it would mark you for death! Alice, too! The Green Bell would kill you so you couldn't tell what you know!"

"Rubbish!" Aunt Nora tried to sound as if she meant it. "They would have no way of telling—"

"Yes, they would, aunty. It looks like they know everything."

Aunt Nora whitened. The tendons stood out on her plump hands.

"Listen, sonny—is the Green Bell aware that you know what you do?"

Jim Cash squirmed, almost losing control of the car.

"I don't know!" he cried shrilly, wildly. "Maybe he does! I'm not sure! The suspense—expecting death any instant, and in the same breath wondering if I'm not safe enough—has been getting me! It's driving me crazy!"

Aunt Nora settled back on the wet cushions. "You're silly not to tell us, Jimmy. But that's just like a man, trying to keep women out of trouble. It don't show good gumption, but I respect you for it. Anyway we'll soon be talking to Doc Savage and you can get it off your chest."

JIM CASH muttered doubtfully: "You seem to have a lot of faith in this Doc Savage."

"I have!" Aunt Nora sounded vehement.

"But you admit you don't even know him."

Aunt Nora snorted like a race horse. "I don't have to know him! I've heard of him! That's enough."

"I've heard a little talk of him, too," Jim Cash admitted. "That's the only reason I let you and Alice talk me into going to him."

"A little talk!" Aunt Nora sniffed. "If you would have kept your ears open you would have heard more than a little talk about him! Doc Savage specializes in things like this. He makes a life work out of going around getting other people out of trouble and punishing lads who need it."

Jim Cash began skeptically: "I don't think any man can—"

"Doc Savage can! Take the word of an old woman who knows enough to discount half of what she hears. Doc Savage is a man who was trained from the cradle for the one purpose in life of righting wrongs. They say he's a physical marvel, probably the strongest man who ever lived. And moreover he's studied until he knows just about everything worth knowing from electricity and astronomy to how to bake a decent batch of biscuits."

"Maybe you've been putting too much stock in wild talk, Aunt Nora?"

"Didn't I tell you I only believe half of what I ever hear?" Aunt Nora demanded.

Jim Cash smiled. The elderly lady's optimism seemed to cheer him.

"I hope Doc Savage is up to expectations," he said grimly. "Not only for our sake but for those other poor devils back at Prosper City."

"You said a mouthful!" Aunt Nora agreed. "If Doc Savage isn't able to help us and Prosper City, I hate to think what'll happen!"

The touring car rooted on through the rain and gloom for nearly a mile. Then the engine gave a few pneumatic coughs, died, coughed a few more times and silenced completely.

"You're out of gas!" Aunt Nora snapped.

Jim Cash shook his head. "But I just got gas. It must be water on the distributor—"

"Out of gas!" repeated Aunt Nora firmly. "I know how these old wrecks act!"

Easing into the drizzle, Jim Cash got a measuring stick from under the seat, walked to the rear and thrust it into the tank. His gasp was startled.

"Empty! I don't understand how that could happen!"

"Maybe that filling station was a gyp!" called blond pretty Alice Cash. "They might not have put in any gas."

"I guess that was it, honey," Aunt Nora agreed. She opened a road map, peered at it by the glare of a flashlight. "There's a little jumping-off place down the road about two miles. You'd better walk to it, Jim."

Jim Cash hesitated. "I don't like to leave you two."

Aunt Nora opened a capacious leather handbag. She produced two big, businesslike blue revolvers. She gave one of them to Alice Cash, and the blond young woman handled it in a way that showed she could use it.

"Anybody who monkeys with us won't find it healthy!" Aunt Nora said dryly. "You go on, Jim. We'll be all right."

Relieved at sight of the weapons, Jim Cash slopped off through the rain. He walked on the left side of the pavement, where he could see the lights of oncoming cars and evade them.

A few machines passed him, going in both directions. He did not attempt to flag them, knowing it would be useless. Motorists who pick up strange pedestrians late at night are few and far between.

He descended a small hill. At the bottom, he crossed two bridges—one over a stream, the other spanning the line of an electric railroad.

He had barely crossed the second bridge when several flashlights gushed brilliant white upon him. In the back glow of the flashes, he could discern the figures holding them.

Each was a tall cylinder of black. And upon every figure was the green likeness of a bell.

THERE was something hideous in the way the raven figures stood there, saying nothing, not moving. The rain, streaking down their forms, gave them a shiny look.

Jim Cash stood as if blocked in ice. He had been pale before, now he became positively white.

"Green Bells!" he said thickly. "That radio—the tolling was meant for us as a—"

His own words seemed to snap the chill spell which held him. He exploded in action. His right hand dived into his raincoat pocket like a frightened animal. He wrenched wildly at a pistol which he carried there.

Another eerie black form glided out of the murk behind Cash. It whipped convulsively upon him.

Taken by surprise, he was carried down.

The flashlights now went out, as if directed by some occult signal. The cavernous gloom which followed was filled with swishings and slappings, as the ebony-cloaked, green-belled figures charged.

Cash's gun was dislodged, and went *clank-clanking* across the pavement.

His raincoat tore. He tried to scream. The yell was throttled, and ended in a sound which might have been two rough rocks rubbing together.

The fight noises trailed off. Several moments of ominous quiet followed. Then the entire group moved back to the bridge spanning the railroad.

They turned off and came to a high fence. There was another short, terrific fight while Cash was being put over the fence. Then they descended to the railway tracks.

Once a light came on briefly. This disclosed the darksome figures in a compact wad, with Cash helpless among them.

The railroad was electrified. The current, instead of being carried by an overhead line, was conducted by a third rail which ran close alongside the track. Use of such third rails was common in the vicinity of New York, where the presence of numerous switches and sidings made overhead wiring too intricate. The charged rail was protected by a shedlike wooden shield.

A light came on. A wad of black cloth between Cash's jaws kept him from crying out.

He was thrown headlong at the electrified rail. With a frenzied contortion of his muscles, he managed to avoid landing upon it.

The somber figures pounced upon him, and again hurled him at the rail. Again he saved himself. He was fighting madly for his life. The shed protector over the rail helped him.

But one touch upon the strip of metal beneath, which bore a high voltage, would mean instant death.

The third time, Cash got an arm across the wooden shed and preserved his life. He tore the gag from his jaws with a desperate grasp and emitted a piercing bleat for help!

The Green Bells swarmed upon him, silent, murderous. This time, they pitched him at the rail feet first. One of his legs fell across the highpowered conductor.

There was a tiny hissing play of electric flame. Cash's body seemed to bounce up and down. It convulsed, tying itself in a tight knot around the rail of death.

It stayed there, rigid and still. A wispy plume of brownish smoke curling upward might have been the spirit departing from his body.

The Green Bells eased away in the rain-moist night like dread, voiceless ghouls from another existence.

Chapter II
VISITORS

THE Triplex was New York's newest, gaudiest, and most expensive hotel. It catered to its guests with every comfort and convenience.

Guests arriving by taxi, for instance, did not find it necessary to alight at the sidewalks and enter before the stares of *hoi polloi*. There was an enclosed private drive for the cabs.

This drive was a semicircular tunnel done in bright metals and dark stone, after the modernistic fashion. In it, a taxi was disgorging a passenger.

The newcomer was a tall snake of a man. The serpentine aspect was lent by the fact that his body was so flexible as to seem boneless. His hair was carefully curled, and had an enameled shine. His eyes were ratty; his mouth was a crack; his clothes were flashy enough to be in bad taste.

He paid the taxi with a bill peeled from a fat roll. Entering the lobby, trailed by a bell boy bearing two bags, he leaned elbows on the desk.

"I'm Mr. Cooley," he said shortly. "I wired you for a reservation from Prosper City."

The man was conducted to his room. The bell boy was hardly out of hearing when he picked up the telephone.

"Gimme Judborn Tugg's room," he requested. Then, when he had the connection: "That you, Tugg? ... This is Slick. What room you got? ... O.K. I'll be right up."

The man rode an elevator up six floors, made his sinuous way down a corridor, and knocked at a door. The panel opened, and he said familiarly: "Howzza boy, Tugg!"

Judborn Tugg looked somewhat as if he had found a wolf in front of his door—a wolf with which he must, of necessity, associate.

"Come in," he said haughtily.

Tugg was a small, prosperous-appearing mountain. His dark pin-stripe suit, if a bit loud, was well tailored over his ample middle. His chins, big mouth and pale eyes rode on a cone of fat. A gold watch chain bridged his midriff, and formed a support for several lodge emblems.

"Slick" Cooley entered, closed the door, and said: "We don't have to worry any more about Jim Cash."

Judborn Tugg recoiled as if slapped. His head rotated on its foundation of fat as he glanced about nervously.

Slick quickly folded his arms, both hands inside his coat, where he carried automatic pistols. "What's the matter? Somebody here?"

"Oh, my, no! It would be too bad if there was! You should be more careful!" Tugg whipped out a silk handkerchief, and blotted at his forehead. "It is just that I cannot get used to the cold way you fellows have of handling things."

"What you mean is the Green Bell's way of handling things." Slick leered.

"Yes, yes; of course." Judborn Tugg ground his handkerchief in uneasy hands. "The Green Bell will be glad to know young Cash is satisfactorily disposed of."

Slick took his hands away from his armpits, and straightened his coat. "I didn't get any time alone with Cash, so I couldn't question him before he was tossed on that third rail."

"Your orders were not to question him," Judborn Tugg said smugly.

Slick sneered slightly. "You don't need to pretend to be so damned holy with me, Tugg. We understand each other. We'd both like to know who the Green Bell is. Jim Cash knew. By questioning him, I might have gotten the low-down. But I didn't dare. There was too many guys around."

"Ahem!" Judborn Tugg cleared his throat and glanced about nervously.

"One of these days, we're gonna find out who the Green Bell is!" Slick said grimly. "When that happens, we'll rub him out, see! And, presto, we've got the gravy."

Judborn Tugg shuddered violently.

"Oh, goodness, Slick!" he wailed. "Suppose the Green Bell—suppose someone should overhear us! Let us not talk about it!"

"O. K.," Slick leered. "What're me and you to do now?"

JUDBORN TUGG put his handkerchief away, and fiddled with the ornaments on his watch chain. "Have you ever heard of a gentleman by the name of Doc Savage?"

"Kinda seems like I have." Slick smoothed his coat lapels. "New York is not my stompin' ground, and this Savage bird hangs out here. I don't know much about him. Kind of a trouble buster, ain't he?"

"Exactly! I understand he is a very fierce and competent fighting man, who has a group of five aides."

"A muscle man with a gang, eh?"

"In your vernacular, I believe that is how you express it. The Green Bell had me investigate Doc Savage. I did not learn a great deal about him, except that he is a man who fights other people's battles."

"Yeah? And what about this guy?"

"The Green Bell has ordered me to hire Doc Savage. I am to obtain the services of the man and his five aides for our organization."

Slick swore wildly. He stamped around the room, fists hard, mean face twisted with rage.

"I won't stand for it!" he gritted. "I was to have charge of the rough stuff in this business! I was to be third in command—takin' orders only from the Green Bell and you! Now the Green Bell is fixin' to ring this Doc Savage in!"

Judborn Tugg patted the air with both hands.

"My dear Slick, you misunderstand," he soothed. "You are to retain your position. Doc Savage is to work under you! The Green Bell made that very clear."

"He did, eh?" Slick scowled, but seemed mollified. "Well, that's different. But that Doc Savage has gotta savvy that his orders come from me!"

"Of course. That will be made clear."

Slick lighted an expensive cigarette. "Supposin' Doc Savage considers himself a big shot, and don't want to take my orders?"

"Any man will take commands, if the pay is sufficient," Judborn Tugg said, with the certainty of a man who has money and knows its power.

But Slick was still uncertain. "What if Doc Savage ain't the kind of a guy who hires out for our kind of work?"

"There, again, my statement about payment applies. Every man has his price. The Green Bell needs more men, needs them badly. He does not want ordinary gunmen. Therefore, I am to approach Doc Savage."

"O. K. Where'll we find 'im?"

Judborn Tugg shrugged. "I do not know. We shall see if the telephone information girl can tell us."

He put in a call. The swiftness with which he was given Doc Savage's address seemed to daze him. He blinked his pale eyes and hung up.

"Doc Savage must be rather well known!" he muttered. "The phone operator had his whereabouts on the tip of her tongue. Come, Slick. We shall go see this man."

The two quitted the hotel room.

THE skyscraper before which Slick Cooley and Judborn Tugg eventually alighted was one of the most resplendent in the city. It towered nearly a hundred stories.

"What a joint!" Slick muttered in awe. Doc Savage ain't no cheap skate if he hangs out here!"

"These surroundings show Savage is good at his business," Judborn Tugg replied stiffly. "That is the kind of a man we want. You, Slick, will wait in the lobby."

"Why?" Slick demanded suspiciously. "How do I know but that you'll pay this Savage more money than I'm gettin'?"

"Nothing of the sort, Slick. You will stay here in case Alice Cash and Aunt Nora should put in an appearance. They were coming here to hire this Savage to do their fighting. They cannot pay Savage as much as we can, but it would be better if they did not see him."

"Yeah," Slick agreed with bad grace. "I'll stick below, then."

An express elevator which ran noiselessly and with great speed lifted Judborn Tugg to the eighty-sixth floor. He strutted pompously down a richly decorated corridor.

Sighting a mirror, Tugg halted and carefully surveyed his appearance. He wanted to overawe this Doc Savage. That was the way to handle these common thugs who hired themselves out for money.

Tugg lighted a dollar cigar. He had another just like it which he intended to offer Savage. The fine weeds would be the final touch. Doc Savage would be bowled over by the grandeur of Judborn Tugg.

Tugg did not know it, but he was headed for one of the big shocks of his career.

He knocked on a door, puffed out his chest, and cocked his cigar in the air. The door opened.

Judborn Tugg's chest collapsed, his cigar fell to the floor, and his eyes bulged out.

A mighty giant of bronze stood in the door. The effect of this metallic figure was amazing. Marvelously symmetrical proportions absorbed the true size of the man. Viewed from a distance, and away from anything to which his stature might have been compared, he would not have seemed as big.

The remarkably high forehead, the muscular and strong mouth, the lean and corded cheeks, denoted a rare power of character. His bronze hair was a shade darker than his bronze skin, and it lay straight and smooth as a skullcap of metal.

The thing which really took the wind out of Judborn Tugg, though, was the bronze man's eyes. They were like pools of fine flake gold, alive with tiny glistenings. They possessed a strange, hypnotic quality. They made Judborn Tugg want to pull his coat over his head, so that the innermost secrets of his brain would not be searched out.

"Are—are—you Doc Savage?" stuttered Judborn Tugg.

The bronze giant nodded. The simple gesture caused great cables of muscle to writhe about his neck.

Tugg felt an impulse to shiver at the sight. This bronze man must possess incredible strength.

In a quiet, powerful voice, Doc Savage invited Tugg inside. Then he gave him a cigar, explaining quietly: "I hope you'll excuse me, since I never smoke."

That cigar was the final shock to Judborn Tugg. It was a long, fine custom weed in an individual vacuum container. Tugg happened to know that cigars such as this could not be obtained for less than ten dollars each.

Judborn Tugg was a pricked balloon. Instead of overawing Doc Savage, he was himself practically stunned.

SEVERAL moments were required before Judborn Tugg recovered sufficient aplomb to get down to business.

"I have heard you are an—er—a trouble buster," he said, in a small voice, very unlike his usual over-bearing tone.

"You might call it that," Doc Savage agreed politely. "More properly, my five companions and myself have a purpose in life. That purpose is to go here and there, from one end of the world to the other, looking for excitement and adventure, striving to help those in need of help, and punishing those who deserve it."

Judborn Tugg did not know that it was a very rare occasion when Doc Savage gave out even this much information about himself.

Tugg did not like the speech at all. He mulled it over, and reached a conclusion—the wrong one. He decided this was Doc Savage's way of hinting that he and his men hired out their services. The man, of course, could not come right out and say he was a professional thug.

"My case is right in your line," Tugg said, managing a faint smirk. "There are people who need help, and some others who need punishing."

Doc Savage nodded politely. "Suppose you tell me the situation."

"It's this way," said Tugg, lighting the costly cigar. "I am one of the leading business men in Prosper City. I own Tugg & Co., the largest cotton-milling concern in the town."

Tugg folded his hands and looked pious. "Some months ago, because of terrible business conditions, we were forced to cut the wages of our employees. Much against our wishes, of course."

"I thought business was picking up," Doc remarked.

Tugg acquired the expression of a man who had been served a bad egg unexpectedly.

"Business is terrible!" he said emphatically. "It's worse now, too, because all of my employees went out on a strike! And the workmen in the other factories and mines went on strikes. It's awful! Conditions are frightful!"

Doc Savage asked gently: "Did the other concerns cut wages before or after you did?"

Judborn Tugg swallowed a few times. He was startled. With that one question, Doc Savage had grabbed the kernel of the whole situation in Prosper City.

The truth was that Tugg & Co. had cut wages first, and the other concerns had been forced to do the same in order to meet the low prices at which their competitor was offering goods for sale. Tugg & Co. had turned itself into a sweatshop, paying their employees starvation wages.

When this had happened, there had been no necessity for it. Business had indeed been picking up. The whole thing was part of a plot conceived by that mysterious unknown being, the Green Bell.

Other concerns in Prosper City had been forced to cut wages, although not as much as Tugg & Co. But the cuts had been enough to give agitators hired by Tugg & Co. an argument with which to cause numerous strikes. The hired agitators had even been directed to urge the strike at Tugg & Co., who paid them.

For months now, the agitators, under the direction of Slick Cooley, had kept all business at a standstill. Any factory which tried to open up was bombed, burned, or its machinery ruined. Every workman who sought to take a job was threatened or beaten, or if that failed, the Green Bell had a final and most horrible form of death, which was in itself an object lesson to other stubborn ones.

The whole thing was part of the scheme of the unknown master mind, the Green Bell. No one knew what was behind it. Judborn Tugg, if he knew, was not telling anybody.

Tugg carefully avoided Doc Savage's weird eyes, and decided to handle the bronze man warily.

"We were all forced to cut wages about the same time," he lied uneasily. "But the salary whacks were not at the bottom of the trouble. It is all the fault of the agitators."

WHEN Tugg paused, Doc Savage said nothing. He had settled in a comfortable chair. Several of these were in the outer office. There was also an expensive inlaid table and a massive safe. A costly rug was underfoot.

Adjoining was a library containing one of the most complete collections of scientific tomes in existence, and another room which held an experimental laboratory so advanced in its equipment that scientists had come from foreign countries, just to examine it. The presence of these rooms was masked by a closed door, however.

"Conditions in Prosper City are pitiful," continued Judborn Tugg, secretly wondering if he might not be entirely mistaken about this bronze man. "People are starving. There have been bombings, beatings, killings. It is all the fault of these agitators."

Doc Savage maintained a disquieting silence.

"Aunt Nora Boston is the leader of the agitators," Tugg said, telling an enormous lie without blinking.

Doc might have been a figure done in the bronze which he resembled, for all the signs of interest he showed. But that did not mean he was missing anything. Doc rarely showed emotion.

Tugg sucked in a full breath and went on: "Aunt Nora Boston is aided by Jim Cash, his sister Alice, and a young man named Ole Slater, who is hanging around Prosper City, pretending to be a play writer gathering local color for a manufacturing-town drama. Those four are the ring leaders. They're the head of a gang they call the Prosper City Benevolent Society. That organization is back of all the trouble. They're just low-down trouble-makers. I'll bet they're paid by some foreign country."

This was so much more falsehood.

Judborn Tugg had not intended for his talk to follow these lines. But he was afraid to broach the truth. It was those eyes of the bronze man's. Tugg would have been glad to get up and walk out, but he feared the wrath of the Green Bell.

"I want to hire you to—er—punish Aunt Nora Boston and her gang," he said bluntly. "I'll pay you plenty!"

"My services are not for sale," Doc Savage said quietly. "They never are."

Judborn Tugg's head seemed to sink in his fat cone of a neck. What manner of man was this?

Doc went on: "Usually, individuals who are assisted by my five men and myself are generous enough to contribute a gift to worthy causes which I name."

Tugg stifled a smile. So this was the dodge the bronze man used to make it seem he was not a hired thug. Tugg thought he saw the light. This Doc Savage could be hired, all right!

"Just how big a gift would you want?" he asked cannily.

"In your case, and provided conditions are just as you have outlined," Doc replied promptly, "the gift would be a million dollars."

Judborn Tugg narrowly escaped heart failure.

DOWN in the skyscraper lobby, Slick Cooley was also experiencing a shock; but from a different cause.

Slick had caught sight of Alice Cash and Aunt Nora Boston.

The two women were mud-spattered, bedraggled, and sodden from the rain. They left wet tracks across the polished lobby tiling. Their faces were pale, frightened, and they seemed overawed by the magnificence of the giant building.

They trudged for the elevators, Aunt Nora in the lead, strong jaw thrust out.

Slick gave his brain a mental whipping. He had best do something! Should the two women get upstairs, they might complicate things. Aunt Nora would do that, at least. She was an old war horse when she got mad.

A brilliant idea hit Slick. He dashed forward. Before the two women saw him, he grabbed them savagely and jerked.

Aunt Nora's big purse sailed to the floor.

Slick pounced upon the bag. He had his roll of bills concealed in one hand. Furtively, he got the purse open. He slipped the money inside. In doing this, he saw the two revolvers.

He now seized the women. A violent tussle ensued.

"Robbers!" Slick bellowed. "These two dames held me up!"

Aunt Nora gave him a poke in the eye which made him bawl in real agony. Pretty Alice Cash administered a few blows of her own.

A policeman dived in from the street. In a moment, he had stopped the fight.

Slick jabbed a hand at the two women. "These women held me up tonight! I recognize 'em! Search 'em, officer! I'll bet they've got the rods they used, and my coin!"

The officer opened Aunt Nora's bag, found the guns and the money. He counted the latter.

"How much did you lose?" he asked.

Slick gave him the exact amount of the roll.

"This is it!" the patrolman said grimly. He collared the two women.

Alice Cash shrieked angrily: "We did not rob him!"

"Evidence says you did!" rumbled the officer. "Even if you didn't, you're carryin' guns, and that's against the law in New York."

"You scut!" Aunt Nora flared at the smirking Slick. "You framed us! You low-lifed, slippery-haired sneak! I'll wring your snaky neck!"

She jumped for Slick, who back-pedaled hastily.

"None of that!" shouted the officer. "It's into the jug for you!"

He propelled his prisoners for the door.

Chapter III
THE COMEBACK

AS the women were leaving, the gorilla ambled upon the scene.

This personage had, to give him his due, some manlike qualities. His fingernails were manicured, even if the job had been done with a pocketknife. His little eyes glistened with keen intelligence in their pits of gristle. His face attained that rare quality of being so homely that it was pleasant to look upon.

His clothing was expensive, although it did look like it had been slept in. He would weigh every ounce of two hundred and sixty pounds, and his hairy arms were some inches longer than his bandy legs.

He ambled up and stopped in front of Slick.

"I saw you slip the money in that purse," he said in a voice so mild that it might have been a child's.

Then he hit Slick. Hit him on the nose!

Slick's curly hair was varnished straight back on his head. The blow was so hard that it made the hair stand out suddenly in front, as if blown by a wind from behind.

Describing a parabola, Slick lit on his shoulders and skidded a score of feet. His nose had been spread over most of his weasel face.

Aunt Nora began to bounce up and down in ribald delight, and to shout: "Glory be! Just what I wanted to hand him!"

Entrancing Alice Cash bestowed a grateful smile on the fellow who looked like a furry gorilla.

The cop shouted: "You say this squirt planted that roll of bills?"

"He sure did," said the hairy man.

Growling, the officer rushed for Slick.

Slick shoved up dizzily from the floor. He sprinted for the door. Glancing around, he saw the policeman was sure to overhaul him. He spaded his hands inside his coat, and brought out two automatics. Each was fitted with a compact silencer.

The guns began to *chung* out deadly reports. The bullets missed the fast-traveling patrolman. But he veered for shelter, tugging at his own weapon.

Slick hurtled through the door. A taxi chanced to be cruising past. With a wild spring, the fleeing gunman got into it. He jammed the hot silencer of a revolver against the shivering driver's neck.

The cab jumped down the street as if dynamite had exploded behind it.

The officer raced out, but did not shoot because of the traffic. He sped back into the skyscraper and put in a call to headquarters, advising them to spread a radio alarm for the taxi.

"The guy as good as got away!" he advised the huge, furry man and the two women, when he rejoined them. "Now—you two ladies! We've still got to settle about them guns you were carryin'!"

"The ladies tell me they were on their way to see Doc Savage," the hairy fellow advised in his babylike voice.

The cop blinked. Then he grinned from ear to ear.

"That makes it different," he chuckled. Then he walked away, acting as if he had never seen the two women.

Alice Cash looked prettily incredulous at the magic which mention of Doc Savage's name had accomplished.

Aunt Nora gulped several times, then smiled. "Bless you, you homely monkey! How'd you get us out of that? I know they're very strict about people packin' guns here in New York."

The human gorilla laughed. "The fact that you were goin' to Doc Savage made it all right."

"Doc Savage must have a big reputation in this town," Aunt Nora said wonderingly. "You ain't him, are you?"

"Who, me? Hell—I mean, oh, my—no! I'm just one of Doc Savage's five helpers."

"What's your name?"

"Lieutenant Colonel Andrew Blodgett Mayfair."

Aunt Nora snorted. "I'll bet you're not called that much!"

"Not enough for me to know who's bein' wanted when I hear it!" the hairy fellow grinned. "Call me Monk."

"Monk" might have added that he was a chemist whose name was mentioned with reverence in scientific circles of both America and Europe. But he was not addicted to blowing his own horn.

THE speedy elevator lifted them to the eighty-sixth floor. When they were near the door of Doc Savage's office, the murmur of a voice within was distinguishable.

Aunt Nora gave a start of angry surprise. "I'd know that voice anywhere!" she gasped. "It's Judborn Tugg!"

Monk's little eyes showed interest. "Who's he?"

"A fat, conceited jaybird! He's no friend of ours! Slick Cooley—the fellow you pasted downstairs—follows Judborn Tugg around like a Man Friday. They're tarred with the same brush—both crooked!"

Monk considered this, then waved the women back. He opened the office door, and stood in the aperture. His big, hirsute hands moved nervously, as if he were embarrassed.

"Oh, excuse me! I didn't know you had company." He started to back out.

No one, other than Doc, had noticed that the apparently aimless movements of Monk's hands had spelled out a message in the deaf-and-dumb sign language.

"Come out here without alarming your visitor," Monk had signaled.

Doc arose, saying to Judborn Tugg: "If you will excuse me—I wish to speak with this man!" He strode rapidly to the door.

For all of his great weight and swiftness of stride, he made no appreciable sound. There was an uncanny silence about his movements, a natural lightness which indicated enormously developed leg muscles.

Fat Judborn Tugg, instead of suspecting anything, was rather glad to have Doc step outside for a moment. Tugg had not yet recovered from the shock of having Doc suggest that his services would call for a million-dollar donation. He welcomed the chance to regain his balance.

Doc closed the corridor door. Shortly later, he was in the presence of the two women.

Aunt Nora let her mouth hang open in unashamed astonishment at sight of the giant bronze man. Then she cocked her arms akimbo and smiled, wrinkles corrugating every inch of her motherly face.

"Glory be!" she chuckled. "You're the answer to this old girl's prayers!"

Alice Cash did not exactly let her jaw drop, but

her lips parted slightly, and her blue eyes became round with amazement. Her next act was to glance down disgustedly at her muddy, disheveled raiment.

Doc Savage usually affected pretty young women like that—set them wondering about their appearance. Feminine eyes were inclined to be quick to note that Doc was unusually handsome, a fact which escaped men after they saw his amazing muscular development.

Monk performed the introductions.

"What has Judborn Tugg been tellin' you?" Aunt Nora questioned anxiously.

"A great deal," Doc replied quietly. "He is one of the most profuse liars I have ever encountered."

This would have pained Judborn Tugg exceedingly, had he overheard it. It was his belief that he could tell a falsehood as smoothly as the truth. He would have been shocked to know that Doc Savage, by close attention to his voice tones, had spotted almost every lie.

Aunt Nora clenched her work-toughened hands, and gave Doc a look of genuine appeal.

"I need your help!" she said earnestly. "But I haven't got a cent with which to pay you!"

DOC'S strange golden eyes studied Aunt Nora and attractive Alice Cash. His bronze features remained as expressionless as metal.

Without speaking, he turned. He entered his office.

"I do not think I am interested in your proposition," he told Judborn Tugg.

Tugg picked the costly cigar from his pursy mouth, as if it had suddenly turned bitter.

"I can pay you plenty," he pointed out. "I might even pay you that million, provided you can do the work that I want done."

"No!"

Judborn Tugg purpled. To him, it was inconceivable that any man would dismiss a million so abruptly. He would probably have keeled over had he known that Doc intended to help Aunt Nora Boston, who had admitted she could not pay him a copper cent.

"If you change your mind, you'll find me at the Hotel Triplex!" Tugg said in a loud, angry tone.

"There will be no change of mind," Doc said, reaching out and grasping Tugg by the coat collar.

Before Tugg knew what had happened, he was hoisted off the floor. His coat tore in two or three places, but held.

Helpless as a worm on a stick, Tugg was carried into the corridor and deposited urgently in an elevator.

"If you want to retain your health, you had better not let me see you again!" Doc advised him in the tone of a physician prescribing for a patient with dangerous symptoms.

The elevator carried Tugg from view.

Monk, an innocent expression on his homely face, ambled up and asked: "Didn't I hear that bird say he was staying at the Hotel Triplex?"

Doc nodded; then invited Aunt Nora and Alice Cash into his office.

Grinning, Monk ambled to a public telephone in the corridor. He got the number of the Hotel Triplex from the phone book, then called the hostelry. He asked the hotel operator for the night manager.

"You have a guest named Judborn Tugg," Monk informed the hotel man. "Doc Savage just threw this fellow out of his office."

"In that case, we'll throw him out of the Hotel Triplex, too," Monk was advised.

Hanging up, Monk fished an envelope out of his pocket and addressed it to the Unemployment Relief Fund.

From another pocket, he produced Slick Cooley's fat roll of bills. Monk had managed to harvest this in the excitement downstairs. He sealed the money in the envelope, applied stamps, then put it in a mail box. The envelope was so bulky that he had to insert it in the lid marked for packages.

Whistling cheerfully, Monk tramped for Doc's office.

WHEN Judborn Tugg reached the Hotel Triplex, he found his bags waiting for him on the sidewalk. The night manager in person was watching over the valises.

"I am sorry," the manager said coldly. "We do not want you here."

Judborn Tugg, after nearly choking, yelled and cursed and waved his arms. He threatened to sue the Triplex for a million dollars.

"Get away from here, or I'll have you arrested for disturbing the peace!" snapped the manager. Then he walked inside.

A moment later, a dark limousine rolled up to the curb. The rear was heavily curtained.

The driver leaned from behind the wheel and advised: "Get in!"

It was Slick Cooley, partially disguised by a raincoat and a low-pulled hat.

Judborn Tugg placed his bags in the front, then got in the back. At this point, his hair almost stood on end.

The rear seat held a figure incased from head to foot in a black sack of a garment. On the front of the raven gown was painted a big green bell.

The unholy apparition in black held two silenced revolvers in dark-gloved hands.

"Do not mind the guns," said a hollow, inhuman voice from the murksome form. "I am the Green Bell, and the weapons are merely to remind you not to snatch at my hood in an effort to learn my identity."

The limousine now rolled out into traffic.

"I was walkin' down the street when *he* called to me from the back of this car," Slick advised. "There wasn't any driver—"

"I simply parked the car ahead of you, before donning my hood," interposed the sepulchral tones of the Green Bell. "Incidentally, this machine is stolen. But I do not think the owner will miss it for some hours. Tugg—what happened to you?"

Judborn Tugg started. He had been cudgeling his brain in an effort to identify the Green Bell's voice. But there was nothing the least familiar about the disguised tones.

Rapidly, Judborn Tugg explained the unhappy outcome of his visit to Doc Savage.

"You have served me very inefficiently!" Anger had come into the booming voice of the Green Bell. "This Doc Savage is not at all the type of man you thought him to be!"

Tugg, still smarting from his reception at the hotel, said angrily: "This is my first mistake!"

The Green Bell gazed levelly at him. The eye holes in the jet hood were backed by goggles which had deep-green lenses. The effect was that of a big, green-orbed cat.

"I do not care for your angry tone!" said the dark being. "You are fully aware, Tugg, that I can get along without those who do not cooperate fully with me. You are no exception! You are of service to me only as an agent, a figurehead through which I can work. You pretend to be Prosper City's leading citizen, and I choose to let you. Your milling concern, Tugg & Co., was ready to fail when I came upon the scene, thanks to your bad management. You have retained control of the company only because I have furnished you money with which to pay the interest on your loans. You are but a cog in my great plan."

Judborn Tugg collapsed like an automobile tire which had picked up a nail.

"I did not mean to offend you," he mumbled. "I was excited because of the treatment Doc Savage gave me."

"I am going to take care of Doc Savage!" the Green Bell said ominously.

Tugg shivered. "The man is dangerous—especially if he has the brains to match his unbelievable physical strength!"

"We do not want Savage against us," replied the Green Bell. "I have already put a plan in operation which will keep Savage so busy that he will have no time to stick a finger in our pie."

"I'd like to see him dead!" said Judborn Tugg savagely.

"You may get your wish!" tolled the Green Bell.

"My little scheme will undoubtedly result in Doc Savage dying in the electric chair!"

Ordering Slick down a dark street, the Green Bell eased out of the car, and was swallowed by the drizzling darkness. A bit farther on, Judborn Tugg and Slick Cooley abandoned the stolen limousine.

Walking away from the car, they could see in the distance what appeared to be a tower of gray freckles in the wet gloom. This was the skyscraper which housed Doc Savage's aerie.

Chapter IV
THE MURDER WITNESSES

IN his eighty-sixth-floor headquarters, Doc was listening to Aunt Nora Boston and Alice Cash tell their story. The homely Monk lingered in the background, furtively admiring Alice Cash's loveliness.

"My brother!" Alice said, whitefaced. "He has vanished! We ran out of gas in New Jersey, and Jim walked ahead to find a filling station. That was the last we saw of him!"

"We thought we heard Jim scream," Aunt Nora amended grimly. "But we couldn't find him."

Alice put her fingers over her pale lips and said between them: "And just before that, we heard the Green Bell from the radio!"

Aunt Nora grimaced. "The sound of the Green Bell over the radio nearly always means some innocent person is to die!"

Alice shuddered, wailed: "Poor Jimmy! I have a feeling something terrible happened to him!"

Doc Savage could do remarkable things with his powerful voice. He now made it calm and soothing, a tone calculated to quiet the excited women.

"Your story is a bit disconnected," he told them. "Suppose you start at the first."

Aunt Nora clenched her hand and stared steadily at them as she talked.

"The trouble in Prosper City started many months ago, when Tugg & Co. cut wages. That caused the first of a series of strikes—"

"Judborn Tugg told me about that," Doc interposed. "All business in Prosper City is at a standstill. A gang of men, pretending to be agitators, bomb or burn every factory and mine which attempts to start operations, and terrorize all men who want to go back to work. Tugg said you were the chief of the agitators."

"The liar!" Aunt Nora flared, "All I have done is organize my Benevolent Society to help some of the poor souls who are out of work."

"Aunt Nora has kept lots of people from starving!" Alice Cash put in. "She has spent all of her money, and all she can borrow, in feeding those unfortunates."

"You shut up!" Aunt Nora directed gruffly.

"I will not!" Alice snapped, "I think Mr. Savage should know the truth! You're an angel!"

Aunt Nora blushed and stared at her big, muddy shoes. "I ain't no angel—not with them feet."

"What about these agitators back of the trouble?" Doc asked.

"They're hired thugs, of course!" Aunt Nora declared. "But just who they are, nobody knows. When they appear they're always in robes that look like black sacks, with green bells painted on the front."

"Their leader is not known?"

"No!" Aunt Nora made a fierce mouth. "Alice and her brother and Ole Slater have been helping me try to find out who the Green Bell is."

"Who is Ole Slater?" Doc Savage wanted to know.

"A nice young lad who thinks he can write plays. He's stricken with the charms of Alice, here. He's gathering material for a play, and he stays at my rooming house. I forgot to tell you that I run a boarding house."

Doc asked: "And you think Judborn Tugg and Slick Cooley are in the Green Bell's gang?"

"I ain't got no proof!" asserted Aunt Nora. "But they could be! One of them might be the Green Bell, himself."

MONK entered the conference, asking gently: "Hasn't the police chief of Prosper City done anything about all this?"

"That old numbskull!" Aunt Nora sniffed. "His name is Clem Clements, and he thinks Judborn Tugg is the greatest man alive and the soul of honor. I don't think Chief Clements is crooked. He's just plain downright dumb!"

"How come Tugg exerts such a sway?" Monk wanted to know.

"Judborn Tugg tries to make himself out as the leading business man of Prosper City!" snorted Aunt Nora. "He's fooled a lot of nitwits, including Chief Clements. Tugg has been spreading the story that I am behind the Green Bell. He has made Chief Clements and plenty of others believe it. I've thought several times they were going to throw me in jail!"

"They haven't quite dared do that!" Alice Cash explained. "The poor people Aunt Nora has been helping would tear down the jail if she was in it. I don't think they've dared harm Aunt Nora for the same reason."

Aunt Nora laughed grimly. "I've told everybody that if anything happens to me, it'll be Judborn Tugg's doing! If the Green Bells should murder me, or drive me insane, my friends would lynch Tugg. That's why I haven't been harmed."

"What's this about insanity?" Doc interrupted.

Alice Cash shivered. "It's something that happens to workmen who are persistent about going back to their jobs. No one knows how it is done. The men simply—go crazy. It's happened to more than a dozen of them."

For a few moments, Doc and Monk mulled over what they had been hearing. It was an amazing story, the more so because the motive behind the affair was unclear.

"Why hasn't martial law been declared?" Monk demanded.

"Chief Clements claims he has the situation in hand!" Alice Cash replied. "The distressing situation in Prosper City has come about gradually. To an outsider, it merely looks like strike trouble."

Aunt Nora had maintained a short, tense silence. Now she exploded.

"Jim Cash as much as admitted he had found out who the Green Bell is!" she announced. "And that very thing makes me think he has been killed!"

Alice Cash gave a soft, grief-stricken moan, and buried her face in her hands.

Monk got up as if to comfort her.

There was a loud interruption from the corridor outside. Blows chugged. Men grunted and gasped.

Doc gilded over and whipped the door open.

Two men stood in the hall, hands lifted, facing a third man who held a flat automatic.

The hands which one of the men held up were so huge it seemed a wonder they did not overbalance him. Each was composed of considerably more than a quart of bone and gristle. He had a somber, puritanical face.

This man of enormous fists was Colonel John Renwick, known more often as "Renny." Among other things, he was a world-renowned engineer, a millionaire, and loved to knock panels out of doors with his big fists.

The other fellow with upraised arms was slender, with a somewhat unhealthy complexion. He had pale hair and eyes. Alongside his big-fisted, rusty-skinned companion, he seemed a weakling.

He was "Long Tom." The electrical profession knew him as Major Thomas J. Roberts, a wizard with the juice.

Renny and Long Tom were two more of Doc Savage's five aides.

The man with the gun was a chap Doc had never seen before. He was tall, athletic, and not unhandsome.

The fellow backed to an elevator, sprang inside, and the cage sank.

RENNY and Long Tom looked sheepishly at Doc.

"We came upon that bird listenin' outside the door!" Renny said, in a roaring voice, suggestive of an angry lion in a cave. "We tried to grab him, but he flashed his hardware on us!"

Doc was gliding down the corridor as these words came. He reached the endmost elevator. His sinew-wrapped hand tapped a secret button. Sliding doors whistled back.

This lift was a private one, which Doc maintained for his own use. It was fitted with special machinery, which operated at terrific speed. The ordinary express elevators were fast, but compared to this one, they were slow.

The floor dropped some inches below Doc's feet, so swiftly did the descent start. For fully sixty stories, he hardly touched the floor. Then came the slow, tremendous shock of the stop. Doc's five aides, all strong men, were usually forced to their knees when this happened.

So powerful were the bronze man's thews that he withstood the shock without apparent effort.

He flashed out into the lobby of the towering building. The cage bearing the young man with the gun had not yet arrived.

But it came within a few moments. The young man got out, backing so as to menace the elevator operator with his weapon.

Doc grasped the fellow's arms. Bronze fingers all but sank from view as they tightened.

An agonized wail was forced through the man's teeth. He dropped his gun. The excruciating pressure on his arm muscles caused his fingers to distend like talons.

He tried to kick backward. But pain had rendered him as limp as a big rag. His head drooped; his eyes glazed. He was on the verge of fainting from the torture.

Doc tucked the slack figure under an arm, entered the speed elevator, and rode back to the eighty-sixth floor.

Aunt Nora, Alice Cash, and the others were waiting in the corridor.

Doc's prisoner was hardly able to stand. His knees buckled. Doc grasped him by an arm, not too tightly, and held him erect.

Aunt Nora stared at the captive, popeyed.

Amazement also engulfed Alice Cash's attractive features as she gazed at the young man.

"Know him?" Doc asked quietly.

"He is Ole Slater!" Alice exclaimed. "My—er—the boy who likes me!"

HALF carried into the office, and deposited in a deep chair, Ole Slater found his tongue.

"I got worried and followed you to New York," he told Alice and Aunt Nora.

"You should not have been sneaking around that door," Aunt Nora informed him severely.

"Don't I know it!" Ole Slater touched his arms gingerly, then eyed Doc Savage's metallic hands as if wondering how they could have inflicted such

torment. "I stopped outside the door a minute to listen. I was just being cautious. Then these men jumped me. I guess I lost my head—I thought they were Green Bells!"

Aunt Nora smiled at Doc. "This young man is our friend. I'm sure he didn't mean any harm."

"Of course he didn't!" Alice Cash added her defense.

"I'm terribly sorry about this," Ole Slater said meekly. "I was, well—worried about Aunt Nora and Jim and Alice."

Grief returned to Alice Cash's refined features. "Jim has vanished, Ole."

Ole Slater now received the story of what had happened on the New Jersey road, beginning with the awesome belling sound which had come unexpectedly from the radio.

Aunt Nora Boston added a few more details about conditions in Prosper City. Although Doc questioned her closely, he learned little that had not been brought out already.

Alice Cash, it developed, was private secretary to Collison McAlter, a man who owned the Little Grand Cotton Mills. The Little Grand was the main competitor of Tugg & Co., in Prosper City, but was now closed down, like all the rest of the industries.

The master mind, the Green Bell, for some reason as yet unclear, was keeping all Prosper City business at a standstill by use of a reign of terror. That was what it amounted to.

They had been talking the situation over for about half an hour when two men dashed excitedly into the office.

One gesticulated with a slender black cane, and barked: "Doc! You're in a frightful jam!"

THE cane which the man waved looked innocent, but it was in reality a sword cane with a blade of fine Damascus steel. The gentleman who carried it was slender, with sharp features and a high forehead. His clothing was of the latest style and finest cloth.

He was Brigadier General Theodore Marley Brooks—"Ham" to Doc's group, of which he was a member. He was by way of being the most astute lawyer Harvard ever turned out. He was also such a snappy dresser that tailors sometimes followed him down the street, just to observe clothes being worn as they should be worn.

"You've been accused of a murder, Doc!" exclaimed the second of the newcomers.

This man was tall, and so thin he seemed nothing more than a structure of skin-coated bones. He wore glasses, the left lens of which was much thicker than the right. The left lens was a powerful magnifying glass. The bony man had lost the use of his left eye in the War, and since he needed a magnifier in his profession of archaeology and geology, he carried it in the left side of his spectacles, for convenience.

He was "Johnny"—William Harper Littlejohn, one-time head of the natural science research department of a famous university, and possessor of an almost universal reputation for proficiency in his line.

The addition of these two completed Doc Savage's group of five unusual aides. Each was a man with few equals at his trade. They were men who loved excitement and adventure. They found that aplenty with Doc Savage. The strange bronze man seemed to walk always on paths of peril.

Undoubtedly the most amazing fact about this remarkable company of trouble busters was the ability of Doc, himself, to excel any one of his helpers at his own profession. Doc's fund of knowledge about electricity was greater than that of Long Tom, the wizard of the juice; the same supremacy applied to the others in their fields of chemistry, geology, law, and engineering.

"What's this about me being a murderer?" Doc asked sharply.

"The New Jersey police have a warrant for you!" declared Ham, still flourishing his sword cane. "They have four witnesses who say they saw you throw a man against the third rail of an interurban line and electrocute him!"

"And they're bringing the witnesses over here to identify you!" Johnny added. Excitedly, he jerked off his spectacles which had the magnifier on the left side. "They'll be here any time, now!"

Ham nodded vehemently. "They will! A police officer in New Jersey, knowing I usually take care of the law angles in our troubles, called me and tipped me off about the thing."

"Who am I supposed to have murdered?" Doc queried dryly.

Ham tapped his sword cane thoughtfully. "A fellow I never heard of. His name was Jim Cash!"

Alice Cash sank soundlessly into a chair and buried her face in her arms. Her shoulders began to convulse.

Monk, who had prowled over to the window, and stood looking down, called abruptly: "Look at this!"

Doc flashed to his side.

Far below, a car was sweeping in to the curb. Men got out. In the darkness and rain, it was impossible to identify them. They numbered nine.

Faint light spilled from the front of the skyscraper, revealing, painted on top of the car for easy identification from airplanes, the lettered symbols of New Jersey State Police.

"The New Jersey officers with their witnesses!" Monk muttered.

Chapter V
PERIL'S PATH

DOC backed from the window. Without apparent haste, but none the less with deceptive speed, he crossed to the massive table and touched several inlaid segments. These depressed under his fingers, but immediately sprang back into place, so as to conceal the fact that the table top was one great cluster of push buttons.

"Monk, you and Ham stay here and stall these fellows!" Doc directed.

Monk surveyed the sartorially perfect Ham and made an awful grimace. "O. K. I'll try to put up with this shyster!"

At that, Ham glared and hefted his sword cane suggestively. His expression said that nothing would give him more pleasure than to stick the blade into Monk's anthropoid frame.

"Some of these days, I'm gonna take that hairy hide of yours home for a rug!" he promised.

This exchange, accompanied by fierce looks, was nothing unusual. Ham and Monk were always riding each other. Their good-natured quarrel dated back to the Great War—to an incident which had given Ham his nickname. To have some fun, Ham had taught Monk some highly insulting French words, telling him they were the proper adjectives with which to curry the favor of a French general. Monk had used them—and landed in the guardhouse.

Shortly after Monk's release from the military calaboose, the dapper Brigadier General Theodore Marley Brooks had been haled upon a charge of stealing hams. Somebody had planted the evidence. The nickname of Ham had stuck from that day.

What irked Ham especially was the fact that he had never been able to prove it was Monk who had framed him.

Monk only leered nastily at Ham, and asked Doc: "Where are you goin'?"

"If you do not know, you can tell the truth when those fellows ask you where we are," Doc informed him dryly.

Everyone but Monk and Ham now left the office. They entered the high-speed elevator. A breathtaking drop followed. Doc sent the cage to the basement level.

The New Jersey officers and their four witnesses had undoubtedly been passed somewhere en route.

Doc led his party along a white passage. They entered a private garage which the bronze man maintained in the basement. This held several cars, all excellent machines, but none in the least flashy.

Doc stepped to a large limousine. He produced two objects from a door pocket. One of these resembled a greatly overgrown wrist watch. The other was a flat box with numerous dials and switches, and a harness by which it could be carried under a coat, out of view.

The two objects were joined by a flexible conduit.

Doc flicked switches. On the glass dial of the oversize wristwatch contrivance appeared a picture of the office upstairs.

Aunt Nora looked at this picture, noting the presence of the big, furry Monk and the dapper Ham. Her eyes threatened to jump out of her head when she saw the two go to the door and admit a string of men.

"Land sakes!" she gasped. "A television machine! I didn't know they made 'em that small!"

"The only ones of that size are in Doc's possession," Long Tom advised her, with the natural pride of an electrical expert discussing a remarkable accomplishment in his profession. "Doc made them. The transmitter is concealed in the wall of the room upstairs."

"But I didn't see it turned on!"

"Doc did that when he pressed the inlaid table top."

There was a radio set in the limousine. Doc spun the dials. The words which came from the loudspeaker showed the set was tuned to a transmitter relaying sounds picked up by secret microphones in the office room above.

Between the televisor and the radio, Doc and the others were able to follow what went on above almost as perfectly as if they had been present.

FOUR of the men who had just arrived wore uniforms of New Jersey State Troopers. A New York detective was also with them. If an arrest was to be made, he would have to make it, jailing the prisoners until they were extradited to New Jersey.

Any waterfront dive might have been combed to get the other four. They were attired in suits, neckties, and hats which looked brand-new. This was productive of a suspicion that they had been dressed up for the occasion.

"Where is Doc Savage?" demanded one of the troopers.

Monk's homely face was very innocent. "Search me, officer."

"This is a regretful mission for us," said another of the policemen. "Knowing Doc Savage to be a man of fine character—"

"He ain't so damn fine!" sneered one of the four somewhat sinister witnesses. "We saw 'im murder a man!"

Ham beetled his brows and bent a hard stare on the quartet. This was Ham's element. As a lawyer, he had handled many lying witnesses.

"You saw the murder?" he challenged.

"Yeah!" they chorused sullenly.

"And you are sure it was Doc Savage?" Ham's tone of voice called them frauds as plainly as words could have.

"Yeah! We've seen the bronze guy's picture in the newspapers! It was 'im!"

Ham leveled his sword cane dramatically at the four. "The Green Bell showed you Doc Savage's picture, and gave you money to swear that he murdered Jim Cash! Isn't that right?"

This blunt accusation failed to have the desired effect. The spokesman of the quartet winked elaborately at one of the troopers.

"This guy must be nuts!" he said. "We don't know anything about any Green Bell. We saw Doc Savage push that poor feller onto that third rail. Like honest citizens should do, we told the police!"

"That's right!" snarled another of the four. "We don't have to stand here and listen to this little snort of a mouthpiece razz us, either!"

"Shut up!" growled one of the officers. Then, to Ham: "Can you tell us where we can find Doc Savage?"

"I do not know where he is," Ham said. This was the truth to a letter.

Ham now stepped into the library. He came back, bearing a large group picture. He held the print up before the four men who claimed they had seen the murder.

"Let's see you pick out Doc," he invited.

Doc Savage was not in the picture at all. Ham hoped to trick the men into a false identification.

It failed to work.

"What d'you think we are!" jeered one of the men. "Savage ain't there!"

Ham wondered if he looked as worried as he felt. These charlatans, he was now sure, had been shown a picture from which they could identify Doc.

This meant that Doc was certain to face a murder charge.

The police of both New York and New Jersey held the bronze man in great esteem. But that would not keep Doc out of jail—not with four witnesses saying he had committed a murder.

There was no such thing as bail on a murder charge.

"Can you tell us whether or not Doc Savage will give himself up?" asked one of the officers.

"Naw—he won't!" Monk rumbled. "Not to get himself throwed in jail on a fake charge!"

The officers became somewhat grim at this. "Then we'll have to spread a general alarm for him."

"Don't pay any attention to what this hairy dope says!" Ham interpolated, glaring at Monk. "He hasn't got good sense, so he don't know what Doc

THE CZAR OF FEAR 19

will do. I am sure Doc will take every measure to help the police."

The troopers showed plainly that they were distressed about the whole thing.

"This is—a case of murder, you know," the New York detective said reluctantly. "I am afraid we shall have to issue an immediate pick-up order for Doc."

The officers and the quartet of mountebank witnesses now took their departure.

"You had better watch those four closely!" Ham warned the police.

"Don't worry," replied the trooper. "We're going to pop 'em in the can an' keep 'em there!"

DOC SAVAGE gave the officers an interval in which to get out of the building. Then he went to a telephone in the garage and called the office upstairs.

"The thing looks pretty bad!" he advised Ham. "If I surrender myself now, I'll have to go to jail. I couldn't get bail on a charge that serious."

"That's right," Ham groaned.

"The thing to do is to get out of town. So we're leaving for Prosper City at once."

"Great!" Ham brightened. "We'll go and clean up on this Green Bell right in his own belfry!"

"*You* are not going!" Doc advised.

Ham squawked in disappointment. "But listen, Doc—"

"Someone must stay in New York and fight this murder charge," Doc pointed out. "You're elected."

Ham was groaning loudly when Doc hung up. The thought that he might miss out on some excitement was a big blow to Ham. He was the logical one to remain behind, however, because of his profession.

It was Doc's custom to assign his men tasks for which their particular profession fitted them. This was an emergency calling for a lawyer, which happened to be Ham's specialty. It was his hard luck if he was forced to remain behind and miss anything.

Monk soon entered the basement garage. His homely grin was so wide that it threatened to jam his little ears together on the back of his head. He was well aware of Ham's disappointment—and tickled in proportion.

"We shall leave for Prosper City in half an hour," Doc stated. "Can you make it?"

The query was directed at Aunt Nora, Alice Cash, and Ole Slater. As for his own men, Doc knew they would have no trouble getting away in that interval.

"Our bags are in our old car in a parking lot near here," Aunt Nora told him. "When we get our grips, we'll be ready to hike."

"It will not take me long to get my Gladstone from the railway station check room, where I left it!" Ole Slater offered.

As guards to accompany Aunt Nora and Alice Cash, Doc dispatched Renny and Monk—much to Monk's pleasure. A pretty girl always took Monk's eye.

Ole Slater declared he would need no protection. "I doubt if they know I am in New York, anyway."

It was noticeable that Ole favored Monk with a faint scowl when the homely fellow offered the attractive young lady a gallant arm.

Each of Doc's men assembled equipment which they might need. This was their usual procedure.

Monk, for instance, had a marvelously compact little chemical laboratory which he took. Long Tom had an assortment of parts from which he could assemble an almost unbelievable number of electrical devices. Big-fisted Renny had a few engineering instruments.

Johnny, the archaeologist and geologist, carried most of his equipment in his head in the form of knowledge. So he burdened himself with machine guns, ammunition and grenades, as well as a set of bulletproof vests.

The machine guns which Johnny packed were remarkable weapons. They resembled slightly oversized automatics, with big curled magazines. Doc had perfected them. They fired shots so swiftly that they sounded like gigantic bull fiddles when they went into operation.

These weapons were carried more for the terror they caused foes than for lethal use. Doc and his aides never took human life if they could help it.

However, Doc's enemies had a way of perishing in traps which they themselves had set for the bronze man.

THE group gathered in the skyscraper basement and entered the large limousine. A special lift carried the car to street level. Few persons, other than the building attendants, knew of the presence of the garage.

Ham, tapping his sword cane disconsolately against a polished toe, saw them off from the curb. He figured he was in for a dull time.

As a usual thing, when there was danger, Doc rode either in an open car or outside, clinging to the running board. He did this as a matter of safety. The manner in which his strange golden eyes could detect a lurking enemy was uncanny.

Doc broke his rule this time, and ensconced himself in the rear seat. To ride outside, where he could be seen, would mean difficulties with the police.

With Renny at the wheel, the car rolled toward the Hudson River.

Except for an occasional lonely drop, the rain had ceased. The streets glistened wetly. Out on the wide Hudson, two tugboats were hooting deep bass whistles, each stubbornly contesting for the right of way.

Warehouses loomed—flat, monster hulks.

Renny drove directly toward one of these. The headlights brought out a name on the front of the structure.

THE HIDALGO TRADING CO.

If one had taken the trouble to investigate, he would have learned the Hidalgo Trading Co. owned nothing but this one warehouse. Also, Doc Savage was the whole concern.

At Doc's quiet warning, no one got out of the limousine. By now, they had all noted that the windows were bulletproof glass more than an inch thick, and the body of the machine itself was armor-plate steel.

Renny depressed a switch on the instrument board. This produced no visible phenomena. But big doors in the front of the warehouse opened silently.

Actually, Renny had turned on a lantern which projected ultraviolet rays invisible to the human eye. These had operated a special photo-electric cell concealed in the front of the great barn of a building. This cell had set the door mechanism in action.

As the car glided forward, the lights illuminated the warehouse interior. Aunt Nora, Alice Cash, and Ole Slater emitted three gasps of surprise which blended as one.

The place held several planes. These ranged from a vast, tri-motored craft which was streamlined to an ultra degree, to various small gyros and auto-gyros. Every ship was an amphibian—capable of descending on land or water.

The automobile heaved gently over the threshold, and rolled several yards into the vast warehouse hangar. Everyone alighted and began unloading the duffel.

"Hey!" Monk ripped. "Lookit what's comin'!"

Seven ominous figures materialized soundlessly from the darkness outside. There was barely room for them to come abreast through the large door. They resembled a charge of crows.

Each was mantled from crown to toe in a black sack of a garment. The bells, painted on the fronts of the gowns, had a green hue which seemed particularly vile.

Three figures held automatics; the others gripped submachine guns. Extra ammunition drums for the rapid-firers were suspended around their necks by thin strings which could be broken with a jerk.

THE seven sinister figures ran a few feet within the warehouse.

"Give it to 'em!" snarled one.

Automatics and machine guns opened up in a hideous roar! Empty cartridges chased each other from the breeches of the automatics, and poured in brassy streams from the ejectors of the rapid-firers. Powder noise cascaded through the capacious warehouse in a deafening salvo.

Alice Cash shrieked, and shoved Aunt Nora into the shelter of the sedan. Quick thinking, that! Ole Slater followed them with a leap.

Doc Savage and his four friends merely stood there empty-handed, and watched the exhibition of murderous fury.

Something mysterious was happening to the bullets. A few feet from Doc and his men, the slugs seemed to stop in mid-air and splatter like raindrops. Some halted and hung in space, strangely distorted.

None of the bullets were reaching Doc's group.

The truth dawned on the gang of Green Bells. They ceased shooting as abruptly as they had started. They goggled at the bullets which seemed suspended in the air.

Their leader tried to yell a command. Amazement had gripped him so strongly that he made several unintelligible choking noises before he could get words out.

"Beat it!" he gulped. "This joint is hoodooed, or somethin'!"

As one man, the seven veered around and pitched for the outer darkness. What had just occurred was startling. But what happened now was far worse—at least to the Green Bells.

They seemed to smash headlong into an invisible wall. Bruised, noses spouting crimson, they bounced back. Two piled down on the floor, stunned.

The survivors now realized what had happened. Walls of glass—thick, transparent, and bulletproof—had arisen in front and behind.

The one in front must have been up when they entered; the rear panel had arisen after their feet had operated a hidden trip in the floor.

Howling in terror, they flung themselves against the transparent barricade. They shot at it. The bullets only splattered, or stuck. They could see tiny cracks radiating like cobwebs from points where the bullets made contact. This fact had escaped their notice before.

They skittered their hands along the cold, vertical expanse, seeking an escape.

Doc Savage glanced at his companions, and said quietly: "Hold your breath—at least a minute, if you can."

Drawing several small glass globes from his clothing, Doc advanced. The bulbs were thin-walled, and held a liquid.

Before the almost invisible barrier, Doc sprang high into the air and flung a fistful of the glass balls over the top. The tiny squashing noises as they broke was lost in the frightened wailing of the trapped Green Bells.

Doc waited. He was holding his breath; his friends were doing likewise. The two women and Ole Slater had followed suit, without knowing what it was all about.

The Green Bells began to act like men who had gone to sleep on their feet. They collapsed in quick succession. Some fell heavily; others reclined with more care, as if tired. The two who had dazed themselves by butting the glass wall, ceased their nervous twitchings.

Perhaps a minute elapsed.

Then Doc gave a signal, and his companions began to breathe.

Chapter VI
FEAR'S DOMAIN

"LAND sakes!" Aunt Nora sputtered. "What happened? I don't mean the glass walls! What put 'em to sleep like that?"

The homely Monk took it on himself to explain, probably for the benefit of pretty Alice Cash.

"There was an anaesthetic gas in the glass balls. It spreads quickly, and produces instant unconsciousness if breathed. After mixing with the air for something less than a minute, the stuff becomes ineffective."

Working rapidly, Doc Savage operated small levers at one side of the warehouse. The glass walls sank noiselessly.

"Put the Green Bells in the big plane," he directed. "The police will be drawn by those shots, and we want to get out of here before they arrive."

This order was carried out with swift efficiency.

Aunt Nora bounced about, highly excited by the lightning speed of recent events.

"This disguised hangar—these planes—that office of yours!" She waved her arms. "These things have cost a lot of money! You must be rich as sin!"

The bronze man only gave her one of his rare smiles.

The somewhat fantastic truth about Doc's wealth was destined to remain a mystery to Aunt Nora, just as it was an enigma to the rest of the world.

Doc possessed a fabulous hoard of gold. The trove lay in a lost valley in the remote mountain fastness of a Central American republic. Descendants of the ancient Mayan race lived in this valley and mined the treasure.

When Doc was in need of funds, he had merely to broadcast, at a certain hour, a few words in the Mayan language. This was picked up by a sensitive radio receiver in the lost valley. A few days later, a burro train laden with gold would appear in the capital of the Central American republic.

The cargo was always deposited to Doc's credit in a bank. It was a slim trip when one of these burro trains did not bring out a treasure of four or five million dollars.

The warehouse floor sloped downward. The outer end, a concrete apron, was underwater. The big plane was quickly rolled down and set afloat. Electric motors pulled great doors back on oiled tracks.

Doc took the controls. The motors started. They were equipped with efficient silencers, and made only shrill hissings.

A few minutes later, the giant plane was streaking over the surface of the Hudson; it cocked its nose up in a steep climb.

Looking backward, using binoculars, Doc's men could see red lights crawling about in the vicinity of the warehouse. These were police cars putting in a tardy arrival.

Prosper City lay to the westward, but Doc flew north. He soon turned the controls over to Renny. All of the bronze man's aides were expert airmen.

MOVING to the seven sleeping prisoners, Doc stripped off the green-belled black gowns.

Aunt Nora eyed the faces which were disclosed, and snapped: "I've seen those rats loafing around Prosper City!"

Alice Cash nodded, then relapsed into a white-faced silence. She was grieving over her brother's murder, and saying very little.

Ole Slater scowled, causing his features to lose some of their handsomeness. "I've seen them around town, too!"

Doc now used a hypodermic needle and administered a stimulant to one of the captives. This soon revived the fellow.

The man quailed from the bronze giant and began to whimper in terror. "It was all a mistake—"

Doc grasped the craven's face between muscular palms and began to stare steadily into the wavering eyes.

The onlookers soon understood what he was doing. Using hypnotism! But the victim was too frightened to realize what was occurring, or to combat the effects of the weird golden eyes.

The fellow finally became still, staring at Doc like a bird at a big serpent.

"Who is the Green Bell?" Doc demanded in a compelling tone.

"I dunno," the man mumbled tonelessly. "None of us knows."

Under normal conditions, Doc would not have believed a word the man told him. But now he knew he was hearing the truth.

"Who told you to spring that trap at the warehouse?" he persisted.

"The Green Bell telephoned us," was the droned answer. "He just said for us to follow you and kill you and your men when we got a chance. We were not to harm the two women and Ole Slater."

"Glory be!" exploded Aunt Nora. "Why didn't he want Alice and Ole and me done away with?"

Doc relayed this query to his source of information.

"It was on account of the effect their death would have on their friends in Prosper City," mumbled the Green Bell hireling. "They'd lynch Judborn Tugg. Tugg is important in the big scheme, whatever it is!"

Doc queried: "Do Judborn Tugg and Slick Cooley belong to the Green Bell's gang?"

"I dunno—I guess so. I don't know much. I'm a new man."

Doc tried one more question. "Did the Green Bell send you to New York, in the first place, to murder me?"

"I don't think so. He just sent us so we'd be handy in case something went wrong. His first idea was to get you on his payroll. He thought you were a common muscle man."

"Did you and this gang here murder Jim Cash?"

"No. Some more of the Green Bell's men done that."

This summed up the information Doc was able to secure from the man. He awakened the other six, and put questions to them, but learned little more. Nothing, in fact, that was valuable.

RENNY veered the giant plane inland, toward the mountainous, thinly populated upstate portion of New York.

The huge speed-cowled motors were almost wide open. The ship was making a speed considerably in excess of two hundred and fifty miles an hour. It was one of the fastest craft for its size to be found.

Doc went to the radio transmitter and sent a brief message.

Later in the night, when they landed in a clearing in the northern wilderness, three ghostly ambulances were waiting. These had been summoned by Doc's radio message.

White-clad men, their faces lost in the shadows beneath their cap brims, loaded the seven prisoners into the ambulances. Few words were exchanged.

The ambulances departed. Doc took his plane off. The whole incident had been grim and spectral.

Aunt Nora was bewildered. "What'll happen to those seven men?"

"They will be taken care of," Doc said, and did not clarify the thing further.

Doc did not advertise what happened to wrongdoers whom he captured. The bronze man maintained a strange institution in this mountain wilderness. There, the seven men would undergo brain operations which would cause them to completely forget their pasts.

Next, they would be taught upright citizenship and a trade. They would be turned loose—honest men, unaware of their past criminal careers.

No crook, once treated in this manner, had ever returned to evil ways.

Doc's institution would have caused a worldwide sensation, had its existence become public.

A hissing meteor, the plane hurtled through the night, bearing the remarkable bronze man, his four unusual aides, and the three unfortunates whom he intended to help.

PROSPER CITY—crisscrossed strings of street lamps far below—appeared some time before dawn.

"The airport is north of town!" Alice Cash advised.

The drome was unlighted. It was situated in the middle of an area of ripening grain which looked yellow in the moonlight—there was a moon shining on Prosper City. The flying field was turfed with grass, which was very dark as seen from the air.

Three rusty hangars were hunched at the edge of the tarmac. A junked plane stood behind one shed. Faded pennants of fabric clung to its naked skeleton.

As far as could be seen, there was no one about.

Doc cranked the landing wheels down out of the wells, into which they had disappeared for greater streamlining. He planted the big ship on the ground as lightly as if it had been a glider. They coasted to a stop perhaps two hundred feet from one of the hangars.

The sliding door of this hangar scooted back and let out a flood of men. They wore police uniforms.

An incredibly tall, rawboned man led the policemen. He had an enormous mustache, and a small red face. The combination was remindful of a cherry with a large brown caterpillar on it.

"The police chief—Clem Clements!" Aunt Nora snapped. "I'll bet someone has told him we're criminals, and Clem has believed 'em! Clem is sure pin-headed!"

Chief Clements was flourishing an official-looking document.

Doc Savage needed no close inspection to tell him what this paper was—a warrant for his arrest, perhaps, or a wire from New York, requesting the bronze man's apprehension.

A deduction that Doc would head for Prosper City would call for no great thinking on the mysterious Green Bell's part. But the mastermind had moved quickly to give more trouble to Doc and his friends.

Doc did a bit of fast thinking, and decided the simplest thing he could do was to avoid Chief Clements for the present.

Turning in the pilot's seat, Doc glanced backward. There had been no rain in Prosper City recently. The prop stream was pulling dust from the grass roots, and squirting it back in a funnel. There was much more dust around the hangars.

Doc locked one wheel brake, and slapped the

throttles open. This pivoted the plane. A dusty hurricane slapped the faces of Chief Clements and his men.

They were blinded. They yelled angrily, and fired warning shots in the air.

Doc dropped out of the ship. He seemed to flatten and vanish in the scrubby grass. He left the vicinity like a startled ghost.

CHIEF CLEMENTS dashed up to the plane, rubbing his eyes and blowing dust out of his big mustache.

"You done that on purpose!" he declared irately. He had a metallic, whanging voice.

Renny put his sober face out of a window. The twanging voice of Chief Clements reminded him of a taut barbed wire being plucked.

"We didn't think of the dust!" he said meekly. This was not a prevarication—Doc had thought of the dust.

"We're lookin' for a murderer named Doc Savage!" snapped Chief Clements.

Renny heaved a relieved sigh. The policemen had been blinded by the dust so effectively that Doc's departure had escaped their notice.

"Who put you up to this, Clem Clements?" Aunt Nora shouted wrathfully.

Chief Clements glared at Aunt Nora as if the motherly old lady had horns.

"None of your business!" he retorted, somewhat childishly.

Aunt Nora jumped out of the plane. "Was it Judborn Tugg?"

Chief Clements pulled the ends of his mustache down in a scowl, giving the impression that the caterpillar on the cherry had bowed its back.

"Now don't you start running down Judborn Tugg!" he twanged. "He's an upright man, and the best citizen this town's got! What if he did wire me from New York that you was mixed up with a murderer named Doc Savage, and might show up here? He was doin' the decent thing!"

"Tugg never did a decent thing in his whole evil life!" Aunt Nora said scathingly.

Chief Clements thrust his little red head forward. "I think you're behind this trouble, Aunt Nora Boston! I've just been waitin' to get some proof, so I could throw you in jail!"

Aunt Nora cocked her arms akimbo. "That sounds like some of Judborn Tugg's advice!"

"If I find Doc Savage in that plane, you're gonna be locked up on a charge of helpin' a murderer escape!" Chief Clements yelled.

"If you find Doc Savage in the ship, I'll go to jail willingly!" Aunt Nora snapped.

Chief Clements and his men now searched the giant tri-motor. Their faces registered a great deal of disappointment when they found no bronze man.

"We'll hang around the airport!" the Prosper City police chief whanged. "Savage may show up in another plane. I've got a guard around your house, too, Aunt Nora! And you're gonna be shadowed, every move you make. If Doc Savage tries to get in touch with you, we'll nab 'im!"

Aunt Nora sniffed loudly. But her wrinkled face showed concern.

"I suppose it's all right to call a car to take us into town?" she snapped.

"I'll send you in my car!" offered Chief Clements, figuring this would make it simpler for his men to keep track of Aunt Nora and her companions.

"I wouldn't ride in it!" Aunt Nora informed him. "I'll telephone for a hack!"

THE cab which Aunt Nora summoned arrived something over half an hour later.

The driver was a shabby individual, who slouched low behind the wheel. He had a purple nose, bulging cheeks, and he seemed half asleep. He did not offer to open the door for his fares.

The luggage was piled in front with the chauffeur. The two women and Ole Slater got in the rear. Johnny and Long Tom turned down the drop seats. Monk and Renny, the giants of the group, rode clinging to the running board.

The taxi had not rolled far when it passed a pitiful little camp beside the road. There was a ragged tent and a litter of house furnishings which had been virtually ruined by the weather. It was a scene of utter poverty, even when seen in the mellow glow of the moonlight.

"There's a sample," Aunt Nora muttered. "A year ago, that family was happy and buying their own home. The husband was one who wouldn't go out on strike. Driver—stop the car! I want these people to hear something!"

The machine halted; the motor silenced. A sound which came steadily from the ragged tent could now be heard. It was a low, frightful gibbering. It kept up without end.

"That's the poor husband," Aunt Nora said brokenly. "He is insane! The Green Bell made him that way in some horrible fashion! As I told you, there's more than a dozen others like him. They're all men who wanted to stay at work, and keep the mills and mines operating. The Green Bell is trying to break every factory in this town."

Everyone was silent as the car got underway again. To Doc's four men, this incident had been an appalling sample of what they were up against. It brought home to them the sinister power of this mysterious master, the Green Bell.

They soon saw other evidence of the terrible conditions in Prosper City. In more than one alley, there were furtive, slinking figures. These individuals were looking for scraps of food.

"The poor souls are starving!" Aunt Nora explained.

"It's ghastly!" Ole Slater groaned. "If I should put conditions such as these in the play I am writing, people in other cities would say it couldn't happen! And no one knows what's behind it all!"

Johnny, the gaunt geologist, took off his spectacles with the magnifying left lens. "Isn't there a community chest, or some kind of a charity fund?"

"All of those were exhausted long ago," Alice Cash told him quietly. "Nine out of every ten men in Prosper City are out of work. That seems inconceivable. But it is true!"

The car rolled on. It turned several corners, behaving somewhat uncertainly, as if the driver did not know where he was going.

"You're not going toward my house!" Aunt Nora rapped.

The driver shrugged. "Which way is it?"

"You don't know?" Aunt Nora asked incredulously.

"No!" said the driver with the purple nose and fat cheeks.

"Humph! It looks like you have never been in Prosper City before!"

"I haven't!"

Aunt Nora suddenly stood up and thrust her face close to that of the driver. She stared.

"Glory be!" she ejaculated. "You're Doc Savage!"

Chapter VII
CLEMENTS SETS A TRAP

THE discovery that the chauffeur was Doc Savage surprised Monk and Renny so greatly that they almost fell off the running board. Ole Slater jumped as if he had been slapped. Alice Cash made silent whistling lips of wonder.

Long Tom and Johnny both chuckled. This was not the first time the bronze man had donned a remarkable disguise. He was a master of make-up, just as he was a master of innumerable other things.

"I was hanging around, and heard you phone for the cab," Doc enlightened Aunt Nora. "It was a simple matter to stop the machine and bribe the driver to let me take his place."

"Where's the driver?" Aunt Nora wanted to know.

"He is going to sneak past the guards, and be waiting in your house to take the car away. That will get me into your house without the knowledge of the watching policemen."

Aunt Nora settled back with a sigh which almost attained happiness. "If you ask this old girl, I'm betting Prosper City is soon going to see the end of its streak of hard luck."

The rooming house operated by Aunt Nora Boston was a large, rambling white structure of two stories and a set of garret bedrooms. Much neatly

trimmed shrubbery surrounded it. Doc and his men thought the old-fashioned place rather attractive.

Doc's ruse for gaining admission to the house was carried to a successful completion. The real driver drove the taxi away, leaving Doc behind.

Chief Clements' cops, stationed just outside Aunt Nora's grounds, did not smell a mouse.

Aunt Nora's house stood on the outskirts of Prosper City, at the foot of a range of high, wooded hills, which the local citizens called mountains.

Coal mines were located in the mountains, Doc soon learned. Long galleries from these mines underlaid much of Prosper City itself.

Alice Cash grasped an opportunity to impart the information that Aunt Nora had secured a small fortune from the sale of this coal. The kindly old lady had expended all of her funds in providing for the needy, however.

The sun flushed up redly. With dawn, a fresh shift of policemen went on duty. There were four of the officers observing the house.

Doc was careful to keep out of sight.

The bronze man took his first steps aimed at improving conditions in Prosper City. From a pocket, he produced a sheaf of bank notes.

Aunt Nora rubbed her eyes when she saw the size of the bills. Some were hundreds, but most were of thousand-dollar denomination.

Doc passed the small fortune to Aunt Nora, along with instructions.

Aunt Nora paid a visit to the Prosper City merchants who had been most generous in contributing to charity. Each received a tremendous order for food and clothing, with cash on the line.

The delight with which the merchants greeted this business was moving. One old groceryman, who had been carrying his whole neighborhood on credit because he could not bear to see former customers in want, sat down and cried.

Before noon, arrangements were completed for the delivery of more than a score of truck loads of food and clothing to Aunt Nora's capacious yard. "By night," was the time insisted upon.

There were a few skinflint merchants who had given credit to none of the impoverished, and who had not contributed to charity. These fellows did not get a penny of Doc's business.

A circus was stranded in town. Aunt Nora leased the big top and the menagerie tent, and ordered them erected in her yard to shelter the supplies.

Working under Doc's directions, Ole Slater rented several open cars. These rolled through the streets. Slater, Alice Cash and Doc's four men stood in the back seats with megaphones, broadcasting the fact that there would be a food distribution and a meeting at Aunt Nora's place that night.

"Tell them," Doc directed, "that at this gathering

a plan will be presented which will put every man in Prosper City back to work within the next two weeks."

To say this information created a sensation in Prosper City was putting it mildly. Few believed the thing could be done. But every man, his family, and his dog would attend the meeting to see what it was all about.

THE mysterious mastermind, the Green Bell, was not dormant. Hardfaced men—the agitators who had been prominent in the trouble from the first—mounted soap boxes at street corners, and began to label Aunt Nora as a sinister woman, and Doc Savage a murderer and worse.

The elderly lady, they said, was in league with "The Interests." Just who The Interests were, they neglected to mention explicitly, but included mill and mine owners in a general way. Aunt Nora was going to try to persuade men to go back to work at starvation wages, they declared. Why go to work and starve anyway, while the pockets of the rich were lined?

This argument would have been good, had it had any foundation in truth. These fellows did not give a hoot about the welfare of the workmen, although they claimed they did.

They were on the payroll of the Green Bell. Their purpose was to keep the factories and mines closed. Why? Only the Green Bell knew.

The hired agitators held themselves up as protectors of the workers. They voiced threats against all who attended Aunt Nora's meeting.

"We ain't gonna go to work until we get decent wages!" one orator proclaimed. "You're fools if you listen to the soft-soaping words of that lying old lady—"

At this point, one of Aunt Nora's admirers knocked the spieler off his soap box. A dozen policemen were required to break up the fight which followed.

This was not the only incident of its kind. The day was marked by a dribble of bruised and battered agitators into the hospitals.

Chief of Police Clements appeared at Aunt Nora's house. His big mustache was a-bristle with rage.

"I forbid this meeting tonight!" he yelled. "You're just fixing to start more trouble! Even now, there's fightin' all over town!"

"Judborn Tugg must be back home!" Aunt Nora jeered.

Chief Clements became purple. It was a fact that Judborn Tugg and Slick Cooley had alighted from the noon train.

"What's that got to do with it?" he gritted.

"Didn't Tugg tell you to stop my meeting?" Aunt Nora countered.

This was the truth, and Chief Clements was not ashamed to admit it. Chief Clements was an honest soul, if a dumb one, and pompous Judborn Tugg was an idol in his eyes.

"Mr. Tugg is the best citizen this town has!" he declared with the firmness of an ignorant man with one firmly fixed idea. "It is true that he thinks your powwow will only cause trouble. I think so, too! And I'm going to break it up!"

"You're going to get your head broke if you try it!" retorted Aunt Nora.

This was hardly the argument to use on a bull-headed man such as Chief Clements. It only made his determination the firmer.

Pretty Alice Cash came forward with the argument which really swayed the boss of the Prosper City police.

"We are going to distribute food to the starving tonight," she said gently. "Surely, you are not going to be cold-blooded enough to stop that?"

Chief Clements squirmed uncomfortably. He might be thick-headed and a worshiper of Judborn Tugg, but he was also a kindly man. If any hungry person was to be fed, he would be the last one to stand in the way.

The upshot was that he agreed to let the meeting be held.

"But I'm gonna have plenty of cops here," he warned.

DOC SAVAGE had eavesdropped from the concealment of another room. He complimented attractive Alice Cash when she joined him.

"You were clever enough to avoid what might have been a nasty bit of trouble!" he told her.

Alice gave Doc a ravishing smile of thanks. She was, it could be seen plainly, experiencing a great attraction for the giant bronze man. Signs already indicated that, once grief over her brother's death was dulled by the passing of a little time, she was going to fall for Doc in a big way.

Ole Slater could see this. He failed to conceal a worried look. He was obviously enraptured with the entrancing Alice.

He might have been relieved to know that Doc Savage made it a policy to steer far wide of feminine entanglements. His perilous, active career made that necessary. Should he encumber himself with a wife, she would not only be always in danger of becoming a widow, but enemies would strike at Doc through her. He could let no woman lead a life like that.

Late in the afternoon, Ham telephoned from New York. He reported that he was investigating the past lives of the four men who had sworn falsely that they had seen Doc murder Jim Cash.

"I may be able to get something on them that will make them tell the truth," he said hopefully. "But, frankly, I'm not doing so hot."

Since Doc was forced to keep under cover, his four aides in Prosper City handled preparations for the night's conclave.

Big-fisted Renny, who had superintended construction of skyscrapers and bridges as an engineer, directed raising of the circus tents. Long Tom, the

Renny lunged in and flung a fist that was as big and hard as half a concrete block.

electrical wizard, installed a public address system, so that every word spoken from a rostrum at one end of the big top could be heard. He also erected powerful flood lights.

Gorillalike Monk, who had learned to command men as a lieutenant colonel in the army, organized a score of Aunt Nora's friends into a corps to handle the distribution of food and clothing.

Two banks remained open in Prosper City. The gaunt Johnny visited one of them, after ascertaining Judborn Tugg was a director in the other. The one Johnny entered was the smaller one.

When Johnny departed, he left a stunned set of bank officials behind. They held a check deposited in Doc Savage's name. The amount of this check crowded the space providing for writing in the figures. The bankers telephoned New York before they would believe the draft was good.

A rumor of this enormous deposit got out. The Prosper City *News* telephoned New York newspapers, asking who this Doc Savage was. They were informed that he was a bronze man of mystery, who possessed an unknown source of fabulous wealth, and who devoted his life to fighting other people's battles. They also learned that Doc now stood accused of murdering Jim Cash.

The *News* carried both stories on its front page that evening. The paper also printed an editorial, beginning:

"Who is Doc Savage—Midas or murderer? Is he a being whose might and wealth is to save Prosper City? Or is he a charlatan and a killer with a sinister purpose?"

Indications were that almost everyone in Prosper City was going to attend Aunt Nora Boston's meeting in hopes of learning the answer.

LONG before sundown, men, women, and children began trickling into Aunt Nora's great yard. The first comers were ragged, pitiful figures with pinched faces. Hunger had drawn them.

Some of the Green Bell's hired agitators appeared and started voicing threats. Monk's corps of trained helpers lit into these fellows with clubs. A pitched battle ensued.

An agitator drew a pistol and tried to kill Monk. The first shot missed.

Renny lunged in and flung a fist that was as big and hard as half a concrete block.

The gun wielder dropped, his jaw broken like so much gravel.

Chief Clements appeared magically, leading a squad of at least thirty officers. The latter had long billies, tear-gas bombs, and gas masks.

"I knew there was gonna be trouble here!" Chief Clements howled. "Every blasted one of you are under arrest!"

Monk waved at the agitators. "You mean those clucks are pulled, don't you?"

"I don't mean them! They're within their rights in makin' speeches! This is a free country! I mean *you!*"

Ole Slater was in none too good a temper, probably because he had been worrying all day over the unmistakable signs charming Alice Cash gave of falling for Doc Savage. Rage got the better of Slater.

He drew back and pasted the handiest cop.

Two policemen sprang upon Slater and belabored him with their clubs.

"Everybody's under arrest!" Chief Clements repeated shrilly. "Then we're gonna search the house! We got a tip that Doc Savage is in there!"

Monk rammed his homely face forward. "You what?"

"Judborn Tugg said one of his friends saw a bronze man hidin' in the house!" growled the police leader.

Doc Savage was stationed near an open window in the house, where he could listen. His strange golden eyes betrayed no emotion at Chief Clements' words.

The report that Doc was concealed in Aunt Nora's home was a puzzling angle, however. Indirectly, it had emanated from the mysterious Green Bell, of course. But how had he known Doc was there? Or had he only made a wild guess?

Doc glided to a rear window. Darkness had now fallen, but the grounds were brilliantly lighted by Long Tom's flood lamps.

Police were stationed in a cordon around the house. They stood close together. It was doubtful if a mosquito could escape past them without being discovered.

Doc was in a trap!

BACK to the open front window, Doc moved. The wall of one circus tent was not many yards distant. He faced this. The remarkable muscles in his throat knotted into strange positions.

He spoke loudly, using ventriloquism. His words seemed to come from the tent wall. They were strange words—a not unmusical stream of gutturals.

It was the language of the ancient Mayans. Doc's men had learned it on their adventurous visit to the lost Central American valley which held Doc's golden trove. It was one of the least-known tongues on earth. Certainly Chief Clements did not understand it.

"Face the tent wall!" was Doc's first advice.

Monk and the other four instantly began staring at the tent. This enhanced the impression that the voice was emanating from that source. Doc knew very well that half the success of ventriloquism lies in getting the hearer's attention on something he *thinks* the voice is coming from.

Doc now added further commands, speaking rapidly. He got them all out before the policemen came to life.

Chief Clements dashed to the tent, lifted the wall, then looked baffled when he found no one. He spun on Monk and the others.

"Put your hands up!" he twanged. "You're carryin' them funny-lookin' little guns! We don't allow gun totin' in Prosper City!"

The "funny-lookin'" guns which he referred to were the tiny machine guns which would fire with such terrific speed.

Monk ignored the order.

"I gotta talk this over with my friends," he said in his small voice.

"You ain't gonna do nothin' of the kind!"

Monk and the others now drew their weapons. "Oh, yes, we are! If you don't let us talk, there's gonna be plenty of trouble!"

Chief Clements hedged angrily, eyeing the weapons. Finally he gave in.

"All right. But you gotta stay in plain sight!"

Monk and the rest did not follow this order to the letter. They retired within the tent. Monk entered the house and came back with hands empty, but with a suspicious package bulging his coat.

The conference lasted perhaps another minute. Then everyone came out of the tent. They threw down their weapons.

"That satisfy you?" Monk demanded.

"We're gonna search you!" whanged Chief Clements.

The officers advanced. Counting Doc's four aides and the score of recruits for the food distribution, there came near being one prisoner for every policeman.

The search got underway. Monk coughed loudly. Instantly, every captive brought his right hand in contact with the face or hands of the lawman who was frisking him.

The Policemen toppled over like mown bluegrass. They lay where they fell, snoring loudly.

Highly elated, Monk and the rest removed tiny metal thimbles from their fingers. These were fashioned to blend closely with fingertips. Only an intent inspection would disclose them, and the unsuspecting officers had failed to note the things.

Each thimble held a tiny hypodermic needle, which, upon contact with the skin, injected a drug producing a sleep of several hours' duration.

Doc, when he had spoken Mayan, had directed this operation to overpower the police. These thimbles were devices of his own invention.

Chief Clements and his men were carried to their parked cars and dumped on the cushions.

Onlookers, vastly puzzled, agreed to drive them away.

"We're shut of that guy until midnight, anyway!" Monk grinned.

THE crowd gathered with increasing speed. Among those coming now were substantial citizens—owners of mills and mines which were being thrown into bankruptcy by the enforced idleness.

It was a strange situation. The owners were anxious to operate their plants; the workmen wanted jobs badly. But the odious organization of the Green Bell was holding both at a standstill. To open a factory meant it would be bombed or burned. For a workman to take a job meant he was in danger of beatings or—worst of all—the weird, horrible insanity.

That there was some cold, relentless purpose behind it all, many realized. But they could not fathom the reason.

Why was the Green Bell trying to bankrupt every industry in Prosper City? Was he a fiend with a mad hate for the town? No one knew.

The crowd seemed reluctant to enter the tents. More than one man there had felt the vengeance of the Green Bell. They gathered in knots outside and talked. A few became frightened and left.

The agitators on the Green Bell's payroll had not spoken entirely without effect.

In order to quiet fears, Long Tom tuned in a portable radio set and stood the loudspeaker near the microphone of the public-address system.

Dance music was now audible all over the grounds, and for some distance along the suburban roads in either direction. The tune came from the local Prosper City station.

Unexpectedly, an unearthly wail burst in upon the lilting of fiddles and the muted moaning of saxophones. The sound rose and fell, changing its tone. It was like the death cries of a monster, pouring from the loudspeakers.

A deep-throated, reverberating boom lifted over the bedlam of wailing. The throbbing sound seemed to fill all the night, magnified a thousand times by the address-system speakers. More of the weird notes came. A death-walk procession!

It might have been the tolling of some cataclysmic dirge.

The sound ended, and the jazzy dance tune poured from the loudspeakers as if nothing happened.

On the grounds men milled, grim of eye and pale of face. Women clung to their husbands, or mothered their children. The hideous tolling had stricken stark terror.

"The Green Bell!" a man mumbled.

"It means death or insanity to somebody! It nearly always does!"

Doc Savage, a motionless statue of bronze, surveyed the scene from the house. He had seen savage tribesmen in far countries, living in apprehension of something they did not understand. He had seen passengers on a great ocean liner aghast at approaching disaster.

He had never seen quite the depth of fear which was here before his eyes, induced by the gonging sound with which the Green Bell had associated himself.

The unknown brain back of this strange trouble—the being who was reducing a city to poverty for some secret reason of his own—had progressed far toward accomplishing his aims. Prosper City was a realm of fear, and he was its czar.

Chapter VIII
VOICE FROM THE EARTH

SOME two hundred yards from Aunt Nora Boston's house, a man perched in a tree, laughing heartily. He was getting great glee out of the terror which the Green Bell's sound had wrought.

Slick Cooley held his side with one hand, and a limb with the other. He finally stifled his unholy mirth.

"That'll hold 'em!" he chuckled.

He pocketed a pair of binoculars and clambered out of the tree. Carefully avoiding the road, he strode northward. On his right, the low mountains frowned in the pale moonlight. He paralleled them.

When he had covered some distance, he veered over to the road, where walking was easier. A dog ran out and barked at him. Slick threw clods at the dog.

He went on. The dog had come from the last house; ahead was a large area of marsh land. A wealthy farmer had once tried to drain this swampy section to cultivate it, but had been forced to give the task up as a bad job. Great weeds and brush had overgrown the wasteland.

A car came up behind Slick, and stopped when it was alongside him. The machine was Judborn Tugg's flashy roadster. Tugg in person sat back of the wheel. He inquired: "Lift?"

Slick got in.

"The bellin' noise scared that crowd plenty!" he boasted.

"I cannot understand what happened to Chief Clements!" Tugg snapped. "I visited the man at the hospital! He seems only to be asleep. But they can't wake him up!"

"If I was you, I'd lay off Chief Clements!" Slick leered.

"Why?"

"Some day he's gonna wake up to the fact that you ain't the goody-goody he thinks you are. When them knot-headed guys turn on a man, they can be just as strong agin' him as they were for him!"

"Nonsense!" Tugg retorted grandly. "Chief Clements is too dumb to ever suspect anything. And he is very valuable to me."

Slick squinted curiously at Judborn Tugg.

Noting the glance, Tugg added hastily: "Valuable to the Green Bell, I mean!"

The roadster pulled into a narrow lane through the brush. They soon parked the machine and went on afoot.

Slick walked in silence. He was wondering if Judborn Tugg could be the Green Bell. True, there were occasions when a hooded man appeared before them both and said he was the Green Bell. This had happened in the car in New York.

But such appearances might be made by members of the gang. Slick himself had once been ordered to don a black gown and play the part of the Green Bell. Tugg might be the mastermind, Slick reasoned.

Suddenly, he recalled the remark he had made in New York about slaying the Green Bell, once he learned the fellow's identity, and substituting himself as the unknown leader.

Slick was serious about that. But he wished now that he had been more reticent with his words. He shivered several times. If Tugg was the Green Bell, Slick had a feeling he was as good as a dead man.

A ramshackle old barn appeared in the moonlight. They rapped on the door, giving a peculiar, drumming signal.

"Come in!" said a weirdly hollow, booming voice. They entered.

THE ancient barn was concrete-floored. A black, ominous figure sat cross-legged in the shadows at the rear. The smoky robe sheathed it from head to foot. Although the form was seated, it also leaned back slightly against the rear wall. Through cracks in this wall, strings of moonlight were visible.

Most of the luminance within the structure came from two candles a few feet in front of the seated apparition. These candles were green, and their flame was sputtering and green. They cast a bilious light on the green-bell design of the seated one's robe, and on the green goggles which masked the eyes. The effect was eerie.

No other word was spoken.

Slick Cooley and Judborn Tugg both drew black hoods from within their clothing and donned them.

In the distance, a crashing of brush denoted men approaching. They filed in—eight in the first group, then by twos and threes and fours. Every man was draped in a sepian masquerade.

No word was spoken. They stood in a half circle, keeping their distance from the strange seated figure. The latter did not move in the slightest, or speak. Nor did the arrivals voice anything. They had come, these followers of the Green Bell, in answer to the summons tolled over the radio. The sound had warned them to gather here for orders.

"Are all present?" asked a voice from the seated form. It was hollowly booming, that tone! It seemed incredible that it could come from a human throat.

Slick counted the assembled men.

"All but about half a dozen," he said. "I guess they didn't hear the call."

"Speak louder!" commanded the sepulchral voice.

Slick fairly yelled a repetition of his statement.

"Very well!" came the croaked reply. "Judborn Tugg—are you there?"

Tugg came forward and shouted: "Yes!"

Slick backed away. It was always like this—the Green Bell pretending he was partially deaf.

The gloomy figure might not be the Green Bell, either, Slick reflected. It could conceivably be some member of the gang who had been ordered to serve in the Green Bell's place.

"I am far from satisfied with certain work done today!" tolled the seated form. "Chief Clements, for instance, was to have been persuaded to seize Doc Savage."

"Could I help that?" Tugg protested. "I did my part. But Chief Clements is so stupid that he let Savage run a whizzer on him!"

"I am not sure that Clements being stupid is entirely to blame," came the dull voice. "I sent seven men to get Savage in New York, and they vanished completely. They were not dumb fellows. Savage is a very dangerous foe!"

Tugg wiped at his fat forehead. His features were, of course, mantled in the black hood, and the wiping gesture upon the cloth was somewhat ludicrous. Savage dangerous! Did he not know it?

"I been doing my best!" he yelled.

"And that was not good! Slick Cooley—I'll talk to you now."

"Sure!" Slick shouted.

He scuttled forward, a spooky vision in the green-belled hood. He did not mind the mention of his name. He knew everyone here, anyway. Many of those present, however, were unacquainted with one another.

The seated figure had not moved perceptibly at any time.

"You did good work in noting Savage's reflection in a mirror in Aunt Nora Boston's house, when you were watching with binoculars!" said the fantastic voice.

Slick was slightly shocked. It was the first time he had heard the Green Bell bestow praise. It made him uneasy.

"I was just doin' my best!" he bellowed.

A SHORT silence ensued. Uncanny quiet lay in the old wreck of a barn. No one moved. The creamy strips of moonlight in the cracks had a spectral quality.

"I need a trustworthy man for the work ahead!" tolled the Green Bell. "So I am selecting you. For this work, if you complete it successfully, you will receive a bonus, over and above your regular pay, of fifty thousand dollars."

Slick's startled gasp puffed out his hood like a small balloon.

"Concealed in the weeds beside the door of this barn you will find my device which produces insanity!" continued the Green Bell. "You will place this where Doc Savage will come close to it, preferably near the head of his bed."

"But I dunno how to work the contraption," Slick muttered.

"What?"

Slick had forgotten to yell. He did so now. "How d'you work it?"

"That is very simple. There is only one switch upon the box. You throw it. Be careful that the switch is not operated accidentally while you are carrying the container. And once you do work it, get away quickly. It takes only a few seconds for the thing to disrupt the functions of a human brain!"

"O. K.!" Slick bellowed.

"With the box, you will find a package of money—ten thousand dollars," continued the voice. "You will take the sum to Chief Clements' office after you plant the box. Wait for Chief Clements to appear; then post the ten thousand dollars as a reward for Doc Savage—dead or alive. This precaution is in case you fail."

"O.K. to that, too!" Slick barked. "I won't slip up!"

"That will be all, then. You other men remain in close touch with Slick or Judborn Tugg, so that you can receive orders quickly."

The men bobbed their hoods in understanding, then departed. They went swiftly, as if eager to quit the ghostly presence.

Slick Cooley remained behind, making a pretense at examining the box which he found in the weeds beside the door. The box was not large. It was shiny and black, with a tiny single-pole switch on the top.

There was also a bundle of money, which Slick pocketed.

He carried the box to the nearby brush and waited, eyes fixed on the barn door. He was watching for the Green Bell to appear. Slick intended to follow the mastermind and learn who he was.

Minutes dragged by. No one put in an appearance. Almost half an hour passed.

Impatient, Slick crept to the door and peered in.

The eerie black form had not moved. The sputtering green candles had burned quite low.

Slick debated, then decided to stake all on a desperate chance. He fished the two silenced guns from his armpits and shoved through the door.

"Put 'em up!" he gritted.

The seated figure did not stir.

Slick ripped another command. No response! He became excited. Both his guns coughed bullets!

The slugs hit the black form and the wall with smacking reports which were much louder than the *chung!* of the silenced weapons.

The apparition in black still remained motionless.

Frankly terrified, Slick pitched forward and brought a gun crashing down on the hooded head.

The whole figure collapsed, amid a loud cracking! It was nothing but a framework of sticks!

CURSING feverishly, Slick bent to examine the thing. A hole in the concrete floor came to view. This had been partially concealed by the black gown.

Slick lighted a match and held it over the hole. He saw the moldy red walls of tile.

Comprehension dawned on Slick. The farmer who had once tried to cultivate this marshland had put in an intricate system of tile drains. The hole in the floor admitted to one of these underground pipes. Or so Slick had decided.

Doubtless there were many other exits. The Green Bell might have been speaking from anywhere in the vicinity.

This, then, accounted for the necessity of yelling. It took a loud tone to carry through the tile labyrinth.

Using his flashlight, Slick carefully rebuilt the framework which supported the black gown. It was just as well, he realized, that his treachery should not be discovered.

SOME time later, Slick appeared in the vicinity of Aunt Nora Boston's home.

Distribution of food and clothing to the needy was well underway, from the looks of the situation. There was a multitude in the two big tents and on the grounds.

Those who had received an allotment of necessities were not departing. They wanted to attend the meeting which was to follow. Especially did they want to see and hear this remarkable bronze man, Doc Savage.

The food in their hands was concrete evidence that the mystery man meant business. Doc had known the distribution would have this effect, hence he had ordered it to be made before the speeches. He needed every ounce of cooperation and confidence from these people.

The battle against the insidious forces of the Green Bell was just starting.

Presence of the crowd made it simple for Slick to snap his hat brim over his eyes and mingle among them. He worked to Aunt Nora's house. All attention was directed on the tent. It proved easy for Slick to enter the house, unobserved.

He made his furtive way to the room where, during the day, he had been lucky enough to observe Doc Savage's reflection in a mirror. He reasoned this was Doc's quarters.

Certain articles of the bronze man's attire hanging in a closet told Slick he was correct.

Numerous intricate mechanical and electrical devices stood about the room. Of these, Slick identified only a portable radio outfit. The other stuff was too complex for his rather limited understanding.

Slick disturbed nothing. He was too canny for that. Nor did he show a light. The moon furnished sufficient illumination.

Behind the head of the bed stood a large, dilapidated cabinet. To all appearances, this was not used. The front had no doors, but was masked by a gaudy print curtain.

"Just the place!" Slick whispered to himself. "I'll plant my toy there, then go to Chief Clements' office and wait for him to turn up!"

He placed the black box behind the curtain, and threw the deadly switch; then all but ran from the room.

Much to his relief, Slick was able to leave the house without being observed.

Just before he faded away into the night, he glanced at the circus tent. The canvas sides had been tied up because of the warmth.

Doc Savage was taking the speaking rostrum.

"That guy will be a gibberin' nut before mornin'!" Slick leered. Then he crept out of the neighborhood. Somehow, even a distant look at that bronze man made him feel like having a good shiver.

Chapter IX
PLANS

THERE was a great deal of talk in the big top, but it snapped into the silence of a graveyard when Doc appeared. In two spots, babies cried. The night breeze puffed the tent top and sucked it down with a hollow booming.

The quiet was a tribute to Doc's appearance. The giant bronze man, in the glare of a spotlight, was an arresting figure.

Alice Cash, also occupying a chair on the rostrum, seemed unable to take her eyes off his figure.

"This is not going to be a longwinded discussion," Doc announced, speaking in a modulated tone which the public address system could handle with most efficiency. "You people who have received food and clothing here, tonight, do not need to embarrass yourselves with the idea that you are taking charity. Your names have been filed, and the stuff charged against you."

"Fat chance you have of collecting!" someone called grimly. "We haven't any jobs!"

"There'll be plenty of jobs!" Doc retorted.

"How soon?"

"I set the time limit at two weeks; but we should be able to beat that. Probably most of you will be drawing pay by tomorrow."

In the rear, a man jumped up and shrieked: "That's just wild talk! You're only a crazy murderer from New York!"

This fellow was one of the Green Bell's agitators who had managed to slip inside. He fled wildly when a dozen angry men charged him.

After the excitement subsided, Doc resumed speaking.

"Will the following individuals please come forward," he requested.

He now read a list of names which Aunt Nora had furnished him. It included practically every factory and mine owner in Prosper City.

The designated men seemed reluctant to assume the limelight—until the lead was taken by a sparse, gray-haired man who had a determined face.

"That is Collison McAlter, my employer," Alice Cash whispered to Doc. "That is—he was my employer when there was a job."

Other men followed Collison McAlter's example. They were quietly dressed, substantial-looking fellows, all of middle age.

The desperate situation in Prosper City was mirrored on their faces. Some were pale, nervous, openly worried. Others carefully masked their concern.

Doc Savage counted them. About two thirds of the list he had called were present. But he had not expected unanimous attendance. That even this many had attended Aunt Nora's meeting was remarkable.

"Will each of you sell me your factory or mine holdings?" Doc asked bluntly. "Provided I give you the right to buy them back at the same price any time within a year."

Jaws sagged among the worried industrialists. The proposition was a bit sudden for them. They were incredulous.

The idea that they should be recipients of an offer so strange was too much for their mental digestions.

"Understand me," Doc told them; "I am not taking any man's plant off his hands at a handsome profit. The purchase price must be what is fair in the judgment of an impartial board."

Collison McAlter ran fingers through his graying hair. "I should like to know what your purpose is in making this offer."

"Your plants are simply being taken off your hands," Doc told him. "We intend to start everyone working. If they are damaged, or we fail, you don't stand to lose anything."

"You mean that you're going to buy them, get them operating profitably, then let us have them back at what we sold for? Why, that's not good business! You won't make any profit!"

Aunt Nora Boston sprang up and said loudly: "You men get this through your heads: Doc Savage don't go around trying to make money! He goes around helping people! You fellows never met anybody like him before! He's probably the most remarkable man in the world!"

"THIS is too good to be true!" Collison McAlter smiled widely. "There must be a string tied to it."

"The only string is an agreement that the wages and working hours in effect, when you take the plants off my hands, must be maintained," Doc replied.

"The kind of a deal you are proposing will take millions!" Collison McAlter muttered doubtfully.

Doc now summoned the banker with whom Johnny had deposited the check for such an enormous sum.

"I want you to advise these gentlemen the size of my account with you," Doc requested of him.

The banker, more than glad to please the largest depositor his institution had ever seen, complied with the request.

The owners of Prosper City's inoperative factories and mines were becoming a bit dizzy. They looked like men who were having a pleasant walk in their sleep.

But they were hard-headed, conservative individuals. They began discussing the matter among themselves. Some wanted time to think it over. A week! Thirty days! Two months!

Doc's powerful voice stilled the babble of words.

"This requires swift action!" he announced. "You men know very well that a mysterious mastermind known only as the Green Bell is behind this trouble! We must begin fighting him without delay!"

Doc knew human nature. If they got to talking about the thing, they might hem and haw for months.

For the second time that night, it was Collison McAlter who took decisive action. This might have been due largely to the persuasive nod given him by his pretty secretary, Alice Cash.

"I'll take you up, Mr. Savage!" he declared. "I'd be foolish not to. I don't stand to lose anything. I shall give you a bargain price on my concern, the Little Grand Cotton Mills."

Doc Savage stepped down and shook hands heartily. Getting the Little Grand concern was half his battle. It was second in size only to Tugg & Co. among Prosper City's industries.

Most of the other owners now came forward with oral agreements to surrender their properties. A few men, still suspicious, were reticent. But Doc had no fear that they would fail to come around, once public opinion was aroused.

This entire discussion had been picked up by the sensitive microphones of the public-address system. The vast throng within the tents and upon the grounds had heard each word.

Doc now addressed the crowd. "You have just heard an agreement entered into which will put most of the industrial plants in Prosper City in my possession. It will be two or three days before these sales are completed and money changes hands. Opening of the plants will have to wait that long. How many of you are ex-service men?"

All over the tents and the grounds a surprising number of hands shot into the air.

"Fine!" Doc called. "How many of you fellows are willing to go to work right now?"

Practically every hand stayed up.

"That's still better!" Doc told them. "You've got jobs. You'll draw pay for today. The salary is ten dollars a day."

Mention of the rate of remuneration called forth several pleased howls. The sum was well over the prevailing scale for labor in that section of the state.

"You fellows are going to earn that money," Doc told them. "You are going to form an armed guard to protect the plants as we open them. Some of you may be killed. But the family of any man who dies in the line of duty will receive a trust-fund income of two hundred dollars a month for the balance of life."

Perpetual monthly payments was the kind of insurance that appealed to the men. It was something their widows could not be swindled out of.

A VISIBLE change had swept over the crowd as developments chased each other. Earlier, the attitude had been the dull hopelessness of beings who felt themselves helpless victims of some Gargantuan monster which they could not understand. That was now changed entirely.

The concern of each man was naturally for himself. Where was the next meal for himself and his family coming from? What had caused the factories and mines to close down was something too vast, too vague and abstract, for them to grasp, unused as they were to thinking in large terms. Nobody, for that matter, understood the reason for this trouble.

They were like cattle caught in a hailstorm. They could feel the hail pelting them, but what had caused the clouds to form and the hail to fall, they did not comprehend clearly. What they wanted was a shed or something for protection.

Jobs which Doc was offering were figurative sheds. The men were overjoyed.

Doc had more bounty to distribute.

Four armored trucks lumbered into Aunt Nora's great yard. These were the type of vehicles used to convey factory payrolls. Each had a grilled pay window.

Lines were formed, the ex-service men superintending operations. Each person to pass a barred window received a moderate sum of money. In return, they signed vouchers saying the amount was advance salary on jobs they were to get.

Through Johnny and the banker, Doc had summoned the money trucks, some of which had come from neighboring cities.

Distribution of this money was the climaxing sensation. Charity to the tune of a few dollars was one thing; philanthropy on such a stupendous scale as this was something else again. Such a thing had never before been heard of here.

Reporters from the Prosper City *News* ran around like chickens with their heads off. Down at the newspaper plant, an extra press was dusted off. It was decided to double the size of the paper, and fill it all with news about Doc Savage. Stories about Congress, European troubles, and the murder of a big gangster were consigned to the wastebasket.

The insidious mastermind, the Green Bell, whoever he was and wherever he was, had something to think about. The pall of fear which he had built up so painstakingly was being, in a single night, almost completely wiped away by the remarkable power of this man of bronze.

Doc knew very well, though, that the battle was just starting. The Green Bell's organization was still intact. The sinister czar's followers were now certain to concentrate on their bronze Nemesis.

This was as Doc wanted it. The innocent workmen of Prosper City would not suffer.

THE night was far along when Doc went up to his room to get a few hours of sleep.

Doc's eyes roved the room as he stood in the door. Nothing suspicious met his eyes—there was no detail to show that the little black box of insanity was concealed near the head of his bed!

Doc strode over, seated himself on the edge of the bed, and started to kick off his shoes.

He became rigid; his mighty body seemed to solidify into the metal it resembled. He brought both corded hands to his ears.

Then he leaped erect and whipped out of the room. He stopped in the hall and waited there, tense. He shook his head a time or two. His expression was strange, curious, puzzled.

Through the open door, his eyes roved the room. They rested finally upon the curtained cabinet, near the head of the bed. This was the only logical hiding place.

Doc entered the room. He flashed to the cabinet, stripped back the curtain, and discovered the dark box. He clicked the switch off. His whole movement had taken but the flash part of a moment.

Curiously, Doc began examining the box. He loosened small screws and lifted the lid off.

Long Tom, the electrical wizard, came in.

"What in blazes is that, Doc?"

"The devil's own machine! Take a look at it!"

Long Tom scrutinized the device closely.

"Huh!" he ejaculated. "This is a mechanism utilizing quartz crystals and high-frequency electric currents for making ultra-short sound waves."

"Exactly," Doc agreed. "Sound waves which have strange effects upon many substances. There is not the slightest doubt but that this is the explanation of the strange cases of insanity in Prosper City. The sonic waves affect certain centers of the brain, rendering them inoperative, I believe."

Long Tom nodded. "But how'd you find the thing?"

"The waves are inaudible to a normal ear. Fortunately, I was able to detect certain sounds of peculiar nature. It is doubtful that these were the sonic waves themselves, but more probably they were heterodyne beats caused by some refracting phenomena."

It was perfectly clear to Long Tom how this could happen, although a scientific discussion lasting for days could have been waged over the subject.

No doubt the main explanation of Doc's escape was his remarkable hearing. From the cradle, Doc had each day taken certain sound exercises calculated to develop his auditory senses. For this purpose, he used a device which made sound waves inaudible to an ordinary ear. Through long practice, Doc was able to hear these notes.

Ole Slater, Aunt Nora, and the others soon arrived, anxious to see the hideous black box and hear how it worked.

Doc borrowed the magnifier in the left lens of the gaunt Johnny's spectacles, and went over the interior of the brain paralyzing device.

Strange little lights came into his golden eyes as he examined it.

INTO the room there came abruptly a low, fantastic sound. It was like the song of some exotic bird of the jungle, or the mellow trilling of a breeze filtering through a forest. It had no tune, though it was entirely melodious.

Those present stared. They looked frightened. Ole Slater backed nervously for the door, thinking the deadly sonic device was in operation. The weird sound was in all the room, seeming to emanate uncannily from no particular spot.

Doc's four friends showed no fear, however. They had heard this uncanny note before. They knew it was the sound which was a part of Doc—a small, unconscious thing which he did in moments of utter concentration. In the present case, they were sure it presaged an important discovery.

"What'd you find, Doc?" rumbled the big-fisted Renny.

"Fingerprints," Doc told him. "The fellow who made this thing might as well have signed his name."

Collison McAlter came upstairs, along with some of the other Prosper City factory owners. He listened in amazement to Alice Cash, as she told him about the sonic device.

Doc Savage placed the black box on a table near the bedroom window. He walked to a rather bulky metal box which stood to one side of the chamber. This was decorated with various knobs and switches, together with circular glass lenses.

Doc opened it. Inside, mechanism was operating slowly. Two large magazines held a narrow movie film.

Collison McAlter's eyes popped. "A movie camera! And it's been operating in here all the time?"

"Doc had several of those," volunteered the homely Monk. "They operate silently, and they're handy to leave standing around to photograph prowlers. I'm betting the fellow who planted that black box got his picture taken!"

Collison McAlter wiped his forehead. "But it was too dark to take pictures in here!"

"This movie camera operates on ultraviolet light," Monk explained. "The rays are invisible to the human eye, but they affect photograph film of the type we use. In other words, that camera can take pictures in pitch darkness. And it carries enough film to run all day."

Monk further announced that the film, immediately after passing the lens, ran through a tank which automatically developed it.

Doc now put the film through a tiny projector. The images were thrown on the white plaster of the wall. The pictures were not attractive to the eye, since highlights and shadows contrasted starkly.

As portrayed by the film, the room seemed unreal, horrible. The creeping figure of Slick Cooley appeared. Every detail of his features was plainly discernible.

He was facing the camera at the moment he whispered to himself; then he planted the box and fled.

"So he is the culprit!" barked Collison McAlter.

Doc stopped the projector. He indicated the black sonic box on the table. "Make sure no one carries that off. The finger prints in it are important."

He glided for the door.

Collison McAlter gulped: "But where are you going?"

"To get Slick Cooley," Doc said dryly.

"But how do you know where to find—"

Collison McAlter fell silent, for Doc was gone.

Doc's four aides exchanged knowing glances. They had a good idea how Doc knew where to locate Slick Cooley.

Slick had been facing the camera when he whispered: "I'll plant my toy there, then go to Chief Clements' office and wait for him to turn up!"

Doc Savage was a proficient lip reader.

THE group now left Doc's room. Renny took up a position outside the door, armed with one of the tiny, high-speed machine guns. The room was on the second floor, and the grounds were flood-lighted.

Even if the Green Bell did know of the fingerprints, it did not seem possible that he could get to the black box to destroy them.

Renny had not been on guard before the door for long, however, when certain portentous events transpired.

A tree, lifting between Doc's window and one of the flood lamps, cast a shadow over the portion of the house that was between the window and the roof.

Directly above Doc's room was the window of one of the garret chambers. This lifted silently.

A small package appeared, tied to the end of a string. This was lowered. A swinging movement caused the package to sweep in through the window of Doc's quarters. It was dropped within.

The string was permitted to hang between the two windows. It was small and dark and not likely to be noticed by anyone.

In the garret cubicle, the murksome figure which had lowered the package now made for the door. This being wore a long black gown, on the front of which was a bell design in bilious green.

The little room under the roof chanced to be the one which had formerly been occupied by unfortunate Jim Cash.

The black-hooded personage quitted the garret.

A few minutes later, the group of factory owners took leave of Aunt Nora's house, discussing Doc Savage and his men, and the things they had seen that night. Collison McAlter was with them. He seemed greatly pleased with the events of the night. His step was jaunty.

Chapter X
THE MURDER SNARE

THE Prosper City police station was a dingy, red-brick building, constructed in the shape of a "T." The stem of the "T" contained the barred cells for prisoners. The crosspiece held offices, including the one used by Chief Clements.

Chief Clements did not keep a very sightly office. Circulars concerning wanted criminals stuck to the walls like stamps. There were metal filing cabinets, all large and rusty.

On top of the scarred flat-top desk stood a box of five-cent cigars. About two thirds of them had been smoked.

Slick Cooley occupied the swivel chair back of the desk. His weasel face was screwed into a grimace over the cigar. Slick considered five-centers below his station in life.

Back of Slick, a window was open. He did not worry. This was the second floor. A night breeze rushed softly in through the window and pulled strings of gray smoke off his cigar end.

Suddenly, the breeze seemed to bring in a great bronze cloud. This cloud tied around Slick and became as real and hard as banding steel cables.

Air tore loudly out of Slick's lungs as he was squeezed. He made no other sound. He was planted, helpless, upon the desk, and relieved of his two silenced guns.

Slick tried to struggle, but he might as well have been a mouse in the clutches of a big cat.

The brick wall of the police station had offered no great obstacle to Doc Savage. It was not the smooth type of wall, but one which had fairly deep grooves between the bricks. Doc, with his tremendous strength and agility, had come up it much as another man would climb stairs.

Doc maintained a purposeful silence, not speaking even after he had disarmed Slick.

Cabled bronze fingers seemed to flow over Slick's person. They administered a wrench here— some pressure there. Slick found himself mysteriously relieved of the power of speech by some weird paralysis of nerve centers.

"You're going to die," Doc told him—but neglected to mention the mortal date.

Slick naturally presumed Doc meant immediately. Doc had no intention of slaying Slick. He had merely stated a natural truth, and let Slick draw his own conclusions.

For some seconds Doc worked on Slick's frame with incredibly strong hands. His manipulations produced excruciating agony. So great was the torture that Slick began to think he was actually dying.

"Who is the Green Bell?" Doc demanded.

The bronze fingers kneaded Slick's nerve centers again, and he found the use of his tongue had magically returned.

He tried to bluff. "Honest, mister, I don't know anything about any Green Bell!"

"A lie!" Doc told him quietly. "You are one of the Green Bell's hirelings. You might be the Green Bell himself—except that you don't show any signs of having that many brains."

"You're crazy!" Slick snarled.

"Not as crazy as you hoped I would be when you planted that sonic device in my room."

"I didn't—"

"A movie camera was hidden in the room! It registered your actions!"

SLICK did not doubt this. Remembering the intricate electrical apparatus standing in the bedroom, he wished he had investigated more closely.

"They won't hang a man for that," he mumbled.

"No!" Doc agreed. "They'll never hang you!"

Thinking this was a threat, Slick shivered. He changed his tactics.

"Now listen, Savage; maybe we can get together!"

"Who is the Green Bell?"

"I don't know! Honest, I don't!"

"But you are one of his men?"

Slick knew there was no use denying this. "Yeah!"

"You were one of the gang who murdered Jim Cash," Doc said.

That was merely a guess on Doc's part, stated as a fact. But Slick goggled at the bronze man's features, saw no expression there, and came to the mistaken conclusion that Doc had learned of the deed in some mysterious fashion.

"What if I did? You can't prove it!" Slick squirmed desperately. "You can't prove anything on me!"

"Judborn Tugg is one of the gang," Doc said calmly.

"Sure." Then it suddenly dawned on Slick that he was being tricked. He cried desperately: "You can't prove a thing I've been telling you!"

The door opened, and a twanging voice said: "He don't need to prove it."

Chief Clements of the Prosper City police stood on the threshold. His cherry of a face was somewhat pale, and his bristling caterpillar of a mustache drooped slightly, making it seem smaller. Otherwise, he appeared none the worse for the hours of sleep induced by Doc's drug.

No surprise showed on Doc's metallic face. A few moments ago he had heard someone approach the door. This had escaped Slick's notice.

"You should have stayed outside a while longer," Doc advised Chief Clements. "You might have learned other facts."

Chief Clements' face wore the expression of a man who had suddenly discovered that his house had burned down. Jerkily he mopped at his small features.

"I've been played for a sap," he mumbled.

"All of us are taken for a ride occasionally," Doc assured him without malice.

This did not seem to relieve Chief Clements. He knotted his bony hands, captured a part of his dark mustache with his lower lip, and nibbled it, goat fashion.

"I talked to some people on my way here, and read an extra edition of the *News* put out," he twanged. "I found out what you done at that meeting tonight—passing out food and clothing and money to them starving people. A lot of them poor devils you helped were my friends."

Chief Clements was an honest, stubborn man, who had learned he was wrong. He was trying to apologize.

Doc helped him out. "Forget it! You were doing what you thought was right. No man can do more than that."

Chief Clements smiled gratefully. His knobby shoulders lost their droop.

"From now on I'm working with you," he said grimly. "What I just heard proves you didn't murder Jim Cash. I'm not going to arrest you. And I'd like to see anybody from out of town pinch you. Furthermore, I'm going to arrest Judborn Tugg. Slick's talk proved Tugg is mixed up with the Green Bell."

"I'm afraid such slender evidence would not convict Tugg in court."

Chief Clements stared dismally at Doc. "You mean that we had better not throw Tugg into the can?"

"Tugg may be the Green Bell. Suppose we watch him closely. If he is not the Green Bell, he might still lead us to the mastermind. With your very valuable help, we'll be sure to solve this."

The last statement was partly flattery. Undeniably, though, having Chief Clements on Doc's side would greatly facilitate matters.

"I'll slap this guy in the hoosegow, then we'll talk things over," Chief Clements said, and snapped handcuffs on Slick's wrists.

The lithe, snakelike Slick was led off in the direction of the cells in the rear.

DOC had been smiling in friendly fashion for Chief Clements' benefit. Left alone, his strong features now settled into repose. A warm light in his golden eyes indicated that he was well satisfied with the way things were going.

Chief Clements returned, stepping sprily.

"I wish you would tell me what you know about conditions here in Prosper City, Mr. Savage. I must confess I have been blinded by that flashy bluffer, Judborn Tugg."

"My facts are meager," Doc told him.

Then, without squandering words, he imparted his facts. He told of the capture of the Green Bell's seven thugs in New York City. But he made no mention of what had finally happened to them. No one, other than those connected with the place, knew of the strange institution in upstate New York.

"So Jim Cash was rubbed out because he got wise to who the Green Bell was!" muttered Chief Clements. "Cash was a good kid. I knew him. His sister is swell, too. That young Ole Slater has been rushing her lately."

"Know anything about Slater?"

"He's all right. I investigated him mighty close."

"How come?"

"That was when Tugg had me thinkin' Aunt Nora Boston was at the bottom of this trouble. I combed their records. I didn't find nothin' on Slater. He's written a couple of plays that have been produced on Broadway."

The discussion veered to plans for the future. Chief Clements suggested that the ex-service men guard for the mines and factories should be commissioned as members of the Prosper City police force.

This was an excellent idea, Doc agreed.

"I can supply most of them with guns!" Clements declared.

"I should like to have all the prisoners," Doc requested.

"I don't get you! What do you want with the Green Bell's bunch, if we catch 'em? Why not let 'em go to the pen?"

"My treatment is more effective than penitentiary terms or the electric chair," Doc said.

Chief Clements looked at the bronze man's face and squirmed uneasily. He had received the impression that Doc meant to slay the prisoners.

"No one will be put to death," Doc promised him.

"It's irregular," Clements said, "but if you want them, you can have them!"

BACK in the jail, a shot banged. The sound was hollow—like a single grain of popcorn letting loose in a popper.

Doc whipped for the door. His movements seemed easy, but were executed with a swiftness which caused Clements to stare in amazement. This phenomenon of a man moving with such unearthly speed all but made Clements forget the shot. He heaved out of his chair and followed Doc.

A long, bare, cold corridor ended at a sheet-steel door. Chief Clements unlocked the panel.

A concrete alley, barred cells on either side, stretched beyond. Faces were jammed against the bars; excited questions babbled.

An iron stairway sloped down to the first-floor cells.

"I put Slick below!" Chief Clements shouted, and hammered his heels on the stairs.

Halfway down the passage, a steel grid of a door hung open. Two turnkeys huddled before it, peering into the cell. Both were rigid, bent forward grotesquely.

Doc and Chief Clements raced the corridor's length.

Light blazed in the passage, but not in the cells. The bars cast striped shadows on the cement floor. The shadow stripes seemed to crawl like black snakes over two figures in the dungeon.

One man was a jail flunky. He held an automatic. An empty cartridge glittered on the floor, and the place reeked of cordite.

The second man was a twisted pile. His position was so contorted that it seemed his body had been pulled apart, then dropped in a heap.

There was an ugly froth on his lips. His eyes were rolled in their sockets until they resembled white marbles. A bullet had knocked the top of his head out of shape. It was Slick Cooley.

The man with the automatic backed stiffly away from the body.

"Something went wrong with him!" he cried shrilly. "He was havin' a fit. He grabbed my gun and got shot when we were fightin' for it. He was stark, ravin' crazy, if you ask me!"

Wheeling, Doc Savage sped back the length of the passage. He reached a metal door. A tiny, glittering tool appeared in his hand. He used this briefly on the door lock, and the panel opened as if he held a weird power over it.

Chief Clements ran to the door. His jaw was sagging. The door had been locked, and he would have sworn that it was burglar proof. He stepped out into the night, bobbing his small red head like a blinded chicken. It was a long minute before his eyes accustomed themselves to the gloom, and he could see Doc Savage.

The lots around the police station were vacant. On them someone had sown grass—and grown a profuse crop of weeds. Doc was wading through these, using a flashlight.

Rows of tiny windows, heavily barred, admitted to the cells. Doc Savage lingered under one from which came the low voices of the turnkeys gathered about Slick's body.

The ground bore faint marks where feet had recently trod. The earth was too sunbaked to retain definite footprints, but weeds, crushed by a recent tread, were slowly straightening.

Doc joined Clements.

"The Green Bell got Slick with one of his sonic devices which produce insanity!" he imparted.

Clements wailed: "We've lost our only witness who could prove you didn't kill Jim Cash."

Doc seemed not to hear the statement. He started away, hesitated, turned back.

"I'm going to Judborn Tugg's home! Want to drive me? You know the town."

"You bet!" Clements ran for his car.

PROSPER CITY'S most pretentious residential district was located on a knoll known to the local wags as Plutocrat Knob. As befitted a man who was not backward in holding himself up as a leading citizen, Judborn Tugg occupied the most flashy dwelling in the section.

The mansion was white, after the Spanish style—a thing of tiled roofs, overhanging balconies, and wrought-iron railings. Shrubbery was plentiful.

Several blocks from the place, Chief Clements got up speed, kicked out the clutch, and cut off the ignition. He coasted to a silent stop two blocks from the white castle.

Doc lifted out.

"Thanks," he said. "You might as well go back to the station."

Chief Clements jerked at his bristling black mustache. "But listen—"

He clamped his teeth on the rest. The bronze man had faded away silently into the night!

Chief Clements stood up, intending to call loudly, then thought better of it. The sound might alarm Judborn Tugg. He sat there, blanketed in disgust. He had hoped to be in on whatever investigation Doc contemplated.

The bronze man fascinated Clements; he wanted to see more of him.

Clements fiddled with the ignition, then made an angry finger-snapping gesture. This was provoked by recollection of how he had fallen for Judborn Tugg's trickery.

Clements suddenly decided to do some investigating on his own. If he could learn the identity of the Green Bell, his stupidity would be less reprehensible.

The thought occurred to him that he might interfere with some plan of the bronze man. Well, he would be careful not to do that.

Leaving his car, he eased through the shrubbery. He managed to make little noise.

The shadow of a manicured hedge led him close to a side door of the white palace. He crouched there, not ten feet from the door, wondering what he should do next.

The problem solved itself.

The door opened, and Judborn Tugg came out. Apparently he was getting a breath of the night air before turning in.

Tugg lit one of his dollar cigars and threw the match away. It landed beside Clements. Not extinguished by the fall, it flared up. The light disclosed the Prosper City chief of police.

Tugg dashed forward, drawing a pistol. Then he perceived the interloper's identity.

"My good friend, Chief Clements!" he exclaimed pompously. "What on earth are you doing here?"

Chief Clements heaved up on his knees. Within the last hour, he had acquired a great hate for this flashy man.

Clements was not only a slow thinker; he had a temper.

"Don't you call me a friend!" he snarled.

TUGG jumped as if kicked. His head seemed to dive down into his fat neck. He had been warned that Clements would be a deadly enemy if he ever learned the truth. And the police leader was now acting as if he had glimpsed light.

Armoring himself with dignity, Tugg began: "My dear man, what—"

"You damn murderer!" gritted Clements. "Don't you try to soft-soap me!"

Tugg appeared to swell in girth and shrink in stature. A paleness bleached his pursy jowls.

Chief Clements had only spoken rashly in his rage, but Judborn Tugg thought the officer was stating a charge, which he could prove. Fear crawled in Tugg's veins like red ants. He was desperate. He decided to try a trick.

"Call your other officers!" he snapped. "I surrender!"

"There's nobody else with me," rapped Chief Clements, falling neatly into the trap.

This was what Tugg had wanted to know. Jutting his gun at arm's length, he worked the trigger. The reports banged thunder. The bullets sledged Clements backward, tunneling through his heart and lungs.

Tugg continued shooting until his gun was empty. Then, from the corner of an eye, he glimpsed what to him was a terrible sight. A giant man of bronze! The figure came volleying across the lawn toward him.

Tugg snapped his empty gun twice at Doc, then veered around into the house.

"Help!" he called.

Several men, aides of the Green Bell, were in the house. Some had attended the sinister meeting in the dilapidated barn. Others were merely agitators, who did not work in the Green Bell's black robes, and, as a consequence, were paid less money. They were loafing in Tugg's company.

Flourishing weapons, these men rushed to Tugg's aid. When Doc Savage loomed in the door, their guns loosened a volley.

Lead gnashed splinters out of the door, or screamed on to slap into distant houses. None of the slugs touched Doc. He had seen the danger in time to twist away.

The Green Bell's gunmen, weapons ready, sidled nervously through the door, or dropped from nearby windows. Their bronze quarry was not visible. But there was much shadow-matted shrubbery nearby, which could hold him.

Inside the house, Tugg ran to a phone. He called the Prosper City police headquarters.

"Doc Savage has just murdered Chief Clements out at my place!" he screamed. "I got half a dozen witnesses to it!"

The words were loud enough to reach Doc Savage, where he lurked in the shrubs. He glided rapidly away from the vicinity.

Five minutes would see half of Prosper City's police department on the spot.

The officers did not know Doc and Chief Clements had made their peace. They would be ripe to believe Judborn Tugg's lie. A terrific manhunt was certain, with Doc Savage as the quarry.

Hardly a flicker appeared in Doc's eyes when they caught the reflection of a street lamp. Their gold was dull. The charge of murdering Chief Clements was going to be a hard thing to combat.

At a rapid run he made for the outskirts of the town, where Aunt Nora Boston's house stood.

Chapter XI
DESTROYED CLUES

ROOSTERS were crowing four o'clock from distant farmhouses when Doc Savage neared Aunt Nora's rambling dwelling.

To one side of the house, Monk was drilling a determined squad of ex-service men.

On the other side of the house a score of individuals stood in a knot, staring upward. Their curious attention was centered on the window of Doc's room.

The window was wiped clean of glass. Part of the frame had been ripped out and hung dangling. Around the aperture, weather-boarding was splintered and torn until it looked furry.

Monk yelled, lumbering over to meet Doc. Monk's gorillalike face was hard and wrathful.

"There was an explosion in your room, Doc! The blast put the kibosh on a lot of your equipment."

"What about the Green Bell's sonic device?"

"Blown to smithereens!"

Doc received this news as expressionlessly as if it had been a comment on the weather. He had developed perfect control. He could take the greatest misfortune without emotion.

Why the black sonic box had been destroyed was perfectly clear. It had held the fingerprints of the Green Bell, or someone who knew the evil czar's identity.

"The bomb was planted from inside the house," Monk grunted. "It was lowered on a string from an attic window and swung into the room. We found the string!"

Doc walked to the house, entered, and went upstairs.

The door was not only off its hinges, but lay in fragments along the hallway.

"Renny was on guard outside the door," Monk explained. "He got knocked head over heels!"

"Was he hurt?"

"That guy?" Monk snorted. "Nothin' can hurt him!"

Doc examined the room. Practically all his scientific devices had been ruined. This damage alone amounted to many thousands. Some of the mechanism was of such a complex nature that only Doc Savage's skilled hand and unique brain could recreate it.

Scummy brown stains smeared the floor, walls, bed—almost everything in the chamber. These seemed to be devouring whatever they covered. An acrid odor reeked in the place.

"Don't touch anything!" Doc warned.

"Yeah—I know!" Monk agreed. "The brown stuff is acid. It would eat the flesh right off a man. There must have been several bottles of it tied in with the bomb."

"It was intended to eat the fingerprints off the sonic device in case the explosion failed to do the job," Doc decided.

Doc sought pieces of the sonic apparatus. The only segment of any size was the split end of a coil mounting.

This trophy Doc carried into the bathroom and washed thoroughly to remove the acid. He also scoured the voracious liquid off his own shoes soles. It was dissolving the leather.

Some moments later, Doc's hands abruptly became idle upon the towel he was using. He glided to a window and leaned out, listening.

In the distance, toward the center of town, he could hear spattering shots. The fusillade died in a banging series which might have been periods.

Monk lumbered over.

"That sounds bad!" he muttered. "It may mean Renny and the rest are in trouble!"

"Where did they go?"

"I forgot to tell you. Ham telephoned from New York that he had sent the body of poor Jim Cash by train. Renny and everybody else accompanied Alice Cash down to the station to get it. Everybody but me, that is. I didn't care about seeing the girl's grief."

"Let's get downtown!" Doc rapped.

THEY loaded into a touring car in front of the house. This was one of several fast machines which Doc had rented and was keeping on hand for general use.

Doc crouched out of sight on the rear floorboards. Monk drove.

Tire treads shrieked as the phaeton careened onto the road. The exhaust moaned; the rush of air popped the top fabric against the bows. Doc braced himself in position, watching street lights bat past like white eyes.

"Angle over a bit to the right," he advised.

Keenness of hearing had enabled him to place the source of the shots.

A cop tweedled frantically on his whistle as the car went past like a meteor. Dwellings ceased; business blocks veered ahead.

Prosper City had erected a new Union Station when times were good. It was a lumpish gray building, with long train sheds radiating like fingers in the rear. The place resembled a mausoleum.

In the gloom in front of the station, Doc found a hearse, two cars, and an excited crowd. Blue uniforms of policemen freckled the assemblage.

Monk drew in close and stopped the car. Doc got out. He worked forward, almost brushing the elbow of a policeman, who was too occupied with craning his neck to notice.

Although dawn was threatening redly in the east, it was gloomy in the vicinity of the station. This, and the fact that all attention was focused on the hearse, aided Doc in avoiding discovery.

Big-fisted Renny and handsome Ole Slater stood near the rear of the hearse, talking to officers.

In one of the parked cars huddled Alice Cash, sobbing on Aunt Nora's ample shoulder.

Long Tom and Johnny were keeping the crowd from getting too near the two women.

Doc found a fat man, and did a good job of masking himself in the gentleman's shadow. He threw his voice in the direction of the hearse. Not wishing to betray his presence, he spoke in Mayan.

"What happened here, Renny?" he inquired in the lost language.

A tightening of Renny's big fist betrayed his surprise. He pondered briefly on how to give the explanation without it seeming suspicious. Then he got it.

"I want you fellows to get this straight," he told the officers loudly. "We came down here to receive the remains of young Jim Cash. They had been shipped down from New York, one of the railway officials accompanying them. We had no more than—"

"You told us all that, before!" snapped a policeman.

"Shut up!" Renny thundered. "We had no more than taken the coffin off the train when a gang attacked us. They all wore black hoods with the green, bell-like design on the front. They started shooting, and we had to hunt cover in a hurry!"

Renny made his voice even louder to emphasize the words which he particularly wanted to reach Doc. "The Green Bell's gang just examined the body. It didn't look to me like they took a thing."

This ended Renny's explanation.

Doc drifted a bronze hand into his clothing and brought out a bundle of small objects which might have been red sticks with strings sticking from the ends.

He touched a lighted match to one of the strings, and dropped them. So great was the crowd's interest in Renny and his story, no one noticed Doc's act.

Careful not to attract attention, Doc drifted nearer the hearse. A moment later, a series of loud explosions came from the spot which he had just quitted.

Doc always carried a few ordinary firecrackers with long fuses. These had proved convenient on many occasions.

A yelling hubbub arose over the fireworks. This hypnotized all eyes. No one observed a bronze figure which slipped into the hearse.

WITH a flashlight that spiked a white thread of a beam, Doc made an examination. His search was brief.

On Jim Cash's body, on the arm above the right elbow, were words.

From their metallic color, these letters might have been printed with the lead snout of a bullet. But Doc knew that they had been put there by a chemical—to remain unnoticed until the application of a second chemical brought them out.

They read:

IN MY FACTORY LOCKER

This, then, was what the Green Bell horde had sought.

Doc dropped out of the hearse. At that point, he lost the good luck which had attended his brazen efforts. A policeman saw him.

The officer gasped. Then he flashed his service pistol, and recklessly tried to put a bullet in Doc's bronze head.

The slug went a yard too high. Doc dropped to all fours. Keeping down, he torpedoed through the forest of legs.

A wake of yelling, overturned men marked his progress. Several individuals sought to seize him. They either missed their clutches entirely, or were shaken off. Some launched kicks, only to bruise their toes on a frame which was almost as solid as metal.

In the phaeton parked nearby, Monk drew one of the tiny machine guns and began to rip bullets into the air.

Renny, Long Tom, and Johnny sent up deafening yells, and thrashed aimlessly about. These two disturbances were aimed at aiding Doc's escape.

Doc dived out of the crowd, raced for the station, and almost made it before a policeman saw him. It was necessary for the officers to fight clear of the crowd before they could use their guns. And long before they could do that, Doc was inside the depot.

The station was cleared of waiting travelers, porters, and loafers, thanks to the excitement outside. Doc crossed the colored tile floor and ran out under the train shed.

A line of Pullmans and day coaches stood under one of the shelters—evidently a train which was to depart at a later hour.

Doc crawled into one of the coaches. He ran between aisles of green plush seats encased in white protecting cloths. Through coach after coach he passed, shutting the intervening doors so the officers could not sight him by looking the length of the train.

At the far end he dropped off.

Although dawn was imminent, enough gloom remained to simplify the rest of the escape. Doc hurdled sidings, whipped under freight cars, and cleared a low concrete wall.

As if to climax recent ghoulish events, he found he had entered the stockyard of a monument concern. Grave markers of white marble, and more elaborately carved headstones, stood all about.

A long alley beyond the monument yard precipitated him into a side street.

UNTIL Collison McAlter's Little Grand Cotton Mills had been forced to close, Jim Cash had been an employee of the concern.

The strange words on Cash's arm undoubtedly referred to his locker at the Little Grand plant.

For the Little Grand Mills, Doc set his course. They were many blocks away on the south side of Prosper City. Doc ran, haunting alleys and side streets.

He made no effort to get a taxi, after noticing that policemen were stationed at prominent corners, stopping passing cars and examining the interiors.

Doc had been without sleep or rest for many hours, yet his stride lacked nothing in elasticity. Through a lifetime of intensive exercises—two hours of it each day—Doc had developed a strength and stamina which was almost superhuman, as compared to that of other men.

The Little Grand Mills were situated like a gaudy blossom on a sweeping stem of railroad sidings.

The buildings were gray, red-roofed, neat. Grass on the ground was cropped so close it might have been a coating of green paint.

A high fence, of wire as thick as a lead pencil, surrounded the plant. A barrier of barbed strands circled the top. There was a wide entrance, steel gated, flanked by a watchman's turret. This latter structure had a small, barred window.

A man peered out of the watchman's box—a pale man who looked scared.

"Who are you?" he quavered. "What do you want?"

"Let me in!" Doc commanded. "It will be all right with Collison McAlter!"

The watchman hesitated.

"Mr. McAlter is here now," he muttered finally. "I'll go with you and find out if he wants you around."

The watchman stepped out of the box, closing the door behind him. He wore a white linen suit badly in need of laundering. He kept his hand in his coat pocket, and the bulge in his pocket was longer than his hand should have been.

He unlocked the gate.

Doc's gold-flake eyes seemed to give the man the briefest of glances.

Then he suddenly flashed a corded arm.

Like a hard cleaver, it descended between the man's arm and his side. The pocket tore open. The fellow's hand and a stubby pistol were forced out.

Doc's sinew-wrapped fist seemed to gulp the gun from the fingers which held it. The watchman tried to flee, but a shove—it made him think of the nudge of a locomotive—sent him reeling against the wall of his cubicle.

Doc opened the door, hurled the man inside, and followed after him.

Propped in a corner, where he had been invisible from the barred window, sat a man. He wore greasy coveralls. A time clock, suspended from his neck by a strap, proved him to be the genuine watchman. He was unconscious from a head blow, and would remain so for some time.

Doc's prisoner gritted: "This fellow is my buddy—the assistant watchman! Somebody beaned him—"

"Did you have on your Green Bell hood when you struck the watchman down?" Doc asked dryly.

The man began to sputter. "I don't know what—"

Doc sent a hand to the man's shoulder, plucked away a long black thread.

"This is not the kind of thread which would come from your suit," he murmured. "It's silk."

"It's from my necktie!" the other barked desperately.

"Your necktie is a particularly unlovely shade of yellow," Doc reminded.

The man pitched backward, desperate to escape.

Doc started a swift gesture, aimed at recapturing him. His gaze, always alert and nearly all-seeing, went beyond the false watchman to the factory buildings. What he saw caused him to duck swiftly.

THE factory walls were largely of glass, after the modern fashion. The windows were great tilting panels. Three of these had opened silently since Doc's last inspection. Ominous black rods were protruding.

The rods lipped flame. They were machine guns, and they trip-hammered mad strings of reports.

Bullets slashed completely through the thin walls of the watchman's turret. They chopped the planks off. A drawer under the little inspection window was hit. It jumped out of its groove and spilled its contents on the floor.

Gloves, a lunch pail—stuff belonging to the watchman—and a Green Bell hood! Evidently this last had been hidden there when Doc was sighted.

The fake watchman was slain by the first storm of lead. The slugs doubled him up, spun him around and around, knocking him out of shape.

Doc grasped the feet of the genuine watchman, who was slumbering from the blow over the head, and jerked. The limp form skidded flat on the floor.

The floor was of painted concrete. Around it ran a foundation wall, also of concrete. It would turn bullets.

The machine guns continued a deadly chatter. The men using them were coldblooded, intent on ridding themselves of the bronze man. In their blood lust, they had coldly sacrificed their fellow crook.

From the walls chunks of wood fell. Shingles were scooped off the roof; gray dust spurted from the concrete foundation walls. The wall cracked at one point, then another. But it held, furnishing protection.

The barrage ended. Silence reeked for a moment. Then men could be heard leaving the factory.

Doc lifted his head. Two men were running forward to see what kind of work their fire had done; both were armed. Both wore the gloomy hoods of the Green Bell.

Doc reached for the pistol which he had taken from the fake watchman. He rarely carried a gun himself. He held the opinion that a man who carried a firearm would come to put too much dependence on it, and accordingly, would be the more helpless if disarmed.

An ear could barely divide the twin roar which his shots made. The charging pair seemed to go lopsided, reel, then topple down, two loose bundles of arms and legs.

It was not because of any lack of skill in their use that Doc did not carry firearms. He had winged both men in the legs.

Machine guns promptly opened up again from the factory. Doc threw himself close to the floor. It would be suicide to shoot back.

The gunfire kept up for what seemed an age. The concrete foundation wall was getting thinner and thinner. A bullet lunged through.

But once more the shooting stopped.

Chancing a look, Doc saw that the two men had been moved to safety under cover of the fire. He could hear one of them wailing faintly in agony.

Two or three mysterious volleys of shots soon sounded somewhere in the rear of the factory.

Doc exposed himself briefly. He was not fired on. Quitting the turret he ran for the factory. He reached it and veered around a corner.

It was as he had guessed: the men in the Green Bell hoods were retreating. They had used their rapid-firer to batter the lock off a small gate in the rear fence.

They fled, carrying the two wounded. Tall weeds and small brush received them. They were lost completely to view.

Motors came to hooting life in the brush. A car lunged out of a thicket like a frightened black hawk. Another followed. The two streaked down a side road, pursued by a tumbling snake of dust.

Doc entered the factory. He knew the general layout of such textile plants as this. It did not take him long to find the room which held the workmen's lockers.

The lockers were tall, green metal boxes. Each bore a small frame which held a name card. One of the lockers was upset.

Doc turned it over so that he could see the name plate:

JIM CASH

Whatever had been concealed under the locker was now gone.

A sharp, brittle voice somewhere behind Doc rasped. "You will put your hands up!"

Chapter XII
THE BODY IN THE VINES

THE lockers stood in a row, like drab metal teeth. The one which was upset left an opening.

Doc dived through.

The factory floors were rubber composition. This explained how the man had approached unnoticed. Too, the newcomer was not very close—at the end of the locker room, a good fifty feet away.

There was no shot. Light in the cavernous place was too dim to permit accurate marksmanship. It was even a bit too dark to identify faces. But Doc had recognized the new arrival's voice. It was Collison McAlter, owner of the plant.

Doc lighted one of the firecrackers and threw it. It was concealed from McAlter by the lockers. Striking the wall near him, the cracker exploded with a terrific report!

Collison McAlter cried out, fired his revolver—both at the same instant. Firecracker and gunshot were about of an equal loudness.

Doc Savage, big and bronze and grim, stood very silent. It was quite dark in the corner where the firecracker had loosened. Collison McAlter probably could not tell what he had shot at, or whether he had hit anyone.

Doc was puzzled. Was Collison McAlter one of the Green Bell's men? Was he the Green Bell himself?

To determine the truth, Doc decided on a small ruse. He glided silently along the phalanx of lockers until he stood as close to McAlter as he could get, without being discovered. Using the voice which he employed in ordinary speech, but making it small, choking, and thin, Doc said: "McAlter— you wanted—to kill—me."

Collison McAlter's gun slipped from his fingers and planked on the floor.

He cried shrilly: "Doc Savage—good heavens! I thought you were one of the Green Bell's gang!"

Doc waited. If Collison McAlter was the Green Bell, this might be a sly trick to draw him into line for a bullet from another gun.

But McAlter came stumbling to the spot where he thought he had shot Doc. The bronze man drew his flashlight, gave the lens a twist to spread the beam widely, and splashed luminance.

Collison McAlter's hands were bare of weapons. He was trembling, pale. He looked worried.

Doc Savage showed himself. "It's all right; you didn't hit me."

McAlter spluttered. He swabbed a cold dew off his forehead, leaning flaccidly against the locker.

"What a horrible mistake I made!" he gulped.

"Did you just get here?" Doc demanded.

"I've been here at least two hours."

McAlter paused, apparently waiting for Doc to make a remark. The result was a dead silence.

"You see, I must confess I'm not a very brave man when it comes to physical danger," McAlter mumbled. "After I left the meeting at Aunt Nora Boston's tonight I went home, but couldn't sleep. So I came out here to the factory to look things over. I saw the Green Bell's men arrive and overpower the watchman."

He paused, shuddered violently, and drooped even more limply against the lockers.

"Frankly, I was afraid to show myself!" he groaned.

"I would hardly call that lack of nerve," Doc told him. "There were too many of them for one man to handle."

"Yes, that's what I thought," McAlter agreed. "Anyway, I don't know why they were here. They started shooting, but I couldn't see their target. I guess it was you! Even then I was afraid to open fire on them. I'll never forgive myself for that!"

McAlter peered anxiously in the gloom, trying to ascertain from the expression on Doc's bronze features whether or not his story had been accepted as true.

What he saw gave him little satisfaction one way or the other.

"What in the world could they have been after?" he asked.

"Jim Cash evidently had documentary proof of the Green Bell's identity," Doc replied. "He concealed the evidence under his locker here in the plant. He wrote the name of the hiding place in invisible ink on his arm. Just why he should follow that procedure is a mystery. How the Green Bell learned of the message is also unexplained."

Both these enigmas were answered indirectly when Doc appeared at Aunt Nora Boston's house.

COLLISON MCALTER used his limousine as a conveyance to Aunt Nora's. Doc crouched on the rug in the ample tonneau. The police did not dare to stop a man of Collison McAlter's prominence and search his car.

Ham was calling by long distance from New York, when Doc arrived at Aunt Nora's.

"How's it coming, Doc?" he asked.

"It could be a great deal better," Doc assured him.

"I thought I'd report something queer!" Ham said rapidly. "It may be important. Our mail carrier here was kidnaped yesterday by men in black gowns. He managed to escape during the night. The object of the kidnaping seemed to be to get mail he was bringing us. He said there was only one letter. It was from Prosper City."

"That explains what just happened here, Ham! Jim Cash hid his evidence against the Green Bell, and marked the hiding place on his arm! He must have written me a letter from Prosper City, suggesting that, in case he was killed, I should look on his arm for the information."

"Confound it!" Ham gritted. "We're sure having our setbacks in this mess."

"Some of the Green Bell's men may still be in New York," Doc warned. "You'd better watch out for them!"

"Don't worry, I've been doing that," Ham said wryly. "I think I'm going to be able to scare those four lying witnesses into telling the truth, too."

"When you get that done, you can come down here and clear me of the charge of murdering Prosper City's chief of police!"

Ham snorted. "O. K. How is that hairy missing link, Monk, coming along?"

"He has his eye on Alice Cash," Doc said, knowing this was exactly what Monk would wish him to tell Ham.

The conversation terminated with a loud groan from the distant lawyer. If there was anything that pained Ham, it was to see his sparring enemy, Monk, making a hit with an attractive young lady.

Monk himself soon arrived. Renny, Ole Slater, Aunt Nora and the others accompanied him. Alice Cash was quiet, and her eyes were continuously downcast.

They had consigned her brother's body to a local funeral home.

MONK looked at Doc and shook his head slowly.

"The cops sure are combing this man's town for you!" he declared. Then, in a low tone which did not reach Alice Cash, he added: "They even followed us into the funeral home and searched the coffin, thinking we might be pulling some kind of hocus-pocus! And they frisked our cars two times on the way here."

"That's not half of it!" Renny put in grimly. "They're liable to show up here any minute!"

Johnny stepped out. He came back with the latest extra edition of the Prosper City *News*. Through his spectacles with the magnifying lens, he stared owlishly at the headlines.

"They've got a decent crowd on that newspaper!" he grinned. "They carry a story saying Chief Clements was shot, but they don't mention Doc's name in connection with the affair! They simply say that there is not enough evidence to name the slayer."

Absently, Renny knocked his big fists together. This made a sound as if bricks were colliding.

"What about the gun with which Tugg shot Clements?" he pondered.

"Tugg will be too wise to keep it," Doc told him.

Ole Slater came dashing in from outdoors.

"Mr. Savage!" he ejaculated. "The police!"

Doc went to the door. Down the road somewhere, loud voices were making angry demands, and getting just as angry refusals. The gang of ex-service guards had evidently stopped the police.

Monk offered: "I told them to do that."

Doc nodded. "Fine! That gives us a few moments to work which should be enough."

Monk looked uneasy. "It's going to be plenty dangerous getting away from here!"

"I'm going to stay right on the grounds!"

"Holy cow!" exploded Renny, using an expression which came to his tongue whenever he was greatly surprised. "How're you going to manage that?"

Without answering, Doc stepped outdoors and circled the house. He did not know how he was going to remain without being ferreted out by the Prosper City lawmen.

He was looking for a hiding place which would not be suspected. Before he was halfway around the house, he discovered it.

A large galvanized iron tank stood at the rear of Aunt Nora's rambling old house. Eave spouts emptied into it. Aunt Nora Boston was a thrifty soul who did her own washing. She believed there was nothing like soft rain water for this.

The tank was two thirds full.

"Give us a shoulder!" Doc directed, and bent his efforts to moving the tank some distance away from the house. "Don't spill the water!"

A skeptical laugh escaped Ole Slater. "You can never avoid them by submerging yourself in the tank. The police are sure to prod around in the water with sticks."

"Dry up, sonny," Monk advised him. "Doc's scheme ain't anything as simple as that."

Ole Slater flushed angrily. He was not in a mood to take any cracks from Monk—piqued as he was because Monk had been giving charming Alice Cash marked attention.

DOC called Monk. They ran inside the house. Although Doc's equipment had been destroyed by the explosion in his room, Monk's chemical supplies were still intact. With a great clanking of test tubes and a fizzing of liquids, Monk went to work.

Doc entered Renny's quarters. Among other things the big-fisted engineer had brought from New York were compact diving "lungs." These consisted of little more than oxygen tanks with hoses running to a mouthpiece. The outfit included a clip like a clothespin for holding the nostrils shut.

Monk appeared. He was carrying two bottles—one small, one large. They held liquids of a widely different nature. He gave Doc the smaller bottle. They hurried outdoors.

The bronze man now picked up a large rock and immersed himself carefully in the tank. He sat on the bottom, the rock on his lap to hold himself down.

Monk dumped the chemical in the large bottle onto the water. Striking a match, he applied it. The stuff blazed up brilliantly, making a brownish smoke.

Homely Monk gave Ole Slater his best leer.

"This chemical burns without hardly any heat!" he chuckled. "The police will think we're burning trash in the tank. They won't know there's water in it. Now, do you believe they'll prod with sticks?"

Ole Slater looked sheepish. "No, of course not! But suppose Mr. Savage should want to get out of there? How could he do it without being burned?"

"Didn't you see the small bottle I gave him?"

"What's that got to do with it?"

"It's filled with an extinguishing fluid that floats. All Doc has to do is uncork the bottle—and the fire goes out."

Ole Slater rubbed his strong jaws. "Isn't there any limit to the number of tricks you fellows have up your sleeve?"

"Listen!" Monk grinned. "Nobody has ever put Doc in a jam he couldn't get out of!"

Word was now dispatched to the ex-service men, advising them it was perfectly all right for the police to approach. When the officers arrived,

Long Tom and Johnny were making a great show of dumping trash into the flaming tank. They ceased this before the cops came close enough to observe that the "trash" was only tin cans, which would not add to the heat of the chemical fire.

"We're gonna search this joint!" a police sergeant declared loudly. "We're gonna search it good!"

"Go ahead!" Monk told him. "Just one thing, though! Don't start intimidating Alice Cash and Aunt Nora!"

"I'm gonna make damn sure they ain't seen Doc Savage!"

Monk gave a signal. His three pals crowded up threateningly. They were a grim-faced fighting crew.

"You can ask all the questions you want to!" Monk grunted. "But whether anybody answers them or not is something else!"

"Where's Doc Savage?"

"That's one we're not going to answer!"

The lawman glowered blackly. "You won't answer because you're afraid of givin' your pal away!"

"I ain't afraid of nothin' or nobody!" Monk hammered his chest like a bull ape. "I just don't feel like answering your damned question!"

AT this point more policemen arrived. Three carloads! They bristled with sub-machine guns and double-barreled riot guns. A cordon was stretched around Aunt Nora's grounds.

The officers pushed their search. Beginning at the circus tents, they tore into every bale and box. They even climbed to the top of the tents to see that there were no trick pockets.

They ignored the flaming barrel, except to toss an empty cigarette pack in the flames.

They reached the house. At front and rear doors guards were posted. The scrutiny started in the basement. Walls and floor were brick. The bricks were examined, literally one at a time, to make sure no trapdoor gave into a secret room.

Other officers scattered over the remainder of the house.

Approximately two dozen newcomers arrived. These were the men who owned the mills and the mines of Prosper City. They had evidently held a conference, and had come in a body to discuss measures which would give Doc control of their property.

When they found the bronze man was being sought by the police, they exploded indignantly. No one would entertain the idea that Doc Savage had shot Chief Clements.

They landed on the officers with a verbal barrage. For a few moments the house was a bedlam of angry shouting. The police perspired and their necks became red. They could not tell these men to shut up and clear out. They were Prosper City's powerful citizens.

"The suggestion that Savage murdered anybody is preposterous!" insisted a mine owner. "We've been investigating! Savage is known all over the world for his remarkable deeds!"

Pompous Judborn Tugg had come upon the scene from somewhere. He entered the argument.

"My dear fellow businessmen and comrades," he said bombastically. "This man Savage is twice a murderer—probably worse."

"We do not believe that!" someone advised.

"I saw Savage murder Chief Clements!" Tugg shouted. "Half a dozen others witnessed the horrible crime, too! Furthermore, Savage is trying to buy your properties for a fraction of what they are worth! Can't you see that? He's not only a killer—he's a gigantic swindler!"

Renny's great voice roared: "When the time comes, Tugg, we'll either prove that you're the Green Bell, or that you're on his payroll."

Both fists up and clenched, Tugg started forward as if to strike Renny. However, he stopped well out of reach of the enormous blocks of gristle which Renny called hands.

"Your lying words won't hurt me!" he said, with the air of an injured man.

After this, Tugg subsided. He could see plainly that everyone but the police was against him.

"Go ahead with the search," commanded the sergeant in charge of police. "We're going to scour this place from top—"

He never finished. Feet rapped the porch. A uniformed officer dived inside.

"One of our men!" he yelled. "Hanging in the vines under a window! A knife is sticking out of him!"

THERE was an excited rush around the house. Vines which the excited officer had mentioned were wistaria. The creepers draped over a lightly constructed trellis.

Under one second-story window there was a vertical streak where the leaves were wet with dull, thick red. The blue-clad body of a policeman was the mountain from which this streak of crimson spilled.

The cadaver hung from the window by a rope around the neck. The officer had been stabbed several times, judging from the places where he had leaked blood. The knife had been left protruding from his chest after the last blow.

One of Aunt Nora Boston's carving knives! It had a black stag-horn handle. From below, the hilt looked not unlike the head of a black serpent peeping from the vest pocket of the dead man's coat!

Homely Monk stared at the window—and began to feel as if he was standing in a pool of ice water. It was *his* room from which the body was dangling!

"Holy cow!" Renny breathed in Monk's ear. "Why on earth was he murdered? And right under our noses, too!"

Monk tied his furry hands into knots, then untied them. He was visioning the inside of the Prosper City Jail.

The chances were good that everyone present would be arrested. It was only in detective-story books that a houseful of people were kept on the scene after a murder, in order that the detective hero might trap the villain. These hardheaded cops would throw everyone in jail.

Made silent and grim by the presence of murder, the officers ran into the house and upstairs.

The rope which suspended the slain man was one Monk had used to tie around a case of chemicals which he had brought from New York. It was not long enough to lower the body to the ground.

They hauled the corpse in through the window.

There was nothing to indicate why the bluecoat had been slain; no bruises to indicate a struggle.

"There couldn't have been a fight, anyway," Monk pointed out. "We would have heard it from downstairs. The fellow has been dead only a few minutes."

"Whose room is this?" demanded the police sergeant.

"Mine," Monk admitted. His small voice was even more tiny than usual.

The officer yanked a pair of handcuffs from his pocket, and bore down on Monk.

"Listen, big hairy, you're under arrest for murder!" he snapped.

Monk beetled his brows angrily. "You're forgetting something."

"What!"

"I haven't been out of your sight a minute since you arrived. The slain man was one of the men who came with you, so I couldn't have killed him."

Marked disappointment was registered by the policeman. He wanted to put Monk under custody. But Monk was obviously not the guilty person.

"Bring everybody up here in the hall!" the cop shouted. "We'll get to the bottom of this!"

The group of men, who represented Prosper City's mines and factories, protested vociferously to being herded about by the police. This, however, had no effect.

"This is mighty serious!" the bluecoats growled. "We got to investigate everybody!"

"That is exactly right, officer!" Judborn Tugg agreed loudly. "I will gladly submit myself to any examination. Personally, I think anyone reluctant to do that, under the circumstances, has something to conceal."

Numerous dark glares rewarded Tugg for his speech. He replied with a smug smile. He knew the words had lifted him in the estimation of the officers.

BETWEEN ten and fifteen minutes of catechizing now ensued. The servants of the law did a rather thorough job. The information they obtained, however, only added to their perplexity. Almost anyone, it seemed, could be the killer. Indeed, Doc's four aides were almost the only men who had been continuously at the side of some officer during the time the slaying must have occurred.

Collison McAlter, Aunt Nora, Ole Slater, Alice Cash—all others, in fact—found difficulty in proving exactly where they had been.

The little flock of Prosper City businessmen became frankly worried. Their efforts to prove by one another that they were accounted for at all times, were almost frantic.

"All of you stick here in the hall!" commanded the sergeant. "We're gonna finish our search of the house. Doc Savage may be around, and may have murdered the cop!"

Tall, bony Johnny had been using his spectacle magnifier on the hilt of the knife which had slain the bluecoat.

"It has been wiped clean of fingerprints," he announced regretfully.

The police search progressed up from the basement. Plaster was scrutinized; walls were rapped; books and magazines were examined.

"You've got strange ideas of hidin' places!" Monk snorted.

"Don't get sassy!" he was ordered. "We're lookin' for the gun that shot Chief Clements!"

Monk gave a pronounced start. "Say, officer, did somebody suggest the gun might be here?"

"We don't broadcast the source of our tips!" snapped the sergeant. But a movement of his eyes toward Judborn Tugg was significant—the gun hint had come from Tugg.

A hoodoo seemed to have settled in Monk's room for it was there that the next unpleasant development occurred.

Monk had brought along a spare suit. It hung in the closet. From its pocket was produced the gun which had slain Chief Clements.

Proof that this was the particular gun would have to await examination of ballistics experts, though. Identification numbers had been filed off. Judging by the shiny condition of the file grooves, it was a safe bet this had been done since the fatal shooting.

Monk entertained no doubt about its being the murder gun. Someone had planted it in his room. He proclaimed this fact loudly.

"It explains the murder of the policeman!" he declared. "The cop happened to find the Green Bell or one of his men hiding the gun in this room! That's why he was killed!"

"The gun bein' here shows Doc Savage has been here," the sergeant insisted. "He could have done the killin'!"

Monk subsided. What was the use of arguing?

A FRESH stream of objections now came from the Prosper City business men. If Doc Savage was guilty, they asserted, why arrest everybody? Some of them made the ominous prediction that, if this kept up, Prosper City would soon find herself with an entire new set of policemen.

The officers relented—partially. It was agreed that everyone should remain at Aunt Nora's place under careful guard, Doc's four men—thinking of their bronze chief concealed in the water tank—were not pleased at this turn of events.

Flames still leaped from the top of the tank. It was the nature of Monk's chemical to burn slowly—it would blaze for another hour. Then what?

Doc stood an excellent chance of being discovered, and none at all of escaping from the grounds.

"We ought to warn Doc how things are stacking up," Monk whispered to pretty Alice Cash.

Alice now showed that she carried around something besides good looks on her shoulders. She secured permission from the policemen, and retired to the privacy of her room. On a sheet of stiff white paper she wrote a brief summary of what had occurred. She sealed this in a large-mouthed bottle which had once contained stick candy.

The roll of paper pressed against the walls of the bottle, due to its own stiffness. Hence the words it bore could be read through the glass.

Alice found a heavy paperweight, and tied this to the bottle to serve as a sinker.

The current fashion in gowns tended toward full sleeves. She was wearing the latest. She concealed the bottle in a sleeve, then managed to make her way outdoors without attracting suspicion.

She maneuvered toward the flame-crowned tank and tossed her message inside, without seeming she was doing anything unusual.

Descending through the water, the bottle and its weight landed on Doc's right knee. He grasped it. The fire above lighted the water more brilliantly than sunlight would have. Too, although the burning chemical was not supposed to make much heat, the water was getting unpleasantly warm.

Peering through the wall of the bottle, Doc read the message.

He reached a swift decision. Indeed, he seemed hardly to consider the matter at all, so rapidly did his brain analyze the situation and ferret out the best procedure.

The cork left the neck of the bottle which held the extinguishing compound. It was a milky fluid.

In wreathing streamers, which resembled the smoke from a small fire, it climbed upward. The chemical flames were promptly snuffed out.

Removing the rock anchor from his lap, Doc got up and clambered from the tank.

Yells of surprise greeted his appearance. Alice Cash pressed her hands to her cheeks and looked startled.

The police sergeant dashed forward, gun in one hand, handcuffs in the other, shouting: "You're arrested! If you bat an eye, you'll get plugged!"

Chapter XIII
PIPED COMMANDS

WITHIN surprisingly few seconds, Doc was centered in a bristling ring of gun mules.

Judborn Tugg bounced up and screamed: "Kill him, officer! Don't let him escape! He's the devil who murdered your chief!"

Long Tom chanced to be near Tugg at that instant. The electrical wizard—slender, pallid, unhealthy-looking—did not seem half a match for the portly Tugg. But he sprang upon Tugg. His fists delivered a smacking volley.

Before Long Tom was hauled off, Judborn Tugg had lost three front teeth. His nose was awry. Both his eyes had received a pasting which would soon turn them a beautiful black.

Long Tom swung his fists recklessly at officers who grabbed him. Two dropped. The electrical wizard had the appearance of a weakling, but his looks were highly deceptive.

Ordinarily, Long Tom kept a level head; but on rare occasions, he flew into a great rage. He was having one of his tantrums now. The accusations against Doc had heated him to the exploding point.

A lawman got behind and whipped the back of Long Tom's head repeatedly with a blackjack. The electrical expert tumbled over, unconscious.

Doc Savage was now conducted into the basement of Aunt Nora's house, and ordered to undress.

Every piece of his clothing was taken. This indignity was suggested by bruised, trembling Judborn Tugg.

"You don't want to take any chances," Tugg told the police. "There's no telling what kind of weapon this bronze fiend might have hidden in his clothing."

An old pair of overalls and a blue shirt were handed Doc. His feet were left bare. The officers conducted him to a large police touring car.

The top was up, but there were no curtains. Doc sat in the rear, an officer on each side. Three more cops occupied the front seat.

When they headed for town and jail, two cars rolled ahead. Three came behind. In one of the latter Long Tom languished. They were going to jail the electrical wizard for his performance on Tugg.

Everyone else was, it seemed, to be permitted liberty. Now that the police had Doc, they seemed to think everything was settled.

The official cars were driven slowly. Their motors were rather silent for such big machines.

As they entered a part of town where residences were more plentiful, a metallic squeaking of radios in houses could be distinguished. Evidently the Prosper City broadcasting station put on a program at this hour which was very popular with the housewives. A majority of sets were tuned in.

The autos progressed several blocks. Suddenly, all about them, a wailing and screaming came from the radio speakers.

The uproar had an eerie, banshee quality. Intermingled with the bedlam, rising above it, came a procession of dull gonging notes. These persisted for only a few moments, then the whole clamor died.

"The Green Bell!" a cop gulped.

The police looked at Doc as if suspecting the bronze man might have made the noise.

Doc showed by no sign that he had heard. His hands reposed on his knees. They rested close together, snugged by handcuffs. His ankles were also manacled.

Three railroads entered Prosper City. To avoid dangerous crossings, the tracks lay on high grades. Overhead bridges spanned the streets.

The police cavalcade crawled toward one of the bridges. Two passed under. Doc's machine came up within a score of feet of the structure. It traveled at a leisurely pace.

The cadaver hung from a window by a rope around the neck.

Flinging both fists above his head, Doc sprang upward. Driven by tremendously developed leg muscles, his body burst through the top fabric as if it were paper.

He twisted out on top. The bows were stanch enough to support his weight.

The shackles on wrists and ankles seemed to hamper him hardly at all. By the time the car reached the bridge, he was standing erect.

Springing upward, he grasped the bridge beams. A flip outward and upward hooked his toes over the rail. An acrobatic swaying—and he was atop the bridge.

HAD Doc sought to make an escape in any direction other than upward, the police would have been in a position to riddle him. As it was, the tops of the cars spoiled their aim. Before they could lean outside, Doc was gone—sheltered by the high steel side pieces of the bridge.

In concealment, Doc tested the handcuffs against his bronze sinews. It was no mean feat of muscle he was attempting. The handcuff links were not undersize, nor were they of a special metal, so brittle it would snap easily—two dodges sometimes employed by professional strong men.

His sinews seemed to bunch, and crawl like animals under his bronze skin. *Snap!* went the links joining his ankles. Then another straining tug, and those on his wrists went the same way.

Down the tracks he ran, doubled as low as possible between the rails. Policemen were shooting, yelling, and scrambling madly up the grade!

It would have been an excellent time for a train to come along. But never was a horizon more barren of a snorting locomotive. Doc scooted ahead until a bullet squeaked dangerously close, telling him officers had gained the track.

He pitched right, and literally slithered down the grade on his stomach. The railway section men had sown a plentiful amount of clover on the slope—it was a sweet variety of clover which grew rank and offered excellent concealment.

Doc gained a fence, left pennants of his overalls on the barb wire getting through, and dived behind someone's chicken house, just as bullets began to smack the boards.

He crossed the yard, surrounded by a young tornado of frightened chickens. Racing past a small dwelling, he glided down the street.

He was safe. He made directly for Aunt Nora Boston's place.

THE brief, hideous clangor of the Green Bell over the radio was the reason for Doc's escape. He had no proof as to the meaning of the unearthly radio noise, but he had concluded it could have only one purpose.

Rumor said the noise always presaged death or violence by the Green Bell's men. Therefore, Doc reasoned, the gong was a summons to bring the evil, hooded tribe to some point where they received orders.

Doc was certain that Judborn Tugg was one of the clan—if not its chief. He intended to watch Tugg's reactions to the radio call.

Doc reached a tall tree some distance from Aunt Nora's home. This was a lofty elm. It chanced to be the same perch from which the ill-fated Slick had watched. Small scuffs on the bark, a clinging thread or two which had been wrenched from Slick's suit, told Doc this part of the story as he climbed upward.

He stationed himself at the end of a large limb.

Some sort of disturbance was going on near one of the circus tents. Judborn Tugg was waving a fat arm and shouting. Monk and Johnny were dancing about him with threatening gestures.

Tugg's actions showed he was insulting Doc's two aides in studied fashion.

In a moment, Monk and Johnny seized the pompous man and threw him bodily out of the grounds.

Doc Savage, witnessing this bit of drama, felt a new respect for Tugg's sagacity. The fat man had managed to get himself kicked out so that his departure, so soon after the radio clangor, would not be suspicious.

Doc silently lowered himself from his perch and followed Tugg.

The fat man entered his limousine. However, he drove only a short distance, and that very slowly. Parking near a wide flat field which was overgrown with brush, he made for the ramshackle barn.

The sunlight was brilliant. At no time did Tugg take more than half a dozen steps without glancing alertly around. Yet Doc was hardly fourscore feet behind when his quarry ducked into the old barn.

Doc sidled near the structure, only to be forced back as he heard the approach of other men.

The Green Bell's pack was assembling!

They came by twos and by threes. Once, half a dozen in a group. The last arrival closed the door.

Each man to come to the spot had been encased in a long black garment with a green bell painted on the breast. No one remained outside on guard. That exotic masquerade would have been sure to attract attention of any chance passerby. No doubt more than one watching eye was pasted to the cracks, however.

In assembling the vast knowledge which his remarkable brain held, Doc had made it a practice to learn from masters in each line; then, by intensive study, to improve on the best they were able to give. He had gone to animal hunters of the jungle to learn woodcraft, for these were the masters of stealth.

As noiselessly as a cloud-cast shadow, he drew near the ramshackle building.

A hollow, earthy voice mumbled within the structure. The words, as they reached Doc's ears, were almost too distorted for understanding.

The thing Slick Cooley had learned only by use of his eyes, Doc's keen ears discerned instantly! The voice was pouring from an underground pipe!

"Is everyone here?" it was asking.

"Yes, sir!" Judborn Tugg shouted in answer.

"You are here for orders!" came the sepulchral tones of the Green Bell. "Each of you, of course, made sure he was not followed?"

To this, there was general clamor, evidently meant for assent.

"Good!" boomed the voice from the ground. "We finally got Savage in jail. His men remain. It is to hear their fate that you were summoned."

DOC SAVAGE listened with only half attention, for he was worming a slow way through the weeds, pressing an ear to the ground at frequent intervals. Due to the marshy nature of the earth, he did not believe the tiling could be deeply buried. Otherwise it would fill with water.

The Green Bell—wherever he was—must of necessity shout loudly to make his voice carry with volume. Doc thought he should be able to locate the tile by ear.

"Judborn Tugg!" donged the Green Bell.

"I am here!" Tugg shouted.

If he did not know the figure to which he spoke was a dummy of sticks and cloth, he must be very puzzled at being asked to identify himself.

"You will recall that, nearly a week ago, you were commanded to make certain preparations near Aunt Nora Boston's home!"

"Yes," howled Tugg.

"Just what did you do? I want to be sure!"

"I hid a big bottle of poison in a brush patch on the mountain slope, close to Aunt Nora's place! You can't miss the brush! Four large trees grow out of it. They're in a straight line—as if they'd been planted."

"Exactly where is the bottle?"

"Buried halfway between the middle two trees."

"What kind of poison?"

"Cyanide! The most deadly stuff I could find!"

Outside, Doc Savage dug silently with his fingers. His sensitive hearing had guided him well, for the hole he sank landed squarely on top of the tile. He spaded rapidly with his hands, lengthening his excavation along the tile.

The big clay pipes were not long.

The Green Bell's voice boomed: "Tugg, you will get that poison and go—"

In the midst of the gonging words, Doc struck a sharp blow with his fist. The pipe was not of very strong construction. It collapsed, eggshell fashion.

The Green Bell interrupted himself, roared: "What was that noise?"

"It sounded as if—it came from under you some place," Tugg yelled.

"Never mind," the mastermind said hastily, apprehensive lest his hirelings learn the figure in the barn was only a stuffed dummy of wood and fabric.

Doc hastily cupped palms over the hole. This was to prevent escape of too much voice sound. Picking up several pinches of fine dust, he let it trickle slowly into the opening.

Entering the tile, the dust streams were sucked away from the barn. This showed a draft, and gave him the direction.

It was possible that the string of tiles turned before they reached their destination.

"Tugg, you will get the cyanide which you secreted near Aunt Nora's!" continued the Green Bell. "There is, I presume, a large quantity of it in the bottle."

"A lot!" Tugg shouted.

"Good! You will get it! Tonight you will take a group of men and dig up the water main which supplies Aunt Nora's home. I happen to know that, due to the house being in an outlying district, the water line is very small—two-inch pipe. You will insert the poison. I am sure you can handle the mechanical details."

"I guess so!" Tugg replied uneasily.

DOC SAVAGE glided away from the barn, following a trail used by the masked men. His gaze switched here and there—always on the ground.

Soon he found what he expected—a cigarette stub. He picked it up, then continued his hunt. He added two remnants of Judborn Tugg's dollar cigars to his assortment.

The prize find was a discarded paper matchbook—one match remaining. Doc had feared it was going to be necessary to start a fire Boy Scout fashion, twirling one stick upon another.

He moved back toward the dilapidated building. The cigarettes, cigars, and matches had been discarded by the Green Bell's men as they donned black hoods upon nearing the rendezvous.

Back at the tile, Doc crumpled the tobacco into a loose fistful. He put a match to the papers off the cigarettes, then added the tobacco. The draft made it burn.

A wisp or two of smoke escaped the baked clay pipe. This was not enough to lift above the weeds and be seen by the watchers in the barn.

Doc listened. Judborn Tugg was talking, giving a recital of what had happened at Aunt Nora Boston's. Doc felt there was no need of Judborn telling the

Green Bell what had happened at Aunt Nora's. The Green Bell had been upon the scene, and had murdered the policeman, Doc believed.

Collison McAlter—the group of Prosper City factory and mine owners—the others who had been on hand—one of these must be the Green Bell!

Doc circled widely, sensitive nostrils expanding and contracting as he sniffed the air. Tobacco smoke possessed a marked odor. He hoped to locate it where it escaped from the end of the tile. Daily from childhood, Doc had taken an exercise calculated to develop his olfactory organs. His sense of smell was phenomenal.

He ringed the place, without finding what he sought. The second time, he went entirely around. The last circle was wider. Doc quickened his pace; he had expected better luck.

Over toward the barn, he heard noises. Brush cracking. The Green Bell's gang leaving the trysting place! The seance had ended.

Doc let them go. Judborn Tugg was the important member. He would not be hard to locate. Doc concentrated on trying to find the mouth of the tile.

Judborn was one of the first to leave the barn. He walked swiftly from the vicinity. It was a hot day; his black hood was uncomfortable. He removed it as soon as he got out of sight.

Although his name was spoken freely at these sinister meetings, Tugg was always careful to keep his face hooded. This was merely a coincidental precaution. If anything came up in court he could swear he had never attended the conclaves, but that the culprit must have been someone else masquerading under his name.

Entering his expensive car, Tugg drove back to town, taking his time. He smoked one of his costly cigars. There was nothing ahead of him for the remainder of the day.

As for getting the poison from the cache near Aunt Nora's home, that would wait until darkness.

TUGG eventually wheeled his machine up before his great white house. A few months ago, there had been a flunky to open the door; but there was none now. Tugg had dismissed all his servants, pleading financial stringency.

The real reason was that he did not want servants around where they might pick up dangerous information. Tugg was unmarried, and took his meals at Prosper City's leading restaurant.

He entered his sumptuously furnished library. The minute he stepped through the door, he jumped a foot in the air.

A somber black crow of a figure was perched in a deep armchair. The green of the bell insignia and the green of glass goggles were almost the same hue.

The apparition held a leveled gun.

The firearm alone was enough to tell Judborn Tugg that he was now facing the Green Bell in person. The czar sinister always held a gun when he showed himself, to make sure none of his followers took a notion to yank off his hood.

"W-what do you want?" Tugg spluttered. "I—I—I was just talking to you."

"And a fine mess you made of it, too!" The Green Bell's tone was deep, angry.

Tugg dropped his cigar, and it lay unnoticed, charring the rug. "What do you mean?"

"Savage followed you to the swamp! He listened to everything that was said!"

Tugg shook his head violently. "Impossible! The police have Savage!"

"He escaped!" The Green Bell's gun never wavered from a line with Judborn Tugg's heart. "The police—helpless fools—let Savage get away. And he followed you to the meeting in the barn."

"Me!" Tugg choked. "Surely not!"

"We will not argue about that!" the Green Bell clanged. "Savage was there! I heard him! I am certain! You will take the orders which I came to give you! Then I will go!"

"What is it?"

"You will ignore all orders pertaining to the hidden bottle of cyanide!"

Tugg blinked. Then his quick brain grasped the possibilities.

"Say, boss, if Savage overheard us talking about that poison, he's sure to go to destroy it. We can lay an ambush—"

"The ambush is already set!" intoned the Green Bell.

"But I didn't know you had gotten hold of any of the men—"

"This is a trap which does not use men. And it is the more effective for that!"

The Green Bell now took his departure, fading into the shrubbery.

Judborn Tugg, watching from a window, swore in disgust and wished he had not landscaped his place so profusely. He would have liked to follow and learned the identity of this fiend who was behind Prosper City's difficulties.

Chapter XIV
THE SUSPICION PLANT

HAD Doc Savage been able to witness what had just occurred at Judborn Tugg's home, he would no longer have retained a suspicion that Tugg was the Green Bell.

However, Doc was not considering Tugg very seriously for the part of villain. His reason for this was simple. Tugg was too obviously connected with the Green Bell organization. The man actually behind the thing was too clever to let suspicion point at him in that fashion.

Doc had now made five circles around the barn ruin. He had detected no faintest odor of tobacco smoke. He was frankly puzzled. It was hardly possible that the Green Bell had been this distant from the rendezvous.

Disgusted, Doc returned to the ramshackle old farm building. By now, his bird had flown. He concluded to follow the tiling and learn where it actually did go.

The baked clay pipes were not buried deeply. By jabbing a sharp stick, he traced them. They ran perhaps two hundred feet, turning sharply at two points. Then they suddenly ended.

He dug. The discovery he made was unexpected. The tiles simply elbowed straight downward. After a depth of three feet, the shaft was steel pipe.

Doc compressed a small ball of clay, dropped it. The lump fell, he judged accurately, at least two hundred and fifty feet.

With great care, Doc now wiped out all traces of his presence, filling in the holes he had excavated, and scattering leaves and trash about.

He left the vicinity. His steps were careful; his progress noiseless. This, although there was no apparent danger. His was an instinctive caution.

Many days had passed since the last rain at Prosper City. Yet the ground underfoot was soft, wet. In some spots it was muck which oozed over his shoes.

It was not ground through which one could readily drive a tunnel. A few feet beneath the surface, the earth must be literally a thick soup. Yet the tile line had ended in a vertical shaft which sank straight downward more than ten-score feet.

Doc had a theory to explain this. He hoped it might play an important part in the eventual capture of the Green Bell.

Something over an hour later, the bronze man turned up in the vicinity of Aunt Nora Boston's home. Evading a covey of searching policemen had delayed him somewhat.

Numerous blue uniforms were scattered in Aunt Nora's yard. Others could be glimpsed occasionally, moving within the house.

Doc set a course for the mountain slope which began almost at the edge of Aunt Nora's abode. He had no trouble locating a patch of brush from which grew four perfectly aligned trees. This, from what he had overheard, was the hiding place of the deadly poison.

What he did not know, though, was that the Green Bell had set a death trap at the spot.

Old leaves made a gray-brown carpet under the brush and smaller trees. These would show tracks, for the undersides were dark and moldy, while the upper surfaces had been washed and bleached by the weather.

As Doc progressed, the brush thickened; trees of moderate size became more plentiful.

Doc crouched, then sailed upward in a great leap. His sinewy fingers trapped a limb. He swung easily to another branch, flipped atop it, glided its swaying length, and seemed to float outward in space to the next tree.

It was a remarkable exhibition of agility. Few jungle anthropoids could have done better.

THE four extremely tall trees, he discovered, jutted from the midst of a thorn thicket. Moreover, a path grooved between the second pair. From the condition of the carpeting leaves, it was evident this trail received only occasional use.

Directly between the spindling trees, there was a small opening in the thorny trail walls. Almost a pit! This seemed a logical hiding place for the poison.

Doc balanced out on a branch of a smaller tree, some yards from the four giant sentinels. Lowering, he dangled from sinewy hands. Back and forth, he began to flip, after the fashion of a trapeze artist getting his swing going. The bough gyrated.

Releasing his clutch at the proper instant, the big bronze man arched upward through space. He made a perfect landing on the lowermost limb of a tall tree.

It was then that he encountered his big discovery.

A machine gun was lashed to the tree. Its ugly snout angled downward. Doc sidled along the limb, examined it. He sighted down the barrel. It was aimed at the tiny recess in the thorns, which probably held the poison.

A flexible wire, attached to the trigger, ran down through tiny, greased pulleys. A death trap! Anyone who grasped the poison bottle would be instantly riddled.

Doc thought swiftly. He detached the trigger trip of the gun. Then, with a long, descending leap, he landed on the path.

Searching under the leaves, he quickly found the poison. He untied a small wire from the neck of the bottle. This was the trip for the rapid-firer.

A glance showed him the poison was genuine. The stuff was not in crystal form, but was an odorless, volatile liquid. Cyanic acid! One of the most deadly of poisons!

Doc carried the bottle some distance away, got rid of its contents in a hole which he dug in the ground, then refilled it with water from a stream trickling down the mountainside. This stream, due probably to the presence of mines above, had a foul color, not greatly different from that of the cyanic.

Replacing the now harmless bottle took only a moment.

Moving with the ease of a squirrel, Doc clambered into the tree which held the machine gun. He altered the position of the weapon slightly.

Doc took great pains with the work. Several

times, he sighted along the fluted barrel. Then he replaced the wire on the trigger.

He quitted the vicinity as noiselessly as he had arrived.

In the distance, a freight train was whistling and puffing as it pulled out of Prosper City. It got underway slowly, and its snorting and bleating became fainter and fainter.

The freight was still audible when Doc appeared in the brush which fringed Aunt Nora Boston's spacious yard. He waited, watching.

A car approached from the direction of town. It rolled into the yard, bearing Long Tom.

The slender, pale, temperamental electrical wizard must have put up bail and received a quick release on the charge of battering Judborn Tugg.

Perhaps five minutes, Doc waited, in order that the jubilation caused by Long Tom's return might subside. Then the bronze man's strange, mellow, trilling note saturated the vicinity.

Musical, yet entirely without tune, it ran up and down the scale. A bystander, looking at Doc's lips, could not have told it was from thence that the fantastic sound came. Yet the weird resonance possessed remarkable carrying qualities.

It penetrated across the lawn and soaked through the innermost reaches of the vast old house. Policemen glanced about wonderingly, with no idea where the cadence was coming from.

Doc's four men gave no indication that the eerie note meant anything to them. But a few minutes later, the quartet sauntered casually into the house. They used binoculars from upstairs windows.

It was gaunt Johnny, spectacles containing the magnifier cocked up on his forehead, who discovered Doc.

A strange bit of pantomime followed. Johnny's binoculars were powerful. Hence, Doc was able to converse with him by using deaf-and-dumb sign language.

DOC explained fully what he wanted. Then he eased away from the region.

Patrols of cops had taken to prowling the vicinity. He wished no contact with them which could be avoided.

The sun had marched two hours nearer meridian when Johnny, driving down the road in one of the rented cars, passed a certain culvert. Without stopping, he flung a paper-wrapped bundle from the machine. This hopped end over end, coming to a rest directly before the culvert.

Johnny drove on as if nothing had happened.

An arm—it looked like a beam wrapped with steel hawsers and painted with bronze—reached out of the profuse weed growth and snared the packet.

Both bundle and arm disappeared.

This seemed the end of the incident. The tops of the weeds shook a little; but that might have been caused by the breeze.

About eight minutes later, and about eight blocks distant, a householder's dog dashed madly through his back yard, barking. The householder looked out.

He saw, or he thought he saw—for he was not quite sure—a mighty bronze figure vanishing along the alley. The householder went back and sat down to his dinner, grinning widely. The police were after that bronze man! What of it? The viands on the table before him were some distributed by Doc Savage the night before.

The next incident of this sort occurred well on the other side of town, when a merchant, coming home to his lunch, was astounded to have a giant bronze man step from a grape arbor ahead of him, and calmly cross the street.

The merchant ran after the apparition. It was not in his thoughts to give an alarm. He wanted to thank this bronze man for a morning's business, which had practically saved his store from bankruptcy.

This merchant had been carrying scores of impoverished families on credit, and these, practically without exception, had been grateful enough to make a substantial repayment with the money which they had received from Doc.

The merchant, however, was forced to withhold his thanks. He failed to find the bronze figure which he had glimpsed. The form had vanished magically in a garden.

These two spots where the metallic giant was sighted were on a direct line between Aunt Nora Boston's home and Judborn Tugg's palatial white mansion.

JUDBORN TUGG had just partaken of an excellent dinner at Prosper City's leading restaurant. He returned to his home, driving his luxurious limousine.

Pausing before the front door, he made an elaborate ritual of clipping the end from one of his dollar cigars, and applying a match.

He opened the door, entered, stopped—his jaw seeming to disappear in his fat neck as he gaped.

He made an absent gesture at putting the cigar in his mouth, but missed that cavity fully four inches.

"I thought you—goodness gracious!" he stuttered uncertainly. "What is the trouble now?"

A figure in a raven-black robe occupied one of the living-room chairs. A green bell was painted on the front of the hood. The eyes were practically invisible. There were eye holes in the hood, but the wearer's face seemed to be bandaged heavily in white.

"Nothing is wrong!" snapped the somber figure in a hollow, gonging voice.

Tugg blinked, lifted his chin out of his fat neck, and found his lips with his cigar.

"You look much different than you did this

morning!" he mumbled. "I guess it is because you are not wearing your green goggles. You have your eyes bandaged! I hope you have not met with an accident?"

"Don't worry about my health!" tolled Doc Savage, imitating the Green Bell's macabre tones.

At the same time, Doc wished he had known about those green goggles. He had resorted to the white bandages to disguise the distinctive gold color of his eyes, knowing they would give him away instantly.

This Green Bell gown had been in the bundle which Johnny had flung from his car. Johnny himself had tailored it.

"What do you want with me?" Tugg demanded anxiously.

"About the bottle of poison!" Doc returned, angling for anything which would give him a lead.

Tugg's head dived into his neck and came up as he nodded. "Yes, yes! When you were here this morning, you told me not to go for the poison, but that Doc Savage would probably appear on the scene and be caught in a death trap!"

This was illuminating. It told Doc nearly all he needed to know. The Green Bell had learned Doc was eavesdropping in the vicinity of the old barn. The czar of fear himself had later visited Tugg and countermanded the barn orders.

"That plan is changed!" Doc said in his assumed tolling voice. "The new scheme is for you to go get the poison, just as you were ordered at first."

"You mean I'm to go ahead—"

"Exactly! You are to poison the water main leading to Aunt Nora's place!"

"Oh, my goodness!" Tugg gasped. "Didn't Savage fall into the trap?"

"Entirely unforeseen developments came up! Savage, I regret to say, did not tumble."

"But maybe he'll be watching the hiding place of the poison?"

"He will not harm you!"

Tugg shivered, said: "I'm kinda worried—"

"You, Tugg, are to get that poison!" Doc ordered in his assumed tolling. "You are to go in person. Above all things, you are not to send anyone else! Understand!"

Tugg squirmed. "Very well."

Doc Savage, in his masquerade as the Green Bell, had accomplished his purpose. He did not want to stretch his luck. Consequently, he now took his departure.

His going was quite effective. Judborn Tugg, determined this time to follow the master mind, flung wildly to a window the instant the somber figure exited. Quick as he was, the sepia form had been swifter. The visitor had vanished, as if gifted with supernatural powers, or an agility which would put him across fifty feet of lawn while a fat man was crossing a room.

EXASPERATED, Tugg turned on an electric fan and seated himself in its windy breath. The taste of his excellent dinner had been ruined, and his digestion hampered.

Sometimes, he wondered if any good at all would ever come from his association with the Green Bell. He had, in fact, pondered this on numerous occasions.

He wished Slick Cooley was still alive. Slick had been intent on learning who the Green Bell was, then killing him.

That would have been highly satisfactory to Tugg. Slick had expected to take over the Green Bell's organization. Judborn Tugg smiled wolfishly, and mused how easily a bullet from his own hand would have finished Slick.

This brought an unpleasant thought—Slick's death!

Tugg snapped up very straight in his chair. Then he scrambled forward and shut off the fan. He was cold enough now without any artificial refrigeration. His spine, in fact, felt like ice cubes joined with a string.

The newspapers had said Slick Cooley had gone insane in his jail cell, and had been shot while trying to escape. Insane! That was the Green Bell's trademark!

Slick Cooley had been killed because, in the hands of the law, he was a danger to the organization. That was clear!

Judborn Tugg's head crawled in and out of his neck. Doc Savage suspected *him* of being one of the gang. Did that not make him—Judborn Tugg— a menace to the organization?

This was a frosty thought, for it suggested the possibility that the Green Bell might find occasion to dispense with Judborn Tugg.

Throughout the evening, Tugg wrestled these thoughts around in a mire of unease. He would go through with the poisoning—it was often fatal to ignore the Green Bell's commands—but he would be very careful.

JUST before dark, furtive, slinking figures began dropping in on Tugg. These were disciples of the Green Bell—the fellows who were to help with the poisoning of the water main.

Tugg directed each of them to meet him at a spot some distance from Aunt Nora's house, then bundled them out. He considered it a strain on his dignity to associate with such riffraff.

An hour and a half after the street lamps of Prosper City had been turned on, Tugg neared the four sentinellike trees on the mountain slope. He was rushing the job. He wanted to get it over.

He carefully scouted the vicinity of the trees and the thorn patch. No lurking figure was flushed out by this strategy.

"Maybe I am wrong in thinking myself in danger," Tugg argued with himself. "Of course I am! The Green Bell will not murder a man of my importance to the organization. I would be hard to replace."

His mental balloon received a big prick when, a few moments later, he bent over and picked up the bottle of poison.

There was a deafening clatter behind him! It was as if a gigantic iron turkey had started gobbling. Bullets swooped over Tugg's head, chopped branches, and clouted the earth.

Tugg flattened, instinctively spinning. He saw the fire-lipping snout of the machine gun.

He had no way of knowing Doc Savage had aimed the weapon high enough that it could not possibly hit a man on the path. He had no way of knowing Doc Savage had been here at all! His only thought was—he had been doublecrossed!

The Green Bell had tried to murder him!

Judborn Tugg's actions for the next few moments were those of a frantic man. He scuttled down the trail, collecting numerous thorns in his haste.

Sweat bubbled from his forehead like grease from a cooking bacon rind. He fell to cursing the Green Bell.

"Tried to kill me like a dog!" he snarled.

It did not occur to Tugg that he might have been tricked. Up until a few minutes ago, he had held an evil admiration for the Green Bell. That had evaporated. Rage had taken its place. Rage, and a lust to turn the tables.

Revenge! The thought flamed Tugg's brain. But how to get it? Tugg knotted his fat hands.

He reached a momentous decision. The attempt on his life meant that he needed protection from the Green Bell. Where better to get this than from the Green Bell's Nemesis, Doc Savage?

Judborn Tugg decided to go to Doc Savage, tell the bronze man everything, and ask sanctuary. If there was any safety at hand, the bronze man was it.

This was the exact train of thought which Doc Savage had foreseen when he had re-aimed the machine gun and set the trickery trap for Tugg. Doc was psychologist enough to guess that Tugg, in protecting himself, would turn upon his master.

Doc Savage, in fact, was at that moment gliding along not fifty yards from the frightened and enraged Tugg.

The portly, terrified factory owner bee-lined for Aunt Nora Boston's home, so Doc let him go.

MONK, a towering, furry form in the night, challenged Tugg. Seeing who it was, Monk smiled grimly, reached out, and trapped Tugg's fat neck.

Tugg wriggled, squealing: "Now, don't hurt me! I came to see Savage!"

"Yah!" Monk growled. "I hope you don't expect to find him here, after your lying charge that he murdered Chief Clements!"

Desperately, Tugg pulled at the hirsute hands clasping his neck. But at the same time, his active little brain raced. Since he had himself murdered Chief Clements, he would have to make some sort of a deal. Any kind of a deal!

If it came to the worst, Tugg was willing to go to trial on a murder charge. With his influence in Prosper City, he believed he could get off. Tugg was a supreme egoist. He did not realize his influence was practically nil.

Better yet, he might strike a bargain with Doc Savage whereby, for his services in trapping the Green Bell, he would be permitted to go free.

Tugg was also always the optimist. If he had known Doc Savage's true character, the iron determination of the bronze man, he would have entertained scant hopes of a deal.

"I think I made a mistake about that killing!" Tugg wailed.

Monk loosened his clutch. "You what?"

"I might have made an error!" Tugg said evasively. "If I can see Doc Savage and talk to him in private, I can tell whether my identification of him as the killer was correct!"

To all appearances, there was not room for a spoonful of brains in Monk's knot of a head. But he possessed a keen intellect. He perceived instantly what Tugg was driving at.

"You wanta make a deal?" he demanded.

Tugg did not commit himself. "If I could see Doc Savage—"

Monk shook him and said: "You'd what?"

Tugg remained stubbornly silent.

The mousy tufts which Monk wore for eyebrows crawled together as he thought deeply. The upshot of his reflection was that he conducted Judborn Tugg to the house.

They sought out the sergeant who was in charge of the detachment of Prosper City police.

"Prosper City's leading citizen thinks he made a mistake in calling Doc a murderer," Monk declared, elbowing Tugg roughly. "Ain't that right, fatty?"

The indignity galled Tugg's pompous soul. But he was desperate.

"I've got to see Savage!" he gulped.

"There ain't no need of that unless you can swear he wasn't the killer!" Monk said cannily.

Tugg writhed, perspired, and pulled nervously at his gold watch chain until he broke it. He had reason to know his own peril was desperate. In his extremity, he was willing to make almost any concession to get in touch with Doc Savage.

"I—I think I made a mistake!" he groaned.

"You think?" Monk scowled.

"I—I'm sure I did!" Tugg gulped. "Savage wasn't the killer!"

Monk whistled loudly. Renny and the others raced up, together with policemen.

Tugg was conducted into the house. Monk—his small voice for once a great roar—announced vociferously that Judborn Tugg was willing to swear Doc Savage was not Police Chief Clements' slayer.

Monk was exerting pressure, not giving Tugg a chance to back up. The proclamation broke up a meeting which the Prosper City businessmen were holding in the house.

This conclave was for the purpose of discussing the transfer of their holdings to Doc Savage. Although Doc had, of necessity, been absent all day because of the police, his four aides were rushing his plans for the salvation of the manufacturing community.

Collison McAlter was a prominent figure in this conference.

Monk left Tugg inside, went out on the porch, lifted his voice. "Doc!" he bellowed. "Tugg is willin' to clear you! But he wants to talk! What'll we do?"

As if it were answering his howl, a shot banged loudly within the house.

Chapter XV
THE GREEN TRAP

MONK veered around. The screen on the front door had a patent lock which defied his fingers. So he walked bodily through, bearded hands pawing fine wire.

Inside the house, the only thing lacking to make the situation a perfect one for murder in the dark, was the lack of darkness. The lights were on brilliantly.

Collison McAlter and Ole Slater rushed up to Monk, crying questions. Other Prosper City industrialists boiled about.

"The shot was upstairs!" somebody yelled.

Big-fisted Renny came lumbering from somewhere. He grunted at Monk, and the two giants shouldered each other up the stairs. In the hallway, burned powder made a tang.

Since the evening was warm, most of the room doors were open to secure cross ventilation. The cordite reek was coming through one of these. Renny and Monk split, each popping their heads into a row of doors.

They fully expected to find a corpse. They were equally as certain that it would be Judborn Tugg.

"The Green Bell croaked Tugg before he could talk!" Monk wailed.

Their expectations were not realized.

In the first place, there was no body in any of the upstairs rooms. Nor was there a lurking gunman.

In the wall of Aunt Nora's room they discovered a gouge in the plaster. This held a bullet. The slug was not distorted, and obviously had not hit the wall with much more force than could have been developed by a small boy's slingshot.

The explanation of the puny blow was scattered over a dressing table—the mangled remains of an ordinary electric toaster.

Monk snorted loudly. "Lookit!"

"The bullet was laid in the toaster, and the heat exploded it," Renny agreed.

"Sure! A plant! Somebody did it to draw attention!"

Monk and Renny had come up the stairs in haste, but they went back down with a great deal more speed. Indoors, a swift search was started.

Racing outside, Monk bellowed for every guard to keep his eyes on the house.

Both hunts drew blanks. Not only were there no murdered bodies around, but nobody had the slightest idea what the excitement was about.

However, the mystery lost its profundity before long.

Judborn Tugg, somewhat pale, his pudgy form drawn up in a stiff dignity, walked toward the door.

Monk collared him. "Where you goin', fat boy?"

"I wish to take my departure!" Tugg replied in a voice which he could not quite make pompous.

Peering at the fat man, Monk observed that a remarkable change had taken place. Tugg was still frightened, but he was no longer anxious to talk to Doc Savage. His greatest concern was now to get out of the vicinity.

Monk looked fierce, but groaned inwardly. He realized what had happened. The shot had been a trick by the Green Bell to secure an opportunity to speak with Tugg in private.

"So you've changed your mind!" Monk gritted.

Judborn Tugg's answer was an angry squirm for his freedom. Monk let him go. He had a hunch that, if he did not, Tugg would immediately reverse his previous declaration that Doc was not guilty of Chief Clements' murder.

Tugg left the vicinity in great haste. He made directly for his palatial white home on the other side of town.

Monk's conjecture that Tugg had received a communication from the Green Bell was correct. What Monk had no way of knowing, however, was that Tugg possessed no idea of who had delivered the words. They had been whispered through the crack of a partially open door, when every one was interested in the banging noise upstairs.

The verbal interchange had been short. In a single angry sentence, Tugg had told of the machine gun. With equal terseness had come the reply that the whole thing must be a clever plot by Doc Savage.

Tugg was to lie low! That was the word. For the immediate future, he was to conduct himself as Prosper City's leading businessman, and nothing else.

There was a catch to this.

"I will attempt to dispose of Doc Savage by other means," the Green Bell had advised. "If that fails, it may be necessary for you to serve as a bait to draw Savage into a trap!"

THE Green Bell had not upbraided Tugg for nearly turning traitor. But Tugg was not deceived. He was live bait. The minute Doc Savage was slain, that bait would no longer be needed.

Tugg shuddered, perspired freely. He was in the jam of his shady life!

A giant, silent bronze shadow dogged Tugg's footsteps until the fat man was ensconced behind the locked doors of his palatial home.

Doc made certain that Tugg showed no sign of immediate activity. Then he retraced his spectral way to Aunt Nora Boston's.

The place, from a distance, had all the aspects of a circus. The giant tents, brilliantly lighted from below, seemed many times their actual size.

Curious individuals were swarming the vicinity, although there was to be no food distribution tonight. The money payments of the night before had made that unnecessary. But they were greatly interested in the negotiations over the factories.

If Doc Savage was given control, they got jobs. If he was refused, there seemed nothing but hard times ahead. So they came to loiter and snap up the latest gossip.

Two of these loafers were arguing hotly about the Chief Clements slaying; suddenly, they fell silent. They gaped slightly; their eyes roved the night.

For upon the scene had come a fantastic note, a nebulous, wind-borne sound which might have been the song of some exotic bird, or the trilling of the night breeze. Up and down the scale, it chased a musical crescendo; yet it was without tune.

"What's that?" demanded a man. "Where'n blazes is it comin' from?"

No one knew—except Doc's four aides. Almost at once, they drifted casually into the darkness. They met a short distance away, where they were well concealed in the brush.

They gave no signal—Doc had, without a doubt, followed their departure closely. For Doc's strange sound, trilling in the murk, could have but one meaning—a meeting was desired.

Doc appeared like a wraith at Monk's elbow, causing that furry individual to all but jump out of his hirsute hide.

"What have you fellows been able to learn about that fake shot?" he demanded.

The four blinked owlishly. Doc had not been glimpsed around the house, but he seemed to know what had happened.

"I've been drifting around in the darkness, listening!" Doc explained. "I've heard a dozen different versions of what occurred."

"It was simple," Monk muttered. "It made us look like numskulls! A cartridge in an electric toaster! *Bang!* We all fog upstairs! And while we do that, somebody slips Tugg the word to keep his trap shut."

"What got Tugg in the notion of talkin', anyway?" pondered the gaunt Johnny, fumbling with his eyeglasses.

Doc told them about the machine-gun trick with which he had deceived Tugg into thinking his master was thirsting for his life.

"Now—you have no idea who talked to Tugg?" he finished.

RENNY made rocky sounds by tapping his knuckles together.

"It's the darnedest thing I ever saw, Doc!" he rumbled. "We questioned everybody. It seems Tugg, being shy of friends because of his attitude toward you, was standing apart from everybody when the shell exploded in the toaster. Nobody knows who talked to 'im!"

"It could've been Collison McAlter!" Monk put in. "It could've been Ole Slater, Aunt Nora, Alice—anybody! I'm tellin' you, this Green Bell is slicker'n greased lightnin', as we used to say back home."

"And there's somethin' funny about Collison McAlter turnin' up at that factory this mornin'," added Long Tom, the electrical wizard. "It looked kinda like he might've been there with the hooded gang who came after the papers Jim Cash had hidden! He could've stayed behind!"

"Was there any proof of that?" Renny demanded of Doc.

"There was no proof either way," Doc replied. "Except, of course, Collison McAlter's word that he had come out to the plant when he found himself unable to sleep at home!"

"What gets me is this—what's behind this whole mess?" Renny boomed. "Is this Green Bell somebody who hates Prosper City—hates it so that he's tryin' to wipe it off the map?"

"Hate does not work like that," Doc pointed out. "Men hate other men, rather than such inanimate things as towns. You might dislike a town, but I don't think you'd try very hard to destroy it."

"I wouldn't!" Renny grinned. "But this Green Bell might. If you ask me, he's crazy!"

Doc shook his head. "Wrong!"

"Holy cow!" Renny exploded. "Have you got an idea who he is?"

"I have," Doc imparted dryly, "a faintest of suspicions!"

"Who?"

"I haven't enough on him to justify pointing the finger at him," Doc replied. "But as to why he is ruining Prosper City—that is as plain as the nose on your face. But, again, there's no proof as yet."

Long Tom shook a pale fist. "I'm all for divin' right into this thing! Doc, ain't there somethin' we can do?"

"That's why I called you out here!" Doc told them.

GRINNING, the four aides of the bronze man drew a bit closer. They knew, from past experience, that the plans which Doc propounded had an uncanny way of working.

"Johnny," said Doc, "your profession is knowing the earth and what it's made out of! This job is in your line. I want you to get me a geologic map of this region!"

"Right!" echoed Johnny. "There's a firm of mining engineers right here in town that'll have 'em!"

"Get them tonight!" Doc directed. "I want the best—maps showing rock formations, coal veins, the different faults and fissures—all that stuff."

"Want charts of the mines?"

"Of course! Not only the late workings, but old ones as well!"

"O. K."

"Tell nobody about this. Not even Aunt Nora Boston!"

"Aunt Nora—sure! I won't tell her!" Johnny's voice sounded a bit queer. Did Doc suspect Aunt Nora?

Doc wheeled on Long Tom, the electrical expert.

"Long Tom, it's your job to work on that gonging noise with which the Green Bell summons his men over the radio! You know, of course, how he makes the noise?"

"Sure I do, but I ain't told anybody!" Long Tom chuckled grimly. "That noise simply comes from another radio station, hidden somewhere. It's on the wavelength of the Prosper City station, and it's much the more powerful of the two. It simply blankets the Prosper City wave out almost completely."

"That's right."

"I learned from Aunt Nora that the United States government had radio inspectors in here, trying to find the interference," Long Tom continued. "They didn't get to first base! Once, they got a line on it. But they didn't find a thing."

"Where did they trace it to?"

Long Tom seemed reluctant to answer. "To Aunt Nora Boston's house—or at least, right in that vicinity!"

Doc's four men were uneasily silent. They liked Aunt Nora. They hated to see this evidence piling up against the motherly old lady.

"I don't like that Ole Slater!" Monk grumbled, to break the tension.

"You wouldn't!" snorted big-fisted Renny. "If you don't stop makin' eyes at his girl, he's liable to smear you!"

Doc said: "How about it, Long Tom? Can you find the secret radio station?"

"If it can be found—I can!"

This, Doc and the others knew, was not a boast. There was probably but one other living man knew more about electricity in all its branches than did Long Tom. And that other man was also in this group. It was Doc Savage.

"Go to it!" Doc advised him. "And the same thing I told Johnny goes for you! Don't tell Aunt Nora, Alice Cash—or anybody else!"

"Right!" Long Tom mumbled.

Doc now addressed the group as a whole. "What's your idea about the attitude of the police toward me?"

There was thoughtful silence.

"They're on the fence," decided Renny, the engineer. "Tugg's backing up helped things a lot."

"Tugg will return to his original story that he saw me shoot Chief Clements," Doc said with certainty.

Renny rumbled a humorless laugh. "The police won't be so ready to believe him. Even they can see Tugg is acting queerly. If that murder charge from New York was quashed, I believe you'd be safe in showing yourself, Doc."

"That's the way I sized it up," Doc agreed.

Monk's tufted brows crept together as he thought deeply. "Doc, I've been thinking about Judborn Tugg. I sure thought the Green Bell would croak Tugg. But he didn't. Don't you reckon that means that the Green Bell hopes to use Tugg to decoy you into a trap?"

"The idea occurred to me," Doc said wryly. "You can rest assured that I'm going to be very careful of Tugg. But here's a point you can check up on when this is all over—I think the Green Bell has another very good reason for not killing Tugg!"

THIS ended the conference. Doc's four aides would have liked very much to know what theory the bronze man did hold. But they knew it would do no good to ask questions.

Doc never put important theories into words until they were proven facts.

Monk and the others tramped back through the moonlight toward Aunt Nora's rambling house. Doc accompanied them part of the distance—they never did know exactly how far. Somewhere en route, the bronze giant faded silently from their midst. Shadows, soaking the undergrowth like puddled ink, had swallowed him.

Policemen eyed Doc's gang suspiciously when they appeared. Just a bit too late, it had dawned on the officers that these men might have gone to meet their remarkable chief. The fact that no mention was made of the incident was an omen.

One of the most powerful forces in existence was working in Doc's behalf—public opinion. The food and money he had distributed, the jobs he had promised, had put the working folk of Prosper City on his side.

This meant nine out of every ten men in town. Such a preponderance of sentiment could not help but sway the police.

For that matter, practically every officer had relatives who hoped to get jobs through Doc's great work.

Easing his gaunt length into one of the rented car fleet, the gaunt Johnny drove off in the direction of town. The geologist was going to locate one of the firm of mining engineers and get hold of maps showing the rock and mineral formation under Prosper City.

The flotilla of rented cars was parked along the road in front of the house. The yard lacked room for them. Floodlights in the yard did not reach the spot. Tall trees lifted nearby. This combination made it rather gloomy around the machines.

Long Tom soon came up. Monk accompanied him, as a matter of safety. Long Tom unlocked the rear compartment of the roadster and stowed various packages of electrical equipment inside.

"I'm goin' back to the house to get a bite to eat," Long Tom declared. "Then I'll pull out."

The two men swung jauntily back past the flood-lighted circus tents.

Shadows covered the cars like black cloths. Little sound was about, except for talk from the nearby house.

Metal on metal made a tiny, mouselike squeak. This came again. The engine hood of Long Tom's roadster lifted.

The sheet-steel covering was raised only a moment. An arm—it might have been only a darker string of the night—deposited something atop the engine. It withdrew.

The hood now closed down. A wad of murk flowed stealthily away from the roadster.

Then things began happening. A flashlight spiked a blinding rod into the night. This waved, seemed to lick like a hungry, incandescent tongue. Then it fixed.

Impaled in the glare stood a somber figure—it might have been a black six-foot tube of flexible India rubber, except that it had arms and legs.

The breast of the weird form bore a bell in green. The eyes were the lenses of goggles—snakelike, with a green glitter.

The Green Bell himself! Only the sinister czar wore those green goggles to shield his eyes.

Chapter XVI
THE MAN WHO VANISHED

FOR ten or fifteen seconds there was a silence in the stricken dead. Night insects droned and buzzed. On the distant horizon, heat lightning jumped about, a gory blushing.

The flashlight beam in which the Green Bell was embedded held as steady as if cast in steel. It threw a dull back glow which faintly disclosed the big bronze man who held it.

Doc Savage had been watching his four aides—against just such an incident as this.

Slowly, the bronze man advanced on the sable figure of the Green Bell.

The darksome form suddenly lifted a clenched, black-gloved fist. The fist rapped against the bell design done in green on the mantle. And the bell rang! Dull, muted—but it rang!

Some sort of a small gong was mounted under the black cloth.

A signal!

Nearby darkness came to rushing life. Dusky figures popped up like evil genies. Their arms waved, tentacle fashion, and yellow-red sparks leaped out of the ends. Gun sound convulsed the air.

Doc doused his flash. For all his sharpened senses, he had been unaware that the Green Bell's henchmen were standing by for an emergency.

Whipping right, then left, he evaded lead slugs which hunted him like whining, ravenous little animals. He headed straight for the spot where the Green Bell had stood.

A man besmocked in black, triggering a pair of pistols in wild aimlessness, got in Doc's path. The bronze giant, hardly pausing, snapped a casehard-ened hand to the fellow's spinal nerve center. The man dropped—marked by no wound, but absolutely incapable of further movement.

In learning this strange paralysis which he employed, Doc had delved deeply into the mysteries of chiropractic pressures and their effects on the muscular system.

Doc reached the spot where the black czar had stood. The nigrescent bird had flown. Doc felt disappointment, but no surprise.

The Green Bell had saved himself by having his men present. He had, while flaming guns harassed Doc, faded into the night from which he had come.

Dark-hooded forms whipped among the parked cars, hunting. Two of them bumped each other. Guns gulped thunder—each thought the other an enemy, so edged were their nerves.

Both sagged down, cursing, clawlike hands digging into their own flesh where bullets had torn.

Over toward the circus tents, big-fisted Renny raced to a floodlight, picked it bodily out of its mounting, and turned the great calcium spray on the road.

The light ended the battle. The Green Bell's men were creatures of the night. Also, Renny, Monk, and the rest were charging from Aunt Nora's house. They were a fighting crew with which nothing less than a young army could cope.

The black-frocked men fled.

Doc haunted their retreat. Twice, he descended upon stragglers, to compress and knead his corded fingers, and leave his victims—limp and helpless—in his wake.

The light, as he had fully expected, showed no trace of a hooded figure with green goggles.

The czar sinister had managed his escape.

DOC SAVAGE soon abandoned the pursuit of the fleeing black forms. He could not hope to corral all of them in the night.

Picking up the two he had just overcome, he carried them back to the parked cars. Three more of the darkly masked men lay there—the one Doc had paralyzed, and the two who had shot each other.

Doc's aides, police, and ex-service men swarmed the spot. With loud yells, hoods were torn off the Green Bell hirelings, and their faces revealed.

"Just bums from around town!" grunted Ole Slater, after eyeing the unveiled features.

"Here's two more!" Doc called from the darkness. Then he left the vicinity with great speed.

Policemen ran to the spot from which he had spoken. They found the two prisoners; nothing else. The officers were excited, but more by events of the last four or five minutes, than by the presence of Doc Savage.

The police made no effort to pursue Doc.

This was significant. There was a warrant out for Doc's arrest on the charge of murdering Chief Clements, but the police were rapidly getting in a frame of mind where they did not care much about serving it.

The prisoners were picked up and carried toward the house. A physician was summoned to patch up the pair who had shot each other. All five were in for a night of questioning.

No one paid the least attention to Long Tom's roadster. Certainly, no one lifted the hood. Whatever object the Green Bell had placed upon the engine, still reposed there.

In the house, Monk bowed his great, sloping shoulders. Small kegs of muscle seemed to spring out on his gorilla frame.

"I know how Doc charmed these eggs," he said softly, the eyes boring the prisoners. "I can snap 'em out of it. I'm gonna do that. And, brothers, I'm gonna make 'em talk like phonographs!"

Renny blocked his huge fists and clanked them together. "Yeah! We'll make 'em talk!"

A policeman chuckled loudly. "You know, all of us guys are beginnin' to think alike!"

Monk made a homely grin. "Meanin' you're beginnin' to believe Doc Savage didn't murder Jim Cash or Chief Clements, or even the cop who was found hangin' in the vines?"

"Somethin' like that," the officer admitted.

This was just one policeman's opinion. But the same attitude seemed to be general.

Long Tom sighed. He would have liked to remain behind and take a hand at questioning the captives. The process of eliciting information was likely to be extremely rough. These prisoners probably did not know the identity of the Green Bell, but they might know other things.

For instance, could they swear Doc had not murdered Chief Clements and Jim Cash? And the bluecoat found slain and hanging in the vines?

"Sorry I can't attend the show!" Long Tom grumbled. "I've got a little errand to perform! It can't wait!"

The electrical wizard headed for the kitchen to finish his interrupted lunch. He had no idea how long he would be away, or how busy he would find himself. It was no simple task, this rigging of apparatus which would locate the Green Bell's secret radio station.

The mysterious transmitter was never on for more than half a minute. In that short space, it was very difficult to get accurate readings with an ordinary radio direction-finder.

Long Tom, however, had an intricate scheme which he intended to use.

He grinned as he ate. Things were looking up. Most of the town was on Doc's side. The police were approaching the point where they would ignore all charges, however heinous, faked against the remarkable bronze man. The Green Bell's agitators were afraid to open their mouths in public.

"We've got 'em on the run!" Long Tom chortled.

He did not know that the Green Bell had planted some mysterious object under the hood of his car.

THE food consumed, Long Tom burdened himself with additional pieces of electrical equipment. He swung outdoors.

Around the cars, things were once more quiet and dark. Mosquitoes buzzed like small airplanes.

Long Tom swatted at one, chuckled: "Jersey canaries!" He was feeling very good.

He unlocked the rear compartment, leaned down to insert the articles he was carrying—and his jaw dropped.

A small slab of glass rested in front of his eyes. It was, he saw, one of the windshield wings which had been taken off the roadster.

The glass bore written words which glowed with an unearthly, electric blue. The script was machine perfect. There was a message of some length on the glass, yet it occupied little space.

The communication was from Doc, of course. The bronze man often left missives in this fashion—written on glass. He used a chalk of his own compounding, a chalk which left a mark invisible, not only to the naked eye, but also to all but the most powerful of microscopes.

When subjected to the glow of ultraviolet light—rays also invisible to the eye—the chalk marks glowed with this uncanny blue luminance.

A tiny ultraviolet lantern reposed on the compartment floor, its beam focused on the glass slab. Long Tom read the message:

The Green Bell placed a chemical on the engine of your roadster. This, when heated by the motor, would have made a deadly gas.

The chemical has been removed.

Suppose you leave the impression you were slain by the gas, Long Tom. If the Green Bell believes you dead, you can work in peace.

Long Tom hastily switched off the ultraviolet lantern. The communication was unsigned, but there was no need for an appended name. Only one hand could write a script as perfect as that—Doc Savage's.

Reading of the note had taken only an instant. No onlooker would have dreamed Long Tom had done other than stow his burden in the compartment.

He got behind the wheel, started the motor, and drove off. He racked his brains. Too bad Doc had not suggested how Long Tom could fake his own death! But then, Doc usually left details of their respective jobs to his men. They were supposed to be the most astute in their individual professions.

Long Tom put a grin on his somewhat unhealthy face. He had it!

Prosper Creek ran along the south edge of Prosper City. This was not a large stream, but it had dug itself a deep ditch down through the centuries. A concern had installed a dam for a small hydroelectric plant. This backed the water up rather deeply.

A bridge spanned the creek where some of this back-water stood.

Long Tom zigzagged about town to shake off possible shadows, and finally headed for the bridge. He was certain no one was on his trail.

A few hundred yards from the bridge, he unloaded his equipment and concealed it in a weed patch. Then he rolled the roadster to the bridge, yanked the hand throttle open, and jumped out.

Motor thundering, the machine dived for the wooden railing of the bridge! It crashed the stringers! They gave. The car seemed to try to climb a steel beam which formed the bridge frame. The beam bent; metal screamed, rent!

The car rolled over and disappeared beneath the water.

AFTER the roadster sank, bubbles came up with a loud gurgling and sobbing. It was as if the monster of rubber, iron, and fabric were a drowning, living thing.

A man, a resident of the neighborhood, came racing along the road, drawn by the crash sound. He peered down at the hideous sobbing in the water, lighted several matches and dropped them, then whirled and ran madly to call help.

Long Tom grinned and worked away from the vicinity. He gathered up his apparatus, such of it as he could carry.

He intended to locate two directional radio devices at widely separated points. These differed from the conventional apparatus in that the directional focusing was done automatically.

Compasslike, they would indicate the source of a radio wave. Long Tom intended simply to tune them in on the regular Prosper City broadcaster, and leave them. When the secret station came on, the indicators would swing to it, pulled by its stronger wave. An inked marker would show the exact direction.

In the distance, an ambulance siren wailed like a lost hound. Long Tom, listening, nodded. That would be an emergency crew coming to rescue his supposed body from the sunken roadster.

Not finding it, they would conclude it had been carried downstream by the slight current.

The Green Bell would believe the gas had overcome Long Tom at just the right moment for his car, running wild, to leap the bridge.

Chapter XVII
THE TOUCH THAT YELLOWED

LOUD and blaring was the siren on the ambulance speeding to the spot where the car lay in water under the bridge. A police emergency truck followed it. This had an even noisier siren.

Many ears heard the uproar—among them, Doc Savage's. He was satisfied. The noise meant Long Tom had lost no time putting across his deception.

At the moment, Doc was loitering in the murk near the cars. Sounds from the house reached his sensitive ears. Howls of pain, curses, moans! The prisoners were being questioned.

Doc did not fancy the sounds. On occasion, he inflicted exquisite torture himself, but it was always of the type which did no lasting harm.

Too, administering physical pain was not the way to get information from hardened thugs such as these disciples of the Green Bell. Fist blows, the smash of gun barrels, they could understand. Men are less likely to fear what they can comprehend.

Doc's methods on the other hand, were so unusual that they impressed the average man, steeped in ignorance as he was, as smacking of the supernatural. And men fear what they cannot understand.

Leaving the darkness, Doc stalked boldly into the zone whitened by floodlights.

The bronze man wished to question the prisoners in person. But more important, he had plans—a trick to try. This trick required his presence in the house.

His appearance created a commotion equal to that of the recent fight. Policemen ran up. They did not flash guns, however. Nor did any handcuffs come out of pockets.

Questions volleyed.

Doc ignored them. A towering, metallic giant in the flood glare, he made for the house.

Collison McAlter jumped like a stricken man when he saw Doc, then sank in a chair.

"They'll arrest you!" he gulped. "Oh, why were you so reckless as to show yourself?"

Monk and Renny snorted in unison. They knew Doc's methods. The bronze man could, they were sure, escape from the police practically at will.

Aunt Nora Boston gave Doc a wide smile, and said warmly: "I think we can persuade the police to permit you to remain at liberty, Mr. Savage." She jabbed a plump hand at the prisoners. "Especially if those rats cough up the truth."

Charming Alice Cash also gave Doc a radiant smile. She was glad to have the bronze man in their midst again, and made no effort not to show it. Of late, she had seen very little of this strikingly handsome man of such amazing marvels.

Ole Slater grinned widely at Doc, but the grin was unnatural. He glanced covertly at Alice. Ole, it was plain to be seen, was getting more worried about losing his girl as each hour passed.

"Any luck?" Doc asked, indicating the captives.

Monk chuckled, pinched a hard-faced villain, and produced a lusty wail.

"A lot of that kind of music!" explained the homely fellow. "But nothin' that does us much good!"

Doc's weird golden eyes prowled the prisoners, appraising their faces and their nervous condition. He selected the weakest of the lot.

He said no word. He merely stood over the man and stared steadily. From his lips began to come the strange, mellow trilling note which was part of Doc. It seeped through the room, with nothing to show from whence it arose.

Doc had long ago learned this sound facilitated his efforts at hypnotism.

The man on the floor was a coward. He did not even wait to be mesmerized.

"Damn you! Damn them eyes!" He squirmed madly, gnashing the links of his handcuffs together. "What d'you wanta know? I'll spill! Only turn them glims the other way!"

ASTOUNDED expressions settled on the faces of those in the room. They had seen this man on the floor defy blows and threats of death. But he had succumbed to the mere stare of the bronze giant.

Monk and Renny showed no emotion. They had seen things like this happen before. Doc's presence seemed to have an uncanny effect upon evildoers—especially after they had come to know what a frightful foe he was.

"Who's the Green Bell?" Doc queried.

Collison McAlter shifted his feet nervously; his eyes roved to the doors, the windows. Aunt Nora shivered, put her hands to her plump cheeks. Alice Cash watched Doc, fascinated.

Ole Slater drew a revolver and seemed to be trying to watch everyone present. Most of the Prosper City businessmen were there. Someone here, in this room, was the Green Bell.

Slater acted as if he were alert to seize the culprit, should his name be disclosed.

"I don't know who the Green Bell is!" groaned the man on the floor.

Doc had expected that. "Who killed Chief Clements?"

A minor convulsion seized the fellow as he made up his mind whether to answer or riot.

"Judborn Tugg!" he wailed.

Several policemen charged for the door, yelling: "That settles it! We'll nail Tugg!"

"Who killed Jim Cash?" Doc demanded.

"I don't know nothin' about that!" moaned the prone man.

"And the policeman found hanging in the vines under Monk's window—who murdered him?"

"The Green Bell! The cop came upon the boss while he was plantin' the gun that Tugg used to kill Chief Clements! That was why he was croaked!"

Doc waved an arm which took in every individual present. "Do you think the Green Bell is one of these people?"

"Yeah! Sure, he must be!"

This had the effect of causing each person in the room to shrink slightly from his neighbor. They had, of course, suspected the Green Bell was one of them. But having it put into words in this way was a shock.

Doc now addressed the crowd: "Any questions you care to have answered?"

"Yes!" Ole Slater shouted shrilly. "What is behind all this horror? Why is the Green Bell tryin' to ruin Prosper City? Is he a madman who hates the town?"

Eyes rolled in the head of the man on the floor.

"I dunno!" he mumbled. "None of us knows what's behind it all!"

THIS was the extent of the information secured. The other four prisoners insisted sullenly that they knew no more than their companions.

"Which is probably the truth," Doc commented. The bronze man now employed a small hypodermic needle upon each prisoner. This caused them to go into a trance-like sleep, from which only the application of another drug could arouse them.

The five were loaded into an ambulance which Doc called. To the ambulance driver, Doc gave secret directions, and a neat sum of money. The machine started off, ostensibly for a Prosper City hospital, where the men were to go into the prison ward.

The ambulance, however, never reached there. In fact, it was fully a year before the five prisoners were again seen. Then, it was in a distant city, and, had an old acquaintance hailed either of the five, they would not have been recognized.

The captives went into Doc's institution in upstate New York, where they were subjected to brain operations wiping out their past, and given training which fitted them to be honest citizens.

The policemen who had gone to arrest Judborn Tugg now returned. They were a disgusted lot.

"The bird flew the coop!" they explained. "There wasn't no sign of 'im!"

"Any of his clothing gone?" Doc asked.

"Didn't look like it! We'll spread a general alarm for 'im!"

"You're wasting your time!" Doc assured them. "Judborn Tugg is a man who likes flashy clothing. He would not have fled town without taking some."

"Then what became of 'im?"

Doc did not answer this, much to the puzzlement of the officers. Doc had an idea what had happened to Judborn Tugg. But that idea was part of the theory as to who the Green Bell was. Lacking proof, he was not yet ready to reveal it.

Johnny, the bony geologist, appeared. He carried a long, circular blueprint case. Catching Doc's eye, Johnny nodded—thereby affirming that he had secured the geologic survey maps of the region under and around Prosper City.

Doc received the maps, but did not immediately consult them. Instead, he went upstairs. He secured, from where it had lain in Monk's room, the small segment of wood which was the chief remnant of the Green Bell's sonic device for producing insanity.

He worked over this perhaps half an hour. Then he carried it back downstairs, mounted a table, and made a speech.

"This"—he held up the bit of wood—"may lead us to the Green Bell. In fact, it is almost certain that it will!"

This pronouncement, coming without any previous dramatic build-up, was breathtaking. The crowd surged close. Word was passed outside, and everyone sought to get into the room.

"As you all know, or, at least, have heard," Doc continued, "the Green Bell sought to drive me insane with a peculiar sonic device. The upshot of the attempt was that the device came into my hands!"

Monk, Renny, and Johnny swapped puzzled stares. What was the bronze man up to?

"We found that the box held fingerprints of the person who made it—probably the Green Bell," Doc continued. "That they were the Green Bell's was made fairly certain by the fact that he sought to destroy them."

"Sought!" yelled a cop. "You mean that there's fingerprints on that piece of wood? It's a hunk of the sonic box, ain't it?"

"It is!" Doc replied gravely. "And it bears proof which is almost certain to trap the Green Bell!"

MONK looked at Renny.

"That's the first lie I ever heard Doc tell!" he grinned.

"Lie?" Renny asked. "What was a lie?"

"When he said there were fingerprints on that piece of wood. There ain't any! I examined it. Doc examined it. And there ain't a speck of a print."

"Doc didn't say there was a print on it!" Renny pointed out.

Monk scratched the top of his bullet head.

"Huh!" he snorted. "That's right—he didn't! But he sure gave the impression there was!"

"I guess he hopes the Green Bell will try to get the stick, and betray himself in the process," Renny hazarded.

This conversation had taken place in whispers which no one could overhear. In addition, both men had cupped palms over their mouths, so that, should the Green Bell be a lip reader, he could not eavesdrop by sight.

Doc Savage now waved everyone away from the table on which he stood. He was carrying his prize tenderly in a handkerchief.

"We must be careful that the Green Bell does not get this bit of wood!" he warned, and placed the piece on the table top.

The policemen promptly formed a circle around the table, keeping everyone at a distance.

"Hm-m-m!" Monk breathed. "Doc's makin' it awful tough for the Green Bell to get that wood!"

"Bring a microscope!" Doc called. "Also a camera for taking fingerprint photos. You police have such devices handy, I presume."

"Huh!" Renny whispered to Monk. "D'you reckon there *is* a print on that thing?"

As if to answer him, the lights went out. Bulbs in the house, floodlamps on the grounds—all blotted simultaneously. The current had been shut off at the main switch, probably in the shed at the back of the house.

A stunned silence followed the first gush of blackness.

It was interrupted by a low hissing noise, a *clunk!* Neither sound was loud.

"The piece of wood!" a man bawled.

Excitement exploded in the room. Policemen yelled, drew their service weapons. Men elbowed their neighbors in their perturbation, and the neighbors, thinking it was the Green Bell seeking to escape with the woolen fragment, lashed out with fists. In a trice, a dozen fights were in progress.

Monk, Renny, and Johnny stood in the background. Whatever was going on, they did not think it had caught Doc napping.

Flashlights came out of pockets, spitting white funnels. The fighters discovered their opponents were friends, stopped swinging blows, and began profuse apologies.

"It's gone!" squawked a cop. "The chunk of wood is gone!"

COLLISON MCALTER held up both his hands, shouting: "I want to submit to a search! And I think everyone present should do the same!"

Ole Slater came elbowing through the crowd and agreed: "I second that suggestion!"

Aunt Nora Boston grumbled: "I'm agin' it!"

Alice Cash gasped in surprise: "Why, Aunt Nora!"

"Ain't no use searchin', child," said Aunt Nora. "This devil ain't fool enough to keep that thing on his person."

The hunt went forward, nonetheless. Even the police submitted.

Monk maneuvered over behind Doc, eyed the table, then asked: "How on earth did the guy get it? There was a ring of cops around the table!"

Doc pointed at a tiny cut in the table top.

"He simply tied a penknife to a thread, leaned over a cop's shoulder, and speared the piece of wood. Harpooned it, if you like."

Monk groaned. "He put over a fast one on you, Doc!"

The bronze man smiled slightly. "Not so you could notice, Monk!"

A loud shout came from the kitchen.

They dashed for the spot.

Aunt Nora Boston was crouched over the coal-burning kitchen range. Her jaw was slack, her eyes were bulging a little. She was peering into the firebox of the stove, from which she had removed a lid.

In the firebox, barely recognizable so charred had it become, lay the fragment of wood from the Green Bell's sonic device.

With it was a small pocketknife. This had had celluloid handles, but they were burned away.

"I was gonna put more wood on the fire," mumbled Aunt Nora. "And I seen this—"

"Recognize the knife from what is left?" Doc questioned.

Attractive Alice Cash answered the query. "I do! It is one I keep on my desk to sharpen pencils."

More inquiries followed, in which the police took a hand. But this got no results. Who had deposited the fragment and the knife in the stove?

Investigating, Doc learned what had happened to the lights. Someone had taken a fork from Aunt Nora's kitchen cabinet and jammed it across the terminals in the fuse box, causing the fuses to blow. There were no fingerprints on the fork.

Monk had dogged Doc's footsteps. While the bronze man was installing new fuses, the homely chemist picked up the conversation which Aunt Nora's discovery had interrupted.

"You said the Green Bell didn't put a fast one over on you!" he whispered. "What d'you mean by that, Doc?"

Doc Savage surveyed the vicinity to make sure there were no eavesdroppers.

"There was no fingerprint on that bit of wood," he said.

"Sure! I know that!"

"But I soaked it in certain chemicals from your collection. Those chemicals were very powerful. If the skin is brought in contact with them, enough will be absorbed to affect the liver, causing an increased production of biliary pigment."

Monk blinked. "So what?"

"The biliary pigment will be absorbed in the blood, resulting in a yellow condition of the skin. In other words, the Green Bell, in touching that wooden fragment, merely contracted an excellent case of yellow jaundice."

Monk all but choked. "You mean—whoever picked up that wood will start turnin' yellow?"

"Exactly! All we have to do is set back, keep from getting killed, and wait for somebody to turn yellow."

"How long'll it take?"

"That is difficult to say. It depends on the individual. A day; perhaps a week. Not over that!"

Chapter XVIII
LULL

THE rest of the night was uneventful. Dawn brought an airplane from New York—a small, speedy machine from Doc Savage's private hangar on the Hudson River.

The dapper Ham stepped out of it. He lost no time making his way to Aunt Nora Boston's home.

The only article of baggage which accompanied him was his slender, innocent-looking black sword cane.

Monk observed Ham's arrival from within the house, and grinned from ear to ear. He had missed his usual diversion of insulting Ham.

Putting a black scowl on his homely face, Monk hurried out.

"Listen, shyster, you had orders to stay in New York!" he growled. "What's the idea of showin' up down here?"

Ham caught sight of pretty Alice Cash. He dressed Monk down with a cold look, swung over jauntily, and bowed to the young lady.

"You are more ravishing than ever!" he assured Alice.

Monk writhed mentally. He usually told pretty young women that Ham had a wife and thirteen children, all halfwits. But he had neglected to tell Alice the yarn. He'd better spill it in a hurry!

Ham guided Alice into the house, where Doc was studying the geology maps of Prosper City's vicinity.

"The murder charge against you in New York is all washed up!" Ham declared.

"How'd you work it?" Doc inquired.

"Simply by putting the fear of Old Nick into the four lying witnesses! I dug up some stuff in their past—burglary and blackmail. That did the trick! They broke down and confessed that they were hired to say they saw you kill Jim Cash!"

Alice Cash flinched at mention of her brother's murder, and left the room hastily. Ham, glancing out of the window a moment later, saw Monk with an arm across her shoulder. Monk was an excellent comforter, especially if the grieved one was as good-looking as Alice was. Ham groaned.

"Who hired the four?" Doc asked.

"They didn't see the fellow's face. He wore one of those trick gowns with a green bell painted on it."

Doc nodded. "Rather thought it would be like that. What did you do with the four?"

Ham smiled fiercely and fiddled with his sword cane. "Got them out on bail when the cops arrested 'em for lodgin' that false charge; then grabbed 'em and sent 'em to our little place in upstate New York."

"Good work!"

After a glance about, Ham grunted: "I see everybody but Long Tom. Where's he?"

"Hiding out," Doc replied. "He has his apparatus all set to locate the Green Bell's secret radio station, once the thing goes into operation."

"I hope he finds it quick," Ham grinned. "I crave some action! That business in New York didn't get me warmed up!"

AS the hours dragged, however, it seemed Ham was to see no action. The Green Bell and his hirelings made no hostile move. Judborn Tugg did not put in an appearance.

The day was marked with events of great interest for Prosper City, however. Practically all factories opened. The mines, as well!

Renny, with his vast fund of knowledge concerning engineering in all its branches, took active charge of this work. He organized crews, demoralized by the recent troubles and inactivity.

Since Doc intended to put the plants on a profitable basis, Renny's work was not easy. In the first place, a high wage scale was introduced in every department of each concern. This made economy of production a prime necessity.

Monk stationed his ex-service men guards over each plant, and made the rounds like a general, keeping things in form.

If he expected trouble, though, he was disappointed. Not a Green Bell agitator put in an appearance. Peace reigned. All was quiet.

"But it's kinda like the quiet of a guy who is aimin' his gun!" Monk muttered pessimistically.

Doc Savage set Ham to work clearing up the final legal details of the deal by which Prosper City's industries were being taken over, literally in the whole. When that was done, Doc visited the ramshackle old barn on the marsh.

He took particular notice that this was hardly more than three quarters of a mile from Aunt Nora Boston's home.

The bronze man did nothing while he was there, except drop a firecracker down the vertical pipe through which the Green Bell had addressed his men. He listened with great interest to the hollow reverberations as the cracker let loose, possibly two hundred and fifty feet below.

These sepulchral echoes seemed to rumble and gobble for fully a minute.

Leaving the spot, Doc visited the men who had suffered more than any others from the trouble in Prosper City—the poor souls who had been driven insane by the Green Bell's sonic machine.

He made a detailed examination in each case, using X-rays, blood tests, spinal-fluid tests—almost every test known to medical science.

Late that afternoon, he made his announcement.

"Sections of the brain are merely in a quiescent state—a form of nerve paralysis induced by the disrupting force of the sonic vibrations."

"Will you put that in plain English?" Aunt Nora requested.

"They can be cured," Doc replied. "It'll take a little time. But there's not the slightest doubt."

Aunt Nora Boston sat down and cried.

"I never did tell you," she said moistly. "But one of the afflicted men is a nephew of mine."

While Doc was telephoning to New York, Chicago, Rochester, and other great medical centers, for specialists to take personal charge of the brain cures, Alice Cash offered her services.

"That's great!" Doc replied. "You can sort of look out for these cases."

"I've been watching your work," Alice told him thoughtfully. "I notice from the way you are organizing it that you are putting others in actual charge. Even Renny, the engineer, is serving merely as a supervisor. What does that mean?"

"Simply that we are going to step out as soon as the danger is past!"

"You mean that you are going to leave Prosper City?" Alice Cash sounded slightly stricken.

"You didn't expect us to remain here? Not, of course, that Prosper City isn't as nice a town as the average."

Alice flushed. "I—I was hoping you would."

DOC SAVAGE saw how the wind was blowing. The young lady was more interested in him than he wished. Unwillingly, he had made another conquest, or was on the verge of making it.

This pained Doc. He did not care to hurt anyone's feelings. So he did something that he rarely did. He took off an hour and explained his strange purpose in life—his life profession of going up and down the trails of the world, hunting trouble and peril, helping those in need of help, and administering punishment to wrongdoers.

He made it very clear to his beautiful listener that such a life precluded any feminine entanglements. When he finished, he believed h e had painted such a picture of horror and danger that a female heart would quail at the thought of sharing them. He thought he had scared this gorgeous young woman off.

"What you need is a loving wife to attend to your needs," pretty Alice Cash said warmly. She did not say that she would like the job, but it was in her voice.

Doc mentally threw up his hands. What could you do in a case like that?

He got away as quickly and gracefully as he could, sought a secluded spot, and went through the round of exercises which he had taken each day.

They were unlike anything else, those exercises. Doc's father had started him on them when he could hardly walk. They were solely responsible for his phenomenal physical and mental powers.

He made his muscles work against each other, straining until perspiration filmed his mighty bronze body. He juggled a number of a dozen figures in his head, multiplying, extracting square and cube roots.

He had an apparatus which made sound waves of frequencies so high and so low the ordinary human ear could not detect them. He listened intently to this—his proficiency along that line had already saved his life on this adventure.

He named several score of assorted odors after a quick olfactory test of small vials racked in a special case. He read pages of Braille print—writing of the blind. This whetted his sense of touch.

Many and varied other parts were in his routine. They filled an entire two hours at a terrific pace, with no time out for rest.

Monk and Ham came upon Doc as he finished.

Monk groaned. "Think of doin' that every day!"

Ham sneered audibly. "You, I suppose, don't take exercises?"

Monk flexed his hairy arms. "Some of these days I'm gonna have a workout on you! That's the one exercise I need!"

Unsheathing his sword cane, Ham flicked it. The fine blade twanged like a guitar string.

"Try it, and I'll do some sculpture work on you with this!" he promised.

The two glared at each other as if they had murder in their hearts.

"What's the trouble?" Doc questioned.

"This furry, lying dead beat!" Ham purpled and jabbed his sword at Monk. "He told Alice Cash that yarn about my wife and thirteen half-wit children! The missing link! I've never had a wife!"

AT nine o'clock that night, there was to be a meeting at Aunt Nora Boston's. Heads of all plants in Prosper City—now actually in charge—were to attend.

At eight thirty, Alice Cash turned on Aunt Nora's radio.

Ten minutes later, the Green Bell's hideous clangor, squealing, and wailing, came from the instrument.

"I know it!" Monk yelled. "We're in for real trouble!"

From Doc Savage's actions, it seemed he had been waiting for just this. He raced upstairs to Long Tom's room. When he came back, he carried two small boxes. One was a radio transmitter, a tiny portable set. The other was a receiver.

Doc gave the receiver to Monk. "Keep tuned in on this! Clamp the headset on that knot of a head, and don't take it off for anything!"

The telephone rang. It was Long Tom.

"My equipment got the source of that secret radio wave!" he barked excitedly. "It came from Aunt Nora Boston's house!"

"It what?"

"From Aunt Nora's! I can't believe it! But it's a fact."

Doc hung up, faced Renny. "Where's Aunt Nora?"

"Dunno! Ain't seen her for a few minutes!"

The maps which Johnny had secured lay on a table. Doc seized them, carried them with him as he ran out of the house. He also bore the radio transmitter.

Doc consulted the charts, then headed due east, mounting the slope of the mountain. After covering a few hundred yards, he added stealth to his pace. He moved with the quiet of a wind-blown feather.

Blackened knots of buildings lurched up in the moonlight ahead. He eyed the maps once more, identifying the structures.

They were surface buildings of a coal mine—a mine which had been closed for several years, the veins below exhausted. For years, however, it had been the largest mine in Prosper City; at one time, it had led the nation in coal output.

Doc posted himself nearby and waited. He was not disappointed.

A group of seven furtive figures crept up. They wore the hideous black gowns of the Green Bell. They disappeared into the maw of the mine.

Other men came, two of them, this time. Then three fellows arrived alone. Eight were in the next group.

The evil clan was gathering.

Doc waited until there came an interval of five minutes when no sinister men put in an appearance. Then he entered the black gullet of the mine.

The tunnel was exceedingly dry for an old working. It sloped downward. Doc sought a recess and used his flashlight on the maps. One of the charts showed every cranny of this particular abandoned mine.

When the tunnel branched, he turned left. The tunnel swept in a vast curve. Doc knew—the map showed it, too—that he was approaching a spot directly under Aunt Nora Boston's house.

He slackened his pace. The drift was long and straight—fully three hundred yards without a turn. A bullet could be fired the length of it without touching a wall.

He covered this direct lane.

Lights appeared ahead. A moment later, he was peering out into a great room. Pillars—coal left standing to support the roof—were a forest before his eyes.

In this forest, black-cowled men were clustered.

Chapter XIX
DEATH UNDERGROUND

ENTERING the underground cavern, Doc glided forward. There was not much chance of discovery. The Green Bell and his men thought themselves safe here.

The Green Bell was present—in person! He sat, cross-legged, as the dummy of sticks and fabric in the distant barn had sat. No doubt some of the masked men before him did not know there was a difference between this figure they were looking upon now, and the form in the dilapidated farm building.

The dummy in the barn! It was that which had given Doc his lead to this underground rendezvous. The pipe diving straight downward two hundred and fifty feet, from which the evil czar's voice had come! It could lead to nothing but a mine tunnel!

Geology maps of the region had shown that a sheet of hard rock underlay the swampy field. The presence of the rock, a great bowl holding water, accounted for the moist nature of the field itself.

And the map of this old mine showed a drift under the swamp. The Green Bell had simply drilled a hole and forced his pipe upward, not a difficult task. Hydraulic jacks and a driving-head on the pipe would do the work.

The Green Bell was speaking.

"Are all of you here?" he boomed hollowly. "That is important, tonight! There must be no absentees! For on our work tonight depends success or failure!"

There was a general wagging of fingers as a count was made.

"Unmask!" commanded the Green Bell. "We must be certain!"

The black hoods came off, some a bit reluctantly. Flashlights furnished a glow sufficient to inspect the faces.

Doc surveyed them with interest. Three men were, he saw to his disgust, fairly prominent factory owners of Prosper City. It was these men who had objected most strenuously to his proposition to take over all plants.

Collison McAlter was not among them.

The Green Bell himself did not remove his hood. He stared, goggled green eyes malicious, glittering in the flash glare.

"All here!" he decided. "Now, we will get down to work!"

The Green Bell arose, strode through the ring of men, and vanished into the blacker reaches of the cavern. A chain rattled.

When the masked leader appeared again, he was leading a forlorn, manacled figure. Judborn Tugg! Tugg's face bore numerous bruises and cuts; dried crimson stains were on his clothing, his hair. His nose seemed to be damaged much more than it had been by Long Tom's blows. Most of his front teeth were missing.

Tugg had obviously been tortured.

"This worm!" intoned the Green Bell, kicking Tugg. "This worm was an unfaithful servant!"

Tugg blubbered: "I couldn't help it if—"

"Shut up! You would have betrayed me! That is regrettable. You were to be the mainstay of the industrial empire which I intend to build, with Prosper City as its center! You were to have been the apparent head of all my enterprises!"

The Green Bell's voice became a shrill tinkling, and he delivered another forceful kick.

"It was through you that I intended to buy all the factories and mines in Prosper City, once I had reduced the owners to a point where they would have to sell for a song!"

THIS information did not surprise Doc. He had surmised that such a scheme was behind the Prosper City trouble. This man, the Green Bell, had money, a lust for more money—a scheming brain. The combination had launched him on this plan of forcing a whole city into bankruptcy, then buying its factories for a pittance.

"You were a fool to go against me!" the Green Bell snarled at Tugg. "I am powerful! I have millions, made by selling stocks short during the great depression! I will have more millions—billions!"

Tugg moaned. "Lemme go, won't you? I can't harm you! I've signed over every stick of my property to you!"

"Not to me!" The Green Bell turned, pointed a black-sheathed arm at one of the Prosper City businessmen, and said: "You, sir, may not know it, but you are now the owner of Tugg & Co. This— this gaudy worm signed his entire holdings over to you for a consideration of one dollar! Incidentally, I will now pay him the dollar!"

The Green Bell produced a bit of silver from his gown, using his left hand. He bent over and offered this to Tugg. His right hand remained out of sight in the robe.

Poor Tugg did not know what to do, except take the dollar. He reached for it.

Like a striking black cobra, the Green Bell whipped out a knife with his other hand. He ran the blade into Tugg's heart. The steel went in easily, as if it had been a hot wire making its way into grease.

Tugg emitted one piercing, lamb-like bleat, then began to kick around convulsively on the floor.

The Green Bell put a foot on Tugg's squirming form and held it steady until all movements had ceased. Then he stepped back.

"You may wonder why I did not shoot him, and why I held him still!" he tolled monotonously. He leveled an arm. "Look! There is the explanation!"

To one side, a small tunnel penetrated. Evidently it had been drifted there long ago, in pursuit of some wisp of coal which had dribbled out.

"There is a room in that tunnel!" said the Green Bell. "It is only a few yards from this chamber. It holds the powerful radio set with which it has been my custom to summon you!"

Doc nodded slightly, where he was concealed in the gloom. This explained why the radio signals had apparently been traced to Aunt Nora Boston's! The room was directly under her house!

"Also, in that room are some thousands of quarts of nitroglycerin!" continued the Green Bell. "It is connected to electrical contacts rigged on a seismograph. Do you know what a seismograph is?"

"A jigger which wiggles when there's an earthquake!" someone muttered.

"That is an excellent description. The contacts are on the jigger which wiggles, as you call it. Any large shock in the earth nearby will cause the explosive to detonate."

There was much uneasy squirming at this information.

"Do not worry!" boomed the voice of the robed man. "The seismograph is adjusted so no distant earthquake will operate it. Only a shock nearby will close the contacts. Such a shock will be the explosion of a small quantity of nitro approximately half a mile from here, which I will arrange."

A hideous laugh gurgled from the lips of the cowled figure who had murdered Tugg so callously.

"Aunt Nora Boston's home is directly above this cache of explosive! Not many yards above it, either! The house and everyone in it will be blown to bits!"

DOC SAVAGE silently unlimbered the radio transmitter. The thing operated without noise, except for the faintest of clickings as he vibrated the key.

The radio waves, of course, would travel through the intervening earth and stone to Monk's portable receiver.

"Is this—necessary?" quavered one of the assembled men.

The Green Bell cursed. "Necessary! Of course it is! It's imperative that we get rid of Savage and the others at once! The devil is clever! Tomorrow he will trap me!"

"Tomorrow—"

"Exactly!"

"But how can he?"

"Shut up!" excitedly boomed the hooded leader.

Doc had finished transmitting, and was listening with great interest. He knew why the Green Bell was positive he would be trapped.

The fellow had found his skin was turning yellow! He had realized that Doc's maneuvering with the segment of the sonic box, the night before, had been a trick.

"I called you here tonight to warn you all to keep away from Aunt Nora Boston's house," said the Green Bell. "Now that the orders are given, you may go!"

As one man, the crowd whirled for the exit.

This took Doc somewhat by surprise. He was given no opportunity to circle the group, so as to remain in the cavern and disconnect the seismograph device. The only thing he could do was to retreat into the tunnel.

He sidled into it. Down the long, straight shaft he sped. Three hundred yards without a turn! He would have to cover that distance before the men behind him cast their flashlights down the passage. He ran as he had seldom run before.

He failed to make it.

A powerful flash scooted a white beam along the straight drift.

A yell! "Savage—it's Savage! There he goes!"

The next instant, Doc seemed to become a bullet in a giant barrel of rock! Lifted by an irresistible force, he was hurled ahead. His eardrums threatened to cave!

Landing, he knotted himself like a circus tumbler. He was helpless to impede his progress. He was pushed from behind by a blast which might have been from a monster air gun!

Rock walls battered him! Dust, boulders, sprayed against him, past him! He crashed into the cross passage and dropped, almost unconscious. All of mother earth seemed to come down on his head!

One of the Green Bell's gang had forgotten the seismograph and the nitro, and had fired a bullet at Doc. The detonation had loosened the explosive.

Even now, the segments of Aunt Nora Boston's rambling, charming old home were probably floating around some hundreds of feet in the air. Anyone in it would be dead.

Dead as those black-cowled men back there in the underground room! There was no possibility that any of them had survived. The sinister czar, who had chosen a green bell for his symbol, was dead—wiped out by his own death device.

His was a fate which had overtaken more than one enemy of Doc Savage.

TEN minutes later, Doc stumbled out of the abandoned mine. He did not feel like coming, even then. He was bruised, battered, damaged as he had seldom been in his life. But deadly gases were loose in the mine, and he had to get out.

Half an hour later, he encountered Monk.

The homely gorilla of a fellow stared at Doc's injuries.

"It looks like you caught yourself an earthquake," he suggested.

"How about the others?" Doc demanded.

"Them—they all got out, after you sent your radio warning, telling them to do so as quick as possible." Monk chuckled mirthfully. "Poor Ham! The overdressed shyster lost his sword cane in the rush. He was about to start back after it when the whole world blew up!"

"How did Aunt Nora take the loss of her house?"

"Swell! She said it was an old wreck that she'd been tryin' to sell for years, anyway!"

"She's a brick!" Doc said, absently fingering various aching muscles. "We'll have to put her in charge of charities here in Prosper City. Of course, we'll reimburse her for her house, and the money she spent on charity before we got on the job."

"She'd go for that," Monk agreed. "But you're forgettin' to tell me what happened down there under the ground."

Doc sketched briefly what had occurred.

"The Green Bell and every one of his followers is finished," he ended. "In a few days we can turn those factories back to their owners and clear out."

"You sound anxious to get away?" Monk said slyly, thinking of ravishingly pretty Alice Cash.

"Well, we should get back to New York," Doc told him. "Something may come up—it always does."

Doc's statement was only a guess, based on the past. He had no way of knowing what awaited them in New York, not being gifted with an inner sight. But it would be there—trouble, peril, mystery! These had always come to them.

Into the black fastness of an underground river, a mystery trail would take them—by submarine! That jaunt into a subterranean cavern, into a black stream which was to carry them they knew not where, was to seem, when they started it, the climax of a orgy of death, danger, and deadly intrigue.

But at the end of that strange, horror-filled voyage was a thing beyond their wildest imaginings!

The Phantom City! Probably the strangest, most fantastic thing ever to be sighted by modern man. A fabulous place, situated in a region which holds the greatest totally unexplored surface on the face of the globe, including the polar regions—the great Arabian desert of Rub' Al Khali.

The Phantom City was to be the object of their next adventure. And vastly different it was from this prosaic American manufacturing locality.

"SO the Green Bell found his hide was turnin' yellow?" Monk ruminated thoughtfully, as they moved through the night.

"There's no doubt of it!" Doc agreed. "And that persuaded him to rush his devilish plan to completion."

Monk grinned. "Ain't you gonna tell me who he was?"

"I didn't get a look at his face!" Doc said dryly.

"You mean we've cleaned this case up without knowin' who he was?"

"I think his identity will come out. It is pretty plain who he was."

"How d'you figure that?"

"Simply from the uncanny way the Green Bell had of knowing our every move. He was very close to us."

They had been striding down the road as they talked.

Pretty Alice Cash appeared. She showed relief at sight of Doc; then registered concern over his bruises.

"Have you seen Aunt Nora?" she asked, a moment later.

"She's around somewhere—I saw her a minute ago," Monk replied. "What'd you want with her? Important?"

"Well, not very," replied Alice. "I wanted to ask her if she had seen Ole Slater."

"Ain't Ole around?"

"No. And I'm curious. You see, Ole seemed a bit ill this evening, when I last saw him."

Monk gulped twice, swallowed, exploded: "What ailed him? Was he turnin' a funny color?"

"Ole Slater seemed to be turning yellow," Alice said. "It was the strangest thing!"

THE END

INTERMISSION by Will Murray

The Great Depression is the theme for this most unusual Doc Savage volume.

We've selected two tales from opposite ends of the 1930s. *The Czar of Fear* first appeared in 1933, considered by many to be the darkest year of the economic depression that cast a pall over the entire decade of the 1930s.

One of the menaces that Doc Savage frequently battled fell into the category of threats to industry. Here, a mill and coal town in the Alleghenies is besieged by the Green Bell and his hooded minions.

Nowhere in the Doc Savage series is the mood and feel of the Depression captured so atmospherically. The magnitude of this collapse is difficult to imagine today. Although the national economy rebounded slightly after the October 1929 Stock Market crash, by 1931 the Depression had gripped the country unshakably. Between 1930-32, an estimated 85,000 American businesses failed, nine million savings accounts were wiped out by bank failures, and a half a million homeowners lost their houses. In modern terms, it was a meltdown.

As a result, by 1933 nearly 13 million people were thrown out of work—120,000 in New York City alone. As early as the spring of 1931, there were 15,000 people without places to live in Manhattan. The newly homeless set up tar paper shacks dubbed "Hoovervilles" in Central Park and along the Hudson River below prosperous Riverside Drive. The out-of-work sold apples on street corners to survive, or shined shoes. At one time, Manhattan boasted 6,000 professional apple sellers. As many as 20 bootblacks vied for business on one city block alone. Soup kitchens and breadlines dispensing free meals to the starving sprang up in major cities. Still, food riots took place in many localities.

To compound the calamity, beginning in 1931, a seven-year drought turned vast areas of U.S. farmland into the arid Dust Bowl. Farm foreclosures triggered an exodus of some three million Americans from the Great Plains. Car caravans snaked all the way to the agricultural promised land of California.

A reference in *The Czar of Fear* to a character having made money by selling stocks short during "the great depression" makes it seem as if it lay in the recent past. This is a good example of the psychology of 1933. After the crash, many Americans felt certain that the slump would be shortlived. By 1931, however, a cold reality had set in. The Depression was here to stay. Still, some felt certain that prosperity lay just around the corner. No one could conceive that the entire decade of the 1930s would feel its crushing weight.

"Old Man Depression" also hit the pulp magazines hard, killing off the giant Clayton chain and temporarily crushing the Fiction House concern. In the writers' magazines, the lists of canceled or suspended pulps read like a list of the war dead.

Street & Smith was also in trouble, but was fighting back.

"The pulps were on the way out in the early '30s," *Doc Savage* editor John L. Nanovic explained. "The only thing that kept them alive was, in my opinion, the character books. They were the only ones that sold. Even the detective books were hurting."

Led by *The Shadow* and *Doc Savage,* the pulp magazine industry would survive another 20 years.

This, the ninth Doc Savage novel, holds many secrets, beginning with Walter Baumhofer's moody and mysterious cover, which shows unmistakable signs of repainting. The salmon-colored background, for example, suggests a redder color scheme originally. And if you look closely, the emblem on the Green Bell's chest looks suspiciously like it was overpainted. A blaze of red seems to be showing through.

This may be because originally Lester Dent called him the Radio Bell and his murderous minions, the Red Bells. As he began writing, he altered it to the Red Bell, then changed the color of his robes in Chapter 3, and moved the dreaded symbol from his forehead to his chest. Why? Probably to avoid conflicting with *The Red Skull,* Doc's fifth adventure, just then hitting newsstands. Baumhofer's cover may have been painted while the story was still in the outline stage.

The name Red Bell could have been an allusion to Red—i.e., Communist—labor agitators of that troubled era. Aunt Nora Boston was almost certainly based on Mary Harris "Mother" Jones, the fearless labor organizer known as "The Miners' Angel" who was involved with aiding mill and mine workers in the early 20th century. And for some unknown reason John Nanovic changed Celia Cash's first name to its perfect anagram, Alice.

Two important firsts are showcased in this novel. Doc Savage's waterfront plane hanger on the Hudson River is given a name: The Hidalgo Trading Company. And for the first time readers are given a glimpse of Doc's growing fleet of private aircraft. And in Chapter 16, Doc employs the chiropractic manipulations that will rob scores of bad guys of consciousness and mobility in the adventures to come, and inspire Mr. Spock's nerve pinch.

Part of the Doc Savage formula in the first year or so of the series involved Doc's men applying their respective specialties to the job at hand. Usually Ham Brooks was odd man out. But in *Czar of Fear,* his legal skills are put to good use— even if that meant he missed much of the action.

The 1939 New York World's Fair was a cultural event meant to mark America's emergence from the Great Depression's economic chains. Nevertheless, ten years after the Crash, unemployment remained an unnerving nine and a half million. The Fair—whose theme was The World of Tomorrow—promised hope for a better future.

Under construction in Flushing Meadows for several years, this new World's Fair captured the public imagination. Its centerpiece was the Trylon, a futuristic triangular pylon that doubled as a radio broadcasting antenna, and the Perisphere—an 180

foot steel globe constructed so that it appeared to be balanced on a cluster of water fountains, illuminated by lights designed to make it seem to rotate. Entering via a sweeping ramp dubbed the Helicline, visitors were shown a diorama of Democracity, a utopia city of one hundred years in the future.

We don't know how *World's Fair Goblin* came to be written in the fall of 1938, six months before the Fair was scheduled to open. But we do know that Fair president Grover A. Whalen and Street & Smith agreed to publicize the Fair through the pages of *Doc Savage.*

That fall, Lester Dent, John Nanovic and Nanovic's number two man, assistant editor William G. Bogart, were given a tour of the fairgrounds, still under construction. Doc Savage had explored lost cities and strange subterranean civilizations, but he was never plunged into a wonderland as fantastic as the World of Tomorrow.

Announcing *World's Fair Goblin,* Nanovic wrote:

> Most of you have heard of the New York World's Fair, which will take place in New York City this year. The promoters, no doubt hope it will go on for another year, even longer. Since the Fair is virtually in our backyard, and since we were rather interested in the work, what would be more natural than to place a Doc Savage novel in that locale?

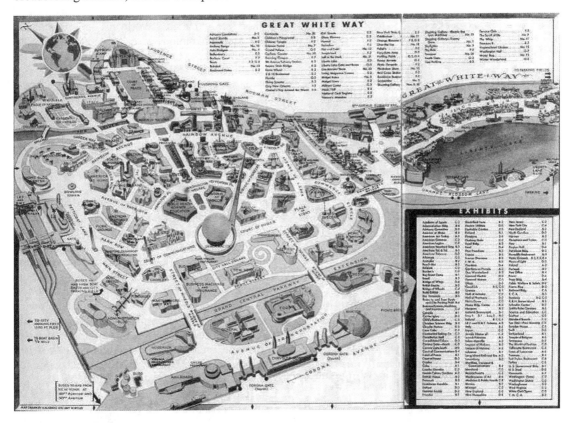

Armed with plenty of little note cards on which to take notes; cameras with which to take pictures; and permission to go through every nook and corner of the Fair grounds, we set out with Kenneth Robeson to look over the possibilities. We were given beautiful and extensive maps of the entire grounds; were hoisted high up inside the Trylon and taken inside the Perisphere. The Perisphere is a huge ball which will seemingly be floating in water. The Trylon is a three-corner shaft, coming to a point almost eight hundred feet in the air. Some people, avoiding the big technical names, merely call it the "ball and the bat," or, if they want to be a bit sarcastic, they call it the "Eight ball and cue stick." Anyway, there it was, and there we were, and right in the midst of our trip, one of the steel workers on the Trylon, in passing comment to us, said, "This should be a honey of a place for Doc Savage to get into!" The net result was a half-hour of enthusiastic talk about Doc Savage, nothing less than an autographed copy of the magazine by Kenneth Robeson—and proof that *World's Fair Goblin* is a real natural.

In reality, a new "Kenneth Robeson" was being groomed. Bogart would ghost the story. Here, the story becomes clearer.

Working under Dent's direction, Bogart drafted a tale he called "Man of Tomorrow." Dent revised it, retitled it "Goblin, Goblin" and Bogart, in his capacity as editor, did further revision work on it in the S&S office.

After doing his part, Dent had returned to La Plata to write *The Freckled Shark,* soon receiving a letter from Bogart:

> I guess you know how I feel about receiving the check in full payment for "Goblin, Goblin." It was just about the greatest thing that ever happened. Though I realized I did a rush job on the yarn, and could have done much better given the time, I had built a pile of hope on it. For it was to be the means of breaking away from the grind down at S&S and making a decent living writing. Even after Nanovic had put the story through for a check, I held my breath, for he had not yet offered an opinion of it.
> Well, he liked it! Thought I did a good job for the first one. So Friday afternoon we had a long talk... He wants me to continue with the Doc yarns at once, saying he knows I can make good.

A note from Nanovic followed, saying:

> Went through the Bogart story, and with some few changes which we can make here quite easily, it should be alright. We will switch the title to WORLD'S FAIR GOBLIN, and build up the goblin idea a little bit more, which ought to make it go over well. Maybe Whalen will not like the idea of us scaring the people over the Fair, but we won't need his help any longer, so we should worry.

In editing the manuscript, Nanovic renamed the General Motors Building, calling it the Motors Building. Street & Smith did not give away any free publicity—not even to General Motors!

The GM Building housed Futurama, a panoramic look at the world of 1960 where miniature cars zipped along cloverleaf highways. It was the most popular attraction of the Fair, which also gave the American public its first glimpse of such futuristic wonders as nylon stockings, electric dishwashers, robots and television. The opening day of the Fair was televised by RCA, whose pavilion displayed the first commercial TV sets ever available to the public. TV receivers were placed in strategic locations all around Manhattan.

World's Fair Goblin ran in the April 1939 issue of *Doc Savage,* published one month before the Fair's official opening on April 30. It was probably no accident that the Camel cigarettes ad gracing that issue's back cover featured a testimonial from an inspector working on the Trylon! Perhaps it was the same one Nanovic mentioned encountering at the Fair grounds.

On the strength of this successful first effort, William Bogart went on to ghost many more Doc Savage novels, ultimately becoming—after Lester Dent—the second most prolific Doc writer.

We don't know which "Kenneth Robeson" conceived this story. Years before, Lester Dent set a novelette at the 1933 Century of Progress Exposition on Chicago. And in 1937, Bogart wrote a short story called "World's Fair." Eventually other pulp champions like The Spider and The Phantom Detective also had their adventures in the shadow of the Trylon and Perisphere. But Doc Savage was there first. As always.

In the summer of 1939, Dent visited The San Francisco World's Fair. He discovered that he could walk through many exhibits without encountering another attendee. Dent pronounced it a "flop." Evidently, America was in the mood for only one great fair that pivotal year.

As for the World of Tomorrow, it closed on Halloween 1940. Despite setting records for the highest attendance of any international fair, it fell far short of projections. Perhaps the growing war sweeping Europe had something to do with it. Nazi conquests cast a shadow over the pavilions of several nations which lost their freedom in 1939 and 1940. More likely, Old Man Depression had not yet let go of America. Only its entry into the Second World War would accomplish that.

While the centerpiece of the Fair, the Trylon and Perisphere, ended up scrapped and converted into armaments for the U. S. war effort, on its exact site another New York World's Fair rose up. The Unisphere, symbol of the 1964 Fair, can still be found on Flushing Meadows. •

WORLD'S FAIR GOBLIN

BY KENNETH ROBESON

"Goblin, Goblin," Was the Cry as a Horrified World's Fair Crowd Cringed with Fear!

A Complete Book-length Novel

Chapter I
THE MEN THE GOBLIN GOT

MAYBE there is nothing to superstition. Maybe it just *happened* to be the thirteenth day of the World's Fair in New York City. The Fair management spent hundreds of thousands of dollars for publicity to let the universe know that this World's Fair was big, bigger, biggest. It covered more acres of ground, offered more means of amusement, had more scientific exhibits. It was worthy of that worn-out word—colossal.

To give some idea:

Doc Savage—scientific man of mystery, muscular marvel, also reported to be an amazing person in other ways—was to give a series of demonstrations of ultramodern surgical skill. Ordinarily, such an event would have been printed on the front pages of the newspapers in the United States, and cabled abroad. But this time, it was just a *part* of the World's Fair daily program.

Incidentally, Doc Savage's first surgical demonstration by mere chance happened to be scheduled for the thirteenth day after the opening of the Fair, which was the day the goblin walked.

Additionally, the Doc Savage demonstration was given before a convention of surgeons and doctors exclusively, which disappointed a lot of people who had heard that the lifework of Doc Savage was really righting wrongs and punishing evildoers in various parts of the earth, a career that had led the Man of Bronze, as he was sometimes called, into some fantastic adventures.

The public had heard that Doc Savage did fantastic things, and it would have liked to see a demonstration of some fantastic feats. But Doc Savage had a great dislike for publicity, and he never cut capers for the public's entertainment.

However, the goblin getting loose was not the first mysterious thing that happened.

Two men had disappeared. That was the initial mystery.

On another day prior to this thirteenth day after the opening of the World's Fair, two hundred thousand visitors paid admission. Exactly two hundred thousand. And exactly two less than that came out.

They had automatic mechanical checking turnstiles at all the gates, and a head gatekeeper whose job was collecting the figures. The head gatekeeper saw from the readings that two less people came out than went in. He decided one of the mechanical contraptions had made a mistake. He was wrong.

Two people went into the Fair grounds and never came out—and it wasn't any mistake of any mechanical contraption.

The goblin got them.

THE white-haired man in the long rubber apron, when he appeared, acted as if the goblins were after him, too.

The white-haired man was Professor Martin Uppercue, reported to be one of the world's greatest scientists. His specialty was electrotherapeutics— he had discovered some remarkable things about how diseases of the human body would react to electrical treatment.

He was a small man, thin, with thick white hair on top of a large head. He made you think of the type of musician slangily called a "long-haired boy."

There was nothing long-haired or old-fashioned about his scientific discoveries. He was fifty years ahead of his time, maybe a hundred. Men of science knew Uppercue as a quiet-mannered, soft-voiced person with keenly bright-blue eyes and a sedate deportment. Especially sedate. He was always dignified.

There was nothing sedate about the way Professor Martin Uppercue came out of his laboratory. Nor dignified, either.

Professor Uppercue's laboratory was situated near the center of the Fair Grounds close to the huge ball of a structure called the Perisphere. It was only a few yards from the laboratory to the landscaped gardens along the Court of Communications. Professor Uppercue dashed wildly into this garden, which was crowded with people.

The natural first thought was that Professor Uppercue was chasing something.

As soon as they saw his face, they knew he was not chasing anything. His face showed terror. His eyes popped until they looked like small saucers stuck, bottoms out, on his face.

He ran headlong, knocking astounded people out of his way. There was blood on his face, quite a bit of it. His mouth was also open, open like the mouth of a dog that has been backed into a corner and is being whipped.

Professor Uppercue wheeled his head in different directions as he ran. He seemed to be looking everywhere, hoping, it was suddenly apparent, for a place to which to flee. He was carrying two articles.

One object that he carried seemed to be his laboratory apron. It was a long rubber apron and he had it in his left hand.

The second item was carried in his right hand, and it was more unusual. It was a cylinder, apparently made of aluminum. It was about three inches in diameter and as long as an average man's arm, and capped at each end.

He kept running, and glaring about in search of some place to run to.

There did not seem to be anything chasing him.

The crowd made the natural mistake. They decided that Professor Martin Uppercue had gone insane. So an effort was commenced to seize the madman.

The attempt to seize Professor Uppercue failed, but it did accomplish two things.

A man snatched Professor Uppercue's rubber apron, and kept it, and later turned it over to the proper authorities, and it proved very important.

Secondly, they learned something about that aluminumlike cylinder that Professor Uppercue carried. He whacked different people over the head with it—the thing was light, and did not greatly damage the recipients of the blows. But several persons were able to testify that a whispering sound came from inside the cylinder.

The sound from inside the cylinder was generally described as a whisper. One man testified it was more like the scuffling of a shoe across a bare floor.

Professor Uppercue got away and ran. He clutched the mysterious aluminumlike tube with both arms.

THE flamboyant heart of the Fair Grounds had been called the Theme Center. Here was locked the great spherical Perisphere that was like a mammoth white tennis ball two hundred feet in diameter, from around its base shooting upward great sprays of water that made it appear the huge ball of steel was floating on a fountain, and circling these fountains was a white, circular promenade bordered by heavy shrubs and foliage.

Professor Uppercue dived into this expensively landscaped brush patch.

There were two impressive structures in this Theme Center. One, of course, was the globular Perisphere—the two-hundred-foot white tennis ball of a thing. The other impressive item was the Trylon, a spike of steel seven hundred feet high coming to a needle point at the top. The minds that conceived the theme of the Fair had been unable to imagine anything more modernistic than this ball-shaped Perisphere and the needle-shaped Trylon, and the two were connected by a rising ramp—a wide sidewalk that spiraled up under the base of the massive ball of steel.

When Professor Uppercue next was seen, he was streaking along this ramp.

He now seemed hardly able to run. He was an elderly man, unused to much physical activity, and the wild running already had him near exhaustion. Once he banked into the side banister of the rising ramp, but he kept going. He was headed for the point where the elevated structure entered one side of the towering Trylon.

The Fair police—the Fair cops wore neat uniforms similar to the New York State troopers—and members of the crowd now set out in pursuit of Professor Uppercue. The crazed scientist—and the impression that everyone now held was that the scientist was insane—had a head start.

A number of people distinctly saw Professor Uppercue disappear into the Trylon.

A few moments later the police and more fleet-footed members of the crowd arrived at the Trylon. Everyone was wheezing from the terrific race up the incline. Puffing pursuers crowded into the Trylon.

There was gloom about them, strange modernistic semitwilight. Stretching upward until it disappeared in the needle point several hundred feet above their heads was the silent network of steel girders which supported the great Trylon. The spot where the pursuers stood was a platform built approximately a hundred feet above the spire's three-sided base.

"Where'd he go?" a man yelled.

They had all become aware of a strange sound—noise as if several carpenters had gone to work simultaneously sawing boards.

"Where'd he go!" The words literally crashed back at them. Everyone jumped, shocked by the increased volume, the impact of the sound.

"Great grief!" a man muttered. "Some echoes."

The sound illusion of carpenters sawing wood, they realized now, was the noise of their own breathing that had traveled upward into the space, and sounded back greatly magnified by the unusual acoustics of the Trylon.

A cop explained, "It's the way the place is built, I guess. But where'd that nut go to?"

"Search me!" grumbled another cop.

They did not search him, but they did search the Trylon—those parts of it where it seemed conceivable that a man might be hidden—and then went over the surrounding grounds.

There was no trace of Professor Martin Uppercue or his aluminumlike cylinder.

THEN the goblin walked.

It happened not over fifteen minutes later. Immediately surrounding the Theme Center of the Fair—the huge ball of the Perisphere and spike of the Trylon—were the most important buildings, which housed exhibits having to do with branches of modern science. These structures were large and, of course, modernistic. They were brilliantly colored, for color was the theme of this vast World's Fair, if one was to believe the words of the men who had conceived the thing.

Prominent among the centrally located Fair buildings was the Hall of Mines.

It was inside the Hall of Mines that the goblin walked.

Men and women spectators began to come out of the Hall of Mines, yelping at every jump. They were frightened. Not as scared as Professor Martin Uppercue had been, but almost.

A Fair cop grabbed one of the runners. "What's gone wrong now?"

The man jerked a thumb at the Hall of Mines. "Dud-dud-dud-damnedest thing in there!"

The cop ran in to see. The Hall of Mines was an enormous structure, well-lighted; it contained exhibits intended to depict the progress of mining and metallurgy from the beginning of things down to the present. There were hundreds of exhibits and as many scared people. A great deal of confusion, in fact.

The cop jumped on top of an ore-processing mill where he could be seen.

"What's going on here?" he yelled.

"Over here," voices told him. "In the mine!"

The mine they referred to was a reproduction of one of the famous gold shafts of the old West. It had been a popular spot, for the artists who had created it had done a very lifelike job. The shaft sloped into an embankment and disappeared into the depths of the earth. There were shovels and picks stacked about.

If the mine shaft had unexpectedly turned into a tiger den, the vicinity could not have been more deserted.

The cop planted himself in front of the shaft. He did not know what to think.

"It come out," someone yelled for his information. "Then it went back in again."

"What did?"

"It looked like a hobgoblin."

"A what?"

"You get a look at the thing," the informant told the cop, "and you'll understand."

The cops rushed into the tunnel.

At this point, the cop heard the sound—and the short hairs on the back of his neck began to want to get up on end. The noise came from the mine shaft. It was a whimpering, a hoarse throat-tearing whimper.

The cop rubbed a hand over his head to make his hair lie down again.

"Hell, that's a dog!" he said. "There's just a stray dog in there."

The cop got a flashlight and a gun and three other cops and went into the shaft. It was very dark. At various points in the old mine, there stood wax figures of miners and these wax men were equipped with miners' caps which bore lights—electric lights that imitated the old-time miner's kerosene lamp. It was observed that none of these lamps were lighted; and the current seemed to be off.

"It was a dog, of course," the cop said, although they had not seen any.

"The people who saw it don't describe any dog," another cop told him.

"Listen, I'll show you. I'll call the dog. Here, doggie—here, doggie—"

That cop never called another dog again. As long as he lived, his vocal chords would freeze when he started to call a dog—because he could not help remembering what he got when he called this dog.

It was probably eight feet high. It was not that wide. It had arms, legs, body. It had eyes that were great and awful, and it had strength that was the most awful of all.

They saw it only an instant, not very clearly at that, for it hurled rocks at them, boulders as large as barrels.

The policemen fled around the corner.

When the policemen had gathered their courage—and ten more cops and four submachine guns, riot equipment and tear gas—they advanced. They found nothing.

No goblin, no way the goblin could have gotten out. No nothing.

Chapter II
HIDDEN TRAIL

RUNNING north and east from the Theme Center of the Fair—the spot where the Perisphere and Trylon were located—were broad avenues and malls branching out like the spokes of a wheel.

The Hall of Medicine was on one of these spokes. It was a long, yellow-colored structure just north of the circular walk bordering the mammoth Perisphere. Inside was the operating amphitheater, built like a small theater, with circular tiers of seats forming an observers' balcony. Seated tense and silent, white masks over their own faces, visiting medical men watched in awe. They were seeing one of the most amazing things of their lives.

Other than the weird panting sounds that came from a mechanical device that looked similar to a punching bag, located near the head of the operating table, there was no other sound. That bag pulsated as oxygen mixed with anesthesia was fed to a small, still form on the white operating table—the figure of a boy from the slums of New York.

A tumor was being removed from the boy's brain. It was a type of operation never done before.

Motion-picture cameras whirred, recording the procedure.

Above that still form only the surgeon's eyes were visible. Amazing eyes. The eyes were magnetic, and like restless pools of rich flake gold. Set well apart, they were compelling and clear, holding the attention of each assistant. No words were spoken. Instead, those eyes directed, gave almost a sharp command when a nurse was a fraction of a second too slow. There was need for swift, sure speed. Remainder of his face was hidden behind a mask of white.

In the observers' balcony, a doctor whispered to a colleague.

"This particular penetration of the ethmoid cribriform has never been accomplished to date. Bet you he don't make it!"

The second doctor said softly, "But that surgeon is *Doc Savage!*"

"Sure, but the boy's been on the table a half hour now."

It did not seem to those seated above in the tiers that the figure of Doc Savage was unusually large. Standing alone, the bronze man's size was deceptive, which was perhaps caused by the symmetry of his physical development—so well proportioned that he seemed no taller than an average six-foot man. But whenever a nurse, who was tall herself, came close, his unusual size was evident. Doc Savage was a physical giant.

Close over Doc Savage's head, a cluster of round operating-room lights sent down powerful light.

A doctor seated in the topmost tier whispered, "Listen!"

Everyone could hear the commotion. An excited man had stopped to yell at the doorman, probably not realizing what a serious thing was going on inside.

"A scientist named Uppercue went crazy, and they're huntin' 'im!" the man yelled. "And they saw some kind of a goblin in the Hall of Mines!"

The skeptical doctors in the tiers breathed, "Good Lord. He'll never pull that lad through now. That'll distract him."

At the operating table, the nurses jerked worried glances toward Doc Savage. But apparently the bronze man had not heard a sound. His capable fingers moved swiftly. His hypnotic gaze flicked to the tiny instruments in the nurses' hands, indicating them as he needed them. For the first time, he made a direct statement.

"Almost through," he said.

But then the cluster of brilliant operating table lights overhead went out.

ONE nurse could not suppress her cry of horror as the big operating amphitheater with only small windows high above, was thrown into gloom down where Doc Savage was working. The bronze man was ready to suture—sew up—the incision close to the boy's brain. One slip now—

A nurse leaped to a wall phone, frantically called the engineer's room in the basement of the Hall of Medicine, announced, "Something mysterious caused the transformers to burn out."

Doc Savage ordered quietly, "Watch the oxygen closely." He stepped swiftly from the room. He always tried to foresee emergencies; there was a flashlight in his equipment case outside in the sterilizing room. He came back in a moment and passed the light to the assistant.

"Hold it steady."

Doc Savage's flake-gold eyes never left the small incision that meant life or death to the small boy on the table; his swift hands made delicate movements, until finally he straightened, said quietly, "See that he has absolute quiet. I shall see him later."

Not until the table with the still form was wheeled from the darkened room, did the famous specialists and surgeons applaud the bronze man's work. The applause was a roar. Only the greatest of them really knew what an amazing feat they had witnessed.

Doc Savage, unmoved by the applause, was taking off the operating gown, white skull cap and facial mask.

Most of the visiting medical men had never seen Doc Savage before he appeared in the room. They stared, for this Doc Savage was a man of amazing physical appearance.

His bronze hair was a shade darker than the bronze man's skin, and it lay flat and smooth, while his mouth was muscular and strong without being severe. Strong facial lines showed power of character.

Doc Savage said, "What was that interruption—about Uppercue?"

The bronze man's voice—calm, yet with a repressed power and tonal inflection that were remarkable—held the attention of everyone, though Doc was only addressing the assistant doctor at his side.

The assistant had unmasked also. It could be seen that the assistant was a young, good-looking man with slender height and delicate features. His hair was straw-blond.

The assistant was Dr. Alexis Mandroff—in charge of the clinic here—and he had willingly offered his services to Doc Savage in performing this operation to demonstrate a method that would save thousands of lives in the future.

Dr. Mandroff replied, "It must be something terrible, sir."

An attendant put in, "I just phoned to find out. They say Professor Uppercue is in trouble or something. They're trying to catch him—"

"Catch him?" Doc asked.

"They say he was acting insane."

There were gasps of dismay, for many of these men knew the famous scientist, Uppercue.

To Dr. Mandroff, Doc said, "See that the printed booklet of the operation procedure is distributed. Also see that each person gets a copy of the motion-picture film."

Dr. Mandroff nodded. *"Da,"* he said. He meant, "Yes."

The bronze giant moved toward the exit. A nurse handed him his coat. As he stood in the doorway, his shoulders almost filled the space.

Dr. Mandroff hurried after the bronze man.

"You were wonderful, sir," he exclaimed. "I've done some work along that line myself, but never anything like you accomplished just now."

If Doc Savage was flattered, he showed no outward indication. Instead, he said, "Any written questions they submit will be answered."

"Perhaps I should go with you," Dr. Mandroff offered. "Professor Uppercue is a friend of mine—"

Doc shook his head. "You stay with the patient, doctor."

The bronze man showed respect for the young, handsome Dr. Mandroff, who had recently arrived from Russia, and was said to be an amazingly clever surgeon who was at the World's Fair to study newest developments in medical science.

DOC SAVAGE went to investigate the mystery of what had happened to Uppercue.

After a few brief questions, Doc knew all that had happened. He learned about the peculiar metal cylinder. The Fair police gave him Uppercue's lab apron, said, "A lot of help this thing is."

They did not realize that the apron was the one clue to Professor Uppercue's trail.

"What about this aluminum cylinder?" Doc asked.

"It made whispering sounds."

"What?"

"Well, that's just what somebody said."

The Fair cops now came from the mine tunnel to tell of the goblin.

"You're crazy!" they were told.

"Maybe it sounds like that. But half a dozen of us saw that thing."

"What you saw were shadows from your flashlights."

"I suppose shadows can throw rocks that weigh two hundred pounds?"

Doc Savage decided to look in the one place that seemed to have been passed up—Professor Uppercue's laboratory, the spot from whence Uppercue had started on his wild flight. Looking at the rubber apron in his hands, the bronze man had noted something.

Blood smears, and long hairs stuck to the inner side of the lab apron.

It seemed sensible to learn the *cause* of Uppercue's flight.

The door at the top of the steps down which Uppercue had plunged from his laboratory was still open. Inside, more steel steps led downward in a steep flight, ending in a long, narrow corridor with only a single dim light at the far end—a passageway that was all of a hundred feet in length.

Moving through the underground passage, Doc

Clark Savage, Jr., otherwise known as Doc Savage, is the great leader of a group of fighters whose fame is on the tip of every tongue.

From the cradle, Doc was intended to be a superman. His knowledge and training began with medicine and surgery, then branched out to include all arts and sciences.

Doc can easily overpower the gorilla-like Monk, in spite of Monk's great strength, and knows even more than Monk about chemistry.

Doc Savage is feared by all who prey on the weak. He rights wrongs.

Savage—his sense of direction was well-developed—knew that he must be somewhere beneath the huge Perisphere. The corridor ended at a heavy-paneled door, and this was also open. The bronze man had to duck as he entered the room beyond.

He was now in a modern laboratory, well-lighted, and containing many of the newest scientific inventions. Doc Savage recognized gadgets that were still supposed to be in experimental state. A scientist himself, he appreciated these machines that Uppercue had designed.

On a workbench nearby was a small model of a generator, and something familiar about the machine held the bronze man's attention for a moment. Then, his observing eyes moved to other objects in the room.

It was blood on the floor that suddenly absorbed his attention. He bent down. His eyes always sought things easily overlooked, such as long reddish hairs that were stuck in these bloodstains. They were the same kind of hairs that had been caught on the rubber lab apron.

The red smears led to another, smaller doorway across the room, an opening that was like the heavy steel entrance to a vault. There was a lever that worked massive lock tumblers. The door was open. Light came from somewhere beyond.

Doc Savage moved forward, and was surprised when he saw what lay past that vault door. Another laboratory. Even greater than the first one. There was a high-domed ceiling, and heavy pieces of machinery made the place look like an electrical powerhouse. Nothing was in operation, though the place was fully lighted. The blood trail stopped at the threshold to this larger room—as though someone had been dragged as far as the doorway and then picked up.

A small sound now came from the Man of Bronze, a sound that was a trilling, low, exotic, as soft as a tropical wind filtering through jungle growth at night; it seemed to emanate from everywhere, yet nowhere, although actually it came from the bronze man's throat, and was a sound he unconsciously made in moments of mental excitement.

It was very strange that Professor Uppercue should have such elaborate laboratories here at the Fair—but Doc's trilling was not the result of that. Nor of seeing the blood trail. Instead, he felt the presence of someone watching him. A slight sound, probably. He stood very still, listening. Then he moved toward a massive machine, located in one darkened corner.

Someone—something—had moved behind that towering piece of steel and gears. The bronze man's footsteps were soundless as he reached the spot and worked his way carefully along one side of the machine.

He heard a faint swishing sound. It could have been the noise a huge person makes when trying to move a foot cautiously. The floor here was cement, and the touch of a heavy foot—no matter how careful—would make such a sound.

Doc Savage was inches away from the rear of the machine now. There was concealing space back there between the wall and the object he was circling.

In one final movement, his muscles, like steel cables, sent him around to the rear of the machine. He got a grip and dragged the skulker out.

It was a small blue-eyed girl who cried, "Wait! Wait!"

Chapter III
GOBLIN

SUCH a small and delicate girl—nicely curved, though—might be expected to be frightened and helpless, especially when swooped down upon by such a giant as Doc Savage. But this one wasn't. She had a small oval face, perky chin, the kind of blue eyes that brought thoughts of the sea at dusk. The eyes were bright and alert, for she was mad.

She kicked, clawed with one hand, stamped at Doc's feet with pointed heels.

"Let me go!"

Her right hand was behind her, as though clutching for support to something at the rear of the machine.

Doc asked, "What are you hiding behind you?"

The girl with the wide blue eyes fought harder for a moment, then stopped suddenly, defeated by the bronze man's strength. She stamped her small foot again.

"I suppose," she snapped, "that if you want to make love to me, I can't help it!"

Doc jumped and released her. He got a little red.

Her soft hair was blond and somewhat curly above her pretty face.

Doc Savage stepped back and waited for the blond-haired girl to come farther out into the room where he could get a better look at her. But she merely stood her ground, while one arm was still pushed behind her.

"Get out of here!" she flared. "Get out of here before I call the—"

Doc said earnestly, "Perhaps you have seen Professor Martin Uppercue? Something has happened to him and—"

He saw that the girl's features tightened. She began looking at him queerly. She was suddenly frightened, Doc decided. Yet her chin remained firm.

She kept her right hand behind her back.

Doc said, "You know Professor Uppercue, do you not? This is his laboratory."

Caution slowly crept into the girl's blue eyes.

She stared up at Doc, began to move carefully around him, one hand still behind her. She started to say, "I don't know you—"

Doc Savage had already surmised that. Many people had never seen the Man of Bronze, though they had read about him in the papers. He was rather pleased. He did not like publicity, and if no one knew him by sight, it would have been better.

And though Doc had never met the girl before, he began to deduce certain things. He had talked with Professor Martin Uppercue several times. Once would have been sufficient for him to have remembered the little scientist's features. This blond girl's blue eyes, the shape of her small face, the way she carried her chin so proudly—there was a resemblance here to the missing scientist, Uppercue.

Doc suggested, "We might stop bluffing."

"I don't know what you mean."

"You might accept my help in finding your father."

"I—"

Swiftly, the wary look came back in the blue eyes.

The girl blurted, *"Father?* I don't know what you're talking about. I'm going to call the police!"

She started backing toward the shadowy corner behind the huge machine again, her right hand still behind her as though feeling the way.

Doc said, "What have you in your right hand?" and moved after her.

The girl cried out, "Get out of here!" She turned to race around to the other side of the obstruction and toward the vaultlike door, and Doc saw the object in her right hand.

It was a metal cylinder such as the bowlegged man on the Trylon ramp had described—the strange tube that Professor Uppercue had been gripping to his chest the last time anyone had seen him. Doc got one view of this, then the girl was through the doorway into the smaller lab.

The girl screamed, "Help me! Put out the lights!"

Then it was suddenly very dark.

REACHING the other room a split second ahead of the bronze man, the blond girl had evidently seen someone whom she expected to help her, and one of them had leaped to a wall switch, plunged the room in darkness.

The person whom the girl had seen must be someone friendly, for a man came leaping at Doc in the darkness. This person landed on the bronze giant's broad back, and began to act somewhat like a wiry, long wild cat.

Doc Savage's powerful hands got fistfuls of legs that felt as if they were coated with piano wire. He yanked the man off his back. The man twisted, squirmed, fought in a way that didn't seem possible of one so fragile in size. The unseen attacker was underdeveloped, but he could scrap.

In the blackness, the girl cried, "Now that you've got him, I'll turn on the lights!"

She switched on the lab lights.

The attacker was an anaemic-looking man. Pale hair dangled about a head that was oversize, and he had bright, pale-blue eyes. From his upside-down position, the thin man looked up at Doc Savage.

"Doc!" he exploded.

Doc Savage seldom showed surprise; in fact he was hardly surprised now, for just before the girl had turned on the lights the bronze man had suspected the identity of the wiry hell-fighter.

Doc Savage, in the strange career of righting wrongs and punishing evildoers which was his real life work, had five assistants. The five were men who loved adventure, as did the Man of Bronze; also the five were, each of them, masters of some science or profession.

This one happened to be the electrical expert of Doc Savage's organization.

He was Major Thomas J. Roberts, better known as Long Tom, a man sometimes called the "wizard of the juice," since he was an electrical genius comparable to Steinmetz and Edison.

Doc released Long Tom. The girl rushed forward. "You know him?" she demanded.

Long Tom said, "Know him? This is Doc Savage!"

"Oh!"

The girl's blue eyes widened.

Long Tom explained, "I had an appointment here with Professor Uppercue, Doc. I was late, and—"

Doc interjected, "You haven't heard about Uppercue behaving queerly, then vanishing?"

As the bronze man spoke, his magnetic eyes shifted to the girl. She stood stiffly, chewing on her lip, saying nothing.

Long Tom noted the girl's suspicious attitude.

"I hadn't heard," he said. "I just drove out here from headquarters."

BRIEFLY, Doc Savage explained to his aide all he knew about the scientist's strange disappearance. As he talked, Doc noticed that the girl backed toward the wall again. There was an expression of fear, of something else in her deep blue eyes.

Long Tom's unhealthy-looking face looked tense. He said worriedly, "Doc, that's funny. Professor Uppercue is one of the finest scientists living. He sent a request asking me if I wouldn't come out here for consultation on some new, important thing he was about to create. I was to meet him here in his laboratory. But now—"

Long Tom's sharp gaze, too, had gone to the girl, who was acting strangely.

She was staring toward the floor, the slender steel cylinder still clutched in her hand. Suddenly she bent down, picked up something long and very thin. She cringed away from the blood that had been on the floor.

The blond-haired girl was holding one of the red, long hairs that Doc Savage had seen stuck in the bloodstains.

Long Tom saw the thing, asked, "What is it? Who—where—"

"Perhaps the young lady can tell us," Doc offered. "Where is that hair from, miss?"

The girl looked scared for a moment. Then her sharp chin came up and she snapped, "I don't know what it is."

Doc's flake-gold eyes were moving restlessly. Apparently this girl was more involved in the mystery than she wanted Doc or Long Tom to believe. She was holding back something.

Doc said quietly, "You're Uppercue's daughter, aren't you? There's something you're afraid of. Why not tell us what it is?"

Long Tom's pallid face brightened. "Sure!" he cried. "That's her—Uppercue's daughter! I saw a picture of her once in the newsreels, and she—"

The metal cylinder now thrust out of sight

Long Tom

Dubbed "wizard of the juice," Long Tom—Major Thomas J. Roberts—is the electrician of the bronze man's little group of fighters. Many are the inventions to his credit that have benefited mankind. As a fighter, Long Tom's looks are deceiving. He is thin, not very tall, has a none-too-healthy appearing skin. But it's just too bad for the man who tries to tangle with Long Tom! He's a wildcat in action.

behind her back, the girl's eyes sparkled and she cried, "I never saw Professor Uppercue in my life!"

"Then how did you get that metal tube?" Doc asked suddenly.

Doc recalled what the bowlegged man had told him on the Perisphere ramp. Doc Savage, of course, did not know about the soft scraping sound that had been heard inside Uppercue's queer metal cylinder.

But the bronze man put out his hand and prompted, "Let us see that thing you are holding behind you."

At first, the girl tried to duck away toward the door. Then meeting the compelling, hypnotic look in the bronze man's eyes, she stopped. She handed the cylinder over quietly.

Both ends of the unusually light object were enclosed with metal caps that were threaded. The whole thing looked heavy, yet was as light as a feather.

Doc unscrewed one of the caps, turned the open side of the long tube downward and waited to see what would fall out.

The Thing struggled with Long Tom ...

Nothing happened.

He unscrewed the other end and peered through the thing.

It was absolutely empty.

LONG TOM was staring at both the girl and Doc.

"What the devil is this all about?" he queried.

"That," Doc said, "remains to be seen."

He turned toward the passageway that led back to the steep flight of stairs to aboveground. "The first thing to do," the bronze man added, "is find Uppercue."

"But how—" the girl started to ask, and then clamped her softly curved lips tight. She looked wary.

Long Tom put in, "When I was talking to the professor on the phone, he said that if I missed him here I might catch him over at the Hall of Mines. He also said—"

There was a small, sharp cry from the blond girl. She said suddenly, "May I go with you?"

The electrical wizard remarked, "I thought you said—"

Doc said, "Perhaps it would be a good idea."

He gave no further indication of what were his thoughts in regard to the girl.

They went out.

Outside in the Fair Grounds, the excitement had died down. There were too many thousands of people here, anyway, for the news of Uppercue's odd disappearance to have reached the ears of more than a few hundred.

World's Fair police had quickly suppressed the rumor of some strange *Thing*—the goblin, a cop had called it—being seen in one of the exhibition buildings. No one really believed the tale, anyhow. Also, Uppercue's disappearance was considered to be the result of the scientist having mental trouble.

No one connected Professor Uppercue's vanishing with the goblin walking, which was unfortunate.

Few people noticed the arrival of Doc Savage, Long Tom and the girl at the Hall of Mines, for visitors were again occupied with staring and gawking at the thousand and one marvels of the Fair.

Inside the long building containing the realistic mine diggings, a lecturer was giving a talk on metallurgy. The crowd was over there, leaving the yawning mouth of the mine shaft deserted.

Long Tom said, "So this is where they saw the goblin?"

"Yes."

"Reckon there's any connection between Professor Uppercue and the so-called goblin?"

The girl jumped forward, gripped the skinny electrical expert's arm.

"No!" she cried. "Wait. I—"

Long Tom and Doc Savage exchanged queer looks. Then they walked into the mine shaft where the goblin had been seen.

AFTER they had gone a few paces, it was very dark and still. Doc Savage's hearing was probably developed beyond that of an ordinary man—he had spent almost two hours daily in regular exercise routine since childhood—which was to a large extent responsible for his unusual physique.

The bronze man still had the flashlight that he had used to complete the brain operation in the hospital amphitheater. He used this light now, and its beam ran over the rock walls like a gray ghost.

When the girl screamed, it startled them both. There seemed no reason for it. They had seen nothing.

"Maximus!" the girl shrieked.

She would have run, but Doc Savage caught her. She struggled, trying to get away.

"What the blazes ails her?" Long Tom exploded.

Doc Savage did not know. He was puzzled. He held the girl and asked her, two or three times, what was wrong, but got no answer.

Long Tom said, "You hold her. Maybe she saw something deeper in the mine. I'll look."

The girl must have been so busy struggling with Doc Savage that she did not hear what the electrical wizard said, nor notice what he was doing. But when Long Tom had progressed some distance down the shaft, she understood.

"Wait!" she shrieked. "Stop!"

She was a little too late with her warning, for at that moment Long Tom let out a howl of astonishment, a howl so astounded that Doc Savage released the girl and raced for the electrical wizard's voice.

The earlier descriptions of the goblin had not been exaggerated. It was, as the cops had said, all of eight feet tall, hunched in stature, and it had arms and legs. It gripped Long Tom closely, and the electrical expert struggled and shouted.

The thing was fleeing down the tunnel and this, coupled with the fact that it struggled with Long Tom and stirred up a cloud of dust, prevented Doc Savage from getting a clear view.

Fast as the bronze man was on his feet, the thing had gained. It rounded a corner. Immediately there was a terrific crash, a sound that turned into a roar.

The roof of the mine shaft had come down. Apparently the goblin, or whatever it was, had jerked loose the supporting timbers and let the roof collapse. Doc Savage waded into the dust and explored with his hands.

Further pursuit of Long Tom and the thing that had seized him was blocked in that direction.

The girl, Professor Uppercue's daughter, was

gone when Doc Savage ran back to the spot where he had left her.

Chapter IV
GARGOYLE ON THE ROOF

IT was now that time of the day when late afternoon was giving way to dusk, and a lull seemed to settle, bringing peace for a few moments to a busy world. The wide shrubbery-bordered walks were less crowded, for most Fair visitors were eating at Fair restaurants throughout the grounds or leaving for home. In the Court of Power, a landscaped parklike enclosure located near the Theme Center of the Fair, it was particularly quiet.

Two people were walking across the Court of Power, a man and a girl. The man was waspish, smartly dressed—in fact, he was probably the best-dressed man on the Fair Grounds that day—and he carried an innocent-looking black cane. His companion was almost as tall as himself.

The very correctly dressed man was making threats.

"If I ever get my hands on Monk," he threatened, "I'll make the hairy ape wish he was back in a nice safe jungle!"

The girl was tall. Her hair was an unusual bronze hue and her eyes an even more remarkable flake-gold tint. She was strikingly beautiful. She laughed softly.

"Ham, you're a clever lawyer," she said, "but you certainly let Monk take you in."

"Gr-r-r!" said the dapper Ham.

"Letting them use you to demonstrate a new man-beautifying machine at Cosmetics Hall!" The girl almost doubled over laughing. "How did you come to volunteer?"

Ham snarled. "I thought it was an invention of yours. There was a sign on it that said so."

"Monk must have printed the sign," the girl said.

Ham said a number of things about the ancestry of a man named Monk, none of them complimentary.

"Monk must have hired the operators of the machine to persuade me to take a trim," he gritted. "The operators were pretty girls. Monk knew I would be susceptible."

The girl laughed again.

She was Pat Savage, the lovely cousin of Doc Savage, as evidenced by her having the same unusual, flake-gold eyes and bronze hair as the Man of Bronze. Owner of an exclusive beauty shop on Park Avenue, Pat's clients were of the Four Hundred. Today she had come to the Fair to see the latest inventions of the how-to-look-beautiful trade.

Her companion was Brigadier General Theodore Marley "Ham" Brooks, the lawyer of Doc Savage's

Monk is the chemist of Doc Savage's little band of fighters. You'd never think he was a scientist—from his appearance. He looks more like the missing link.

Monk is a tough battler, a bruiser who doesn't know when to quit.

He likes the girls, too. In fact, Monk is quite a contradiction all the way through. As witness his almost constant quarreling with Ham, for whom many times he has risked his life.

group of five adventurous associates. Ham's weakness was sartorial splendor, and his hobby was quarreling with Monk Mayfair, who was another of the Doc Savage group of associates. The gag that had just been played on Ham was one that would take a long time for him to live down.

Ham had been given a marcel by Monk Mayfair!

Monk was the clever chemist in Doc's group. Deceived by some pretty girl operators—hired by Monk—that the new marcel machine was a beautifying aid invented by Pat Savage, the lawyer had submitted to a treatment. He had little realized that for some time he would be going around with a very neat "finger wave" in his dark hair!

This explained why Ham's hat was now pulled down tightly over his head; also why he was looking for Monk.

"I'll assassinate that Monk!" Ham snarled.

Pat pointed at the Hall of Mines.

"Excitement."

"Eh?"

"Over at the Hall of Mines."

They could see milling excitement. Then they suddenly glimpsed a giant bronze figure.

"That's Doc!" Pat said.

Ham was suddenly moving forward. "You'd better wait here, Pat," he advised. "Looks like trouble."

But Pat Savage hurried after the tall lawyer. Ever since she could remember, she had wanted to be a member of the bronze man's group. But because of the great danger of their work, Doc seldom permitted Pat to accompany them.

"You don't keep me out of this!" Pat told the dapper lawyer.

Ham looked displeased, but it was no use to argue with a girl as beautiful as Pat.

"This," he murmured softly as he ran into the Hall of Mines, "looks interesting."

DOC SAVAGE was giving building attendants quiet, but imperative orders.

"Shovels! Picks!" Doc directed. "They may be trapped beneath the fallen stone. Get more men!"

A few moments later, when workmen came running with shovels, Doc grabbed one and went to work. At least twenty men took turns, shoveled as furiously as they could.

Ham grabbed a shovel and joined in.

"What's up, Doc?"

"Long Tom is in there—and the goblin."

"What?"

Doc explained the somewhat unbelievable series of events.

"Say!" Ham said. "It looks like the beginning of a darned queer mystery."

The slide was slowly cleared away, disclosing beneath it the solid floor of the tunnel. Beyond this cleared space was a rectangular opening in the tunnel floor. An opening which should not have been there. Everyone moved close. It appeared to be a deep pit in the floor.

A search showed no trace of Long Tom or the goblin in the mine. The searchers came back to the pit in the floor.

The black hole, they could see, was slowly filling up with water that came up from somewhere below. Along with the rising water there was the rock and gravel that had, through power of gravity, slid down into the opening. The whole mess was bubbling and gurgling.

It might have been that this shaft had been caved in by the shock of the tunnel roof collapse.

"No human," Doc said, quietly, "could live in that."

Ham and Pat were silent. As they had worked, the bronze man had briefly explained about what had happened at Uppercue's laboratory; of Long Tom's suggestion that they come here to perhaps find the missing scientist, or Long Tom's strange attacker in the mine shaft.

"Where did Uppercue's daughter go?" Ham asked.

"No telling. She simply fled."

"And you have no idea of what is back of this?"

"None," Doc admitted.

At this point, a man came running into the mine tunnel.

"Something else has happened!" the newcomer barked.

"What?"

HAM

Brigadier General Theodore Marley Brooks — called Ham — is a top-line dresser. Tailors have been known to follow him for blocks, just to see masculine garb worn as it should be worn.

Ham's mind is as quick and flashing as a flaming meteor. He is reputed to be the most astute lawyer Harvard ever turned out.

He is never seen without his slender black cane. That cane can prove a formidable weapon when Ham is pressed.

Ham squabbles with Monk a good deal. And yet when trouble looms, both Ham and Monk turn on the common enemy and always mop up.

"There's some kind of a creature loose on top of the Motors Building. There's a crowd over there waiting for it to come down—"

Ham said, "Motors Building?"

"Yes."

Ham looked uncomfortable. "This may be my fault. I better investigate."

"I'll go with you," Pat said. "I don't want to miss anything."

WHEN Ham and Pat Savage reached the Motors Building, a modernistic structure that housed every possible device connected with the automobile industry, they saw a staring throng at one end of the building.

It was night now, and the Fair Grounds were bathed with myriads of brilliantly colored lights. Groups of buildings each had color schemes of their own, and taken all together, the yellows, blues, bright greens and a dozen other shades combined in a lighting effect that was breathtaking.

An apelike figure was moving around in a spotlight ray that was directed at a cornice of the Motors Building.

Pat Savage stared upward.

"Good Heaven!" Pat exclaimed. "That's Monk, not an animal!"

Ham snorted. "No one could ever tell the difference."

"Let's go to the roof," Pat said, "and see what that crazy chemist is doing."

"I think I know!" Ham muttered under his breath.

It was ten minutes before they could find their way to the rooftop. The building was sleek-sided, and built like a huge letter T. The section where Monk prowled was near a tower at one end of the structure. There was no way up from the outside.

In the building, Ham caught an elevator and rose to the top floor. From there, he ran up a narrow iron stairway to the penthouse. Hurrying out onto the roof, he was momentarily blinded by the floodlights which illuminated the building walls from the ground.

Then he saw Monk, who looked like a burly ape climbing out along the roof edge to a slim ledge that was high above the staring crowd below.

Ham yelled, "Come back here, you hairy misfit, before you break your neck!"

Monk turned and glared. Ham returned the glare. These two liked nothing better than an argument.

Monk was Lieutenant Colonel Andrew Blodgett Mayfair, chemist of Doc's group. Constructed almost as broad as he was tall, and covered with red hairs that bristled like dyed steel wool, Monk looked not unlike a stuffed ape out of a museum

jungle exhibit. In strange contrast to his massive body, however, Monk's voice was a thin squeak.

"Come over here, you shyster," he invited. "There's something you're gonna explain!"

The skilled chemist indicated an object out near the edge of the precarious ledge. Cautiously, Ham moved over to the roof edge and peered.

"I don't see anything at all, you flat-head—"

THEN Ham saw what Monk meant. The object was a grotesquely carved gargoyle, one of the weird-looking figures placed on the upper part of many buildings. In this case, a sculptor had let his thoughts run rampant in designing the homely figure—and, strangely, the head of the gargoyle had an uncanny resemblance to Monk's face.

Ham began laughing.

"A perfect example of prehistoric workmanship," he gurgled unkindly. "In fact—"

Monk's face was red with rage.

"Listen, you marcelled clotheshorse," he piped. *"You* had something to do with this! I'm gonna find the guy that made this thing and ask him where he got the model—"

Ham, as a matter of fact, was responsible for the statue resembling Monk. The well-dressed lawyer laughed until he had to hold his sides.

"So you climbed up here to see yourself?"

Monk stalked to Ham, made a grab for the dapper lawyer's hat, and said, "Wait until you try to wash the curly-girly out of your hair, shyster!"

That silenced Ham.

With a growl of disgust Monk swung and started across the long rooftop.

"Where you going?" Pat called.

"Where they fumigate for lawyers," Monk snapped.

"Wait," Pat said. "Did you know that Professor Uppercue—"

"Let the big clown go!" Ham snapped.

Monk disappeared into the deep gloom toward the center of the wide roof. The building extended for a length of several city blocks, and away from the edges where floodlights played their streamers up from the ground, the place was in stygian darkness.

Ham, still chuckling to himself, started to leave the roof. Far below on the grounds, he noticed two great circular pools that were part of the decorative scheme, and he stopped to admire the effect of colored lights upon the water.

Ahead, in the darkness, there was a shrill yell.

"Ham!" Come here! There's somethin'—"

Monk's voice! It suddenly broke off in a choking gasp.

Ham's first thought was that it was a trick. But no. No, it was no trick. Suddenly worried, Ham started running. There had been a note in Monk's voice that the lawyer had never heard before. Terror, he believed. Utter terror, too.

And the hairy Monk wasn't afraid of Satan himself. Yet the tone had distinctly been of awe— and fear.

Ham banged into an obstruction in the darkness, circled it, then drew up with an open-mouthed gasp. Just ahead, limned on the raised wall along the roof edge, a figure stood. It was vaguely human in form, but of superhuman size. Ham was too far away to see the *Thing's* face, but he was aware of its weird, booming chuckle. That sound was like nothing human. It was hard to think of it even as a *voice*.

Ham thought of the goblin as described by those who had seen it.

As he stared in bewilderment, the *Thing* leaped outward into space.

And it was holding Monk as it leaped.

Chapter V
MAN WITH THE SCAR

DOC SAVAGE had returned to the laboratory of Martin Uppercue. After Ham and Pat Savage had left to investigate the trouble on the roof, the bronze man had spent a little time looking for the small blond girl. He had not found her.

Doc had then gone back to his car, near the Hall of Medicine, and from an equipment case taken a special ultraviolet light used to penetrate fog or water. He had used the light on the rectangular pit that had been found beneath the mine tunnel heap.

Strangely, when Doc Savage had left the Hall of Mines, he did not seem greatly upset about Long Tom's watery grave demise.

The small door at the top of the steps outside Uppercue's laboratory was locked. Doc had closed it when they all had left here a little while ago.

From his pocket he got a key that would open almost any type of lock. A Fair cop, in his natty uniform, was going by and came up the steps to greet the bronze man.

"I understand," he said, "that you are Doc Savage. I've been instructed to give you any possible aid. Can I do anything?"

Doc nodded, told the officer that Ham and Pat Savage might be looking for him. They were to be permitted to enter the laboratory.

Neither Doc Savage nor the officer had heard about the excitement atop the Motors Building.

The cop said, "Say, Mr. Savage, there sure is queer things goin' on around here. Like Uppercue's disappearance. You know, I have a hunch that guy was up to something. I—"

"Has any trace been found of him?" the bronze man interjected.

"Naw. Say, I hope you can find him, though. They say you're good at stuff like that, and—"

"That," Doc finished, "is what we hope to do."

He went inside, down the steep steps and along the narrow corridor to the laboratory. The rubber apron, the empty metal cylinder that the small blond girl had carried, were on a workbench where the bronze man had left them.

He disregarded these now and moved to the table where the model spherical generator was set up. Doc Savage seemed especially interested in the generator.

He noted that it was put together in units that could be quickly dismantled. Soon he had the model apart and was busy examining each part. His metallic features were thoughtful.

Doc Savage had discovered something.

The running feet in the corridor behind him made sharp sounds that knocked about the laboratory walls. Doc Savage turned to face the girl who came dashing breathlessly into the room.

It was the nicely put-together small blond girl, and she cried, "May I stay with you?"

Doc Savage said, "You seem to be a person who changes her mind often. A little while ago you disappeared. You've refused to be at all helpful."

"It was the man." Her eyes were big and round. "What man?"

"The one with the scar. I saw him staring at me over there at the Hall of Mines. That's why I ducked out. He was following me now when I came this way. I ... I'm afraid."

"It could not have been that—goblin—that scared you?"

"I ... yes ... that scared me, too. But it was the man with the scar that caused me to flee."

"What is that 'goblin'?"

The girl said nothing.

"You know what it is," Doc said. "That was obvious. Now, what is it?"

"I won't tell you!" the girl said.

Ham and Pat Savage came back then with the news of Monk's seizure.

PAT SAVAGE'S eyes were bright, and a flush of excitement had climbed into her cheeks.

"Doc," she exclaimed, "that ... that *Thing* I saw grab Monk was incredible. You should have seen its size. I was standing there on the roof when—"

Ham cut in with, "And it jumped right off the roof with Monk gripped in its arms, Doc! I heard Monk yell, and tried to reach him—"

"Jumped?"

Doc Savage was at alert attention.

Obviously the bronze giant was thinking of the height of the Motors Building; that death could be the only end for anyone leaping from its roof.

The Thing was holding Monk as it leaped.

But Pat quickly put in, "They landed in one of those two big pools beside the building. You know, those pools around on the side. There's a lot of shrubbery and gardens surrounding the spot, and by the time I got there that *Thing* had disappeared."

"And Monk?" Doc queried.

"Gone, too," Ham said. He explained. "The spot that *Thing* jumped from was directly over one of the pools. By the time I got down there—by the time *anyone* could get there—both Monk and the *Thing* were gone. You could see the wet tracks where the *Thing* had pulled Monk out of the water."

For once, the smooth-talking, dapper lawyer was upset. He was deeply worried about Monk. Though the hairy chemist and Ham liked nothing better than an argument or fight, either would have gladly forfeited his life for the other in time of danger.

Doc Savage was thoughtful for a moment, saying nothing.

Then with a brief, "Wait here," he went out to where he had left the Fair cop at the outer door.

Doc Savage questioned the man about the blond girl arriving here.

"She was followed," the cop said.

"Followed?"

"I saw the mug who was trailin' her. I started for him. He ran."

"Can you describe him?"

"Well, now"—the officer was thoughtful—"yes and no. He had some sort of scar on his face. And the bloke was grinning like he was happy as hell about something."

Doc Savage said, "Thanks," and went back to the laboratory.

Someone was really trailing the girl. Doc had thought she was lying about that.

As Doc looked at the girl's small oval face, back in Uppercue's laboratory, he was certain that she was terrified. It was in her blue eyes. She sat in a chair near the workbench, her small hands twisting a lace handkerchief in her lap.

Pat Savage moved around to the blond girl's side, placed an arm around her shoulder and said, "I wish you would let us help."

The girl began shaking. "Just get … get me to some place where I'll be … safe. That's all you can do."

Doc Savage said, "We'll take you to a safe place. Ham, escort both girls over to that small building near where my car is parked. They'll be safe there."

Pat would have objected, but Doc got her aside and said, "Gives you a chance to question her."

Pat was satisfied.

Later, Doc said something in an aside to the well-dressed lawyer, and Ham smiled. The place the bronze man had referred to was a small lockup—a jail on the grounds used in case of emergency. Doc Savage knew that a guard was on constant duty there. Thus the girls would be safe.

When Ham had gone out with the girls, Doc Savage stepped through the vaultlike door into the large laboratory, the room with all the machinery that obviously was in readiness to operate something above.

The bronze man stared upward. Across the room, iron steps like those in a ship's engine room led to a catwalk near the high dome of the room. From there, still another iron ladder led to an opening in the ceiling, a trapdoor of some sort.

Power lines, cables, different kinds of wiring also led up to somewhere above. Doc decided that he would later go up and investigate.

The tall dark man who stepped out from behind the vaultlike door Doc had just cleared, said quietly, "Maybe you better stay right here, mister."

There was a lot of gun in the man's fist.

DOC SAVAGE'S right hand was in his coat pocket. He didn't move, but looked quietly at the tall young man who moved around to a position in front of him.

About thirty would catch his age, and he had pleasant brown eyes, darker brown hair, and was wearing pin-striped trousers and a dark, semiformal coat. He reminded one of the alert young men who were members of the diplomatic service in Washington. An embassy attaché.

He looked nothing like a gunman; yet the heavy automatic in his hand was steady on Doc's chest, and the young man's face was quite grim.

The stranger said, "You aren't fooling me. What's the idea of sending that nice kid to jail? I heard what you said—and don't act like a toad, either!"

This last was an exasperated command when the stranger saw what Doc was doing.

The bronze man had taken a deep breath, like a person who is going to be obstinate. Doc was holding his breath and moving slowly back from the black hole of the gun barrel.

The tall man stepped forward, his face flushed with anger as he glared at Doc Savage. "See here," he shouted, "you either start talking or this gun starts blasting!"

Ordinarily, the bronze man would have been wearing a bulletproof vest. He had left it off because of the operation he had been asked to perform this afternoon. If that gun went off, nothing would stop the heavy slugs.

And the young man holding it looked mad enough to fire at any second.

Doc had been holding his breath for fully two minutes. He had backed away from the spot where he first stood.

The brown-eyed man reached that spot now, choked, started to yank at his collar, and suddenly collapsed. His fingers went slack around the gun butt.

Doc Savage caught the man as he fell, picked up the gun, dropped it into his pocket and, lifting the tall man easily into his arms, hurried him out of the room. On the way out, the bronze man reached back with one hand to close the heavy vault door behind him.

Then Doc let out his breath.

He propped the man in a chair and in a few moments the brown eyes opened.

"I—ugh— Say, what the—" the man started to bluster. He climbed to his feet, swung a steaming right fist at the bronze man's head.

Doc Savage, in a swift movement, caught that fist in his right hand and the young man stopped in his forward plunge as though he had run into a brick wall. His eyes looked startled.

Doc said quietly, "Now let's be sensible? That harmless gas has made you light-headed. It will pass in a moment."

WHILE the bronze man's hand had been in his right pocket, he had broken a small bulb that contained a quick-acting anaesthetic gas. Doc had held his breath, thus inhaling none of the colorless, odorless gas. The effectiveness of the gas wore off in a few moments. But as a matter of precaution, Doc Savage had closed the door behind him.

Doc explained about Professor Uppercue; about how he had placed the blond girl with his cousin Pat in a place where they would be safe for the moment. He asked:

"You were upset about Uppercue's daughter, weren't you?"

The young man's face had flushed when he learned that the speaker was Doc Savage. He talked.

He was Adam Ash, a public relations consul at the World's Fair. His job was that of diplomat dealing with various representatives of foreign powers with buildings at the Fair. Doc was impressed by Adam Ash's background, his training.

He queried, "Then this girl is Uppercue's daughter? What is she afraid of?"

Adam Ash's brown eyes looked worried. "Uppercue was readying some great experiment," he said. "Publicity on the thing was being kept from the newspapers until everything was all set."

"What kind of an experiment?"

"I don't know. But something terrific."

"There is some connection between Uppercue's disappearance and this so-called goblin that has been seen, and has seized two of my men. Any idea what the connection might be?"

"No."

The bronze man did not comment further. Often when Doc Savage did not wish to explain an idea that was shaping up in his mind, he maintained silence.

Unexpectedly, he asked, "Who has charge of the attendance records here at the Fair?"

Ash mentioned an official's name, told where he could be located.

Seeing that Adam Ash—who was apparently quite fond of Uppercue's daughter, Kay—was willing to help, the bronze man suggested that he go over and see that the girls were all right. Ash agreed, and then departed.

Doc Savage went to the Administration Building, learned from the gate-keeper about the actual figures on the attendance record sheets.

The masses of figures did not interest Doc Savage, but what did particularly interest him was the two-less-went-out-than-came-in angle.

"Oh, we noticed that," they told him. "But one of the machines must have made a mistake."

As Doc left the official's office, he paused in the open doorway a moment as the gatekeeper again repeated the information. The bronze man's eyes were thoughtful, and he did not see the figure of a man lurking in an L of the corridor.

Doc was thinking as he left the building and walked through a darkened area where cars were parked. The bronze man disliked publicity, and he was taking a route that was away from the wide, well-lighted malls.

Again he did not see the man who was following him, the corridor lurker—an individual with a peculiar scar on his face.

Chapter VI
THE THING CHUCKLES

DOC SAVAGE'S route took him back toward the Court of Communications. This consisted of the broad twin malls that paralleled a landscaped green built between. Evening World's Fair visitors jammed the walks now and it was impossible for the bronze man to avoid the crowds at this point.

Yet there was little possibility of recognition, for everyone was dazzled by the splendor of the long, varicolor-lighted promenade walk. There were too many things for people to stare at.

The crowd was unusually close-packed down near the huge Perisphere. The great white-covered ball looked like a giant round egg in the powerful floodlights.

Someone tugged at the bronze man's arm as he quietly made his way through the crush of human beings. Doc turned.

And just as he did so, Doc Savage felt another jerk at his coat sleeve, near the shoulder.

But it was no one trying to gain his attention.

Instead, Doc Savage had a brief glimpse of a man whirling away from him, of a face that seemed to be drawn into a hell-let's-have-some-fun sort of grin and beaded eyes that were as cold as death. The man elbowed his way swiftly through the crowd.

Doc Savage saw his own torn coat sleeve, and something else.

The object was a long, nickel-plated instrument that was in the man's hand; it gleamed for a brief second in the light. Then the man had ducked through the crowd.

The bronze man did not have to examine his torn coat to know what that tug had meant. The grinning man with the scar near his mouth had tried to jab him with some sort of hypodermic needle.

Doc took out after him.

This wasn't too difficult, for even on the jammed walks, the man's high silk hat bobbed up above heads frequently. The assailant's attire was hardly in keeping with the hard, icy stare in his piglike eyes. For, wearing "tails" and the high silk hat, he appeared, at a brief glance, like one of the many visiting foreign diplomats!

THE chase continued across the wide mall, through the throngs and to a bypath that wound beneath thick foliage near bordering trees. It was not the sort of chase that draws attention, for there were too many people to make running possible.

It was really a case of quick footwork in slipping in and out of holes in the jam of people. The man with the grinning face proved to be quite adept at moving swiftly without drawing any attention.

But when he got away from the walks and beneath the enshrouding trees, he got his legs pumping and looked like an open-field runner going places.

Doc Savage ran just as swiftly, but with no apparent effort.

Doc knew that the running man must have trailed him from the Administration Building. For some reason, the stranger had followed him there, must have overheard the questions Doc had asked of the gatekeeper.

The chase was leading toward the spot where Doc's big sedan was parked near the Hall of Medicine. The man in the silk hat reached another crowded mall again—one of the streets that led toward the Theme Center like the spoke of a wheel—slowed his steps, got into the crowd and disappeared momentarily.

But his high hat bobbed up again over near the long yellow-walled building; he cut around toward the rear.

Doc decided that this had lasted long enough

and quickened his stride. Obviously, the stranger ahead could answer important questions. He was involved in this mystery somehow; otherwise, why the attack?

Beneath the bronze man's coat was one of the special machine pistols that he had picked up when he went back to his car. Like an oversized automatic, the pistol could fire the "mercy" bullets that Doc's aides used. The bullets could bring down a crook, make him unconscious without doing any specific harm.

But there was a possibility of the bullets traveling beyond the darkened parking space back here and striking one of the Fair visitors. Doc Savage figured it would be just as easy to catch the man by hand.

They were now running close to the high walls behind the Hall of Medicine. It was dark back here, after the brilliant lights of the mall behind. But in the gloom, the bronze man's unusual gold eyes held to the streaking figure ahead.

Doc Savage closed in. In three more strides he would be able to bring the stranger down in a flying tackle. The bronze man's powerful legs started to close that gap—

And a man who came out of the rear exit of the Hall of Medicine at that moment opened the door outward right in Doc Savage's path.

THE heavy door was ripped half from its hinges as the bronze giant's form plowed into it. Doc went down.

He was on his feet in a fraction of a second. Doc Savage's quick mind had prepared his trained body for that crash in the heartbeat of time before he had hit the opening door. Muscles had set for the impact. He was unhurt.

But the tall man who gasped with dismay, and who moved forward quickly to aid Doc Savage, said, "I say, but I'm sorry! *Da*. I had no idea anyone was so near this door—"

And then he paused, peered at the bronze man's face and exclaimed, "Doc Savage! What—what's wrong? May I help?"

It was good-looking Dr. Alexis Mandroff, the personable young doctor who had assisted Doc Savage in the brain operation this very afternoon.

It was not necessary for Doc to explain. Ahead, the running man had skidded to a halt in the gravel. His path had taken him toward the huge Perisphere, and he perhaps surmised that there he might be trapped. It would be difficult to circle the mammoth globe with its throng-packed walks.

The grinning man cut across the parking lot, ducked behind a line of machines on the far side of the yard. He was out of sight, but there was the sound of his feet kicking up cinders.

Doc Savage said, "I'm trying to catch him."

Doctor Mandroff, hatless, his straw-blond hair rumpling as he dropped his black medical bag and started running, yelled, "Come on, then! Between us, we'll fool him!"

He went to the left; while the bronze man cut off to the right of their trapped mouse. The victim was somewhere behind the parked machines.

But fifteen minutes later, it was tall Dr. Mandroff who panted, "I guess we've lost him. *Da?*"

"Yes," Doc agreed.

They went back to the bronze man's car.

Doc Savage unlocked the door, leaned inside the car and turned on a switch on his shortwave radio. He waited a moment until the set warmed up, then said quietly, "Ham, you might come over to the Hall of Medicine. Bring the man named Adam Ash who was sent to meet you."

Dr. Mandroff, leaning over to stare at the radio inside the bronze giant's sedan said, "How in the world—" His gray eyes were wide.

"That," Doc said, "is quite a simple device. My men all carry small, portable earphones with them. We use a special wavelength and Ham is expecting to hear from me. You know him, I believe."

Dr. Mandroff nodded, suggested that they wait inside in his office, which he had just left.

Mandroff again made apologies for opening the door so quickly in the bronze man's path. "I'm so sorry, but it was an accident that could not be helped," he said miserably.

Inside the building, Mandroff moved on ahead, and flicked on a light in a modernistically furnished office that was more of a consultation room than anything else. An open doorway on the far side of the room showed a more practical, white case-lined office beyond.

A few moments later cane-swinging Ham arrived with Adam Ash. It seemed that Ash was already acquainted with Dr. Mandroff.

It was Adam Ash who said: "I think this is entirely concerned with his mysterious experiment that Uppercue planned. The thing he was keeping secret."

THEY were all seated in Mandroff's consultation room.

Ham, the smooth-talking lawyer, put in, "But I *saw* the *Thing*—this—whatever it was. I saw it grab Monk and leap from the Motors Building!" Ham's grip was white-knuckled on the handle of his innocent-looking cane—it was really a sword cane.

The lawyer's voice lowered and trembled slightly. "And it got Long Tom, another of our associates."

"How do you account for the seizure of Monk and Long Tom?" Dr. Mandroff asked curiously. "What was the motive?"

"They were investigating Professor Uppercue's disappearance. Somebody didn't want that."

"That might be," Dr. Mandroff said thoughtfully.

Doc said, "Two other persons have disappeared on these Fair Grounds, too."

"Who?"

"As yet unidentified. Attendance records merely show two persons came in and didn't leave."

"That," Dr. Mandroff said gravely, "is mysterious."

"Apparently as important as the disappearance of Professor Uppercue, also."

"Eh?"

"An attempt was made to kill me after I found out that two of the crowd apparently had never left the Fair Grounds."

Ham thought about it for a moment, then rubbed his forehead in an exasperated way.

"The girls are safe, anyway," he said.

"You're sure?" Doc said grimly.

The well-dressed lawyer nodded. "Safe in the Fair jail, with a guard outside the door. Pat is fit to be tied."

Doc Savage looked at Adam Ash. "You look as if something was on your mind."

The pleasant-faced public relations consul nodded.

"I just thought of something that might be important."

"Let us have it."

"It strikes me that part of this mystery has to do with a special metal cylinder that Professor Uppercue was always closely guarding. In it, he had something that he once told me meant the success or failure of an experiment greater than any known invention."

Doc mentioned the cylinder he had opened in Uppercue's laboratory, the tube he had found empty.

"If it was empty, that wasn't the one," Adam Ash said. "He had several other fake ones in case someone tried to steal the real cylinder. Precaution, I guess. He was almost nuts about the whole business."

For several moments, everyone in the room was silent. Through the open windows came the constant soft hum of voices of thousands of people on the Fair Grounds. Each man was thinking to himself that any one of those innocent persons might be seized by the weird creature that was the goblin.

It was stiffly quiet inside the room, until Ham said, "Doc, I called the headquarters of the Fair police. Told them to tell any excited visitors that the leap of Monk and that—that *Thing* from the Motors Building roof was a publicity stunt or something. Otherwise, there might be a panic."

Doc nodded. "That was an excellent idea," he said.

The bronze man stood up, indicating that the talk was finished.

From outside, on the warm night air, came a sound that held every other occupant of the room rigid. A sound like nothing human.

It was a guttural chuckling, and the volume of the sound was enough to vibrate through the whole room.

Ham yelled, "That—that— It's the same sound I heard that goblin of a *Thing* make!"

Chapter VII
MONK'S MEMORY IMPROVES

OUTSIDE, they found no one. Whatever strange being had been out in the darkness behind the building had disappeared as easily as its weird throat sound had come through the window.

Ham said, "It might have been a trick."

"Trick?"

"To get us all steamed up on the mysterious monster theory."

Doc Savage did not comment. The bronze man removed some gadgets from special compartments built into the inside of his big sedan, and these he tucked away in a vest he wore beneath his coat. He also thought it wise to put on one of his bulletproof vests.

Ham asked one more question.

"Doc—about Long Tom? Is he really—"

The lawyer couldn't get the word out. He had been going to say "dead."

But Doc Savage shook his head. He told about the trouble at the mine exhibit. "We examined that pit beneath the mine cave-in. There was water and fallen earth. But no sign of Long Tom."

"Then how in the devil—" Ham started to ask.

"Perhaps we'll have that answer shortly," Doc finished and left.

A few moments later the bronze man was passing over the Bridge of Wheels, a futuristic structure that crossed a busy Long Island parkway separating part of the World's Fair Grounds from the central portion where the Theme Center was located.

Over here was the Motors Building and the two big pools into one of which the *Thing* had plunged with Monk in its huge arms.

The pools were surrounded by landscaped gardens, and what Doc Savage next did was unobserved. He took from his special vest a queer-looking object. It looked like an old-fashioned lantern.

Then he carefully circled one of the pools.

The water marks that the *Thing* had left when it dragged Monk from a pool had disappeared now, yet in a few moments the bronze man had picked up the trail. The lantern device Doc carried employed an ultraviolet light, but it would have been useless for trailing purposes, except for one thing—the chemicals which Monk always carried about his person.

If Monk was conscious, it was a good bet that he had managed to open one of these bottles of chemicals and pour the contents on his captor, where the chemical would mingle with water that dripped—and leave a trail.

Sure enough, there were footprints which fluoresced—glowed as do aspirin and vaseline and other substances—when exposed to an ultraviolet light.

The prints of huge feet glowed with an uncanny luminance at the pool edge. They led off across a sweep of green lawn, cut behind Fair buildings and down a long slope toward an artificial lake that had been especially constructed at the Fair.

The lake looked like any real lake, and was over a mile in length.

The tracks swerved away from the lake and avoided any buildings. Doc Savage finally found himself in a field that was a leftover part of the vast Flushing Meadows, on which the World's Fair had been erected.

The big prints ended at an iron manhole cover in the center of the field.

The ultraviolet lantern showed something else now. Hand prints on the manhole cover. Big prints that no ordinary man could make. They were smudged, useless as a clue—but Doc Savage realized that the creature must have gone below ground here.

The bronze man lifted the heavy iron cover—it was all of four feet in diameter and two inches thick—raised it as easily as though it were a pot lid.

Inside, an iron ladder led downward into a damp-smelling cavern. Heat, a steaming odor floated up and struck Doc Savage's metallic features.

The place was obviously an opening to the underground pipe lines that carried steam from a central heating plant to the various Fair buildings. Electrical conduits were probably under here also, since there was no wiring visible anywhere about the modern grounds.

Deep down in the black pit a squeaky voice grumbled, "Goshamighty! How am I gonna get outta this danged Turkish bath?"

IT was Monk.

Doc Savage removed a powerful flashlight from his pocket and went down the iron ladder swiftly. The ladder ended in a small circular room whose walls were a maze of valves and skinny and fat pipes. The pipes were insulated, but still the thick, choking heat caused by steam made the place like an oven.

Monk was banging his hairy bulk about the place, trying to find a way out. The apelike chemist looked as though he had tangled with a dozen wild cats.

"Doc!" Monk squealed delightedly. "Blazes! I thought I was a gonner sure! I been tryin' to get outta this damned place for half an hour!"

Monk's little eyes were red and inflamed in his homely face. He squinted at Doc Savage through the glare of the flashlight ray. He asked seriously, "Look, Doc, this ain't one of them short-cuts to hell, is it?"

The bronze man's eyes looked slightly worried at the sight of Monk's condition.

Clothes had been half torn from the hairy chemist's powerful torso. He was bruised and scratched. Monk liked nothing better than a good fight, but this time it looked as though he had been set upon by half a dozen thugs.

Fighting his way blindly through the underground pipe lines with their intense, choking heat, it was quite obvious that Monk was almost done for.

Doc said, "We'd better get out of here."

He gave the chemist a boost up the ladder, and a moment later they were out in the fresh night air again. In the distance, the pink-red glow of the many Fair buildings made the heavens bright as day.

Monk straightened out rapidly. The fresh air soon cleared his fogged brain, and Doc Savage had made his aide take a special capsule that quickly brought back renewed strength, after which Monk seemed all right.

Briefly, he told the bronze man what had happened.

"Doc!" the burly chemist piped. "You oughta see that *Thing!* It's at least eight feet tall and strong as a bull. We landed in that danged pool and I tried to drown the *Thing,* but it rapped me over the head and I woke up down there some place."

Monk indicated the manhole which Doc now had covered again.

"Does it have red hair?" Doc Savage asked quietly.

Monk almost jumped. "Then, you ... you've seen it, too?"

Doc Savage shook his head.

He said, "But we found some of the hairs mixed with bloodstains in Uppercue's laboratory."

"Uppercue!" Monk got the name out in a surprised squeak. "You mean, it ... that *Thing* has Uppercue?"

"And Long Tom," the bronze man added.

The broad-bodied chemist was suddenly trembling with fury. "Doc," he exclaimed, "there's somethin' I should remember! I got a hazy recollection of comin' to for a couple moments down there."

To help him, Doc Savage said, "The *Thing* had red hair, and was over eight feet high. What else?"

"It's got the funniest face, Doc. Like a guy who can't think. The eyes look right through you, as though they don't even see you."

Monk shuddered. "And it's dressed in some kind of a cheap gray suit like a ... well, like a convict."

"And the features?" the bronze man prodded.

Both men were walking back toward the Fair buildings now.

Monk's forehead wrinkled as he tried to remember through the nightmare. "Well, Doc, you just can't describe them. They ... they're blank, is all. And there's something else. It seems there should be somethin' I should remember. I—"

Monk's words trailed off, as though he were slipping back into the fog again.

"Yes?" Doc prompted.

Suddenly the hairy chemist gave a whoop and started jumping up and down.

"Doc, we've got to hurry!" he piped.

"Hurry?"

Monk looked as though he had swallowed a grapefruit whole. Startled.

"I remember a little now," Monk raced on. "Someone was talking to this *Thing*—this what-you-call-it. You know, like a person trying to tell a dog to do something. He was saying it over and over, and—"

"Saying what?" Doc Savage prodded patiently.

"It was something about that *Thing* was to go and *kidnap the two girls!"*

THE point at which Doc Savage had located Monk was a good two miles from where the bronze man had left his car. But Doc and his assistant had now reached one of the express highways that circled the World's Fair Grounds.

These roads were also used by the special Fair police in patrolling the various routes that skirted the fringe of the many buildings and smaller crossroads.

Doc hailed a cruising radio car, spoke to the man in trooper's uniform at the wheel. The driver was one of the regular Fair police.

The bronze man identified himself, then asked, "Is this a two-way radio, officer?" Doc indicated a box beneath the dashboard and a microphone hanging from a hook nearby.

The man in the patrol car nodded. The car was painted the color of an army car, and the top was lowered.

Doc asked, "Then call your headquarters and have someone find out if the two girls who were left guarded in that small holdover tank are all right."

While the officer contacted his dispatcher, Doc

Savage explained to Monk about Pat Savage and the blond girl.

In a moment the loudspeaker in the police car

The police car had been cruising the Fair highway while the call had been made to headquarters. Doc thanked the officer, directed, "Drop us here."

The spot at which they left the patrol car was not far from where Doc's own sedan was parked. It was not very late in the evening, and there were still throngs of Fair visitors on the grounds. Cars were not permitted to use the roads inside, in the more congested part of the Fair, while so many people were everywhere.

Avoiding the main thoroughfares, Doc again questioned Monk as they headed toward the medical building parking lot. Doc Savage had told Monk about leaving Ham there with good-looking Adam Ash and Dr. Mandroff.

"Try to remember something else about that place where the *Thing* took you," the bronze man suggested.

Monk's scarred face was thoughtful. "I've tried to, Doc," he said apologetically, "but I only came to for a few seconds and everything was blurry. But I'm gonna find my way back to that damned steam-hole an'—"

"You didn't see the speaker—the one who gave the *Thing* the orders?" the bronze man prodded.

crackled, and then a voice said, *"Car 15 ... Calling car 15 ... We've phoned the officer on guard at the place you mentioned and he informs us that the two young ladies are O.K. That is all—"*

Monk let out his breath.

"Whew!" he sighed. "If anything ever happened to Pat—"

His tone said that Pat Savage was just about the grandest girl living. Monk liked all the girls, but the bronze man's cousin rated far above anyone the homely chemist had ever met.

The "diplomat" pulled a gun ...

"No," Monk stated in his squeaky voice. "It was dark down there, and the place they dumped me must have been off from some kind of larger room. I just heard the voice—"

Monk stopped in his rolling stride. His massive arms, which trailed to his knees at times, came up to clutch the bronze man's own. His face was worried again.

"Doc!" Monk exclaimed. "That voice!"

"What voice?"

"The *dispatcher's* voice just now on the police shortwave. The guy that said Pat and that other dame was O.K. It—"

"Well?"

"Blazes!" Monk squealed in his childlike tone. "It just came to me. It sounded like the voice that told that goblin—or whatever it is—to grab the girls!"

Doc Savage had continued forward swiftly at Monk's startling announcement. They had been close to Doc's big car. In a moment, the bronze man was working with the shortwave radio, a two-way set itself. He got the wavelength of the Fair police.

"Hello?" the bronze man said.

An excited voice replied. *"Hello? Who is it?"*

Doc Savage identified himself.

And the voice—a different one than they had heard over the police car radio—said breathlessly, *"There's been trouble over here, Mr. Savage. We found our regular dispatcher knocked out a few moments ago! He is still unconscious and we can't learn what the trouble was—"*

Doc interrupted with, "Can you contact the small jail where the two girls are being guarded?"

The voice answered: *"Just a moment. We have an intercommunications system here. I'll get the guard—"*

The radio in Doc Savage's car hummed for a few moments. Then the voice came back, and it was excited.

"We can't get any reply from that place!" the police dispatcher said.

Chapter VIII
LONESOME

WHEN Doc Savage had left his very attractive cousin, Pat, along with the equally as pretty blond-haired girl, Kay Uppercue, Pat had at first been furious.

She had figured that for at least once in her life, she was going to be right in the midst of trouble.

But the bronze man had decided differently.

Pat Savage, her unusual gold eyes flaming, had sat stiffly on the edge of an iron cot within the single cell and glared. After a while she became aware of the tenseness of the slender, blue-eyed girl beside her.

Pat's inquisitive nature got to work.

"You *are* Kay Uppercue, aren't you?" Doc's attractive cousin asked.

The small girl seated so rigidly beside Pat Savage nodded. She looked too frightened to do otherwise.

"Yes," she said tremulously.

"Then why not tell me what this is all about?" Pat suggested.

"I … that is … ah—" the girl stammered. Pat's arm went around the small blond girl's shoulders.

"Please let me help," Pat offered.

The girl looked up at Pat Savage, at the frankness in lovely eyes that were like Doc Savage's own. She murmured, "I really ought to. But I … I'm terrified! If that … that *Thing* ever catches me—"

Pat indicated the heavy bars of their solitary cell. She pointed to the policeman who was on guard in the doorway of the small building. The cop was working on his teeth with a toothpick.

"Doc Savage certainly couldn't have left us in a safer place," Pat said cheerfully.

"Well, maybe I'd better tell you," Kay Uppercue finally admitted with a sigh.

But just then they were interrupted by the arrival of someone at the outer door, where the guard was seated.

The man who stepped inside the small jail room just outside the girls' cell door looked like someone of importance. Pat could not get a good look at the arrival, for his back was partly toward them as he talked to the guard.

But she heard the man say, "It ees quite important, *monsieur. Le Docteur Savage* has send these message to his cousin. It ees ver-ry important, *non!*"

The broad-faced guard looked quizzical for a moment, cocking an eye at the man who was talking to him. Then he shrugged. Perhaps he was afraid to offend this messenger from Doc Savage, who wore a high silk hat and tails. These Frenchmen were pretty touchy, the guard knew.

He shuffled across the room, unlocked the heavy iron-barred door that protected Pat and the blond girl, and said, "O.K., mister. Talk to 'em. But make it snappy."

The guard started to go back to his post.

The visiting "diplomat" pulled a long-barreled gun from beneath his coat, stuck it against the guard's back, and snarled, "O.K., copper, push your face inside this cage and don't try tricks!"

The long gun dug into the guard's back. The cop raised his hands. As he moved past the gunman, the stranger quickly lifted the guard's service gun from a hip pocket. Then he brought his own gun barrel down on the policeman's skull.

The guard tumbled face-first into the small cell.

Kay Uppercue leaped to her feet and started to scream.

But Pat Savage put in swiftly, "Stop it! I don't think this guy is fooling!"

For Pat had seen the odd look on the arrival's peculiar face. There was an old scar near the mouth, and it twisted the whole face out of shape, so that the gunman seemed to be grinning happily about something. But the small, fishy eyes were as cold as death itself.

Over his shoulder, the gunman called, "All right, you guys—come and get 'em!" The grinning-faced man then took an apple from his pocket, polished it on his sleeve, and calmly took a bite.

Six more "diplomats" jumped into the cell room from just outside the doorway. Like their leader, they were arrayed in tails and high silk hats. They could have been easily mistaken in a crowd for a committee of visiting representatives of a foreign power.

Close to, they had faces that would have terrified babies.

The men grabbed Pat Savage and the girl with her, quickly placed gags in the girls' mouths, and pushed them ungently toward the door. One thug asked, "Take them to the regular place, Lonesome?"

"Yeah," said the leader, pausing a moment in his apple chewing, and the girls were bundled into a car parked just around the corner of the building.

Lonesome followed, after locking the cell door on the unconscious guard.

Lonesome was the leader whose twisted mouth made him appear like he was tickled pink about something. But there was nothing cheerful about his harsh voice.

PAT

"This," he said flatly, "will sure get Doc Savage's goat."

He took another bite of the apple.

THE bronze man and Monk were still standing near Doc's shortwave car radio when the police emergency dispatcher made his startling announcement.

The apelike chemist got excited. "I'm goin' over there, Doc!" he yelled in his squeaky voice. "Maybe that dame has played a trick on Pat—"

"Wait!" the bronze man said swiftly.

There was a buzzing in the loudspeaker; the police announcer's voice came on the air again.

"Mr. Savage," the voice said, *"we have the intercommunications system switched onto that jail lockup. We should have the guard in a moment ... We're sending a man over there to investigate—"*

Just then another sound faded in behind the announcer's voice. Doc Savage surmised that it was coming from the communications speaker, most likely on the dispatcher's desk.

The sound was Kay Uppercue's screams as the apple-eating kidnap leader named Lonesome knocked out the guard.

The announcer's voice got excited as he started to repeat the information for the bronze man's benefit.

But Doc had heard enough. He flicked off the radio in his sedan. Voices spoke excitedly behind him.

Ham and young Adam Ash had returned, and both had heard the startling news. Monk was almost going crazy.

He leaped at the fastidiously-dressed lawyer and squealed. "You blasted shyster! Doc says *you* were gonna watch the girls. I ought to bounce you so hard on that thing you call a head that it'll take—"

Well-dressed Ham drew himself up stiffly. His eyes gleamed.

"Listen, you hairy gossoon," he snapped. "If it hadn't been for you going native and starting to climb on roofs, we wouldn't have had this trouble. Doc should be looking for Uppercue and Long Tom, but he had to get *you* out of a jam first. Furthermore—"

The battle got off to a nice start.

Quietly, Doc Savage said, "Perhaps it would be a good idea if you tried to find the girls."

That settled that.

Ham and Monk took out in a hurry in the direction of the building where the girls had been left under guard.

Doc started to turn toward Adam Ash, and he saw then that the brown-eyed tall man's eyes were blazing.

Adam Ash said stiffly, "I don't like to be hasty, Mr. Savage, but I must say I'm disappointed in you.

You said the girls would be all right. And now"—
the young public relations consul's usually pleasant
voice rose shrilly—"well, I think I'd better handle
this in my *own* way!"

Adam Ash stalked off furiously.

For a long moment the bronze man merely stood
and watched Adam Ash disappear in the gloom
behind the Hall of Medicine. Doc's metallic features
were thoughtful.

Something in Adam Ash's words had not rung
quite true.

Doc Savage decided to follow Ash, for he
wondered if the dark-haired young man's feelings
for Uppercue's pretty daughter were as sincere as
Ash had pretended.

IT was getting late now, and the extensive
World's Fair Grounds were practically empty of
weary visitors. Display floodlights had been
switched off. Many of the brightly-painted exhibit
buildings were darkened. The glamour, the thou-
sand-and-one sights that held a staring visitor's
attention, were now gloomy-looking structures in
the quiet night.

Across the sweeping Flushing Meadows, a chill,
dank mist was rolling in from nearby Long Island
Sound.

Curiously, Adam Ash's steps took him in a direction away from those of Doc Savage's wrangling
aides. Ash seemed to be headed for the Lagoon of
Nations, the entrance point to building colonies of
foreign countries. It was like being carried on a
magic carpet to far-off lands.

Doc Savage found himself trailing along a narrow, cobbled street in the French Quarter. Building
doorways were dark now; the vague form of Adam
Ash, some distance ahead, was like that of a Dr.
Jekyll stalking the Paris underworld.

Adam Ash made no stops. He seemed to have a
definite goal in view. He left the French quarter,
crossed a white bridge that led across a creek into
the more sedate section that was Great Britain's
exhibit.

The bronze man's steps were soundless as he
followed. He was fairly close behind Adam Ash, yet
so quietly could Doc Savage move his powerful
form that not the barest foot scuff could be heard.

Ash swung around a corner and disappeared.

Doc Savage moved silently up to the building
corner and stood listening. His trained ears told
him that Adam Ash had paused.

Then there was a new sound: the click of a car
door being unlocked and opened. A moment later a
car motor sputtered into life, gears clashed and
Adam Ash took off as though the devil himself
were after him.

Hearing the motor, the bronze man had leaped
silently forward, planning to swing onto a rear

**KAY
UPPERCUE**

bumper of Adam Ash's car. But the young man's
actions had been too surprising. The car got away
before Doc reached the spot where it had been
parked.

The public relations consul's car reached one of
the express highways that circled the Fair Grounds,
and Doc Savage knew that there was no exit from
that highway until one reached the far side of the
Fair.

Behind Doc, someplace, another car was moving
in the quiet night.

Doc hastened back to the corner in time to see
one of the World's Fair police prowl cars cruising
toward him. An officer in the regulation trooperlike
uniform was at the wheel.

The car was the open model, two-seated type of
khaki color.

The bronze man hailed the driver, identified
himself and indicated Adam Ash's coupé in the distance. Doc said, "If you go straight back this road,
we can intercept that other car halfway around the
bordering highway. Hurry."

Doc Savage climbed in the front seat, the driver
got the car in gear again and almost pulled the
wheels off getting away from there like mad.

Doc looked suddenly cautious. "This is the
wrong *way*—" he started to protest.

The man beside him raised his right hand higher, to show the gun in his steady fist, and said, "But
this roscoe shoots one way, bronze guy!"

Two heads rose up from the rear compartment—
the men had obviously been hunkered down there
out of sight—and one of the two snarled, "These
gats work the same way, too, friend!"

His gunman partner chuckled. "Now we're
gonna learn about that metal cylinder!"

Chapter IX
CURTAIN CALL

MONK and Ham were standing outside the small lockup where the girls had been kidnapped. Other police officers had arrived now, and were inside questioning the dazed guard. Doc Savage's two aides had remained long enough to hear a vague description of the crook leader with the grinning face. Then they had hurried out.

Monk's keg-sized arms hung dejectedly at his sides. His little eyes in their pits of gristle were dull.

The hairy chemist looked at waspish Ham and said, "The only reason I don't tear you apart for letting this happen, is on account of the testimonial."

"The testimonial?"

The quick-thinking lawyer was wary.

"Yep. I've sent a testimonial to the company that makes that marcel machine, sayin' how well you liked your permanent. They might want a picture of you!"

Ham snorted, and his fists knotted.

The astute lawyer had a thick shock of dark hair, and was proud of it—but furious at the very pretty wave that was in that hair now.

"You hairy oaf!" he said. He looked at Monk's tattered figure and sniffed. "At least, I'm an attraction to the ladies. But you look like something out of a lost civilization!"

The endless bickering that was forever taking place between the two, got underway again.

But the weird sound that came out of the night cut the near-brawl short.

It seemed to come from nearby, and yet the only things in the vicinity of Monk and Ham were the deserted streets that bordered the long, rectangular Administration Building, a parking lot that was now empty of cars, and vacant rest benches that were placed about for weary sightseers.

The lawyer lowered his sword cane, which had been raised over the hairy chemist's head, and looked startled.

"What was that?" he asked cautiously.

The night air was again stiffly silent.

But Monk was leaning forward strangely, his bulletlike head straining outward. "It sounds like—" he started to say, and then the sound came again.

IT was a throaty chuckling, and it came from a bridge some distance away from them. The bridge was a walk for visitors going from the Administration Building to the Annex, behind, and it was shaped not unlike a yacht's sleek hull.

The chuckling came from up there on the bridge. It was an uncanny thing, deep, far-reaching. Any other person would have been frozen in tense horror.

But hairy Monk suddenly let out a howl and leaped forward. "That's *it!*" he squealed. "What I'm gonna do to that *Thing* this time is tragic!"

It was said that Monk would probably fight a gorilla, given the chance.

But Ham's black, alert eyes had seen the vague figure on the bridge. It was a hulking form that loomed massively in the dark night. Forgotten was the argument. Crazy Monk was headed right for destruction, and it was the lawyer's job to stop him. For when Death stepped close, Ham would have gladly laid down his life to protect the man with whom he argued so frequently.

Calling, "Wait, you missing link!" Ham took out after his partner.

The *Thing* on the bridge turned, swung into a long-strided gait and disappeared toward the wide, darkened Court of Communications. Its chilling throat sound floated back on the damp air.

The chase continued some distance down the wide mall, and then Monk swerved to the left as the huge figure ducked beneath shrubs nearby.

By the time Ham came running up, Monk was tearing his way recklessly through thorn bushes and rare, imported plants.

"Lost it!" he said grimly.

Ham's face was thoughtful.

Then he asked abruptly, "Listen, where did we leave Habeas and Chemistry this afternoon? We parked the car some place—"

Monk let out a whoop.

"Blazes!" he squealed. "I forgot about poor Habeas. They're locked in our car back at that Cosmetics Hall. Say! Maybe Habeas could pick up the—"

"—scent of this—this goblin," Ham finished. "That's why I asked about the pets. Only, that scrawny pig couldn't smell its own dinner. I meant Chemistry!"

Monk scowled.

They hurried back to where their limousine had been left early this afternoon. The two pets—after Ham unlocked the car—leaped out in joyful glee at the sight of their masters.

Then they backed off suddenly and glared at one another. Like Monk and Ham, the pets, too, enjoyed a fight.

THE two pets were remarkable-looking creatures. Habeas Corpus, the pig, had long ears like a jackass, stiltlike legs, and a snout made for boring into gopher holes. Chemistry was a pint-sized model of an ape and, strangely, looked greatly like hairy Monk. The pig belonged to Monk; Chemistry to the dapper lawyer. Sarcastic remarks by either of Doc Savage's aides toward the other's pet were sufficient to start a small war.

The pets were quickly separated before a fight started and taken back to where Monk had lost the dim trail of the man-creature *Thing*. Surprisingly, both Chemistry and Habeas Corpus picked up the trail about the same instant.

The pig scrambled off with its long snout to the ground; Chemistry went bouncing along on hands and feet.

The two aides of the bronze man raced after them.

The chase led far across the World's Fair Grounds, back to a spot somewhat near the lake where Doc Savage had found Monk in the man-hole. The pets cut across to a landscaped stretch of gardens that curved down to a huge, semicircular building.

Ham recognized the structure as the great Marine Amphitheater, built at one end of the long, artificial lake. The side of the white building they were approaching looked like the high wall of a stadium, and on the ground level were entrances leading to the tiers of seats above.

The two pets went scrambling into an open gate, and were heard prancing up steps to balconies overhead.

Monk and Ham were close behind.

Suddenly, as both aides emerged at the head of a long aisle that led downward between the tiers of seats, they saw the pets stopped tensely some rows ahead.

Monk and Ham were in a balcony high above the lake. Like a playhouse theater built on a mammoth scale, the amphitheater faced a huge, circular stage, constructed right out in the lake. The aisle at which they had emerged led downward to shadowy gloom. But the pets were close enough ahead to be seen. They had not moved.

Chemistry was chattering like an excited monkey. The pig snorted.

Monk whispered in his squeaky voice, "They've found it, Ham!"

He started down the steps.

"Careful!" Ham warned.

There was a figure down there, vague in the night light. It was seated in a balcony seat close to the aisle.

Monk again whispered. "You got a flashlight, Ham?"

The lawyer nodded.

"Flick it on the minute I get close to that *Thing*."

Monk kept moving cautiously forward.

But Ham slipped Monk a machine pistol. He rapped softly, "Use this, stupid—and if you can't stop it, I've got my sword ready."

They stalked forward, stealthily approached the seated figure. Then Monk said, *"Now!"*

The little, loudly-dressed man who leaped to his feet as the light ray hit him, exclaimed, "Douse that light, you fools! You're going to spoil everything, I'm telling you!"

The small man was holding binoculars in his hands.

MONK slowly lowered the machine pistol in his hand and stared at what he had expected to be the terrible *Thing*.

He piped, "I ... ah ... that is—Goshamighty, who in blazes are *you?*"

Habeas the pig bristled his back and gawked likewise.

The man they had pounced upon was no taller than the thickset Monk, and thin. His clothes were so loud they almost shrieked. He had bright, dark eyes, white hair and eyebrows that were black. Gold rings with large stones flashed on several of his fingers.

The stranger drew himself up haughtily and asked, "I don't believe I know you two, either, friends. But never let it he said that Shill Burns was one to be highbrow. You gentlemen are now talking to the one and only Burns, who knows everybody and has seen everything. Why, like I always say, gentlemen, like I always say—when better shills are born, Shill Burns will first have to be consulted. Ha!"

The man laughed at his own remark.

Ham said coolly, "He sounds like a side-show spieler—"

"Ah!" cut in the flashy little man. "My friend, you have hit on only *one* of the accomplishments of the great Shill Burns. But now I have been called to this mammoth, gigantic, stupendous World's Fair as a special consultant. Like I'm telling you, friends, like I'm telling you. There is nothing—do you hear?—nothing that the great Shill Burns does not know—"

"Maybe this mug knows about goblins," Monk said.

At the remark, the voluble little man went tense. His voice dropped to a stage whisper.

"Say!" he said cautiously. "You gentlemen look somehow familiar! Would it be possible that you are two of the well-known assistants of the bronze man known as Doc Savage—"

"That about hits it," Ham said.

"Ah!"

Little Shill Burns was suddenly passing the binoculars to Ham.

"Then I can help you," he announced with confidence. "Consider it fate that has brought you two friends to me."

Shill Burns indicated the huge stage out in the lake.

"Look!" he directed.

Ham peered through the binoculars. He saw a dark hole that was the stage proper. It was too dark to make out anything else.

He passed back the glasses and said frostily, "I don't see a thing."

Monk took the glasses and squinted his apelike eyes. Habeas and Chemistry climbed up on the back of two seats and gawked also.

"Blazes!" Monk ejaculated. "What *is* this?"

Shill Burns took the glasses from Monk and also looked.

He announced, "It's gone!"

He swung to look at Ham. "But it's there. It's out there on the big stage. Fate has brought you two gentlemen to me. Come!"

Flashy little Shill Burns started down the balcony toward a stairway that led to the lake edge.

Monk gave the lawyer a sidelong look.

"I can't savvy that mug, Ham. I wonder—"

The two aides of Doc Savage were trailing along.

"He knows something," said Ham.

"But—"

"He's a shrewd cuss. Perhaps he can help us."

Hairy Monk relaxed a little. "Yep. As much as I hate to admit it, I think you're right. Now maybe we'll find that Uppercue and Long Tom. Daggonit, Ham, this mystery is gettin' me."

For once, Ham was quiet and thoughtful.

At the lake edge, they climbed into a rowboat. The pets tumbled in after them.

Shill Burns wrinkled his nose at the sight of Habeas and Chemistry. He started to pick up the oars, but Monk took the rower's seat and went to work with bulging muscles.

Once Ham commented, "Those oars bend, useless!"

But they safely reached a landing ladder for the great stage, climbed to the footlights, stared at the vastness of the structure, and started moving toward the background of scenery.

Monk grumbled, "Dang it! I don't see no signs of anyone, or any goblin—"

Curtains parted backstage and six men with submachine guns cradled in their arms covered Monk and the lawyer.

The grinning-faced leader said sadly, "Here's one play that closes before the curtain goes up, dopes!"

Then he calmly went on taking bites at the apple which he held in his left hand.

CHEMISTRY

Chapter X
DEATH WITHOUT MUSIC

THE dapper lawyer and Monk were caught off guard.

There had been no one on the stage upon their arrival. Both aides of Doc Savage had been staring at the magnitude of this unusual large stage built right out in the lake, and at the looming vastness of the circular amphitheater across the water.

The six ugly black mouths of the machine-gun barrels took their minds off anything theatrical.

Monk exploded, "Say!"

He then jerked his little head around to ask Shill Burns what this was all about. "You dang well better explain this, you double-crosser—" the hairy chemist started to exclaim. But he stopped, stared.

Shill Burns had vanished.

At some point where the three of them had climbed up to the stage proper, Monk and Ham in the lead with the two pets, the overdressed Shill Burns had taken a silent departure.

Ham stared at the menacing gun barrels and commented, "Neat trick, wasn't it?"

Monk grumbled, "Ah!" and started to bellow.

Monk was ready to fight, guns or not. The apelike chemist liked to fight, and when he got into a scrap his squeaky voice always changed to a bull roar and he howled and bellowed. He was getting worked up to a fight now.

Ham advised quietly, "That won't help any, you dunce. Those guns will rip you apart."

But Monk howled, "Dang it—*them Tommies are fakes!*" and dived forward.

When the Tommy guns did not start their chatter of death, the thin-waisted lawyer leaped forward, too. The six gunmen dropped their weapons, grinned out of evil faces and started slugging at the two Doc Savage men.

One thug commented, "Hell, a lotta damage these two birds can do against six!"

The speaker was in error.

Like a cyclone released without warning, the hairy chemist grabbed two of the men, banged their tough heads together three times in quick succession and dropped the dazed figures to the floor. He reached for two more figures.

Ham had whipped his sword from his black cane handle and was using it deftly. That sword point contained a mild anaesthetic drug that, when the point flicked an opponent's body, quickly put him to sleep.

The dapper lawyer put two more of the thugs to sleep.

The "guns" that had been dropped to the stage floor were merely show "props," and were wooden. Monk had seen this in the moment before he had barged into the mêlée.

But Lonesome, the leader of the gang, had leaped clear at the first signs of Monk's fury. He had discarded the apple. He came up behind the two scrapping aides now and snarled, *"This* one isn't a fake!"

There was a roar, and lead slugs tore holes through the flooring at Monk's feet.

The heavy weapon in the grinning-faced leader's big hands was a riot gun of latest design.

Curtains parted backstage and men with submachine guns covered Monk and the lawyer.

Monk and his smooth-looking partner decided that maybe the leader meant business. They drew up short.

The long-eared pig and Chemistry had been scurrying around taking nips out of some of the prone gunmen. But now they, too, sensed danger for their masters. They likewise halted stiffly.

Monk scooped up Habeas and stood squinting at the crook leader's oddly-grinning face. He said blandly, "For a guy that looks like he's gonna bust out laughing, you sure sound gloomy."

Lonesome, the leader, said, "This face fooled the others, too."

"What others?"

"The ones that croaked."

"But who—"

"You two guys won't like the pit either," said Lonesome sadly.

A LITTLE later, the two aides learned what Lonesome had meant when he had spoken about the "pit."

The five dazed thugs were on their feet again—each was that degree of toughness that he had only been knocked out for a moment or two—and now they were in charge of Ham and the hairy-fisted chemist. Real guns taken from shoulder holsters covered Monk and Ham now.

The cut lips and swollen knobs on the heads of the five added none to their hard features. Expressions in the men's fishy eyes said that it was going to be fun rubbing out the two Doc Savage men.

Ham, trailed by Monk with Habeas held in his arms, was pushed down a flight of stairs backstage. There were numerous dressing rooms beneath the large circular stage; but Monk and the lawyer were directed away from these.

One captor said, "You guys get a special room."

The tone of the man's words caused Ham to give his partner a guarded, sidelong look.

But Monk was calmly scratching the porker's back, and looking as unconcerned as a toastmaster being escorted into another banquet room.

The route ended at a small trapdoor built into a wall. Monk had a time squeezing his broad form through the opening.

He put down Habeas, said something in a mumble to the pig and finally got his squat figure through. Ham followed with Chemistry at his heels.

Lonesome's men came in and grinned.

The place was a deep pit—an orchestra pit that was now far below the stage above. The lawyer had seen such places before.

Built along modern lines, the pit was really like a long, narrow room that could be lowered out of sight when the orchestra was not needed. All musical equipment had been removed from the orchestra pit, and now the space reminded Ham of a sleek-sided bear pit at a zoo.

It was fifteen feet up the smooth walls to the stage above, and there was not a single thing that could have been used as a foothold to climb those walls.

One gunman said, "Lie down on your backs."

Monk and Ham lay down.

Another of Lonesome's men said, "That's the right position to die in, anyway!"

He backed out of the wall trap opening, which was of heavy steel, and the others backed out one at a time also. Their leader, Lonesome, had not come down here with his henchmen.

Monk heard the door slam; then some sort of heavy bolt was shot home. Though the muscular chemist could look over his head and see night sky high above, he knew that they were just as effectively trapped as though they had been in a black dungeon.

Monk grinned, "They think they got us fooled!"

Ham looked at his partner sharply, scowled. "Listen, chump, just what *else* would you call it?"

The lawyer had walked around the room once, inspecting the trap briefly. He figured that these orchestra pits were raised by hydraulic water pressure. When he saw something—a small round opening—at one end of the room, his face looked worried.

Ham walked back and faced Monk. The hairy chemist was grinning cheerfully. He added to his statement.

"Yep," Monk said. "Those guys sure were dumb. I worked it right under their noses."

"Worked what, you missing link?"

"I wasn't scratching Habeas' back," continued Monk. "I was writing the words."

Ham scowled. "What words?"

"The message to Doc," grinned Monk. "I told him just where we were and to hurry over here. I whispered to Habeas to hurry back and find Doc. He'll use that powder on the pig's back, and my writing will fl—flour—"

"You mean fluoresce," explained the dapper lawyer.

"Yep. That's it. And now Doc will see the message and get us out of here!"

Ham looked relieved. "Sometimes," he said, "I think you're almost intelligent. You know what?"

Ham was indicating an opening, a small pipelike opening in one wall.

"What?" Monk queried.

"This platform is lifted by hydraulic water pressure," the lawyer explained. "Only now I have a hunch they've connected a water supply to this inlet here. Lonesome and his men plan to flood this pit and watch us drown like rats."

Monk looked undisturbed. "I sure was smart to send Habeas with that message then, wasn't I?" he said loftily.

Before Ham could reply, the bolt slid back in the wall trapdoor, and the grinning-faced Lonesome stuck his head inside for just an instant.

Lonesome's brief words were in strange contrast to his gosh-but-I'm-happy features. He spoke gloomily.

"Sending that message to Doc Savage was a dumb idea," Lonesome said. Then he slammed and bolted the heavy steel door.

He had been holding the pig, Habeas, in his arms.

LONESOME locked the hound-eared pig in a small room beneath the stage and proceeded to another, larger room where his men were waiting. It looked like a miniature League of Nations meeting with the gunmen in their frock-tailed coats and stovepipe hats.

But the circle of grim, bruised faces seemed more like those of a conference of thugs after a prison break.

One man grinned, "Well, chief, that takes care of Doc Savage's crowd. Now we can go ahead, eh?"

The grinning Lonesome said harshly, "How about those dames? Are they still where we left them?"

A second gunman spoke, "Sure, Lonesome. Gagged, too. I gotta hand it to you for efficiency, chief. I—"

"And that skinny bird called Long Tom?" went on Lonesome.

A third henchman grinned. *"He's* with the … the goblin boss. And they're takin' them over to that room where the brains wants Doc Savage brought."

One of the five men facing Lonesome laughed loudly. "Nicky sure fooled that Doc Savage!" he said. "Can you imagine a hood like Nicky posin' as one of them radio-car cops? He even—"

"Don't kid yourself about this bronze guy," Lonesome said icily. "You're never sure when you got him. Has anyone checked to make sure Doc Savage is in the operating room?"

The others shrugged. Apparently, no one had.

Lonesome growled a curse and stepped to a wall phone. He dialed a number and waited some time before there was an answer.

Then an obviously disguised voice said, "Yes?"

"Lonesome speaking," the happy-looking but grim crook said. "We got that Monk and Ham in the orchestra pit."

"Good!" the voice exclaimed. "That about makes it perfect."

"Then you got Doc Savage?"

A nasty laugh floated from the mouthpiece of the telephone. "I'll say we have. Right here in the operating room. The secret one. Those dumb doctors'll never find this place!"

"And Uppercue?" Lonesome continued.

There was a short, tense silence.

Then: "Never you mind about him anymore. *I'm* taking care of that angle."

A second later the voice added: "Don't forget to fasten that big tarpaulin cover over the orchestra pit. That will trap that lawyer and Monk Mayfair when you fill the pit. Those birds can probably swim."

Lonesome asked, "Then we better drown 'em now, huh?"

"You better wait a little," the man giving orders over the wire directed. "We want to make sure this operation works."

That ended the telephone conversation.

Chapter XI
STRANGE EYES

THE last thing Doc Savage recalled before being brought into the formidable-looking room he was in now, was something about an assailant saying, "Now we're gonna find out about that steel cylinder!"

After that, a sharp instrument had jabbed his back and he had remembered nothing. This had taken place in the police car driven by the phony Fair cop.

The bronze man's power of resistance to any kind of sleep-producing drug was unusual. Perhaps his great vitality accounted for this.

Thus he had soon thrown off the drowsiness, and now his senses were already alert as he was carried onto some kind of movable platform. The platform started rising in an eccentric arc. Doc Savage had the sensation of floating in endless space.

He tried to move, to stare about. But he was bound securely hand and foot. His eyes were covered with tape.

The thing he had been placed upon evidently was moving upward as near as Doc could deduce, and from unusual sounds that the bronze man caught with his sharp hearing, he knew that the platform was climbing inside some huge place.

It was a peculiar sensation.

The thing finally came to a stop, and Doc Savage recognized one of his captors' voices as the man said, "Carry the bronze guy into the secret room."

Doc Savage was lifted—it took all three men—and he caught the assorted odors of a hospital operating room. He felt himself dumped heavily on a long table. Immediately rough hands were fastening heavy straps about the bronze man's powerful legs and arms. Then the adhesive was yanked from Doc Savage's eyes.

For a moment, the intense light that struck Doc's unusual gold eyes was blinding. But slowly he managed to adjust his vision to that brilliant glare. Doc turned his head.

The room where he had been carried was some sort of laboratory. Doc saw racks of test tubes, retorts, dozens of shelves with bottles containing various drugs and chemicals. Directly over his head was a huge, convex window that now revealed the dark night above. The window was about twelve feet square and constructed of opaque block glass. But right now a cluster of blue-white colored lights were turned on beneath it, and it was this glare that had struck the bronze man's eyes.

Doc shifted his head again.

In one corner of the laboratory was a strange-appearing machine into which ran all sorts of wiring. The machine was built around a long operating-type table of white. Above the operating table were suspended big glass containers filled with odd-colored liquids. Rubber tubing went from the containers to massive-sized gadgets beside the table. These looked like giant hypodermic needles.

All this weird apparatus surrounded the thin, anaemic-looking figure strapped down on the tabletop.

Doc Savage's eyes widened. The bronze man seldom revealed his emotions, but his metallic features were tense now.

For the helpless figure bound to the operating table was that of the electrical wizard, Long Tom!

A DOOR opened across the room and a figure in white walked in.

Immediately, the three men close to the table where Doc Savage was held captive snapped to alert attention. These three were the two roughly dressed men from the police car rear seat, and the car driver himself—the one posing as a Fair prowl cop. All, from their talk, worked for the grinning-faced Lonesome.

The strong straps were holding the bronze giant across his chest, waist and ankles. But Doc could still lift his head a few inches from the table. He raised it now as one of his captors said, "Well, here's that Doc guy, professor. I guess gettin' him about cleans up the job, eh?"

The figure in white stood silently just inside the doorway. The effect was disturbing.

For the figure was clothed from head to foot in the garb of a surgeon ready to undertake an operation. There was the close-fitting white skull cap, a mask that covered the face, all but the eyes, and the white hospital gown tied in the back. From the elbows down, the arms were covered with long rubber gloves.

The eyes were the most chilling thing about the figure. This was because heavy goggles fitted close above the face mask, and behind the thick-lensed glasses the eyes appeared large and distorted.

Doc knew that the eyes could possibly be small. It was the goggles that gave the enlarged effect.

The figure spoke, "Yes, as far as you men are concerned, the job is about done. But mine has just started. Release the bronze man!"

One guard looked scared. "But, boss! This guy's dynamite! Better we should keep him tied—"

The figure in white showed a large gun that he had been holding concealed in his folded arms. The gun was a big .45 automatic, and now it aimed directly at the bronze giant's prone figure.

"Release him," the masked one rapped. "I've got to use him."

Doc had been straining his ears to catch every tonal inflection of the speaker's voice. It was a voice that held the first rather shrill, falsetto pitch of a person with a twisted mind.

Doc Savage had made an intense study of the human mind. So he knew that the way this person spoke, the somewhat nervous, shrill pitch, was indicative of near-madness.

Either that, or—another, more startling thought hit the bronze man—the figure could be that of a woman!

Doc was untied.

THE guards moved back swiftly, cautiously, as the Man of Bronze swung his feet to the tile floor. Doc flexed his cablelike muscles. In doing so, the insides of his arms felt for the special vest that he wore beneath his coat. The equipment vest with the secreted gadgets.

It was still there.

Apparently in their quick search of him for a gun, the guards had overlooked the vest. One thug was holding Doc's special machine pistol.

His gaze went to the strange eyes behind the goggles again. The figure was watching him closely, the .45 now shifted to train on Doc's head. The masked one addressed as "Professor," said, "I happen to know you use a bulletproof vest. But there isn't anything stopping a slug from entering your brain. So be careful!"

The speaker jerked his head toward another, smaller doorway across the room, and the three guards hurried out. A moment later, Doc Savage heard the strange whirring sound of the movable platform. It seemed to be dropping away into a bottomless pit.

Across the room on the weird-looking operating table, Long Tom's thin figure moved.

The masked one laughed.

"Your electrical wizard is drugged," the shrill voice said. "He hardly knows what this is about.

That, however, makes it all the better for the experiment."

The bronze man's eyes were wary. The gun had not wavered a fraction of an inch from his head.

"What experiment?" Doc asked.

"The Man of Tomorrow experiment," the masked surgeon said.

Doc immediately thought of the huge-sized, awesome figure—the goblin—that had seized Monk. His eyes narrowed imperceptibly, and then his gaze flicked to Long Tom, stirring restlessly on the operating table. Long Tom seemed to be slowly coming out of some sort of stupor. He was mumbling.

Doc asked of the masked figure, "You mean—the goblin?"

"That," said the one behind the magnifying goggles, "is the general idea."

Doc Savage could not help but give a slight start. The figure in white continued, "The goblin is called Maximus. But Maximus is a fool. He has no brain. The experiment ruined that. Maximus can only follow childlike directions. But—"

The shrill voice got thinner, more sharp. "But your electrical expert has a trained mind. His brain is far superior to most men's. It should withstand the terrific shock of the Man of Tomorrow power generation."

"Power?" Doc Savage asked vaguely.

The bronze man asked the question haltingly, as though slow to grasp what the other meant. But in reality, Doc's mind had never been more alert.

"Yes, power!" the masked speaker said. "Long Tom's brain in a body of giant size will produce the greatest man living—the Man of Tomorrow. I need one thing: the secret of producing a certain type of electricity—something that I'll call *animal* electricity, which is probably a by-product of processing tremendous voltages. This *animal* electricity will bring life into body cells of my giant man."

At the statement, Doc's lips showed the faintest trace of a smile. "And that's what has you stumped?" he said.

But the other shook his head.

"Scientist Martin Uppercue knows that secret," the garbed person jerked out shrilly.

"And Uppercue has disappeared," Doc finished.

The bronze giant sensed a feeling of relief. Perhaps, then, there was still a chance for Long Tom and—

Doc's guard laughed oddly. "No, Uppercue is not missing. I have him right here in the next room. I'll say this for him: he has a great scientific mind that cannot be swayed. He has refused to reveal that secret."

Doc Savage nodded. Relaxing slightly, he said, "And so you're stumped. Without that secret, you cannot—"

The figure in white started shaking its head slowly. The eyes looked strangely mad behind the magnifying goggles.

"No," the masked surgeon said slowly. "I was in that audience that watched you and Dr. Mandroff operate this afternoon. I understand your unusual powers, Doc Savage. So I know Martin Uppercue is going to reveal his secret!"

"Reveal—" Doc started to query.

The masked one held the .45 steady and motioned toward the doorway through which he had entered.

"Yes," he finished. *"Because you're going to make him reveal it!"*

THE power of Doc Savage's unusual eyes was not a mystery to many men of science. Those eyes had been known to hypnotize a man within a few seconds. The scientifically trained mind behind Doc's eyes held an amazing control over men of average intelligence.

If necessary, the bronze man could even sway the minds of men of almost equal intelligence to himself.

That seemed to be the white-garbed surgeon's idea in regard to Uppercue.

Doc was at last facing the missing scientist who had disappeared under such queer circumstances.

Small, white-haired Martin Uppercue was tied in a straight-back chair in the room adjoining the laboratory. His birdlike, wiry figure was no longer tense and active; instead, something of the brilliant man's intense energy had gone from his slumped figure.

"Uppercue!" the white-garbed figure rapped. "This is Doc Savage, remember? *Look at him.*"

Martin Uppercue looked like a person who had been beaten until life was uninteresting to him further. He raised his white head slowly and stared at the bronze man out of bleak eyes. For a moment, there was no recognition.

The man in surgeon's garb was standing to one side of Doc, the gun still trained on the bronze giant's head. He said now, "You're going to talk, Uppercue. You're going to tell about that steel cylinder. Where is it? What is in that tube?"

At the words, Martin Uppercue stiffened.

His marvelous brain, the one part of him that had not been conquered by terror or threats, again rebelled.

"I'll never … talk!" Martin Uppercue managed to get out. He looked more directly at Doc Savage now. The eyes had lost a little of their dullness. It was possible that the little scientist recognized the bronze figure, though he said nothing to indicate it.

To one side of Doc, the masked figure snapped,

"All right, hypnotize him. Make him talk. If you don't—"

The man broke off and waggled the .45 significantly.

Doc asked, "Have you got some bright object?"

In hypnotism, it is usually helpful to have the subject center his gaze upon some bright and shiny object.

Acting carefully, keeping well out of the bronze man's reach as he held the gun steady in one hand, the figure in the mask tossed over a ring taken from

Doc's hypnotic eyes raked the masked figure.

beneath the surgeon's gown. It was a small ring with a bright, clear stone, that held and reflected the light from a bulb overhead.

Doc noticed that the fingers of the masked figure, though rubber-gloved, were long and slim like a woman's.

Doc took the ring, glanced at it, rubbed it on his sleeve.

"Careful!" his captor warned.

Doc's hands had been close to his coat. The white-garbed one was taking no chances on the physical giant's unusual capabilities.

Then Doc Savage started talking, holding the bright-stoned ring before Martin Uppercue's gaze. The bronze man's words were soft-spoken, low, yet the tonal inflection of those words held a strange vibrancy. They were compelling, fascinating, gripping.

Slowly, the little scientist's eyes went to the ring and his gaze held there. This was the first step in hypnotism.

As Doc talked, and without an apparent movement of his head, he managed a sidelong glance at the masked figure, to one side of him.

Behind the disguising goggles, the strange eyes were shifting back and forth between Doc and the ring.

The bronze man talked on in a vibrant monotone.

Without a single pause, steadily, like the certain, throbbing beat of a jungle drum, Doc Savage's voice intoned words that would weaken Uppercue's resistance.

Once, the thin scientist shot a swift glance to the bronze man's flake-gold eyes. As though he read a message there, his gaze went back to the ring and its compelling attraction.

Doc was saying, "You are going to tell me of the metal cylinder, Martin Uppercue. Remember? The cylinder that you were carrying when you ran from your laboratory. Think. Think hard! What is the secret of that tube, Martin Uppercue? What is—"

As he spoke, Doc sent a quick glance from the corner of his eyes. The masked one's own gaze was intent upon the ring.

Doc said without a break in his vibrant flow of words, *"Drop that gun!"*

The deadly .45 in the hand of the surgeon slipped to the floor.

Martin Uppercue strained against his bindings, his words hardly those of a hypnotized man.

"You did it, Doc Savage!" Uppercue shouted. *"You've hypnotized him!"*

Chapter XII
ONE-WAY EXIT

MARTIN UPPERCUE'S exclamation was correct. For Doc Savage, instead of hypnotizing the helpless scientist himself, had been cleverly drawing the masked figure's eyes to the ring. The figure in white had, unknowingly, centered his gaze upon the bright stone.

The bronze man had not tried to hypnotize Martin Uppercue. Doc had revealed this in a quick, appealing message to the little scientist as he talked. The masked person had not perceived that glance.

But Uppercue had made one mistake. He had shouted. That was sufficient to break the spell the moment the white-gowned surgeon dropped the deadly .45.

Understanding of his error immediately leaped into the eyes behind the goggles. The masked one moved.

There was no chance to retrieve the fallen gun. Doc Savage was already leaping forward.

So the figure in white twisted, plunged toward a cabinet standing against one wall of the room.

The cabinet contained many sharp-bladed operating instruments. The masked man's rubber-gloved hand plunged through glass door and all, then the figure whirled with a deadly-looking knife in his hand, leaped toward Doc.

Doc Savage had lost the machine pistol to one of the guards who had helped bring him here. To pause and pick up the masked man's fallen .45 would have been fatal. And Uppercue was tied helplessly in the chair.

Doc's agile fingers had gone beneath his coat. They came out with a small object taken from his special equipment vest. Doc hurled the vial.

The thing struck the masked figure's knife hand, burst, and a quick-acting anaesthetic gas enveloped the masked surgeon's face. The gas was a type that should easily penetrate the gauze mask that hid the figure's face.

Doc's assailant staggered, brushing at the air before his goggled eyes. He backed against a far wall, swayed there for an instant, and then started slowly collapsing to the floor.

The bronze man spun toward helpless Martin Uppercue. The scientist's small eyes were bright. "Gracious, now we'll find out who that devil is!" he exclaimed.

Doc quickly untied straps holding the scientist's wrists to the chair arms. He spoke rapidly, briefly.

"You can loosen your own ankles," Doc said. "Try to hold your breath. That gas will float over here shortly. It is harmless. I've got to—"

Doc Savage heard the humming sound of the movable platform. Outside the adjoining room, he could hear the strange object lifting again, coming up from some mysterious depth.

The guards were returning!

The bronze giant whirled toward the operating room and reached Long Tom's prone figure. The electrical expert's eyes were open, staring at Doc; but there was a vacant, stupefied look in their depths.

Doc Savage quickly loosened the table straps, then reached inside his coat. His bronzed hand came out with a shining hypodermic needle. He swiftly jabbed the hypo into Long Tom's arm.

Almost immediately, the aide started reacting to the injection. The hypo was a powerful stimulant that would counteract the drug in Long Tom's system. And though frail-looking, with a pallid color that made him look anemic, Long Tom had never known a sick day in his life. His little skinny form was tough, hard—whipcord and muscle.

Long Tom jerked up on the table and exclaimed, "Doc!"

The Man of Bronze nodded toward the door through which he'd been brought into the room, said, "Gunmen are on the way."

The hum of the strangely rising platform was quite loud now.

Long Tom had stooped, to remove something strapped inside his trousers leg. It was one of the special machine pistols that all the bronze man's aides carried.

"Cover the door," Doc directed, as he whipped back toward the adjacent small room. He had to tie up the masked figure, help Uppercue, return and aid Long Tom before the gunmen arrived.

As Doc neared the doorway, he tossed a small lozenge into his mouth. The lozenge contained a form of concentrated oxygen that would counteract the effects of the gas Doc had thrown in the vial. He took out another capsule to give Martin Uppercue. The gas might have reached the scientist—

Across the threshold, Doc Savage drew up with a jerk. His metallic features went grim. More than the gas had reached the slender little scientist.

Both Martin Uppercue and the masked figure had disappeared.

DOC peered swiftly around.

The only exit from this smaller room was the entranceway back into the operating room. There were no closets; nothing save a couple of chairs, a table and the broken glass instrument case. There was a telephone on the table.

There was a similar opaque glass skylight in the ceiling, as in the adjoining, larger room. Doc had noted a queer thing about those ceilings; they were convex and low.

The only manner in which the masked figure and Martin Uppercue could have escaped would be through a secret panel. Obviously, thought the bronze man, the goggled surgeon had not been completely knocked out by the gas. The gauze face mask must have saved him. Thus he had regained his strength long enough to seize Uppercue and escape.

There was no time to search, for at that moment a bull-fiddle roar cut loose back in the operating room.

Doc Savage hurried that way.

The door leading to the floating platform thing had crashed open and one roughly dressed man had leaped in with a gun in his hand.

But Long Tom had been ready. Mercy bullets from the special pistol in the electrical wizard's hand had caught the first arrival in the legs. The man went down mouthing oaths.

He would not die.

Doc Savage and his men never took a life needlessly. They preferred, when possible, to use gadgets that made a fight bloodless. And Long Tom realized that Doc wanted to capture these men now, to question them.

A second gunman—the fake Fair trooper—swung into the room. His gun was blasting even before he saw the bronze man. The thug was aiming at skinny Long Tom.

The third guard was jumping into the room behind his fake cop partner and, with a snarl, he also yanked out a gun.

Long Tom's queer-looking pistol cut down the second thug. Again the mercy bullets had struck in the legs, and the man would recover, to talk. The special bullets only caused temporary unconsciousness.

But the twisted expression on the third gunman's face said that he would not go down until he had brought death to at least Doc or his assistant.

So the bronze man hurled the powder that brought temporary blindness to anyone in its path.

The gunman choked, batted at his eyes, started triggering his gun recklessly. But he was shooting too high, through the enveloping powder that brought the blindness.

Doc Savage called to Long Tom, "Hold it."

The aide of Doc Savage had been ready to bring down the third and last arrival. But Doc did not want the sound of Long Tom's pistol to draw the blinded thug's fire.

The man fired his last shot through the opaque glass skylight above. A pane of glass crashed downward; a gust of night air came into the room—and blew the powder directly into the faces of the bronze man and his assistant!

They staggered about blindly.

Doc called, "Careful, Long Tom! That gunman is over toward that entrance door."

Doc Savage, even with his unusual eyes temporarily blinded, had an uncanny sense of direction. He headed toward the thug.

Doc heard the door slam and a second later the whirring sound of the movable platform motor.

Doc announced grimly, "He's escaped. Can you see, Long Tom?"

The aide was making growling sounds somewhere nearby.

Both men were so blinded that they seemed to be fumbling around in pitch-black night, though lights were still on in the room.

Long Tom said, "Blazes! I'm kinda mixed up!"

The telephone in the adjoining smaller room started ringing.

MOVING carefully, hands stretched out before him, Doc reached the inner room and the phone. Lifting the receiver, the bronze man imitated the missing masked surgeon's voice.

It was a call from Lonesome, beneath the amphitheater stage. The grinning henchman of the masked surgeon thought he was talking to his chief. He had called again to ask a question about Monk and the dapper lawyer.

Doc Savage thought quickly. He knew now where his two assistants were held captives. Lonesome also spoke vaguely about the girls being safely tied up in some other place.

Lonesome was taking it for granted that his chief knew the location of that hideout. It would not be wise for Doc to ask questions about it. Better to hold Lonesome and his killers off until he and Long Tom could get to the amphitheater stage.

Thus, Doc Savage directed, in the masked figure's voice, that Monk and Ham be kept alive until they were certain the operation on Long Tom was a success.

Lonesome believed these were orders from his chief, the masked one.

Still moving in blind darkness, Doc Savage hung up the receiver. Somewhere behind him, Long Tom exclaimed:

"Say, Doc! I've found it!"

"Found what?"

"A way outa this danged place!"

Doc Savage moved cautiously forward, toward the source of Long Tom's voice. Doc knew that, in a few moments, the temporary blindness would wear off.

He said, "But there's no door."

"It's a panel," said Long Tom. "And it opens outward. I can feel it. Wish I could see, dang it! It swings outward and there's some sort of space behind—"

Suddenly, there was a sharp cry from Doc's assistant. Long Tom started to shout, "Hey, Doc! I'm falling—"

And the words died away as though the thin electrical expert had dropped like a plummet into a bottomless pit.

In his worry for Long Tom, perhaps Doc Savage moved a little too swiftly. Also, he had not realized he was so near the secret panel. Furthermore, the panel had swung open, and remained that way, thus leaving no wall for Doc's sensitive fingers to touch.

Doc stepped through the opening before he realized he had gained the wall.

He went plunging downward.

Chapter XIII
ADAM ASH IS MISSING

BECAUSE Doc Savage was a physical phenomenon who was practically fearless, and who had faced death in many forms, he did not cry out when he plunged into space. The sensation was doubly awful when it is considered that the bronze man was still blinded from the powder.

But in that brief second before Doc's shoulders hit a slick surface and he went skidding downward at a furious pace, he had realized that the secret panel could not possibly lead to death.

For certainly the masked surgeon and Professor Uppercue must have used this exit.

Doc knew that he was hurtling down a long, steep slide, much like the chutes used in a fun house at Coney Island. Only this particular slide must have started at a great height, for the plunge downward was breath-taking, and at train speed.

Finally, Doc felt a slackening in his terrific rush; the chute was flattening out. Built like a highly polished and waxed semishell, there was not a single thing to grasp.

But slowly the bronze man's form was coming to a stop.

Ahead some place, Doc Savage heard a commotion. It was Long Tom, his aide, and he was growling oaths.

A moment later, Doc dropped down beside the thin electrical expert. The slide had ended, to dump the bronze giant man off its end and into some sort of small room. Doc Savage felt his body hit double trapdoors that swung quickly downward. They whipped back into place again as he cleared them.

His large form brushed Long Tom's, and the aide exclaimed, "Whew! I sure thought I was a goner that time, Doc!"

Doc Savage asked, "Can you see yet?"

"I dunno," Long Tom said curiously. "Either I can't see, or this hole we're in is black as night."

Doc said, "Wait."

He took a flashlight from his special vest and flicked it on. Doc could see nothing.

To Long Tom, he said, "How about you?"

"How about me, what?"

"I have a light turned on," stated Doc.

"Then I'm still blind," announced the electrical wizard.

DOC removed a small vial containing a solution from his inner vest. He broke the vial, reached for his aide's hands in the dark and directed, "Here, rub some of this on your eyes."

Both men wiped their eyes with the solution, and almost immediately they were able to see again. The liquid was a special preparation of the bronze man's invention, made by Doc to counteract the effects of the temporary blinding eye powder.

They stared around as Doc Savage directed the flashlight ray.

Long Tom said, "It's some sort of tunnel. There's pipes and all."

Doc nodded. He was directing the light overhead, pointing it at a thin, almost invisible line where the double trapdoors had swung back together. The spot was about eight feet over his head.

"That," Doc said, indicating the closed doors, "makes it impossible to ever reach the secret laboratory again. No one could possibly climb that steep slide. It must have been over two hundred feet long."

"Do you remember how you got into that room where they had me?" Long Tom asked.

Doc shook his head. "They used drugs. But there was the odd sensation of the way that platform moved. It didn't go straight up."

"Yet that room was at some high point," the electrical expert offered. "Remember that funny ceiling skylight?"

Doc nodded.

"What was that masked devil goin' to do to me, Doc?"

The bronze man did not answer. Often, when Doc Savage had hit upon some idea, some explanation of a mystery, he preferred to unravel the whole case before stating his findings. He was turning a clue over in his mind now, and a part of the conclusion he had reached was startling.

Doc said, "For the present, it will be impossible to know where we were just now. Uppercue knows the answers to this mystery. And so does that masked surgeon—or, at least, part of the solution. He is holding Uppercue until he learns more."

"Then we better trail them," suggested Long Tom. He was indicating tracks in the dust at their feet. Apparently the tunnel was one seldom used, and there were scuff marks in the dust.

But Doc Savage shook his head.

"If we don't hurry and find our way out of this place," he went on, "it might be too late to save Monk and Ham."

Long Tom started to say, "Then we better—"

The startling, guttural chuckling of the thing they knew as the "goblin"—the creature called Maximus—came from somewhere ahead in the underground cavern.

USING the light, Doc Savage plunged ahead through the dank tunnel. As Doc explained hastily to Long Tom, "I want to meet this Maximus. I want to see him."

Running at Doc's heels, the electrical expert shuddered.

"Maybe you better not, Doc. That guy, that goblin's got the strength of ten men. Just lookin' at him almost scared me to death—like back there in the mine shaft."

Briefly, Long Tom explained about that.

It seemed there had been a way into a basement cavern through the flooring beneath the mine. Maximus, the electrical expert said, had pulled a supporting timber loose inside the tunnel, then leaped with Long Tom into the trap opening.

Long Tom remembered, vaguely, of passing downward and into some underground room. There a masked man had met them and said something about turning on a water-main valve.

Prodded by Doc for further information, Long Tom stated that he had been knocked out by Maximus, and could recall nothing further until he came to on the operating table.

"Was it a place like this?" Doc asked.

Both men were still running through what seemed to be an endless maze of pipes. They had found no trace of the weird thing that had made the chuckling sound.

"Ye-es," Long Tom said thoughtfully. "It was like this."

"Then," Doc snapped, "that explains it."

"Explains what?"

Doc told about finding Monk in the manhole opening.

He continued: "There are fifteen miles of water mains, thirteen miles of gas mains, and another fifteen miles of electrical conduits beneath these grounds, besides thirty miles of sewers."

Long Tom whistled. "An army could hide down here, then."

"Or be hidden," Doc Savage put in significantly.

And he added: "Many of those ducts—like this one—will probably never be used. Thus it is simple for the villain to duck out of sight easily and appear elsewhere on the Fair Grounds."

The electric expert looked puzzled. "But how are *we* goin' to get out of this danged place, Doc?"

The bronze man had paused, to study a section they had just entered. They had been running stooped over. This part they were now in was higher, though, and was joined by a line coming in at right angles.

"This," Doc indicated, "looks like a way out."

It was.

There was a narrow steel ladder, leading to above. Since they had found no trace of the goblin, Doc reminded his assistant of the predicament of Monk and Ham. Doc hurried up the ladder, Doc in the lead.

It took a man of the bronze man's great strength to raise the massive iron cover that sealed them below ground.

Then they were out in the night again. Both men stared silently around.

Suddenly, Long Tom said, "Listen, Doc!"

Voices were talking. One was sharp and clear. The speaker was rapping: "Look, you hairy baboon, try to raise *this* side!"

Doc said, "That's Ham."

"And he could only be talking to one person that way!" Long Tom added.

Yet the only thing close by was the huge, deserted amphitheater and the lake, calm and fog-shrouded in the night.

THE bronze man and Long Tom had moved around to a point directly in front of the great amphitheater. They were standing near the lake edge.

Though the massive, open-air theater was apparently deserted, the squabbling voices of Monk and Ham sounded clearly. It seemed they were somewhere above, in one of the balconies.

Long Tom asked curiously, "Doc, what could those two guys be tryin' to escape from up there?"

There had been something about, "Trying to raise this danged cover!" Monk's words echoed clearly in the night.

"Acoustics," the bronze man stated. He added: "But Monk and Ham aren't here."

"But where—"

"The amphitheater acts like a great sounding board for any speech out there on the island stage. The voices of Monk and Ham are carrying from there. We need a boat."

Long Tom looked puzzled, but quickly followed Doc as the bronze man moved toward a small dock at the lake side.

Soon they were silently rowing toward the dark stage.

When Doc and his assistant had, a few moments later, climbed the steps to the broad stage, they heard the splashing—a commotion beneath a heavy tarpaulin cover across the orchestra pit.

Monk was heard to squeal, "Hey, shyster! Get this danged Chemistry off my back! He's pullin' me under!"

Doc moved swiftly to the edge of the stage, at a point directly above the disappearing orchestra pit. Beside him, Long Tom could see where the heavy canvas cover was securely tied down. Apparently, Monk and Ham had no knives to slash the tough material, and water that was slowly filling the pit was trapping them like rats.

From his equipment vest, Doc quickly got a sharp-edged instrument. He worked fast with long, sweeping movements. A section of canvas was opened up.

Doc directed, "Over here, Monk."

The bronze man directed the flashlight ray downward.

Shortly, the hairy chemist, with the pet ape clinging to his back, climbed out, helped by Doc Savage. Ham followed. Both aides looked half drowned.

Monk squealed, "Goshamighty, Doc! They filled that place with water, an' it was almost to the top!"

"You mean—Lonesome?" Doc asked.

Monk glared. "Yep. And that grinning devil has Habeas! I'm gonna—"

"Perhaps," Doc warned, "we might use a little caution. We might be able to trap Lonesome and his mob." The bronze man looked at Ham, who seemed to be the less excited. "You know where they are, Ham?"

The lawyer, looking much distraught, because of his wet, expensively tailored clothes, said, "We can reach their hideout from backstage."

He led the way.

But just as they reached the rear of the wide stage, Doc suddenly paused and raised his hand for silence. He said quietly, "Listen!"

The others stood silently.

Behind them, from out on the water, there was the sound of oars, squeaking in oarlocks. And voices. Voices that carried plainly between the massive backgrounds of stage and amphitheater.

Doc Savage recognized Lonesome's voice, and the grinning-faced thug was saying: "So we gotta find him. The chief says he must have the accumulator, and that's the one gadget stoppin' the experiment, now."

A second harsh voice floated across through the foggy night.

"What's an accumulator, Lonesome?"

"It's about the size of a suitcase, and if you birds find it, you better be careful how you handle it. The chief says that dingus could stop the Niagara Falls power plant itself!"

"But—"

The voices were fading. The boat was heard to scrape the side of a dock near the amphitheater. Doc Savage's aides could hear nothing else.

But the bronze man's unusual hearing detected still further conversation.

The last words he caught were:

"So you guys look for Adam Ash!"

Chapter XIV
STORM CLOUDS GATHERING

APPARENTLY Lonesome's men had known of the arrival of Doc Savage and Long Tom at the island stage. Besides, the gunmen had left by some rear exit and their boat had not passed the front of the stage proper.

Monk was all for taking right out after Lonesome's gang in order to get Habeas. And another thought hit him.

"The girls, Doc!" Monk piped. "Daggonit, they've got Pat and that nifty little blonde hidden some place, and maybe—"

Ham said significantly, "The only reason that hairy mistake was worrying about being drowned just now, was because he hasn't had a chance to date that Kay Uppercue."

Monk grumbled, "There's somethin' subtle about that crack, shyster. I—"

Doc said, "Temporarily, I believe the girls—wherever they are—are safe. That masked surgeon figures Kay Uppercue knows something. He doesn't dare harm her. And Pat can take care of herself."

"But—" Monk started to query.

"Lonesome is perhaps on his way to meet the masked man and Uppercue."

Doc Savage looked at his aides, gave brief orders.

"Long Tom will look for the girls. Ham, you and Monk follow Lonesome and try to learn the way into that secret operating room. Uppercue will most likely be taken back there. Get equipment from my car and keep in touch with me."

Ham looked worried. "But Doc, whatever this experiment those guys are planning is—what if they start it—"

Doc and his aides had climbed down from the stage again and were preparing to shove off in the rowboat.

The bronze man interrupted the lawyer's query.

"Apparently they're stalemated," Doc said. "Because of one thing. Something called an accumulator. And the person who has that is missing."

Hairy Monk suddenly remembered the trick played upon him by the little, flashy Shill Burns. He told briefly of the voluble man who had brought them there, and ended with, "Dang it, Doc, I'm gonna find that guy. He's mixed up in this mystery someplace!"

"It might be a good idea," offered Doc.

Back at the shore of the amphitheater, Doc Savage questioned Long Tom quietly. He mentioned the small model generator he had seen in Uppercue's laboratory. The electrical wizard's eyes widened, and he said:

"Doc, Uppercue was secretive about that. I don't think it had anything to do with this Man of Tomorrow experiment on which the Fair people were getting ready to release publicity. It was something else."

"Correct," Doc said. "And in that generator model there was a tiny part missing. Enlarged from scale,

that unit would be about the size of a suitcase. Did you ever hear of an atomic accumulator, Long Tom?"

The electrical expert's eyes went wide, and perhaps a little horrified. "Big electric companies have experimented with those accumulators!" he exclaimed. "Given perfect insulation, an atomic accumulator could store energy equaling millions of volts. Enough for that thing to drain the power of the largest electrical distributing plants. Why, it would even wreck—"

Doc nodded.

"That," the bronze man said, "is the general idea. And the missing metal cylinder that Uppercue was first carrying has something to do with it, also."

Long Tom was abruptly tense. He gripped the bronze man's arm. The electrical expert's scientific brain was swiftly fitting pieces of a gigantic idea together. He gasped:

"Doc, that place where we were taken, that trick, movable platform—I was thinking of that little model you saw in Uppercue's lab. Good Lord, could they be planning—"

The bronze man interrupted quietly, though he, too, was tense. "You're on the right track," he stated. "So, hurry. In the meantime I'm going to locate the man who seems to be holding the key to the whole thing."

"You mean—"

"That person seems to be Adam Ash," Doc finished.

Shortly after this conversation with Long Tom, Doc disappeared on a mission of his own.

BUT by the following night, the mystery still had not been solved.

And a new mystery had developed at the great Perisphere. All during the day, visitors had been refused admittance to the giant globe of steel. The news spread; one stranger told another:

"They won't allow you in the Perisphere!"

"Why?"

"I dunno. But I heard some fellow talking about a goblin."

"What's a goblin—can it hurt you?"

"Danged if I know. But I'd sure like to know what is wrong in there!"

And so it continued. One telling another. People jamming up along the circular mall encircling the Perisphere and causing no end of trouble for the Fair cops. There was confusion, questions, wonderment.

The excitement increased throughout the day. There were two persons, though, who were unaffected by it.

Monk and Ham had followed seemingly endless

miles of the tunnellike pipe line conduits that honeycombed the vast grounds. Lonesome and his men had completely eluded them.

From their car, they had obtained a sound-detector device to use in locating any secret byways in the underground mains. They were also carrying a portable shortwave transmitter and receiver with which to keep in touch with Doc Savage.

Both aides were grimy and tired from their trek through the gloomy, stuffy, narrow tunnels. But Monk never slackened in his rolling stride, as he said: "They got Habeas. And that runt pig is smart. Maybe if Lonesome goes to where the girls are hidden, Habeas will get back with a message, somehow."

Ham snorted. Chemistry, the ape, trailing along at his side, the pet's face dust-smeared from peering into dark places, bristled, too.

"That fool pig couldn't find his own way home," the lawyer said unkindly. "And all that's bothering you is shining up to that blonde, Kay Uppercue. I'll take Pat any day."

"I'll take 'em both," Monk said.

The bickering continued throughout the day.

IN the meantime, Long Tom was on a similar hunt. He had gone back to the manhole where he and the bronze man had left the underground pipe lines, traced his way back to where he and Doc had landed in a heap after tumbling down the long slide.

There seemed to be no way whatever of getting back up above, to the strange operating room where the masked one had held him captive.

The electrical wizard took time out to make careful calculations. He worked his way slowly back to an exit and as he did so, jotted down figures on a piece of paper.

He had also been using a compass.

When Long Tom was outside in the crowded Fair Grounds again—it was late in the afternoon now—he plotted his way back to a spot that should be almost over the point where he and Doc had piled up in a heap underground.

The electrical expert stared. Slowly, Doc's comments of the night before took on great significance in this active mind.

Before Long Tom loomed the massive, round bulk of the Perisphere. He saw the excited crowds and elbowed his way through.

Tense with excitement, Long Tom hurried up to an entranceway to the huge sphere. He had to get inside now, had to—

A uniformed Fair policeman stopped the electrical genius at the door and said, "Sorry, sir, but the Perisphere is closed to all visitors."

"Closed?" skinny Long Tom said.

"There seems to be something out of order. No more visitors will be allowed inside."

The anemic-looking aide of Doc Savage turned hurriedly away. Perhaps he could locate the bronze man back at Doc's car, still in the parking lot behind the Hall of Medicine. Something told Long Tom that there was need for haste. The Perisphere was closed! Closed because—

Long Tom started running through the crowds. *He had to find Doc Savage!*

UNLUCKILY, the bronze man had left his parked sedan only a few moments before Long Tom's arrival. Doc had spent the whole day trailing Adam Ash, the young public relations consul. The last clue had led back here to the Hall of Medicine. There, the trail ended.

Doc tried to raise Monk and Ham on the short-wave set in his car, and receiving no reply, took a few moments' time to visit the youngster he had operated on in the Hall of Medicine.

The boy was in a special hospital room that the bronze man had ordered for him. None would ever know that Doc Savage was paying all the lad's expenses here.

Doc found Dr. Alexis Mandroff in the private room with the patient. Mandroff reported cheerfully:

"He's doing fine, Mr. Savage. But he just dropped off to sleep. Too bad you can't talk to him."

Doc gazed at the small, calm face in the white bed. Color had already returned to the thin features. Gone was the expression of pain and fear that had been on the lad's face such a short time ago.

Beside the bronze man, Dr. Mandroff said, "The nurse says he is picking up rapidly. *Da*—yes, you certainly performed a marvelous feat, sir."

They moved quietly outside to a corridor.

The bronze man told Dr. Mandroff that he was seeking Adam Ash. Doc did not state his purpose, but merely mentioned that the young public relations consul could not be located.

The tall doctor with the straw-blond hair was smoothing fawn-colored gloves over his hands. He picked up a medical bag from a nearby table, looked at Doc Savage out of keenly sharp eyes. "That's odd," Mandroff said. "I don't know why he should be keeping out of the way. He was here only a few moments ago, and said that he was going over to watch that moon-rocket experiment tonight as soon as it gets dark."

Both men were approaching an exit from the building.

Dr. Mandroff asked about the missing scientist, Professor Uppercue, about the mysterious way in which Uppercue had disappeared.

But Doc Savage did not mention the experience in the hidden operating room. He merely said, "The scientist cannot be found. I think it is more important to first locate Adam Ash."

Dr. Mandroff offered brief apologies for leaving. "I wish I could help," he said. "But I have an urgent call into the city. Perhaps I could meet you tonight—"

Doc Savage nodded.

"I'll be looking for Adam Ash over by that moon-rocket tryout," he finished.

Mandroff shook hands and left.

But by nine that night, though the bronze man scrutinized hundreds of faces in the great crowd waiting to view the moon-rocket sensation, he had not located Adam Ash.

DR. MANDROFF had been correct in stating that Adam Ash was going to watch the moon-rocket experiment. Adam Ash was observing the fantastic event now. But he was not in the jam-packed crowds around the tower where the rocket was to be released.

Adam Ash was seated in his small coupé in a landscaped small lane some distance away.

There was a strained look on the slender, brown-eyed man's good-looking features. The place where he had chosen to park was well away from the Fair crowds. Adam Ash seemed greatly worried about something.

Once, he got out of the car to walk around to the rear and unlock the rumble seat. He peered inside. Looking reassured, he closed the rumble lid and relocked it.

The object he had checked upon was a flat, long case of suitcase size.

Some distance ahead, where practically every visitor at the World's Fair was gathered, a great roar suddenly went up.

They were releasing the rocket.

The moon rocket contained no human beings. It was merely a test flight of a torpedo-shaped, huge object of silver color. Inside the rocket had been placed the newest scientific devices for recording the moon rocket's flight. If the rocket ever returned to be gripped by the earth's pull of gravity, special radio-controlled machines would guide it to a landing.

The strange thing left the Fair Grounds with a shrill whistling sound that could be heard for miles.

There was merely a silver streak—though huge floodlights had been rigged up to illuminate the rocket—and then floating down from the heavens came a stream of sparks, cascading like some multicolored comet.

Adam Ash stood beside his coupé, his head strained backward, and watched those trailing sparks with tense fascination. Almost at the same moment thunder rumbled far off, and a flash of lightning cut through the sky.

The grumble of the thunder perhaps covered the heavy step that sounded behind Adam Ash.

Too late, the public relations consul sensed the feeling of some bulky object close to him, and whirled.

The thing was a towering giant of man size, and its hair was red. The facial features were set in a blank, chilling stare, the wide eyes apparently fastened on some distant object.

Adam Ash attempted to leap clear.

But powerful arms seized the young man's slender form, whirled him off his feet; from the giant's throat there came a guttural, weird chuckling.

Adam Ash choked out, *"Maximus*—the goblin!"

Overhead, as though angered by the invasion of the man-made rocket, the heavens loosened a thunderclap that drowned out Adam Ash's frantic cry.

Chapter XV
STAIRWAY TO DOOM

ANOTHER man had observed the trail of sparks from the moon rocket. And then, later, he again peered heavenward as the storm gave muttering warning of its approach.

Doc Savage was that observer, but he was no longer near the crowds gathered to watch the rocket's fantastic flight.

The bronze man had returned to his big sedan. He was able to contact Monk and Ham with the shortwave radio this time, and shortly they put in a bedraggled appearance. For once, the usually sartorially perfect lawyer was dust-smeared and grimy. Even the high polish of Ham's sword cane was dulled.

Chemistry, the ape, looked moth-eaten.

Monk reported complete failure in their search for Lonesome and his men. He spoke sadly about Habeas, still missing.

Doc told about trailing young Adam Ash.

"You found that crook, then?" Monk asked.

The bronze man shook his head. "No," he said. "And it seems apparent that he is not a crook, Monk."

"But—"

"I've been checking up on him," Doc went on quietly. "Adam Ash is Kay Uppercue's fiancé. He is a close friend of Professor Uppercue. Along with his public relations work here at the Fair, young Adam Ash has been helping Martin Uppercue in his experiments at night. Ash is somewhat of a scientist himself."

Monk got his scarred face screwed up in a knot. He looked puzzled.

"But Doc," he said, "I can't savvy why this Adam Ash is hiding out—"

"Because," the bronze man continued, "he was given something by Martin Uppercue to protect. Uppercue was taking no chances. The metal cylinder, which has strangely disappeared, was part of the mystery. Something that resembles a suitcase is another part. I believe Adam Ash has it."

Weary-looking Ham put in suddenly, "Here he comes now!"

ADAM ASH, tall and smartly dressed in his pin-striped trousers and morning coat, walked up to Doc and his aides as though just meeting them casually while out for a walk. He hardly looked like a person who had been attempting to hide from some vague menace.

Adam Ash said quite calmly, "I was looking for you, Mr. Savage."

Doc Savage said nothing for a moment. But his flake-gold eyes were unusually sharp. Some slightest change in the good-looking public relations consul's voice had been only noticeable to the bronze man. That voice seemed just a trifle shrill.

Doc finally said, "I missed you at the moon rocket send-off. Dr. Mandroff told me you would be over there."

Adam Ash nodded. "That's right. I was watching that trail of sparks behind it. Did you ever see anything quite so marvelous?"

Doc Savage admitted that he had watched the show.

Monk, listening curiously, had to get out a question that was bothering him. Out it came with a rush.

"Say, Ash," Monk piped shrilly, "you sure been actin' funny. What's the idea?"

The calmness dropped from Adam Ash's dapper slender figure. He looked worried.

"I'm convinced I can trust you men," he said confidentially. "I have learned of Doc Savage's worthwhile work since I first met you. Yes, I've been keeping under cover. But now I think I need your help—your assistance to help save Martin Uppercue from something terrible about to happen."

"Yes?" prompted Doc Savage quietly.

Adam Ash cast a worried look at the dark sky overhead. The thunder was growing nearer. He said tensely, "If this storm breaks, the person behind this mystery will do everything in his power to work the test tonight."

"What test?" Ham prodded.

"The experiment in the Perisphere!" Adam Ash blurted fearfully. "But first, they'll need the metal cylinder. They've already stolen another necessary unit from my coupé. If we could get into the Perisphere, perhaps—"

The bronze man appeared uneasy. He said, "Monk, try to contact Long Tom from the car."

The hairy chemist leaped to obey Doc's order.

A second later, he returned, to report, "Long Tom's down in Uppercue's laboratory, Doc. Says

he's located that real metal cylinder. Says to send somebody over there quick—"

Adam Ash seemed to reach a sudden conclusion. He addressed Doc Savage.

"I know a way into the Perisphere, even though it's closed," he put in quickly. "Monk and Ham, here, can go and meet your man named Long Tom. But right now, we've got to stop a fiend up there in the Perisphere!"

Doc Savage prepared to leave with Adam Ash. "You mean," he asked, "the Perisphere is the location of that secret operating room?"

Ash nodded jerkily. "And more!" he cried. "Tonight, if the storm breaks, *a new Man of Tomorrow will be created!*"

A moment later the bronze man was hurrying toward the huge, looming Perisphere with Adam Ash. Monk and Ham had gone partway, to circle the globe in an opposite direction and enter Uppercue's laboratory near its base.

Neither Doc nor his assistants could have known of the appearance of Maximus, the goblin, as Adam Ash watched the moon rocket's blazing trail!

IT had started to rain. With the occasional flashes of lightning, the threat of the coming storm, the night Fair visitors were rapidly leaving the grounds. Besides, it was getting late now, and it appeared that the storm was going to be a bad one.

Doc Savage and grim-looking Adam Ash passed an entrance to the globular Perisphere that was guarded by a uniformed Fair officer. This was at the same

ADAM ASH

door that Long Tom had tried to enter earlier today.

But now Adam Ash walked up to the man in uniform, spoke a few words, and the cop turned to unlock a heavy entrance door. He gave a friendly smile as Doc and the public relations consul stepped inside the mammoth globe.

They seemed to be in some sort of walled shell, much like the inner "skin" of a great ocean liner's hold. Within this double-walled shell was a curving ladder that snaked upward into gloom.

Adam Ash abruptly indicated the ladder and said sharply, "You won't walk up that, bronze guy. You'll be *carried* up!"

He stepped aside and a half a dozen assorted gunmen leaped from dark corners of the arc-shaped room. The leader was the man of the beady eyes and the hell-let's-go-out-and-ring-doorbells grinning face. Lonesome! His voice was a harsh snarl.

Lonesome said, "Watch out this bronze mug doesn't go for one of his trick gadgets! Close in on him careful, you birds!" Then he continued eating the apple which he held in his hand.

Six menacing automatics cautiously closed in on Doc Savage. The weapons were in the steady hands of the hardfaced men.

Doc was ordered to put his hands behind his back.

Strangely, the bronze man offered no resistance. And right beneath Doc's armpits, if he moved his arms in a certain way, were hidden small containers that would have sprayed an enveloping black gas into the faces of all.

But Doc Savage allowed himself to be tied hand and foot.

"Get Maximus!" Adam Ash ordered sharply. He referred to the goblin.

A moment later, the huge, shambling thing with the red hair came through a nearby door. It stood before tall Adam Ash, its staring, blank eyes fastened on the public relations consul in a fixed manner.

With a soothing, strange tone, Adam Ash directed, "Maximus, you are going to carry the bronze man to the operating room on top of the Perisphere. Understand?"

The giant creature made a queer throat sound. It moved close to Doc Savage.

DOC was tense, unmoving. His metallic features showed no expression, no indication of his thoughts as he studied the goblin known as Maximus. He saw the bloodshot eyes of the thing, the broad, vacant stare of the set face, the drab-gray, loose clothing that covered the massive body.

Doc was lifted into the huge man-creature's arms. Slowly, monotonously, Maximus started the long climb up the curving ladder.

The bronze man knew that they were mounting the great arc of the Perisphere shell, going higher and higher toward that strange operating room in the very top of the globe. Outside, rain hammered down and beat against the sides of steel. The rumble of thunder increased, and the huge ball seemed to tremble.

Somewhere behind the bronze man, the voice of Adam Ash queried, "All exit doors are locked and barred?"

The gloomy voice of Lonesome replied, "The devil himself couldn't get in, boss. The only escape now is down the chute."

Adam Ash's voice seemed to be dropping back.

He said, "Then we'll go to meet that Long Tom and the others. We sent Monk and the lawyer to meet him." There was a shrill laugh, a satisfied sound from Adam Ash.

Someone said, "Jeez, boss, are you goin' to start the thing?"

"That," came Adam Ash's voice faintly, "is the main idea."

And high up on the upper half of the great globe, still gripped in the arms of the goblin as the creature climbed, Doc Savage recalled that small generator model in the laboratory of Martin Uppercue, beneath this very giant sphere.

The model represented a type of spherical generator which had been developed on a huge scale by various electric manufacturing companies. Its design was known to be more efficient than any other type. Millions of volts had been generated in tests with various ones built.

And now—

Doc Savage's thoughts leaped to different parts of the table model he had inspected briefly. Yet that inspection had been sufficient for the bronze man to retain an exact picture of the whole unit itself.

Martin Uppercue's spherical generator was an exact reproduction *of the giant Perisphere!*

Chapter XVI
MAD MENACE

ONE of the reasons for the success of Doc Savage's constant fight against evildoers throughout the world was the close unity between the Man of Bronze and his aides.

A spoken word from the giant bronze man, and any one of Doc's assistants could be depended upon to follow through with some particular assignment.

Doc Savage had mentioned to Long Tom, the electrical expert, something about the small model generator in Martin Uppercue's laboratory. Immediately the unhealthy-looking aide's quick mind had followed the bronze man's trend of thoughts.

As soon as possible, Long Tom had therefore returned to Uppercue's laboratory, somewhere beneath the great Perisphere.

It was here that he had contacted Monk, at the shortwave set in Doc's car, announcing that he had located the odd metal cylinder.

Long Tom had found the thin tube hidden in a cabinet near a workbench where the model generator was set up.

Placing the cylinder to one side, the quick hands of Long Tom had gone to work on the model itself. It was quickly dismantled. The electrical wizard's sharp eyes widened as he worked swiftly.

He located the small missing part and, from quick calculations, saw that the unit which was needed fitted in at the very top of the spherical motor. In actual size, it would be the shape of a long suitcase.

Long Tom remembered the "accumulator" that the bronze man had mentioned.

Recently, Long Tom had lectured before a group of famous engineers on the possibilities of such an accumulator. The atomic machine was a unit capable of storing unlimited power. Hooked into a power transmission line, an accumulator would be capable of draining the current and putting out all lights in a large-sized city.

One thing had halted the perfection of such an invention. A perfect insulator was needed with which to protect the suitcase-sized unit, when in operation in connection with a huge, spherical generator.

Long Tom was intently studying the one tiny part of the model that was missing. He knew now that Martin Uppercue, fearful lest someone should steal his secret, had left something out of that small-scale model. He had also—

Abruptly, there was a commotion behind the electrical wizard. He whirled to face those who had come into the passageway from outside.

It was the waspish-looking Ham, arguing with hairy Monk as they hurried into the laboratory. Behind them trailed Chemistry, the small chimp.

Monk squealed excitedly, "Long Tom, look! That guy Adam Ash is with Doc, an' he had a clue to somethin'. We're all to hurry and meet them. Maybe we'll find the girls there, too; and like I was tellin' Ham—"

Ham managed a pained sneer. "Wait till that Adam Ash learns you're on the make for his girl, you missing link! There's going to be trouble starting—"

From the vaultilke door leading to the larger laboratory beyond, well-dressed Adam Ash said coldly:

"Trouble has already started, friends!"

TALL Adam Ash stepped into the room with an object in his hand that had been taken from Doc Savage when he was brought, drugged, to the secret operating room. It was the machine pistol, a

deadly weapon when the regular high-powered explosive bullets were used.

Long Tom saw, with a start, that the drum attached to the weapon was loaded.

Hairy Monk's small eyes had blinked rapidly at the sight of Adam Ash. He let out a bull roar.

"You tricked Doc!" the powerful chemist yelled. "You—"

Monk suddenly whipped a pistol from his torn clothing and started blazing away.

But Adam Ash had acted a split second before the gun cut loose. He had leaped back through the protecting, heavy vault door, to take up a position behind the steel casement.

From somewhere deeper in that room, came a shattering roar as one of the gunmen with Adam Ash loosened a hail of machine-gun lead.

Pellets spattered the walls near the heads of Monk and Ham. Long Tom had leaped for a corner of the room and switched off the ceiling lights.

Adam Ash was shouting orders above the roar of gunfire. Another death gun took up its nerve-racking chatter.

And then, from the only other passageway leading out of this underground room, Lonesome's sad-sounding voice yelled, "I'm lockin' the door, boss. Give 'em the gas!"

The door slammed to the passageway that could have been the only possible exit for the three aides of Doc Savage.

Immediately from the vaultlike opening through which an orange-red stream of gunfire was coming, there was the sinister hiss of gas.

Chemistry was squealing.

Monk howled, "Blast 'em! I'm goin' through that door and get that traitor Adam Ash! I'm gonna—"

"Wait, you fool!" Ham snapped in the darkness. "I've got something that will knock those devils out of their shoes. Here, give me a hand."

Monk located the lawyer's voice. Ham was crouched in a corner of the darkened room, out of range of the deadly machine-gun fire.

As Monk crept up to his side, Ham said, "I've got a hand grenade. Picked it up from Doc's car before we came over here. But the pin's stuck. Here, take a hold."

Monk reached out to help, bellowing happily, "For once, shyster, I got to admit you're smart. Wait'll we toss this pineapple at those birds—"

The chemist struggled with the jammed pin in the hand grenade. Luckily, it did not release.

For the knockout-gas fumes that enveloped the three aides and the pet, Chemistry, within the next two seconds put them swiftly to sleep.

DAPPER Adam Ash gave terse orders a few moments later as Monk, Ham, Long Tom and the pet were carried from Uppercue's laboratory.

An exhaust fan—located in one wall of the lab—had been turned on and the room quickly cleared of the gas fumes.

The public relations consul's eyes were cold, and there was a smirk on his thin lips. "This," he said to the grinning-faced thug beside him, "takes care of Doc Savage's crowd. Take them up to the operating room, Lonesome."

Lonesome looked incongruous with the heavy machine gun cradled in his arm. For he was still wearing the high silk hat and "tails." The fixed grin of his mouth hardly went with the menacing Tommy. "Hell, chief, let's give it to them right here."

The eyes of Adam Ash snapped. "You're forgetting the experiment, you fool. Take them above—up the catwalk." The queer, shrill tone that Doc Savage had noted, was now back in Adam's Ash's voice.

The three aides and the pet were carried through the big motor room where Doc had first found Kay Uppercue. The catwalk took the men high above the electrical equipment of massive size. Somewhere in the long, high-ceilinged room, there was the soft, steady purr of a small booster dynamo running.

Gunmen reached the small opening in the ceiling, a direct opening into the huge Perisphere above. Iron steps led upward.

Adam Ash paused to see that everyone was out of the big motor room below. Then, with a twisted grin on his lips, he stepped to a heavily insulated control panel built near the catwalk.

Large contact switches of varying sizes were at his fingertips. Adam Ash started slapping the switches home—closing the electric circuits.

Immediately, the motor hum in the power room increased.

Like the shrill "winding up" of a big transport plane inertia starter, the motor hum increased to an ear-splitting howl.

Adam Ash laughed with almost insane glee. "And now," he grinned, "the *real* generator starts!"

Above him, waiting in the entranceway to the huge Perisphere, the grinning-faced Lonesome commented: "That little dude, Shill Burns, didn't do bad when he led those guys our way, boss!"

They moved on into the place above.

THIS was the vast, awe-inspiring interior of the Perisphere itself. But now a strange transformation was taking place. Levers that Adam Ash had thrown had started a movement of giant-sized units in the two-hundred-foot-high globe.

Sections of a massive machine were swinging out into position overhead. The men carrying Doc's aides paused a moment and stared in wide-eyed wonder. One thug shivered slightly.

"Hell, boss," he gasped, "if this thing ever gets out of control—"

Adam Ash snapped an order. "Move!" he said shrilly. "Take those fools up the curved ladder. The movable platform has been dismantled. Others are guarding Doc Savage and the rest, above."

Lonesome, his own voice a trifle awed, remained behind, to query, "Say, chief, that storm is sure goin' to be a corker!"

Outside the great steel ball, the fury of the universe seemed to have been unleashed against the Perisphere. Thunder cracked ominously; a steady trembling took place beneath the sphere's very foundation.

Adam Ash laughed queerly.

Sounds of the storm seemed to remind him of one more thing to be done. He stepped toward a barred exit doorway near the base of the Perisphere.

Loosening a heavy steel bar, he opened the door to let in a burst of wind and rain. A lightning flash revealed his satanic face for an instant.

Adam Ash said, "I'll get back through the laboratory entrance. Bar this last exit. There's one thing I must do."

Lonesome stood there grinning, his voice gloomy. "But, chief, you better not—"

"That fool, Shill Burns, must be located," finished Ash. "He's just dumb enough to stumble onto something. I've got to get him, also."

The queer laugh that Adam Ash gave as he disappeared into the night sent a chilly feather of ice racing down his henchman, Lonesome's, spine.

Lonesome had been standing polishing an apple on his sleeve. Ready to take a bite, he lowered the apple and stood with his mouth half open.

Chapter XVII
THE GENERATOR STARTS

SHILL BURNS was not a brave man. But the flashily dressed little talker was an opportunist. Any little racket in which he could collect his own ten cents' worth—while still keeping within the law—appealed to the gum-chewing little sharpshooter.

Burns had seen a chance to cash in on the Martin Uppercue disappearance, and the night he had followed the strange figure of the goblin—Maximus—to the Marine Amphitheater on the lake, he had really been sincere when directing Monk and Ham to the stage. Shill Burns had hoped for a nice retainer.

When Lonesome and his men had struck, Shill Burns got scared and ran for cover. He had hidden out throughout that night and the next day.

But now, moving like a little wet terrier in the rain and scary claps of thunder, he was stalking the deserted Fair Grounds, trying to bring himself to call the police. He knew, somehow, that Doc

Savage was in trouble. Yet Shill Burns was afraid to contact the law. He had been mixed in shady dealings in the past.

Shill Burns spent an hour trying to make up his mind.

He went back to his little concession office with the determination that he would put through the phone call. And tall, gray-eyed Dr. Alexis Mandroff was there waiting for him.

Shill Burns had seen the doctor several times, knew him by reputation. He was surprised at this complimentary visit.

Dr. Mandroff smiled and asked, "You're Shill Burns, *da?*"

Shill's chest expanded.

"No other, friend, no other. To whom am I obligated for this—"

Dr. Alexis Mandroff's light features grew suddenly serious.

"Doc Savage, a friend of mine, once mentioned you," Mandroff hurried on. "Now he and some of his aides are missing. I thought you might be able to help me locate them. I'm afraid something has happened—"

Shill Burns suddenly decided that he had kept still long enough.

"My friend," he said confidentially, getting his gum out of the way, "that thought is mutual. I'm telling you, it's something beyond our grasp. And yet I have an idea—yes, an idea—"

"What?" interrupted Dr. Mandroff, trying not to appear impatient.

"Now you take that Perisphere," said Shill Burns. "There's something damned mysterious going on there—"

"Then we should investigate," suggested Mandroff. He was carrying a cane, and wearing the expensive fawn-colored gloves. He stepped toward the door. The doctor was also wearing a cape against the downpour outside.

Shill Burns grabbed a coat and quickly followed. He said worriedly, "Friend, I gotta hunch Doc Savage is somewhere *in* that damned globe."

WHEN Doc Savage was carried into the weird operating room atop the Perisphere globe, and untied, to be guarded by the ponderous, red-haired Maximus, he had made no attempt to escape.

For the bronze man had permitted himself to be brought here. It was in this place that he had hoped to find the others—Martin Uppercue and the two girls.

For the bronze giant had suspected Adam Ash's trickery!

Martin Uppercue was there, tied again in a chair, and close by were also the bound, shapely figures of lovely Pat Savage and the pretty Kay Uppercue.

The girls' faces were pallid, drawn from their dire experience, and yet Pat Savage managed a smile.

Doc, after being searched to make certain he was unarmed, had been permitted freedom by gunmen who stood guard in the room. Besides, the brute-sized Maximus stood towering nearby.

Doc had thought first of the girls.

They were all in the smaller room adjoining the operating room.

Pat Savage said cheerfully, "For once, my dear cousin, I looked for trouble and found it! Are you angry?"

The bronze man was silent. For Doc knew that only one ending awaited all of them now: death!

He turned to little white-haired Martin Uppercue.

The scientist said, "Thanks, Doc Savage, for almost rescuing me once before in this room. But I'm afraid there will be no chance at a rescue again." Uppercue looked significantly at the menacing guns in the hands of the guards close by.

His voice was weary, though no fear showed in the little bright-eyed man's face.

"You know what's in there?" Uppercue asked, nodding toward the adjoining, larger room.

Grinning, the gunmen permitted Doc Savage to look.

The bronze man saw more bound figures laid out on tables near the weird operating platform. Above the heads of the stupefied victims, rain slashed the opaque glass of the convex skylight. Lightning seemed to leap right out of the heavens above and smash against the glass covering. The broken pane had been patched.

Doc returned and spoke to the scientist. "Those are the missing Fair visitors who were jabbed with hypodermic needles in the crowds. I almost got the same treatment from Lonesome, myself. They were to be used to fake the Man of Tomorrow publicity surrounding your own experiment."

Uppercue nodded his bushy white head.

"Correct," he said. "No man can create a man. That poor devil, Maximus, was a Fair visitor himself, once. He was given injections of thyroxine and adrenalin—and changed rapidly into a pituitary giant. But, in the experiment, his will power was destroyed. Now he only follows the directions of that masked devil who has him hypnotized."

Doc mentioned that he was aware of the method used. He had figured something like this when he had checked with the gatekeeper about the missing persons, and when an attempt had been made to jab himself with a hypo near the Hall of Medicine.

He said, "The Man of Tomorrow stuff was merely publicity to draw the Fair crowds—and a shield to cover your own experiments. But the masked surgeon cashed in on it. Obviously he is mad enough to really believe a superman can be created."

Across the room, small Kay Uppercue and Pat Savage were staring in open-mouthed horror.

Doc's metallic features were tense. "Given the proper voltage, life might possibly be brought to body cells," he continued. "That is something of this masked one's idea, I believe."

Just then there was a disturbance at the door.

HAM and Monk, along with Long Tom and the pet ape, were carried into the room. The three aides had started to regain consciousness. Monk was struggling like a bull ape to break loose from several scar-faced captors.

Monk saw the two girls and let out a roar of protest.

"What the hell do you mean, tyin' them girls up like that?" he bellowed.

In the doorway behind them, Lonesome said gloomily, "I'm going to take pleasure in rubbing out that dish-faced guy!"

Before Monk could think of a suitable retort, everyone was held tense by the strange vibration that began to fill the room.

The bronze man's gaze flicked to the scientist, Uppercue, and he saw the look of utter horror in the little man's eyes.

Professor Uppercue stammered, "My God! He ... *he's started the Perisphere generator!"*

The hum of some massive motor was slowly, inexorably increasing into a deep-throbbed whine.

Even several of Lonesome's gunmen looked nervous.

One said, "Say, Lonesome, where's the chief? I don't think it's goin' to be so damned healthy hangin' around here much longer!" The gunman was jittery about the electrical whine below them.

Lonesome rapped, "Shut up!"

But he, too, sounded worried.

As everyone listened in awe to the weird, slowly increasing speed of the mammoth generator in the massive ball beneath them, a guard suddenly appeared and shoved two more figures into the room. He said to Lonesome:

"I caught these two guys snoopin' around!"

The two newest captives were the loudly dressed Shill Burns and tall Dr. Alexis Mandroff.

Chapter XVIII
UNMASKED FIEND

EVERYONE stared at the last two captives brought in.

Shill Burns, protesting volubly, clutched regal-looking Dr. Alexis Mandroff's arm and cried:

"Like I said, Doc, you're important! You got connections here at the Fair. Tell 'em they can't get away with this—"

The blond-haired, tall doctor shrugged his shoulders hopelessly.

"It looks," he said quietly, "as though you and I have nothing to say about that."

The masked fiend, through his chief henchman, Lonesome, now had captured everyone who might frustrate his plans.

It was hairy Monk, kicking up a fuss as he tried to wriggle out of his bonds, who croaked hollowly, "All right, where is he? Where's that yahoo behind all this trouble—that Adam Ash?"

Petite Kay Uppercue, hearing Monk's words, stared out of horror-filled eyes. She stammered: "You ... you said ... Adam Ash—"

Doc Savage knew that the small blond girl had been engaged to the good-looking public relations consul, Adam Ash.

Monk realized his error. The way in which he looked at Kay Uppercue said that he thought she was swell, and now to have blurted that Adam Ash was the real fiend—

It was Dr. Mandroff who interjected with: "Do you mean to say that young Adam Ash is the one behind all this? Why, I never dreamed—" His voice broke off shrilly.

The well-known doctor looked at the bronze man, at others in the room.

Kay Uppercue was crying softly.

Pat Savage, stiffly erect in the chair in which she was tied, looked at Doc Savage.

Like Monk, Dr. Mandroff realized his error.

He said thoughtfully, "I'm sorry, Miss Uppercue. I ... I didn't understand."

Only the bronze man himself had been acting strangely.

DOC SAVAGE appeared not to have heard the others. Instead, he had been intently regarding the massive figure of Maximus stationed near himself to act as guard.

Doc had caught the huge giant's stary eyes, was looking into their depths peculiarly with his own. The bronze man's compelling eyes were like unwavering, accusing pools of restless gold.

Everyone stiffened as the bronze man spoke.

With great tonal inflection, Doc Savage ordered: "Maximus! You are listening to me now, understand? You are to obey me."

The increasing generator vibration that gripped the whole Perisphere seemed to lend power to the bronze man's words.

"Maximus—*bring us Adam Ash!"* rapped Doc Savage.

Slowly, eyes fixed ahead as though in a trance, huge Maximus shuffled step by step to the center of the room.

Fascinated, Lonesome's accomplices stepped

aside, held spellbound. The gunmen had seemed to forget that the bronze man was unguarded, now that Maximus had moved away from his side.

In the middle of the room, Maximus paused. Close above his towering form, the smaller glass skylight of this inner room was within reach. The giant figure reached up, released a catch and slid the panel back on a groove.

Even Pat Savage shuddered slightly as the fury of the storm lashed into the room. Thunder rolled in great waves; jagged streaks of white lightning seemed to leap to the very opening above.

The huge hands of Maximus reached outward into the storm—and dragged from the roof of the massive steel ball a soaked, limp form.

The half-conscious figure of Adam Ash was dragged to the bronze man's feet!

Pat Savage gasped.

Kay Uppercue crowded her small knuckles against her teeth and tried to stifle a scream.

Monk's eyes almost bulged in their pits of gristle. He piped, "Now, how in hell—"

Maximus stood dumbly by, awaiting the bronze man's next order.

The mind of Doc Savage, his great will power, had conquered another sinister brain that controlled the one of the dumb brute!

LONG TOM had been roughly dumped in a corner of the room when dragged into the strange Perisphere hideout. But he had twisted to one elbow now. He asked of Doc: "But ... but if Adam Ash wasn't the masked man, then who—"

Others, too, were asking that question silently. Even the hard-faced thugs of Lonesome were staring at Doc Savage. Apparently none had ever known the true identity of the masked director of crime, and now—

One thug asked, "Then where *is* the masked guy?"

Through the room, even above the ever-increasing moan of the monstrous generator in this sphere underneath them, an exotic trilling note floated. It was the identifying sound the Man of Bronze made in moments of mental stress—or perhaps approach to near danger.

And covered by the generator whine, no one had heard the stifled exclamation, the intake of breath of another person in that room.

Yet Doc Savage had heard—because he had been listening for that very thing.

It was Martin Uppercue who cried, "But the accumulator! It is priceless! Where is it, Doc Savage?"

Again the bronze man looked at Maximus. He said firmly, steadily, in that strangely compelling tone: "Maximus, now get the accumulator."

The huge man-monster again moved toward the middle of the room, leaned one hand on the table and reached upward with the other into the rain that was hammering into the room.

The hand of Maximus paused. He turned uncertainly, his staring-eyed gaze going to Doc Savage, and then shifting away, as though pulled by some other force.

Doc Savage said tensely, "One man in this room has controlled Maximus. He is trying to overcome my power over this dumb servant now. Because that person also needs the metal cylinder—*and someone in this room has it!*"

The bronze man's words must have proved a startling shock to the real villain. For the moment, his control over Maximus was lost. The huge giant again looked at Doc Savage, seemed to nod in agreement—and reached again toward the roof opening.

There was a shrill cry of anger from a person near Doc Savage. A man plunged toward the table directly beneath the open roof skylight.

The well-tailored form of Dr. Alexis Mandroff, his wet cape billowing out behind him, mounted the table in a single swift bound. Agile, slender hands clawed the roof opening and the blond-haired man raised himself swiftly out of sight.

Alexis Mandroff's face had been twisted with maniacal fury.

DOC SAVAGE fired orders.

"Maximus! Help the hairy one. And the man with the sword cane by his side. Untie them. Hurry!"

Spellbound by the sudden exposure of a man they did not even know had employed them, the bulging-eyed gunmen were slow to move. The ropes were yanked from Monk Mayfair's wrists by Maximus, with one powerful twist, and the release of Ham followed.

The hairy chemist dived headfirst into a slow-moving thug, grabbed a gun and let out a whoop.

"I'm sure gonna raise havoc now!" Monk bawled.

Monk blasted away with the gun.

A thug returned the fire, but his aim was wild. Perhaps he, too, had been startled by the form of Dr. Mandroff leaping out onto the very top of the globe of steel.

Uppercue was screaming, "The accumulator! He's after the accumulator, Doc Savage."

But the bronze man had swung with powerful, cabled arms out to the slippery, rain-swept roof. Two hundred feet below lay the lightning-illuminated Fair Grounds. More than a dozen steps either way from that small opening atop the Perisphere, and the bronze man's form would skid to swift doom on the curved, slick surfaces of the sphere.

And towering over all, seemingly only a few feet away, rose the three-sided spire that was the Trylon. It lofted still another half thousand feet above the globe of steel—and from its sides now bombarded flashes of light.

The Trylon, during a storm, was constantly struck by lightning which harmlessly followed its tapered length into the earth.

Doctor Mandroff had whirled back toward the bronze man with an object in his hand. It was a long case, approximately the size of a large suitcase. He snarled shrilly:

"Even you cannot stop me now, Doc Savage. I'm going back down there into the room!"

With his free hand, he fired the .45 automatic.

Doc Savage had been in the act of hurtling at Alexis Mandroff. Weight had been thrown forward on the balls of the bronze man's feet. The heavy .45 slug caught him in the chest, and he pitched sideward, to roll toward the curve of the roof that dropped off sharply to the wide circular mall far below.

OUT here in the storm-lashed night, the weird roar of the Perisphere generator was a thing that penetrated far. It was like the combined bumblebee hum of a thousand bombing planes. It was not a deafening sound, but rather a vibration that sent a strange chill through all.

It was too late for Fair visitors now—yet many had gathered far below the spot where Doc Savage and Mandroff were fighting.

Those persons were the Fair police, attracted by the uncanny sound of the giant generator, and hundreds of late workers and exhibitors who had been on their way home for the night.

Prowl car sirens screamed like insignificant play horns, against the greater noise enveloping all. Armed coppers battered against the heavy, steel-barred doors that had been closed at the Perisphere base. No one could find a way inside.

And as Doc Savage was seen by Mandroff to slip toward a plunge of death, the mad-eyed doctor leaped back into the roof room with the precious accumulator case in his hand.

But Mandroff had not figured on the trained hands, the fingers of Doc Savage. Daily, the bronze man exercised various parts of his marvelous body. Those bronze-colored hands contained a grip of steel.

Doc's fingers had splayed as he struck the curved roof. Fingertips had flattened mightily against the wet steel surface. Like a vacuum-cup tire grips a slippery pavement, Doc's fingertips had stopped his slide.

Slowly, he pulled himself back to the roof opening. He had not been injured by the .45 slug. Doc's bulletproof vest had stopped that bullet.

But the force of the shot, catching the bronze man partially off balance as it did, had been enough to make him slip back on the sleek-surfaced globe.

Doc Savage leaped back toward the Perisphere room.

Chapter XIX
DEATH STRIKES HIGH UP

A TERRIFIC battle was taking place within the room of the Perisphere.

Hairy Monk had taken time out between pile-driver swings, at Lonesome's men, to leap to Long Tom's side. The skinny-looking electrical expert had been lying helplessly in the same corner of the room. Monk swiftly unbound his wrists.

Yet Long Tom made no attempt to get up and join the mêlée. One leg remained stiffly straight before him on the floor, as though broken.

But Long Tom picked up a crook's fallen gun and bopped heads as Monk and Ham sent dizzy victims flying his way.

And huge Maximus, apparently still obeying the will of the great bronze man, joined in to help Doc's aides.

One of Lonesome's henchmen saw the twisted face and figure of Dr. Mandroff plunge back into the room from the roof opening. He took one glimpse at the hurtling Mandroff, and bawled, "Me, I'm gettin' outa here! This damned Perisphere is goin' to shake itself apart any minute!"

The thug went diving through the secret panel wall opening that Doc and Long Tom had once before used. Another gunman followed, yelling in fear. The great sphere of steel was actually vibrating on its base. It appeared that over a hundred thousand tons of metal threatened to collapse at any second.

Monk let out a yell and raced to the wall opening where the thug had disappeared down the chute. He was holding something solid in his hairy fist, jerking at the object with his other hand.

Then Monk bellowed, "I got it, Ham. I got that danged pin outa the grenade. Lookit this, will ya!" He tossed the bomb, and a second later there was a tremendous roar somewhere below in the escape chute that led to the underground pipe lines.

It was Long Tom who cried shrilly, "Fool! That's the only way out of here. We're all doomed now!"

Monk looked startled.

In the excitement, they saw Mandroff for the first time.

The doctor, with the heavy suitcase-shaped accumulator in his hand, had leaped past the fight to reach an outer wall of the room. This roof prison was built between two outer layers of the steel Perisphere, and in that outer wall was another four-foot-wide partition of thin steel.

MANDROFF had pushed a wall lever to raise a partition of that outer narrow room. He plunged inside and yanked something downward with his hand.

He turned, his eyes wild, his face contorted.

"Fools! No one can reach me now. There's an escape ladder in here. As soon as I charge this thing, I'll send you all to doom beneath tons of crushed steel—by letting the Perisphere generator run wild and tear itself loose!"

Monk and Ham drew up short, to stare. Apparently nothing separated them from the wild-eyed doctor.

Doc Savage came hurtling into the room from just above as Monk, with a howl, dived toward nearby Alexis Mandroff.

Monk said, "I'll get that guy—"

And then he gave a yip of pain. The hairy chemist had cracked his head against something that appeared to be only empty space between him and the doctor.

From where he was still tied, Professor Uppercue exclaimed, "It's a sheet of shatterproof, invisible glass. You can't reach him—"

The little scientist's alert eyes suddenly popped like round saucers. "Look! He's putting the accumulator into the slot! My God, we'll all be—"

The bronze man's brain had remembered the model generator construction in that fleeting, precious instant. He said, "But he needs the insulator—the steel cylinder."

Abruptly Doc went into whirlwind action. He started shoving everyone toward the adjoining operating room. He slammed orders at Monk and Ham.

"Get everyone out of here!" yelled Doc. "There's no time to untie anyone. Take them, chairs and all. Hurry!"

The bronze giant had already swung helpless Pat Savage and Kay Uppercue up by a chair in each arm. He plunged through the doorway.

The room was cleared in seconds. The bronze man was the only one to see the crazed Alexis Mandroff's last movements.

Behind the glass screen, the doctor had finally worked the heavy accumulator into a special groove made for it somewhere in the Perisphere generator outer wall.

There was a sudden peculiar humming. And then the ozone smell that electricity makes when burning.

Doc Savage himself moved back into the room with the others.

But from the large glass skylight of this larger room, everyone saw the weird arc of flaming lightning that came from the very heavens above, from the top-most point of the skyscraper-high Trylon that adjoined the great ball.

There was a horrible crash, and the Perisphere seemed to rock and sway. In the outer shell room where Alexis Mandroff was crouched, liquid fire split the thin steel wall at his back. Steel melted around that spot, melted like a thin scrap of tin caught in thousands of degrees heat. Molten steel splashed off the side of the Perisphere at that one concentrated point.

There was a single scream of horror from the doctor.

Then there was only the stench of flesh and the ozone smell.

Alexis Mandroff had died the death of white-hot fire.

BREATHLESS seconds passed. No one moved in the outer room that had been protected by the second inner wall of the great sphere.

Professor Martin Uppercue breathed finally, "We ... we'd better not let the girls look!"

Doc Savage had gone into the small room close to the shell partition where Mandroff had sealed himself in. The bronze man said quietly, "There's nothing to see. Only dust!"

Dust was all that remained of the fiend who had been Mandroff.

Suddenly, Monk yelled, "Hey, Doc! The blasted thing's stoppin'. Listen! The Perisphere generator's dyin' down!"

It was true. The whine that had accompanied the awful trembling of the massive sphere was fading. Vibration slackened.

Doc said, "Perhaps Martin Uppercue can tell you the explanation of that—and of Mandroff's death."

The bronze man had released the small, bright-eyed scientist.

Uppercue said shakily: "The accumulator is my invention. It might be compared to a storage battery. Only it stores power—thousands and thousands of volts of energy. The Perisphere generator—the largest spherical generator ever designed—was needed to *charge* the accumulator. It would only take the massive generator below a matter of seconds to completely charge it."

"But how—" Ham started to ask curiously.

Uppercue went on swiftly, his keen eyes bright. "Mandroff had been to my laboratory often. He had seen that model of the Perisphere generator. I told him, and others, in order to cover my real work, that we were planning a Man of Tomorrow experiment and thus needed greater electrical generation than had ever before been produced."

Ham had to get the question out. "But why was he killed?"

Doc Savage answered the query.

"Because Mandroff failed to use the one thing needed to make the accumulator a success," he explained. "That is the insulator, which Uppercue, here, had in the metal cylinder—the cylinder he tried so valiantly to protect, and which Long Tom found hidden back in his laboratory. The insulator was needed while charging the accumulator, and to protect it *after* receiving that charge. Without it—"

The bronze man indicated the space where Dr. Alexis Mandroff had only a few moments before been.

"Instead," Doc went on, "when no insulation was there to hold that terrific Perisphere charge within the accumulator, the great voltage *kicked back* and drew the bolt of lightning from the Trylon—and at the same time, shorted the Perisphere generator and perhaps saved us all."

Uppercue nodded, said in an awed voice, "Yes. The generator below us, tons of steel and power, would have probably run wild and torn the Perisphere to pieces."

For once in his scrappy life, hairy Monk was silent for two full moments. Then he blurted, "Say—gosh!"

DOC SAVAGE interrupted the questions to take care of Adam Ash. The young public relations consul was still dazed, and there might be a brain concussion. The bronze man showed Ham and Monk how to get back to the narrow steel ladder inside the Perisphere "skin." Unarmed thugs guarded by Monk and Ham were put to work carrying Adam Ash below.

Soon coppers who had been battering at the lower Perisphere locked exits had been admitted and were climbing up here to the secret room. It was not until much later that morning, in Uppercue's own laboratory, that Doc finished with explanations.

Someone had asked about the missing metal cylinder, the tubelike thing that had caused pretty Kay Uppercue to act so suspiciously—as well as good-looking Adam Ash.

The scientist's daughter was there in the lab now, after learning from the hospital that her fiancé would be all right in a day or so. Her brilliant father gave her a warm smile.

"Tell them, Kay," Professor Uppercue said.

"That tube," the small blond girl said, "contained a monatomic film that was to have insulated the accumulator. It was thinner than the thinnest paper. I found the real tube, brought it back here to the lab—"

Ham asked, smiling fondly at the blue-eyed daughter of the scientist, "But where is it now?"

Long Tom looked sheepish. His anemic features, for once, flushed slightly as he looked at the girl. "I found it—before that Lonesome and his mob knocked out Monk and Ham and me, down here! Dang it, I had it hidden in my pants leg, but Monk

got it up there in the Perisphere fight—"

Doc interrupted quietly with, "Well, where is it, Monk?"

Monk stammered, coughed, then got words out. "Goshamighty!" he piped. "That Lonesome had Habeas locked in a closet up there. So I took a swing at that grinning ranny with that tube thing. I guess—well, hell! I guess I busted it all to bits!"

Uppercue sighed. "It is just as well," he said. "I'm afraid the accumulator's possibilities were too great—and also too dangerous. With its unlimited, stored power, it would have always been a treasure sought by men like Mandroff."

Pat Savage was slightly holding well-dressed Ham's arm. She still looked a trifle frightened, though her lovely gold eyes were bright.

She queried, "But the Man of Tomorrow—what about him?"

Doc explained, "It was merely publicity to cover Professor Uppercue's work." The bronze man looked at the white-haired scientist and received a nod of agreement.

"Of course, that publicity would have helped the World's Fair. Later, it could have been announced that something went wrong. But Mandroff, having access to persons stricken on the grounds by the heat and so on, made a pituitary giant out of one man, to scare off everyone and cover his own search for Uppercue's invention, and to throw suspicion on kidnapped Professor Uppercue. Those other victims were being held in readiness should Maximus be killed—to make it appear Maximus was indestructible."

"And Mandroff even tried to get you!" Pat Savage said.

The bronze man smiled. "I suspected him first when he barged right out of the Hall of Medicine side door when I was chasing Lonesome, the man who tried to jab me with a needle. Mandroff's door-swinging was too nicely timed to be an accident. And further, up there in the secret room, and when he was masked, Mandroff cut his hand when he grabbed a scalpel from a glass case. I saw the cut on his right hand when he tried to quickly slip his gloves on at the hospital yesterday."

Queried about Maximus, Doc explained that he had given the giant man the first of treatments that would gradually bring him back to normal. Maximus would forever be of huge size, but in time—after a delicate brain operation—the man would forget his terrible experience and be a normal human.

The other captives, missing Fair visitors, had been given similar treatment by the bronze man at the hospital early this morning.

Doc also produced a set of paper-thin eye shells of brown shade. He told how Alexis Mandroff had disguised himself as young Adam Ash, using the eye caps to cover his own gray eyes. Mandroff had known about Adam Ash going to watch the moon-rocket show, and had quickly disguised himself and taken the public relations consul's place—after having Ash grabbed by Maximus. It was Mandroff who had appeared after the moon-rocket show, instead of Adam Ash.

It was Mandroff's shrill voice that Monk had recognized on the police radio when, disguised, Mandroff had knocked out the dispatcher and taken his place.

Doc produced the ring that had been used to make him try and hypnotize Martin Uppercue. The ring, Doc told, fitted Mandroff's thin, womanish finger exactly.

Behind the group, a familiar voice spoke.

A voice that said, "Well, well, well! I'm telling you, friends, it is a pleasure to be back with you again. As I told them over there at the hospital, I got in a little mess trying to help the famous bronze man. But it was worth it. Oh, yes, indeed, it was worth it! I—"

SHILL BURNS, in a new, screaming checkered suit and a patch over one eye, came like a little gamecock into the room with the long-eared pig, Habeas, and the runt ape trailing along behind.

The voluble, former side-show spieler turned to Monk and Ham, and said with an expansive smile, "Friends, consider yourselves lucky to have ever met the great Shill Burns. I have just this past hour completed arrangements for an exhibit of the two most famous pets in the world—Habeas and Chemistry. Like I always say—"

Hairy Monk let out a howl of rage. He leaped toward Shill Burns, who, suddenly wide-eyed, backed swiftly toward the passageway exit.

Monk yelled, "Exhibit Habeas, will you? Listen, you over-dressed wart—"

Ham, too, had leaped after Shill Burns. But the fast-talking and fast-moving little opportunist had evaded both aides, to disappear madly through the corridor.

Monk and Ham hit the narrow doorway at the same time, and jammed there shoulder to shoulder and face to face.

Monk gave a big-mouthed grin, raised a hairy hand and lifted the hat that had been jammed over Ham's head ever since the hair-waving trick he, himself, had maneuvered.

The lawyer's nicely waved, dark hair was revealed.

Ham strived furiously to bring up his sword cane with which to bat Monk.

The hairy chemist called to demure Kay Uppercue, "What do you think of a guy that waves his hair, Blue Eyes?"

Small, shapely Kay Uppercue moved close to the two aides of Doc Savage. She smiled at both.

"Well, I—"

Monk was beaming, stepping aside at last to face the girl.

"Now if you weren't engaged to that handsome Adam Ash—" Monk started in his childish voice.

"Oh, that doesn't matter!" said Kay. "Adam told me not to be blue while he's laid up. He even suggested that I go to dinner and a show occasionally."

Monk was ready to start at once. He reached for blonde Kay's arm, his eyes as hopeful as a young calf's.

"That's fine!" he piped. "Too bad about Ham, here. Before he can have any dates, he'll have to grow out that wave—"

"Oh!" Kay said. "But you didn't understand. I *have* a date with Ham already. You know, Ham is so mature-looking; thus people are less apt to talk about an engaged woman."

Monk deflated. His shoulders slumped.

Ham called back, "How about that testimonial, sweetheart?"

THE END

James Bama

JAMES BAMA'S WORLD'S FAIR MEMORIES

For this Doc Savage volume, readers have a choice of editions—featuring the original 1933 Walter M. Baumhofer *Czar of Fear* pulp cover, or James Bama's 1969 Bantam Books interpretation of *World's Fair Goblin*.

Bama considers the cover to be his second favorite Doc painting. As he told Brian M. Kane, author of *James Bama: American Realist,* "I was at the New York World's Fair when I was twelve. We went a couple of times and I remember the Trylon and Perisphere so vividly. The other thing is that *King Kong* is my all time favorite genre movie. It has always been a big influence in how I approach compositions. The *World's Fair Goblin* was my chance to get to do King Kong on a cover. You might say it is my version of King Kong at the World's Fair."

The heroic image was made more striking by detonating fireworks which highlight the Man of Bronze in two startling colors. "I remembered them from being at the World's Fair," Bama said. "I thought the use of the fireworks to create the dual lighting would evoke a dramatic tension. Blue and yellow are not complementary colors but the combination effectively created a feeling of strangeness."

POSTSCRIPT by Will Murray

It's a wonderful irony that *World's Fair Goblin* should revolve around an attempt to create a superman called the Man of Tomorrow at the New York World Fair. In fact, it's eerily prophetic.

In the 1938 Doc Savage novel *The Pirate's Ghost*, Lester Dent foreshadowed it through one character's casual comment:

> You have heard of the mythical City of Tomorrow, the ultramodern metropolis of the future? Doc Savage is the Man of Tomorrow. He is a combination of scientific genius, muscular marvel and Sir Galahad. He is today what they hope man will be a few centuries in the future. He is an electrician, chemist, geologist, engineer, surgeon and I don't know what else. Mind you, he's not just an ordinary electrician, chemist and so on. He's probably the best there is in any and all these lines.

No one involved with Doc Savage could have foreseen it, but one of the attractions of the Fair was Superman Day, which set an attendence record on July 3, 1940. Billed as "The Man of Tomorrow," actor Ray Middleton portrayed the Man of Steel—the first actor ever to don a Superman costume. Superman alias Clark Kent would eventually eclipse Clark Savage Jr., the original Man of Tomorrow.

I once asked John Nanovic about the photographs taken at the Fair grounds that day in 1938. He replied: "Re the pictures on World's Fair—Les had the camera; he took the pictures. Bogart shot some; I shot some, so we all got into the act."

Unfortunately, none seems to have survived.

William Bogart worked in the office next to that of John W. Campbell, the legendary editor of *Astounding Science-Fiction.* Just as John Nanovic sometimes would, Bogart consulted Campbell on the scientific aspects of *World's Fair Goblin.*

As Bogart told Dent:

> I went over last chapter and accumulator details with Campbell, that ed of *Astounding.* You met him down here. So any business (I tried to keep it simple) about accumulator stuff is at least based on possibilities. The question was whether to make Mandroff an out-and-out nut or not. Campbell had a grotesque suggestion for such an ending, but I was afraid Nanovic might balk at it.
>
> Nanovic's comments were few. He said to follow your suggestions while editing the story. One spot had him puzzled where I shifted from night to the next day in story. He made a good suggestion for making this bridge, having crowds around Perisphere, staring, anxious about what is wrong, etc. Another was about buildings being air-conditioned, with no open windows, and thus no conversations able to be heard outside. He thought the Goblin idea swell, but suggested Doc and his men call him Maximus, after explaining about Goblin, etc. This was about all, except possibly more color, as you suggested too. I thought I might run out to the Fair next weekend, now that it is nearer completion, and get a better "feel" of the place and work this in while editing.
>
> Your suggestions about Doc, the character tags and all, will be very helpful for future work. Naturally I realize about the tags, but in rushing the work overlooked a lot of this. In the future, I will have time to plan out an action scene carefully, weeding out all extra detail, and getting in more punch and sharper pictures.

Finally, it's also ironic that William G. Bogart's first Doc should carry the title *World's Fair Goblin.* His last name is a corruption of the English folk term, "boggart"—or goblin! •

Photo © Jack Adler, used by permission

Ray Middleton portrayed another "Man of Tomorrow" at the New York World's Fair's Superman Day in 1940.

Lester Dent (1904-1959) could be called the father of the superhero. Writing under the house name "Kenneth Robeson," Dent was the principal writer of Doc Savage, producing more than 150 of the Man of Bronze's thrilling pulp adventures.

A lonely childhood as a rancher's son paved the way for his future success as a professional storyteller. "I had no playmates," Dent recalled. "I lived a completely distorted youth. My only playmate was my imagination, and that period of intense imaginative creation which kids generally get over at the age of five or six, I carried till I was twelve or thirteen. My imaginary voyages and accomplishments were extremely real."

Dent began his professional writing career while working as an Associated Press telegrapher in Tulsa, Oklahoma. Learning that one of his coworkers had sold a story to the pulps, Dent decided to try his hand at similarly lucrative moonlighting. He pounded out thirteen unsold stories during the slow night shift before making his first sale to Street & Smith's *Top-Notch* in 1929. The following year, he received a telegram from the Dell Publishing Company offering him moving expenses and a $500-a-month drawing account if he'd relocate to New York and write exclusively for the publishing house.

Dent soon left Dell to pursue a freelance career, and in 1932 won the contract to write the lead novels in Street & Smith's new *Doc Savage Magazine*. From 1933-1949, Dent produced Doc Savage thrillers while continuing his busy freelance writing career and eventually adding Airviews, an aerial photography business.

Dent was also a significant contributor to the legendary *Black Mask* during its golden age, for which he created Miami waterfront detective Oscar Sail. A real-life adventurer, world traveler and member of the Explorers Club, Dent wrote in a variety of genres for magazines ranging from pulps like *Argosy*, *Adventure* and *Ten Detective Aces* to prestigious slick magazines including *The Saturday Evening Post* and *Collier's*. His mystery novels include *Dead at the Take-off* and *Lady Afraid*. In the pioneering days of radio drama, Dent scripted *Scotland Yard* and the 1934 *Doc Savage* series.

William Gibson Bogart (1903-1977) forsook college and the prospect of being an engineer, and by a circuitous route that included managing a Child's Restaurant, became a prolific pulp writer.

His first sale was a short story to Woolworth's *Tower Mystery Magazine,* but he found filling the back pages of *The Shadow* and *Doc Savage* his steadiest market. He moved to Yonkers in July, 1936, freelanced, and operated a small literary agency for pulp writers. Soon after, he joined Street & Smith, becoming one of editor John L. Nanovic's many sub-editors.

Quitting his Street & Smith staff job in December 1938, Bogart began contributing to periodicals ranging from *Detective Story Magazine* to *Unknown*. His 1940 hardcover novel, *Hell on Friday,* was the start of a series featuring Johnny Saxon, a pulp writer turned private eye.

Bogart committed some of his sub-literary sins under other bylines. Taking the maiden names of his

mother and wife respectively, he became "Russell [sometimes Russ] Hale" for the Spicy pulp chain and "Will Gibson" for the low-rent detective pulps. When Steve Fisher went off to Hollywood, Bogart continued his Danny Garrett shoeshine boy detective series as "Grant Lane" in *The Shadow*. From time to time, Bogart wrote a Skipper or Nick Carter adventure. Writing as "Kenneth Robeson," William G. Bogart ghosted a total of 14 Doc Savage novels.

When Street & Smith's pulp line shrank in 1943, Bogart moved to Chicago, where he worked as a copywriter for N. W. Ayer, an advertising agency. He continued to moonlight as a pulp writer. Lester Dent called him back to ghost Doc Savage in 1946, but after a handful of novels, the series went bimonthly and Bogart hooked up with the Chicago-based Ziff-Davis chain, where he recycled some of his old Doc plots and penned a faux Doc novel called *The Crazy Indian* for *Mammoth Adventure*.

Bogart faded out as a writer in 1947, the year his novelization of the film *Singapore* was published as a Centaur Mystery. His career after that time is unknown. He died in Burlington, Vermont on July 20,1977, just as the Bantam Books reprint of his 1940 Doc Savage novel *The Flying Goblin* was rolling off the presses.

—Will Murray